I0787967

Captive
OF THE
Night

K. Loraine

USA Today BESTSELLING AUTHORS

Meg Anne

ISBN:

978-1-951738-53-2 (Paperback Edition)

978-1-951738-54-9 (Hardback Edition)

Edited by Mo Sytsma of Comma Sutra Editorial

Cover Design by CReya-tive Book Design

Photographer: Wander Aguilar

Model: Liam Black

To Sunday's Ravens. We love you, babycakes.

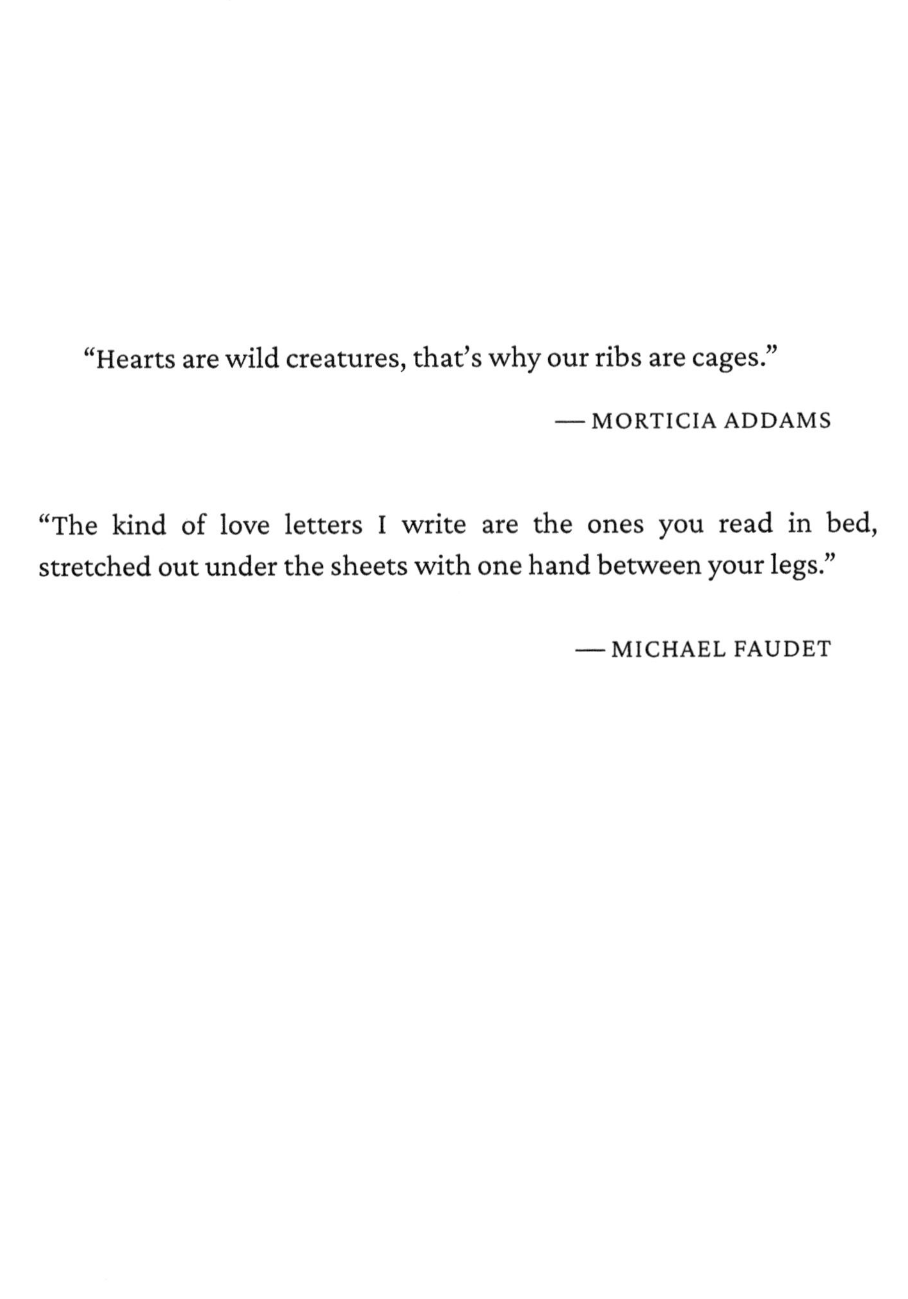

"Hearts are wild creatures, that's why our ribs are cages."

— MORTICIA ADDAMS

"The kind of love letters I write are the ones you read in bed, stretched out under the sheets with one hand between your legs."

— MICHAEL FAUDET

CAPTIVE
OF THE
NIGHT

AUTHORS' NOTE

Captive of the Night contains mature and graphic content that is not suitable for all audiences. Such content includes dubious consent, degradation, impact and blood play, bondage, and more. **Reader discretion is advised.**

In addition to our usual warning, we also wanted to let you know that this book contains a scene some readers may consider to be **extremely dubious consent.** The scene in question can be found in Chapter 28 and occurs between Pan and Rosie. Please protect yourself if this is content you find harmful and skip this chapter.

As always, a detailed list of content and trigger warnings is available on our website.

"We should start making arrangements," Gavin said, his voice cutting through the silence.

We were all gathered in the hacker's living room, the three of them sitting in shock, me biding my time. I had to play the grieving boyfriend before I could execute my plot.

"W-what k-kind of a-arrangements?" Ben forced out.

The vampire sighed and dragged a hand through his thick hair. "For her burial."

Both of the shifter twins stiffened, Remi's jaw clenching as he inhaled sharply. "Burial? She's not even cold, and you want to put her in the ground?" The way his voice broke would have gotten to a more sensitive man. Good job I wasn't a man at all. Just wearing one's skin.

But this was my moment. It was time for my greatest performance to date. I stood, adopting a stricken expression, adding a bit of wobble to my lower lip. God, I was good.

"I . . . I can't believe I wasn't here. She's gone, and I didn't save her." Turning toward the hall, I began a purposeful stride toward the room where they'd placed her.

"Where are you going, Asher?" Remi asked, rising as though he was going to join me.

"I need to see her. I need to say goodbye."

"I'll come with you. You shouldn't be alone right now."

Motherfucker. Take a hint, wolf. This is a solo mission. Wait your turn.

Thankfully the other Mercer got it. He reached out and grasped his brother's arm, holding him back. "L-let him g-go, Remi."

"But—"

"Some things are b-best d-done in p-private."

"I just need a few minutes with her. To apologize for not being here, you know?"

What was *this accent? I couldn't get a read on it. Was I from California? Or the Midwest? Was I a surfer? Or a farmer? Why was this so difficult to figure out?*

"There's nothing you could have done. Aisling got past all of us," Remi said, his eyes bloodshot.

"I know, but . . . it's just something I need to do."

Before her blood goes cold and she's not useful. I want my horns and tail back. And my cock.

Praise Lucifer, the wolf sat down and stopped pressing the issue. I was worried he'd embrace me and try to comfort me. I was a good actor, but not that good. I'd likely kill him simply because I had the opportunity. I didn't do touchy-feely.

The only touchy I liked to do was with Rosie. Between her legs . . . or mine. A pang of loss hit me at the realization that was over. I'd never make her sigh again, or taste her, or feel her warm skin.

Wait . . . was I bloody *sad?*

Must be a side effect of the body. Demons didn't get sad. I shook my head and cast my eyes down. "I'll be back."

In moments I was alone with her, the veil of death shrouded the sparsely decorated room in its darkness.

She was laid out on the bed, clad only in Gavin's button-down shirt. If I didn't know better, I'd assume she was simply sleeping. She looked so peaceful, her hair carefully arranged around her shoulders, her hands at her sides, face relaxed.

I couldn't help myself; I reached out and ran one finger across her brow and down her cheek.

"Hello, my sleeping beauty. Why can you never stay out of trouble, *ma petite monstre?*"

An odd tightening in my chest made my breaths come in harsh gasps as my eyes burned. Was I fucking crying? This human had terrible emotional control. He was broken. I wondered if there was some sort of warranty? Perhaps I could trade him in for a better model, one that wasn't prone to bouts of weeping.

But no. This one was *mine*. My perfect vessel. Wonky wheels and all. Figures my mum would leave me with a junker. She always did have an odd sense of humor.

Demon up, Pan. You might be wearing this human, but you're still the firstborn of a horsewoman. She gave you a job to do and not much time to do it. Best get on with it before you muck up the entire Apocalypse.

Hell was vast, but word spread quicker than a succubus's thighs. Infamy was one thing, but single-handedly fucking up the end of the world really wasn't the sort of thing one wanted to be known for.

Right then. Taking a deep breath, I gripped Rosie's chin in my fingers and twisted her head away from me, baring her throat.

Another foreign sensation took hold of me, this one an uncomfortable weight just beneath my ribs. Was this guilt? What was *wrong* with this vessel? He couldn't go more than a bloody minute without *feeling* something. How pathetic.

"She promised me her blood," I gritted out. "I'm not taking anything she didn't freely offer."

Why I felt the need to justify my actions, to myself of all creatures, was something best left to unravel another time. Preferably whilst sipping brimstone whiskey in my pool. Naked.

She still smelled like Rosie. Bergamot and sugar. *"Death, that hath sucked the honey of thy breath, Hath had no power yet upon thy beauty,"* I whispered in my mind as I lowered myself onto the bed, pressing my lips to her throat as I hovered over her. Romeo who?

Pulling Asher's stupid—but useful—utility knife from my pocket, I sliced into the already chilled skin of her throat, my tongue darting out to steal the first ruby bead. Her blood was still sweet but tainted slightly by the flavor of death. My sense of self-preservation shattered as the ring on my finger seared my skin when the blood was transferred and the magic collected the last drop needed. I didn't stop once my task was completed. I wanted all of her in my veins. She could live on through me. Perhaps her soul would come along. Sure, death could drag me down in its icy clutches if I didn't stop, but what was death but a free ride to hell for a demon?

A low moan filled the air, one I didn't expect, accompanied by fingers sliding through the hair on the back of my head. I broke the seal on her throat and pulled back slightly just as those fingers tightened and pain burst along my scalp.

"Mine." The growled word barely registered before pain exploded in my neck.

Rosie latched onto me like she intended to tear my damn throat out. Her strength was unexpected. Hell, her being alive was unexpected, and I was frozen for embarrassingly long seconds before I began to struggle in her hold.

"Stop," I rasped, my vocal cords already ravaged by her feral bite. "Rosie, stop."

As though I'd slapped her, she released me, her eyes glowing a brighter amber than I'd ever seen in them before. But it was the fangs that drew my focus.

Vampire.

Everything clicked into place. She'd turned.

While extremely rare, it wasn't uncommon for a hybrid to turn after they died. Usually if they didn't turn during their adolescence, it never happened for them, but something about me taking her blood must have triggered her vampiric side.

Look at me saving the day. Well done, Pan. Is this what being a hero feels like? Shall I get a spandex super suit? Captain Aubergine at your service.

"Mine," she growled again, this time softer and lust-addled.

Ah, the newly turned vampire was my favorite kind. Hungry for blood but unable to fully distinguish between their bloodlust and common desire.

"Yours," I whispered. "All yours, Rosie."

She tore my shirt clean down the center, fingers roughly undoing my belt and fly as she worked her way to my—well, well, well, Asher—sizable cock. Bravo. It's no Captain Aubergine, but it'll do nicely.

"Whatever you want, I'll give it to you." I wasn't lying. Having her touch me again was akin to reigniting a fire that had gone cold.

"Mate." Her voice was a breathy plea as I nudged one thigh between hers. "Mark."

"Yes."

I wasn't fully conscious of uttering the word, only that I wanted more of this. Her looking at me like I was the center of her universe, as she'd been mine for so long. Her craving me. Choosing me.

This time when she latched onto my throat, she was more careful. The burn of the bite was accompanied by a wave of absolute pleasure. I moaned and rocked my hips, cock leaking as untameable need careened through every cell in my body. I had to be inside her for this. She was claiming me as hers.

I may no longer be able to mark her in the demonic sense, but I could claim her as a man does his woman. She parted her thighs, welcoming me as she took my cock in her hand and placed me at her entrance.

The silent demand was impossible to ignore. I thrust inside, a frenetic buzz building beneath my skin. It wasn't just my soul reacting to the tendrils of the budding mate bond as they reached for each other. It was my host's too. I could feel Asher right there beside me, stirring as Rosie's soul formed a connection to his. She was knitting us all together, each thread weaving a chain that could only be broken by true death.

I knew what was happening but couldn't bring myself to stop it. She would be as tied to me as I was to her if I let this bond solidify. She'd never be able to escape me, and I never wanted to be rid of her.

I fucked her deep and slow, fighting the desire to hammer hard and fast so I could find my release.

"Yes, Rosie. You're mine. Finally," I groaned, hating that she didn't know it was me, that my voice wasn't my own.

Unbidden, Asher's voice filtered through my brain. *She doesn't want you. This is me she's mating, me she's marking, me who is fucking her.*

No, I mentally snarled. *You're not supposed to be here. Fuck off.* I broke the tether between Asher's consciousness and my own, shoving him so deep inside his mind he'd never break free. I was captain of this ship, thank you very much. He could fuck right off.

But not, unfortunately, before the mate bond snapped into place.

At that point, I was too far gone to do anything about it. I came hard, my breath stalling, heart skipping a damn beat, my cum filling her. I spared a thought for the truth of the matter, because Asher's words had hit a sore spot. It wasn't mine. It was *his*.

All of this was his.

No matter. Once I got my body back, I'd leave my scent all over my mate, because nothing could change the fact that she'd claimed me. The body didn't matter. My soul was hers. Whether she wanted it or not.

CHAPTER

TWO

REMI

Something wasn't right. I could feel it in the air. Asher's pained groan only drove the point home.

Fuck.

I forced myself to walk calmly toward the bedroom, not bothering to tell anyone else I sensed danger. They'd only mock me—well, Gavin would anyway—tell me I was still keyed up on the fight with Aisling. I mean, I'd say the same thing if our positions were reversed. What sort of trouble could Asher really get into with a dead body? Still . . . I couldn't shake that gnawing sense that something was wrong.

I opened the door without knocking, and my stomach churned as soon as I was able to process what I was seeing. Asher with Rosie in his arms, blood running down his spine from where Rosie had latched onto his throat.

As if she could sense me, her eyes opened and locked onto mine.

My first thought was a stunned *she's alive*. Followed by a very frantic *she's a vampire*.

Asher groaned again as his hips rocked into her. He wasn't in pain. He was coming. I knew that sound well, but I also knew this was how vampires killed their victims more often than not. They'd drain them dry while the poor souls weren't even aware their death warrants were signed the moment lips met skin. It was a small mercy, I guessed. Better than the alternative, which Ben and I had narrowly escaped.

Asher was probably too far gone to even know what was happening. I had to save him, both of them, before she did something that couldn't be undone.

"Rosie, stop!" I lunged for Asher, gripping him by the elbow as I pulled him back.

She must've been shocked because she released her hold on his throat, her lips bloodstained, cheeks pink, eyes shining.

Instinct screamed for me to protect Asher as he sat slumped over, unconscious but breathing. I moved to put myself in front of him, getting on the bed and kneeling between her spread thighs. If she killed him, I'd have no options. I couldn't let her hurt him and risk losing them both.

"Mine," she growled.

I barely recognized the raspy, serrated quality of her voice. For a second, I thought she was referring to Asher, like a child who'd just had their toy taken away, but the interested gleam in her eye told a different story.

Then again, so did the way she threw herself at me, fangs bared and aimed straight at my throat. I'd taken away one toy, but given her a shiny new one.

Me.

Her hands reached for me, that touch I craved now sending fear through me instead of love. She'd kill me. She was feral. All new vampires were.

"Rosie," I bit out, but I didn't think Rosie was home just then.

A snarl filled the room as I caught her wrists in my grip, holding her back as she snapped at me.

"We've got a problem in here!" I called out. "I need some fucking backup."

Gavin was there almost immediately. Vampiric speed usually annoyed the hell out of me, though I considered it more of a blessing at the moment. "What—" But there was no need to finish the question; he figured out what happened immediately.

Unfortunately, no one had a chance to explain it to Ben. I knew the second he made it to the doorway. Not just from the heartbroken whimper that escaped my twin, but because of the wave of absolute devastation that poured off him. He didn't see Rosie, his mate. He saw a vampire covered in blood attacking his last remaining family member. The discovery was worse than his mate dying.

Death he might eventually get over. But a vampire for a mate? After what we'd been through as kids, that was going to be an impossible pill to swallow.

I shoved her back until her shoulders were pinned to the headboard, her breaths coming in ragged pants as she mindlessly lunged for me. Asher's blood stained her chin and chest, and her fangs glistened and promised painful pleasure just like he'd experienced. In another life, I'd have been down to let her do whatever she wanted to me, but not like this.

I didn't want to be a mindless conquest. If she was going to claim me, I wanted it to mean something to both of us.

But also, I didn't want to be worried I might die at any second.

Call me crazy, but that was a bit of a boner killer.

"Mine," she growled again, fighting me hard.

"Can you guys please fucking do something? I'm strong, but not feral vampire strong."

"She'll have to be chained. Hold on, I'll be right back," Gavin stated, leaving me without any help.

The fucker.

A panicked glance around the room showed me Ben was gone too. What the fuck? I never thought I'd be the sacrificial lamb in this scenario. I was more of the 'defile someone with holy oil' type.

"Asher? You alive?"

I didn't think the human would be much help either, but anything would be better than trying to do this solo.

He let out a half-hearted grunt that could have been the result of blood loss or coming so hard he nearly blacked out.

I turned my head to check which it was. Rookie mistake. As soon as my focus wavered, Rosie pulled both her legs in and then kicked out, her feet hitting me square in the chest and sending me flying off the bed and straight into the full-length mirror.

Glass shattered, shards splintering and embedding themselves in my back.

"Motherfucker," I rasped, eyes swimming at the unexpected concussion. "Baby girl, I like it rough, but damn, give a guy some warning."

I tried to stand, but that wasn't happening. Nausea curled in my gut, and I had to swallow back the urge to bring up everything I'd eaten today. Shit.

There were two of her crawling across the bed toward me as my brain worked to right itself. *Is this how Rosie feels when she's sandwiched between Ben and me?*

Once upon a time, the thought of two of her at my disposal would have turned me on. Not now.

Her smile was eerie, a mixture of lust and hunger. She crouched like a cat, ready to pounce. Holding my stare, she licked her lips and whispered, "Mine."

This was it. I was going to die. Maybe if I was lucky, she'd take me like she did Asher.

Fuck it. I'd always wanted to go out with a bang.

THREE

My brain refused to accept what was playing out in front of my eyes. Rosie was a monster. No longer my mate, but a *thing*. A feral creature intent only on sating her—no, *its*—need for blood. Just like the rest of those filthy bloodsuckers. Just like Aisling.

Everything hurt as I bolted from the scene, my instincts screaming at me to protect my brother and my lost mate, even though I knew there was nothing left of her to save. Her eyes had been vacant, though the hunger written across her face had been plain enough. I shuddered as the image of her blood-smeared lips and those vicious fangs flashed in my mind. Asher's blood dribbled down her chin, coating her throat and chest as though she'd bathed in it.

My heart twisted. *Rosie.*

"No," I growled. That *thing* wasn't Rosie. Rosie's dead.

A harsh laugh escaped at the insanity of the situation we'd found ourselves in. I'd once claimed only death would make me leave my mate. Looks like I was right. I just never figured I'd live long enough to see it come true. I should have known better than to tempt fate. To think that fickle bitch would give me something good and pure after a lifetime of nothing but shit.

The sound of shattering glass snapped me from my thoughts and brought me back to the present.

Remi's labored breaths triggered my wolf, and it was all I could do to keep from shifting as his pained voice filtered through the hall. "Motherfucker. Baby girl, I like it rough, but damn, give a guy some warning."

I would not let this world take anything else from me, especially not my brother. Remi was all I had.

Spotting a splintered piece of wood from the window frame, I picked it up and looked back at the guest room with pure determination. My hand shook as anxiety shot through my veins. I had to do this. It was the only way. Tears burned my eyes with every step closer. Especially when I saw her on the bed, alone, looking exactly like the woman I loved more than anything.

It's not her. She's gone. You lost her. She's never coming back to you.

Remi's panic was palpable as she crouched on the corner of the bed and growled, "Mine."

No. You can't have him. He was mine first.

Raising my makeshift stake, I took a step forward, blinking away my tears. I hated this. Every part of it.

It's not her. It's not her.

The soft clink of chains startled both me and the fledgling vampire. Her gaze found mine, the pain of the connection between us making me hesitate just as Gavin's hand clamped around my wrist.

"What the hell do you think you're doing?"

"She's t-trying to k-kill us."

"No she's not, you bleeding idiot. She's trying to mark you. She recognizes her mates," he explained with the strained patience of a grade school teacher. "A newly turned vampire runs purely on instinct. Feed. Mate. Fight."

"Kill."

"Yes, and kill. But that's not what she's after, or she would have taken Asher out by now. He's easy pickings, and she's focused on claiming Remi."

"It's true," Remi rasped. "She could have attacked any one of us by now, but she's just sitting there waiting."

Gavin took the stake from me, throwing it to the floor before putting himself directly in her line of sight. "Look at me, petal."

Her gaze snapped to his, posture tensing as though she was ready to leap on him. "Mine."

"Yes, you're right. That's a good girl. I am yours. And you are mine, and you will obey me."

"O-bey." She said the word in two parts, almost like a question. Like she was trying it on for size. Her brow furrowed, her head tilting to the side. "Mate."

Gavin reached out and stroked a thumb down her cheek. "Mate," he agreed, far more calm and tender than I'd ever seen him. Then again, I supposed he was sort of in his element here. I was the only one whose entire world had just imploded.

"Ben, take the chains and secure her." Gavin's command made the hairs on the back of my neck stand up.

"No. I'm n-not t-touching that . . . m-monster."

He rolled his eyes and huffed. "Fine. Have it your way."

The thing that used to be Rosie leaned in a little closer to Gavin and inhaled. "Mine," she whispered, sounding more like my mate than she had any right to.

"We're yours," Gavin continued as he took her wrists and shackled them before securing them to the bedposts.

With her distracted for the moment, Remi pushed to his feet and eased around the bed over to Asher. He reached for Asher's wrist, likely to check for a pulse, and the second his fingers made contact, the hacker let out an indecipherable mumble. My twin sagged in relief and scooted a bit closer, taking a seat beside him and supporting some of his weight.

Without saying a word, he met my gaze and then looked at Gavin. Watching. Waiting. Not wanting to interfere.

He still thought there was a way to save her. That Rosie was in there.

I knew better.

It seemed like I was the only one who saw the writing on the wall.

Our mate was gone.

And a monster had taken her place.

FOUR

GAVIN

My wife was restless. The chains I'd bound her with rattled as she tested them yet again.

"Are you sure those will hold?" Remington asked from his place on the floor beside Asher.

"She's strong," I allowed, "but not that strong. They'll hold."

For now.

"That said, I should probably take her away from here for a while. Newborn vampires are unpredictable. It will be easier for the both of us to focus and for me to help ease her transition without . . . distractions."

"G-good r-riddance," Bentley muttered.

"You don't mean that," his twin snapped, a flash of his wolf in his eyes. "She's ours."

"N-not any-m-more."

I'd predicted this eventuality, that her vampiric heritage would always be a wedge between them. Had hoped for it, even. By all rights, I should have been happy to see the man turn his back on her—that simply freed up a place in her heart—but I wasn't. When she came back to herself, she'd be heartbroken. And as I was unfortunately coming to learn, the things that hurt her hurt *me*.

Bollocks.

"You tend to the hacker. I will secure her elsewhere until it's safe."

Roslyn grunted and tried to free herself from the restraints once more, but I soothed her with my gaze and softly murmured commands as she fell under my compulsion again. As she gained control of herself, my power would be less effective. Better to use it now while I could.

"Where will you go?" Remington asked, proving that his head wasn't actually filled with cotton wool as I'd once expected.

"I have accommodations," I replied vaguely.

"In town?"

I nodded, not missing the way the wolf's gaze narrowed with suspicion.

Holding my hands up in a show of innocence, I said, "Don't worry. I didn't kill anybody. Just convinced them it was time to take a much-needed vacation. Get your knickers out of a bunch."

"I'm not wearing any," he said smugly.

"Why am I not surprised?"

Remington got to his feet as Asher finally appeared to come to.

"Is that safe?" Asher asked, his voice labored.

"Eavesdropping is a disgusting habit," I said by way of answer.

"I'm in the fucking room."

Cocking one brow, I assessed him. "Playing dead. Eavesdropping."

"Whatever. I don't think she should leave. What if she gets out?"

"Do you doubt my skill with restraints? I assure you, I am quite talented."

Bentley shifted in the doorway, drawing Roslyn's attention. She growled low in her throat, her tongue darting out to wet her lips.

"G-get her o-out of h-here."

"You can't kick my mate out of my fucking house," Asher protested.

The reminder that she'd marked Asher seemed to be too much for the usually stoic shifter. He shuddered in disgust, spun on his heel, and stormed down the hall.

"Come along, petal. I'll see you fed. I'll teach you everything you need to know. When I'm through with you, Bentley will be nothing more than a bad memory and a sour taste in your mouth." Not taking my eyes off her, I called over my shoulder, "Remington, be a good lad and remove the chains from the bed?"

He did as I instructed, his usually careless demeanor now shadowed with worry and sorrow.

Scooping her into the cradle of my arms, I kept my throat well out of her reach. "No biting. Not until you're invited, darling. Be a good girl."

She pressed her nose against the artery pulsing beneath my skin and inhaled greedily, following up with a long wet lick up my neck. "Mine," she murmured, the rumble a combination of lust and hunger.

"Yes. Yours. Forevermore."

Another pleasure-filled rumble was her only answer.

"He's like the fucking vampire whisperer," Remington muttered behind me. "Look how calm she is with him. Why isn't she making him shit his pants?"

"Vampire privilege. She must recognize her kind. Animal instinct or what have you."

"Fuck. Does that mean she'll like him more than me now? I don't want her to like him more than me."

"Calm your tits, Remi. No one likes a needy puppy."

"You calm your tits, Asher. She's our mate too."

I glanced back just in time to see the look of intense yearning flitter across Asher's face as he stroked the mate mark on his neck. "Trust me, I know."

"I'll call you if I require your services, gentlemen. For now, I have her well in hand."

"Says the guy who was dueling in the fucking street a few nights ago. Can we really trust him with her?" Remington crossed his arms over his broad chest.

"Do we have another choice?"

"No, you don't," I answered. "She will accidentally drain you dry if she gets her fangs into you again. Bentley is right to be afraid of her, even if he's a disloyal arsehole."

Some of the mistrust on Remington's face crumpled away. "Speaking of brothers, should we uh . . . let Noah know about the situation?"

Balls. I hadn't considered the added complication of Noah Blackthorne, or any of the Blackthornes, for that matter. I'd been too absorbed with the fact that my wife had escaped death. For a second time.

"I'll handle it."

Without giving them another moment of my night, I strode out the open door and stepped over the pile of ashes that was once that bitch Aisling. "Ta, love. I'd say it's been a pleasure, but we both know that would be a lie. Save me a seat in hell."

"What do you mean, she's a vampire?" Noah Blackthorne's furious voice was loud enough to pierce my eardrum. I had to pull the phone away from my ear to spare my hypersensitive hearing.

"Exactly what I said. She's turned."

"You fucking turned her? Are you mad? Why would you do that? Did you even ask her if that was what she wanted?"

I didn't turn her. No one turned her. Roslyn wasn't a made vampire. She was born—which meant her transition would be a whole other beast entirely. Shorter, but intense. She'd require me, her mate, to guide her through it. Teach her and serve her. Let her take from my vein and sate her unquenchable thirst until she could safely hunt. I was up for the challenge.

"Why do you automatically assume I had anything to do with it? She died, Noah. Or did you miss that part? True death. An hour later, we found her—"

"Wait. You're going to have to run that by me again. Did you just say my sister *died*? How could you let that happen?"

I glared down at the little device in my hand, annoyance surging through me. "You act like I simply stood aside and watched."

"From where I'm sitting, you didn't exactly prevent anything."

"Oh, piss off."

"No, I don't think I will. Where is she? Bring her home."

I scoffed. "What, to the burned-out husk of your former manor? Her home is here. With me. Her husband. Her mate." I let the last word hang there for a heartbeat. "I just thought you'd like to know what happened. Excuse me for trying to be polite. This is what happens when I'm nice."

Noah's answering laugh was filled with derision. "You and nice don't belong in the same sentence, Donoghue."

"Don't I know it, *Blackthorne.*"

"What are you doing with her? Where is she? Has she gone feral?"

There was less accusation and more protective big brother in his voice now. A tenderness for her laced with fear. Sometimes newly turned vampires never made it out the other side and were lost forever as bloodthirsty beasts. Well, we were bloodthirsty by nature, but it wasn't long into my transition before I was able to keep them in my mouth, so to speak.

"She's ravenous, as you'd expect. Not yet herself, but I catch glimpses of her. She's in there. She'll come back."

He blew out a heavy breath, and I could practically feel his relief at my words. "When it's safe, I'd like to see her. Rosie never thought she'd turn. None of us did. This is going to be a shock to her."

"I'm aware. Once we come through this, I will let you know. You have my word."

Noah hummed over the line. "What about the others?"

"Who?" I feigned ignorance because God help me, I didn't want to think of the others.

"Her other mates. She'll kill them if she feeds from them too soon."

"I'll take care of her. She needs me. I'm more than capable of seeing to her."

"You won't be enough for her. It's different for those with established mate bonds. You know as well as I do that this is something akin to a shifter's heat. She'll need her other mates, sooner rather than later. The instinct to claim them with her vampire side will overwhelm her otherwise. As uncomfortable a topic as it is, I will not allow you to let my sister suffer—"

"Enough, Noah. You've made your point. I will ensure Roslyn has everything she needs when it is safe enough to do so."

"And you'll supervise—"

"Noah Blackthorne, are you asking me to play voyeur with your sister?"

"Fuck off. I'm asking you to ensure no one gets killed. It would destroy her."

"Unlike you and I, your precious sister will remain untainted by the title of cold-blooded killer. I'd prefer to keep it that way myself. Her light is too bright to diminish."

Noah surprised me by chuckling.

"What's so amusing?"

"You. I'm not sure I'll ever wrap my head around the fact that there's an actual heart beating in that cage you call a chest."

"Well, you better . . ."

A low, pained moan from the other room interrupted my barbed words.

"Noah, I have to go. Your sister needs me. We'll be in touch soon."

I hung up without giving him a chance to say anything further. My heart was a wild racing thing as I rushed to her side. She was writhing from the center of the bed where I'd restrained her, the soft dark waves of her hair framing the face of an angel.

"Mine," she whimpered, eyes locked on me, fangs glinting as she arched her back and tried to get closer.

"Do you remember where you are, petal? Why you're here?"

She tugged again, sliding her knees together, the silk of the nightgown I'd changed her into rasping over her skin.

"Mate." Her thighs parted. "Mine." I caught the scent of her arousal and fought a groan. "Claim."

God, I wanted to fit my hips between those welcoming thighs and drive into her more than almost anything, but now wasn't the time. I could give her one thing, though. I'd slake her thirst for blood, bring her around enough that she called me by my name when I sank deep and filled her with my cock.

"You need me, yes. But it's my blood you'll have, nothing more. Not yet."

She struggled against her bindings, trying to take what she so desperately craved.

"Behave, petal. Or you'll get nothing."

It was a bluff, and a poor one. I could no more deny her need for my blood than I could my need for her. But she didn't know that. All my duchess heard was the edge of command from her mate. Her lord.

Even in this state, Rosie recognized who we were to each other and the power dynamic between us. If that told me anything, it was how deeply ingrained the need to submit was to her.

I crawled onto the bed, allowing myself the simple comfort of pressing my clothed erection against her warm center as I offered my throat. She rocked her hips a second before her fangs made purchase with my skin. The explosion of pleasure was immediate. Absolute.

Euphoria raced through my veins, drowning out reason as she drank.

And drank.

Roslyn's thirst was endless, and I could see now why she was so dangerous. I had next to no resistance against her. I'd happily ride this wave into the arms of death itself.

"Enough. Enough, petal."

She growled low and sank her fangs even deeper.

It was all I could do to shove her away, tearing her teeth from my vein as I separated our bodies. I stared at her, panting and light-headed from blood loss.

"Gavin," she whispered, her eyes glowing, cheeks pink, voice soft.

That one word would have knocked me to my knees if I hadn't been on the mattress already. "Yes, petal."

The blood smeared across her chin did nothing to diminish her beauty. She was more mine now than she'd ever been.

"Hungry," she mewled, leaning forward to try and take another bite. "More."

I leaned away, not leaving her, just enough to stay out of her range. "No, petal. Not now."

"Ache," she protested, squirming beneath me and nearly making my eyes cross as she rubbed against my erection.

"Me too, petal. Me too."

She was nearly impossible to resist, but with each feeding she was coming back to herself. Soon, when she could form proper sentences and really ask for what she wanted, I would make her mine again.

"I'll feed you again, my love. But not until I heal. I promise."

She rattled her chains again and whined. "More, Gavin."

It hurt to deny her, but I'd do her no good drained dry. So I caught her in my gaze and whispered, "Sleep now, Roslyn."

Her eyes fluttered closed, and she instantly relaxed as I staggered off the bed, aching in ways I had never expected. As I shut her away in the bedroom, I leaned against the door and allowed myself one moment to fall apart.

In the space of an hour, I'd watched her die and then come back to life. There hadn't been a chance to wrap my head around any of it, but I knew no matter how many nights I walked this earth, I would never forget the sight of her lying on the ground with her neck broken, eyes vacant.

It brought everything into sharp relief. The lies I'd been telling myself. The things I'd tried so hard to deny.

I loved my wife. Desperately.

I would not survive losing her again.

Why was I shackled to a bed?

The room smelled of Gavin, but he was nowhere to be found as I tugged on my restraints. My stomach cramped and my gums ached. Not like a little twinge, but a heavy ache. Like my teeth no longer fit in my mouth. I was desperately thirsty, my throat burning with the need for something to ease the scratchy rasp.

"Gavin," I forced through dry lips.

There was no immediate answer, which told me he must not be nearby. I couldn't imagine my husband would ignore me for long. Well, not unless I'd earned some sort of punishment. I couldn't recall a reason for this, though. The last thing I remembered . . .

The thread of recollection hovered just out of reach. A teasing glimmer of my past. Asher's blood in my mouth. Brimstone and rich red wine. But why would I have the taste of his . . .

It all came back to me then.

Aisling.

The snap of the bones in my neck.

Darkness.

Attacking Asher. No, *claiming* Asher.

My gums tingled as fangs filled my mouth. Fangs I didn't have before Aisling killed me.

Oh God.

I was a forking vampire.

"Gavin!" I called, a little more frantically this time, pulling hard on my restraints as my panic spiked.

Oh no. No, this could not be happening. I wasn't supposed to be a vampire. I was just Rosie. The hybrid with the fancy blood who was little more than a human. I'd never turn. That was what they all had said. The healer who'd been called to assess me had told my father in no uncertain terms that the chances of me turning once I passed twenty were microscopic. One in a million.

Apparently I was a million.

But newly turned vampires were feral. Creatures fueled by instinct and little else. Which meant that if I was thinking like myself again, I must have lost time. Must have fed. And have no recollection of any of it.

Oh God, Asher. What had I done to him?

"Gavin Donoghue! Get your broody arse in here and unchain me before I scream!"

The door opened, revealing my mate, his usually pristine countenance gone. The man who stood before me was rumpled, hair mussed as though someone had been tugging on the lengths, throat a mass of bruises and bite marks in various stages of healing, white shirt open to the middle of his chest, spots of blood dotting the collar.

"What in God's name happened to you?" I asked.

"You did, darling. It's good to hear you speaking in coherent sentences." In a move too exhausted to be graceful, Gavin propped an arm up on the doorframe and leaned heavily into it. I would have said he was drunk, but that was a near impossibility for our kind.

Jesus. *Our* kind.

"Are you unwell?" I asked, my eyes searching him for a clue as to why he looked so worn down.

"It's not easy being a one-duke blood bank. Your thirst is on par with your sexual appetite, which is to say, petal, that you are fucking insatiable."

Heat flooded my body at the gleam in his tired eyes. He was already working open the remaining buttons on his shirt as he stumbled toward me.

"I've got one more in me before I'll have to feed. Take what you desire. I promised I'd serve you."

I was starved. Ravenous even, but I couldn't take advantage of his offer, not when I could see the toll this was taking on him.

"Gavin, stop."

"You don't want me?" He leaned against the mattress and gave me a roguish smile more appropriate for Remi.

"I can wait. Sit down. I need you to tell me what happened."

He didn't sit so much as flop. I didn't even know Gavin Donoghue could flop.

"Perhaps you should tell me what you remember."

His fingers traced the bones of my ankle as I relayed my broken memories. Aisling. The fight. Asher. Then the flashes of Gavin's visits and his sharing of blood with me. Over and over, he'd come to give me what I needed. Never asking for anything in return.

"Did I . . . kill him?" I didn't want to ask the question, but I couldn't stop myself.

"No. You claimed him as a vampire truly claims their mate. He's yours now."

"I remember that word hitting me like a thunderbolt when I opened my eyes and saw him." I frowned, recalling the distinct taste of brimstone. "But if he's mine, why isn't he here? Where are Remi and Ben?"

"It's not safe for them, petal. You may want to claim them, but you could still kill them."

"I couldn't ever—" My words cut off as the truth hung between us. I absolutely could have killed all of them and never even known I was doing it. I'd seen a newly turned vampire tear his partner's throat out without a second glance.

"You could, petal. But you didn't. I brought you here to ensure it stays that way. Once we both feel you are strong enough, we will see about . . . visitation. In the meantime, you'll just have to make do with me."

He attempted what I thought was a waggle of his brows, but it was so awkward and out of character it seemed more like he'd gotten something in his eye.

"Maybe you should lie down."

"That's what I was doing."

Before I'd interrupted him. Great.

"How long have I been here? Like this?"

"Three days."

"And you have been taking care of me all this time?"

"Of course. I'm your husband, your mate besides. I won't let anything happen to you."

He'd said similar things before, but this was the first time I truly believed he'd meant it. "Who's taking care of you?"

Feeding me was a monumental task. If he wasn't getting his own meals, I could drain him far past what was safe. No wonder he was covered in bruises. He was no longer strong enough for his healing to kick in.

He blinked at me like I'd started speaking in tongues. "What do you mean, caring for me?"

"You look a fright. I've clearly been draining you. You can't go on like this. Have you been hunting?"

"Serving my mate during her time of need is a great honor, Roslyn. I wouldn't have it any other way. I will continue being the only one who feeds you until it's safe for you to hunt."

"That's all well and good until you drop dead on top of me."

He smirked. "I won't."

"I might have been human until recently, but I was raised with vampires. I know mated pairs serve each other when one turns. If you aren't going to hunt, you must take from me."

"You need your strength."

"So do you."

I may like it when he bossed me around, but on this point, I would not budge. Gavin was used to getting his way with me, but I held his stare without blinking. I could be just as stubborn as him when the occasion called for it. This happened to be such an occasion.

"Come, lie with me, Gavin. Take what you need so you can serve your mate again soon." I gave a little rattle of my chains. "And maybe consider untying me while you're at it."

A low moan left him as he crawled up the bed without argument. "I can't give you both hands."

"I only need one."

He raised a brow, but I could see the hunger burning in his eyes, and for once, it wasn't for me. My duke was starving. He'd been denying himself for days.

"Take what you need, Gavin," I said, echoing my earlier words while purposefully turning my head away and bearing my neck to him.

Pulling a key from his trouser pocket, he fumbled with the chains, unfastening one wrist as he laid on top of me, his knee between my thighs, one hand in my hair. "I'll only take a little. Just enough to tide me over."

"Take as much as you want. I seem to have more than enough to spare."

"Fuck, petal, you tempt me."

His lips feathered over my pulse point, and I arched into him as his ragged breaths danced across the tender skin. My newly awakened senses sparked to life, triggered by the scent of him. The bite of tobacco and the richness of leather, all mixed with an underlying aroma—lust. That was new. I didn't recall scenting specific emotions before. Now I better understood what my wolves had meant when they said they could smell my need for them.

"Please, Gavin. I'm aching for you. I'm so empty."

"That's the change. I'll care for you. I'll see to everything you need. I promise, but not until you're ready for me."

"I am. Oh God, please."

He bit down on my neck, fangs piercing me, sending the sensation straight between my legs. His groan was pained, the hard press of his erection against me betraying his desire. If he ran his hand up my thigh, he'd find me wet and ready for him.

I'd known vampire bites could be pleasurable; I'd always enjoyed it when Gavin had fed from me, but this was on a whole new level. The rapid thrum of his heartbeat was loud in my ears, an almost frantic thing. He rocked against me, taking what he wanted, using my vein to heal him.

Almost as soon as he'd started, he tore himself away, my blood glistening on his lips.

"Now?" I asked, parting my legs as he panted for breath.

"No. Not yet, love."

I writhed, whining without a care for how pathetic I might have looked. I needed him. "Yes. Now."

"You're not able to control yourself enough to keep from killing me, or the others, petal. I know what you want, but we're not ready. Not right now."

"I need . . . something." I shifted restlessly on the bed, my body too empty and aching to be filled.

He gave me a long, considering once over. "Perhaps we can compromise. Touch yourself, petal. Make yourself come."

My breath hitched as he leaned back against one of the pillars at the foot of the four-poster bed, one leg down, the other resting on the mattress. The position offered him an unobstructed view of me. And me of him.

"I'll even join you," he purred, freeing that beautiful length of his.

I wanted it in my hands, my mouth, or better yet, in my dripping center. Why was he denying me? Because he was afraid of me. Interesting. I'd never been a creature feared by anyone.

My fangs were extended, lust causing them to release, the combined hunger for his blood and body sending confusing signals through me. He was right. I couldn't be trusted. So I did as he commanded. I slid my fingers between my legs and ran them over my slick folds, moaning as soon as I brushed my swollen bundle of nerves.

"That's right, petal. Pretend it's me touching you. Show me what you like."

I bit down on my bottom lip, hissing when my new fangs punctured the soft skin. The pain added a new, delicious note to the other heightened senses rolling through me.

His nostrils flared. Oh, yes. We both liked that.

I let my free hand drift away from my core before scoring the skin of my inner thigh until blood rose to the surface. His sharp inhale, the clenching of his jaw and the jerking of his fisted erection, all told me one thing. We were going to continue playing just as we always had, but now, we could take it farther than he'd ever dared.

"My lord," I whispered as he slowly pumped his shaft, gaze locked on my thigh.

"My duchess."

"I want you."

"You know the rules. Obey them, or you'll get nothing at all."

This was a dangerous game I was playing. One where I tried to see how far I could push him until he broke and gave us both what we so obviously craved. The scent of my blood was an unexpected aphrodisiac, and I found myself more turned on than ever when I returned my fingers to my aching core.

"Give me what I want, Roslyn."

"What's that?"

"Your orgasm. I want to watch you fall apart as I do."

I nodded, biting my lower lip again and giving myself over to the knife's edge of pleasure I was balancing on. "I'm close."

He didn't answer. He simply continued stroking himself, his breaths coming in tense pants. His dark gaze locked on the place where my fingers feverishly worked.

"Touch me, please," I whispered.

In one smooth motion, he was up and kneeling between my legs, his straining hardness so close to where I wanted him, but not quite touching. But his palm gripped my thigh, his fingers digging into the flesh.

"Stop," he ordered.

"W-what?" I did as he said, but I was in pain because of it.

Then his swollen head slid along my tender clit as he guided himself across my slick center.

"Please, don't torture me."

A wicked smirk preceded his dark chuckle. "It's what I live for, petal."

Rocking his hips forward, he made us both moan. I reached up, needing more contact with him.

He jerked back, and instead of stroking my hand down his torso, my nails sliced through his skin, drawing beads of scarlet to the surface. My reaction was instantaneous. My nostrils flared, my fangs descending, my eyes locking on the trickle of blood over the taut line of muscles.

So hungry.

I need his blood, not his cock.

Take.

Feed.

I shook my head, fighting against the vampire instinct. But it was so strong. Thirst burned in my throat. I pulled at the single shackle holding me chained to this bloody bed. I could get free. I could have what I needed. I could feed, and then I'd be loose in this world where I could have everything I wanted.

I tugged at my restraint, a thrill running through me as the wood creaked. Almost there. So close.

"No, petal. Look at me." Gavin grabbed me by the wrist and held me down, his hips fitted to mine, his eyes hard and determined, pinning me with that intense stare.

My breaths were labored, my body reacting like I'd just run for miles as I fought for control of myself. I warred with the monster inside me that only wanted to kill and drink.

"There you are. Come back to me, wife." His hips rocked into me, drawing the velvet and steel length of him through my folds and reminding me what we'd been in the middle of.

I blinked, the red haze coating my vision dissipating. I hadn't even realized it was there until now. So lost to the hunger was I.

"Come for me, my darling. Let us both get what we desire tonight. There's more to this life than thirst. I'll ensure you remember it if it's the last thing I do."

He rocked again, and the hunger for blood was replaced with a hunger for him.

"Gavin."

"That's right, duchess."

True to his word, he didn't enter me, but he continued that slow glide of his erection over my aching center. It wasn't long before I was on the precipice once more, writhing and bucking against him.

The hand holding me in place gripped tighter until I knew bruises would ring my wrist. The thought of bearing his mark sent me over the edge, and I came with a wild cry of his name.

He followed, the pulses of his release spilling across my lower lips and belly. I wanted more already. He was right. I was insatiable.

The way he stared at me, a mixture of awe and pure lust in his eyes, was disarming.

"Well done, petal. You're very nearly ready."

"For what?" I asked with a moan as he collected his spend and slid his fingers inside me.

"To take your place in the night at my side. No longer a captive, but a queen."

"I'd rather be a duchess."

"As you wish."

SIX

PAN

My eyelids fluttered closed for the third time, my head dipping toward my chest. Fucking human bodies and their incessant *needs*. Lust was one thing; that was at least fun. But hunger. Exhaustion. The constant urge to piss. It was ridiculous. Who had time for all this *nothing*? I had better things to do, an Apocalypse to begin. I couldn't very well do it on the shitter.

"C'mon, Asher. Let's go to bed." Remi reached out for me, but I jerked away, not interested in a cuddle.

"I'm fine."

His eyes were wounded by my dismissal, but he persevered. "You're not fine. You're all but asleep on your feet. When was the last time you slept?"

Never.

"Before she died." I ground the words out, needing him to leave me alone. "How can I sleep when she's not here?"

"She's with Gavin."

"As if that makes it better. Who knows what that bloodsucker has been doing to her for three solid days?"

Remi winced, and I pressed my advantage, trying to get his focus off me and onto someone else.

"He won't even let us see her, for fuck's sake. We're just supposed to what? Take his word for it that she's okay?"

"It's better than her being in the ground. He won't hurt her, not like that. You know it as well as I do."

I rubbed at my chest, the unwelcome ache that accompanied thoughts of her since she claimed me rearing its head again. I didn't like it. I'd assumed being marked as hers would give me more sway, more control over our situation. Instead, it made me weak. At her mercy. Desperate. Whiny.

Oh, I hated this. I couldn't even rail her into next week to rid myself of these emotions. I was sat here like a lovesick sap with a mopey werewolf as my babysitter.

Be human, they said. It's fun, they said.

Fucking liars.

I'd like to get off the ride now and go home, please.

Standing, I shoved my hands into my pockets and stared into the wolf's pure blue eyes. "Do I? What kind of mate are you that you'd let her be out of our sight for even a minute with that sadist?"

"You trusted him enough a few days ago. Hell, you're the one that gave them the literal keys to your stupid dungeon. What is this sudden change of heart?"

"He probably led Aisling right to us."

"He's the one that suggested going to the Council. What reason could he possibly have to side with her after the fact?"

"Are you really that stupid? He wants nothing more than to get rid of all of us so he can have her to himself. He has what he wants. His wife. A vampire. Just. Like. Him."

Remi's eyes widened as though I'd slapped him. "Fuck you, Asher."

A slight stirring at the back of my consciousness made my eye twitch. *Well, well, speak of the devil.* Asher's soul had been putting up one hell of a fight. Seems like he wasn't enjoying the little trip down memory lane I sent him on. Well too the fuck bad for him; I had work to do. He could piss right off.

I shrugged, enjoying stirring the pot. I needed something to let out this pent-up anger. Gavin was living the dream. He had her chained up and at his disposal. No interruptions. All while I was here falling a-fucking-sleep with the wolf twins.

"You know what? Maybe you're right. Maybe I should have a lie-down."

"A lie-down? Who the fuck are you? The King of England?"

Realizing my slipup, I scowled at him. "Maybe I just miss her, okay? Ever think about that? Excuse the ever-loving fuck out of me."

"Asher, wait. I'm sorry."

I flipped him the bird as I strolled out of the room.

There it was again, that uneasy pressure, insistently reminding me he was there. As if I could forget about the pissant when I wore his skin like a costume I didn't want. He was stronger than I'd thought. Perhaps a visit to a hellscape of his own making would teach him to fight me.

A heavy weight pressed on my shoulders after expending the energy I'd needed to send him away. Again. I was knackered after that, and Asher's bed was looking more and more comfortable. Maybe I'd try out this nap thing everyone was always going on about.

Lying on the mattress, I stared up at the dark ceiling, my gaze trained on the small crack snaking out from the light fixture. I rolled over, Rosie's scent wafting up from the pillow next to my head. Bloody hell, I was hopeless.

Sighing, I grabbed the soft downy cushion and pulled it close, burying my face in it and inhaling deep. Fuck it. No one could see me.

Without realizing it, my eyelids fluttered closed, and my mind began to drift. It wasn't long before my breaths evened out and my limbs grew heavy. The haze of sleep crept over me without my knowledge, but as soon as the scent of brimstone filtered to my nose, I knew.

I opened my eyes, glancing down at my perfect, fuck-hot form. I was back. My purple-hued skin fit me better than any other I'd worn. God, I missed myself. My tail flicked behind me, cock heavy and hanging to the left as he should.

"Pan, you sexy fucking demon. It's good to be back."

"Well, where is it?" Mummy dearest's voice threw cold water right on any celebratory wank plans I had in the works.

"Where's what?"

"The blood? Give it to me."

"Give me back my body."

"You seem to think you're the one calling the shots here, Pandemic. Give. Me. The. Ring."

A low rumble of annoyance rattled around my chest, but I did as I was told. "Here, have it." *You nasty old bird.* Tossing the ring at her, I stared daggers at the woman who made me.

"And the body?" she asked, her eyes trained on the spelled metal she held between her fingers.

"The one you gave me? A waste of space with a slightly above average dick."

She rolled her eyes. "No, Pan. *Her* body. Is it disposed of?"

"She's ruined. Not necessarily disposed of."

"What do you mean, ruined?"

"She turned. She's a vampire. This is the last of the sun blood she had in her veins."

She tapped her fingers together. "Hmmmm. Interesting. Very interesting. It seems our supply may not have run out as feared. It may just be a little diluted."

"What does it matter? You have everything you need."

She booped me on the nose. "A horsewoman never knows when she might require a little splash of her most special ingredient."

"A happy accident, then. Jolly good. Now, return me to my body, if you please. I've got hell to raise."

I held out my arms and waited for her to reward me for a job well done.

Instead, she tutted. "Oh, my sweet, stupid child. No. Now that she's immortal, I'll need my eyes on her at all times. I think you'll best serve me acting as a spy for the time being."

"But you promised!"

"I did no such thing. You'll just have to deal with your vessel's . . . shortcomings until I decide otherwise."

"Absolutely fucking not. You fix me right this instant."

"Or what, Pan? What do you think you can do to me?"

I gritted my teeth and clenched my hands into fists. The truth was, my mother had power on a level I couldn't begin to understand. She held all the cards. I was simply a foot soldier.

"Go on. Take your shot. Are you going to kill me? News flash, son. I. Can't. Die. Your pitiful cousin may have bested her mother, but she didn't kill her. Auntie War is licking her wounds, but she'll be back. We always come back."

The lick of fear that sent through me shouldn't have been possible. There was no reason for me to fear my own mother, but I would be a fool not to steer clear of an angry horsewoman. They'd been set with their purpose for a reason, and good fucking luck to anyone who tried to stand in their way.

Instead of answering her, I heaved out an angry breath. "I don't have to be the one to spy. I'm much better suited for other assignments."

"That might have been true before you allowed your obsession with the girl to waste all that glorious potential. Now you're not fit to do more than stay at her side like a well-trained dog. You should be happy. This is what you wanted, isn't it? To be with her. Well, now you can be. Mummy made it all better, just like she promised she would."

"This is not what I asked for."

"No . . . but it's what you've been given."

"I was supposed to be at your side, ruling after the world ends, your crown prince of Pestilence."

"And now you're the sullied, banished one. But thank you for finally getting me what I desired."

It would seem that was the end of the conversation because my eyes snapped open and I found myself in Asher's bed—and body—once more.

"Cocksucking sonofawhore," I bellowed, taking the pillow I clutched like a cherished stuffie and flinging it across the room. It smacked into the top of the scattered items on the dresser, sending them toppling to the floor with a satisfying crash.

Well, at least this realm had *that* going for it.

SEVEN

ASHER

The sensation of being knocked through your own mind is about as unsettling as you'd imagine. I simultaneously felt as though I'd been kicked in the balls and tossed onto a roller coaster upside down without a seatbelt. I had to close my eyes against the swirl of imagery I couldn't make heads or tails of.

My ears rang as the volume around me rose in a deafening crescendo of white noise until everything suddenly stopped and the familiar scent of pot and artificial vanilla assaulted my nose. Man, it was like being back in my bedroom at the haven, the one-room apartment I'd commandeered through a series of fake documents and *repossessed* cash.

I'd decided at sixteen I'd had enough of the foster system and set out on my own. Not a life choice I'd recommend, but we do what we have to do.

"Sam?" My voice echoed in the dark, but I sure as fuck hadn't spoken.

As my eyes adjusted to the light in the room, a sinking feeling took hold in my gut. It wasn't *like* being back. I *was* back. Vanilla sex candle on the dresser, half-used box of Magnums on the floor by the bed, Superman bedspread, and a naked lamp I'd picked up in the alley behind the complex. If there was more light coming in through the window, I'd see the Kate Beckinsale poster on the wall. Underworld Kate. My favorite.

"Sam!"

This time I could feel my mouth open and close, along with the curiosity and faint tendril of panic that accompanied the shout.

"I think we're supposed to discuss safe words before we fifty shades this shit!"

I knew what was going to happen next. I'd tug on my bound wrists, the belts tying me to the bedposts would cut into my skin, and no one would come for me.

"Samantha! What the fuck?"

She didn't answer. She wouldn't. Sam betrayed me and sold me out; the me that was trapped inside my own head was screaming for us to get out of this mess. To escape before it was too late. Fuck, I hated being a captive in my mind.

I'd replayed this memory often, usually in my nightmares. This was the moment that changed everything for me. The single life-defining event that derailed every single plan I'd ever had. No MIT. No Sam in a white dress with a matching picket fence. No three-legged mutt named Tripod I'd rescued from the pound.

I knew what was coming before the door even opened.

"Sam, it's about fucking time! Don't you know the first rule of kinky fuckery? No man left behind. Consent is sexy."

"I'll be sure to tell her that." The cool voice of a woman who was definitely not Sam filled the room. Just as I knew it would.

A chill ran down my spine. I was lucky to be alive after my smart mouth continued to get the better of me. I knew that now as I watched this play out again.

"Did she book a threesome for us? How thoughtful. I'm not really into older chicks, though."

She wasn't that old, not really. Somewhere in her twenties, maybe, but chicks never liked to be reminded of their age, and I was trying hard not to show how fucking scared I was. Being tied to a bed mostly naked was every teenage boy's fantasy . . . until a stranger walked into the room and he was at their mercy. Then it was just scary as hell. Trust me. I'd lived it.

"The only threesome you'll be having is from the pits of hell, you self-serving prick."

"Jeez, you don't have to be so mean about it."

Shut up, past me. Stop poking the vengeful witch.

But it was too late. She lit my sex candle, the room glowing and already smelling more like warm vanilla. It cast into sharp relief the discarded laundry, condom wrappers, and shoes I hadn't cleaned up.

"Beware the black flame candle," I intoned with a nervous chuckle. "Hope you're not a virgin. Witches might come for us."

"The witch is already here."

"Fuck me," I whispered, fear finally taking hold of my stupid ass.

"Pass."

"Haha, yeah, me too."

She smiled, her eyes filled with wicked glee, like she was going to relish whatever she had planned. "Hold still. This might pinch a little."

"Aren't you going to buy me dinner first?"

One hand pressed flat to my chest, she dug her nails into the skin over my heart and began murmuring—no, chanting—in a language I didn't know. The words were lyrical. Ancient. And with each one, something in me tightened until it felt like I was going to break.

I fought the urge to scream until I couldn't keep it in anymore as what seemed like ants crawled through my veins. Stinging started on the top of my hand, though I felt it everywhere. I was on fire. Burning from the inside out.

I was dying. I had to be dying.

Fuck, I was too pretty to die.

Then the scent of sulfur hit my nostrils. God, was I having a stroke?

No, that was toast.

She released me and smirked down at my panting, sweaty form.

"Is that . . . all . . . you've got? Can't even . . . finish the job? Someone call the dojo. Your ninja assassin card should be revoked." I was going to puke. Any second. "Not much of a witch, are you?"

"Oh, the job is finished. But you're not going to die easily, hacker. You're going slowly. Painfully. You'll suffer and remember my mate's name with each pulse of your heart that brings you closer to death's door."

As if she willed it to happen, my arm throbbed, and searing pain wound through me. This time I didn't even fight the urge to scream. It was torn from me, tears pouring from my eyes.

Fuck. It sucked just as much as it had the first time I'd lived through this. The pain was excruciating. I didn't want to see any more, but I couldn't block it out. Thankfully, I knew it didn't last much longer.

Just as the pain reached its climax, purple light swelled in the room, blinding me and sending me tumbling back. Out of the memory. Out of that room. Out into the Wild West of my mind.

EIGHT

I stared at Asher's locked bedroom door, my stomach tied up in knots. This was the third night in a row he'd locked me out. It killed me to think he blamed me for Rosie. But that had to be the cause. He blamed us all for not protecting her when that was our sole job. Keep our mate safe.

"Asher?" I called, knocking on the door. "I need proof of life, man. I'm starting to worry."

I could hear him rustling around in there, doing whatever it was he did when he locked himself away. It sure as shit wasn't sleeping. The guy's bags had bags. He was on a full-blown bender, and this was an official intervention.

At least that's what I was telling myself. Mostly, I just wanted to know that we were okay. He and I. I fucking missed him.

"I'm gonna need you to answer me before I break down the door." I rattled the doorknob. "I'll give you until the count of three. One . . ."

The door swung open, revealing a haggard-looking Asher with nothing but disdain in his eyes. "I'm fine. I just need some goddamned privacy."

Jesus. It was like we'd taken a turn somewhere and ended up back in the pre-Rosie days. No, worse. This wasn't even our hate-fuckship, or whatever it used to be. This was like we barely knew each other. Two strangers coexisting in the same house.

"Listen, I know it's hard having us all up in your space when you're used to being alone . . ."

"No fucking kidding."

Ouch.

"But we're all grieving in our own way. Maybe grieving isn't the right word, but it will be easier if we deal with what these changes mean, you know . . . together."

Look at me, trying to use my words and talk about my feelings.

"I'm not grieving. I'm pissed. I need some fucking space, and no one is giving it to me. Everywhere I look there's a Mercer."

"At least the view is nice."

Not even a smirk. *C'mon, Asher. Throw a guy a bone here. Can't you see I'm freaking the fuck out?*

"Look, we can go. Ben and I can stay at The Tip if you don't want us here. But . . . all of us being together was your idea. I don't get why you're acting this way."

"Great idea. Do you need help packing?"

Whoa. At least put up a little fight, man. What happened to dating? What the fuck's happening right now?

"Wait. Are you . . . are we breaking up?" The wobble in my voice would've been embarrassing if my heart didn't hurt so bad.

"Were we together?"

The complete lack of *anything* in his gaze nearly sent me staggering back.

"What the fuck, Asher? Are you serious right now?"

"Rosie wanted us both. She held us together. She's gone. You should be too. Actually, it would be even better if she was here and you and your sad sack twin fucked off."

"I thought you were ready to stop hiding and face your demons. With us at your side."

He laughed at that. "Maybe I am, and I realized I don't need anyone's help to do it."

My stomach churned as a cold pit formed. So this was what being dumped felt like? It hurt like hell. A cross between whiplash and getting kicked in the dick. *Zero out of ten stars. Do not recommend.*

"I can't believe you're saying this. We . . . you told me things. I said I loved you. I don't understand."

"Did I fucking say it back?"

Oof. He hadn't. He telegraphed it, though. At least, I thought he did. Maybe I'd misread everything. Saw what I wanted to see. Made him—us—into something we never really were.

I ran a hand through my hair, trying to ignore the full-body shakes this interaction caused. I was about ten seconds away from passing out or throwing up. I needed to get out of here.

"You know what, Asher? Fuck this. And fuck you too."

"No thanks. I'm good. You don't have anything I want."

Now I was just angry. Angry at him for hurting me. At myself for believing I could ever be happy. And at Rosie for making me think love was something I deserved. Love and vulnerability only ended in heartbreak and pain. Love was for fools.

Asher had made me into the biggest fool on the planet.

And I was so fucking done.

I spun around, flinching when Asher slammed his bedroom door shut behind me. What had I expected, him to rush after me and say it had all been a joke? The only joke here was me.

My twin was on the couch, his attention lifting as I tore into the room.

"What's w-wrong?"

"Pack your shit. We're leaving."

"I d-don't have any shit."

"Even better."

He raised a brow but stood. "W-where we going?"

"The Tip. I can't be here."

Ben nodded, pulling his keys from his pocket. "I'll d-drive."

That was probably for the best. I was liable to run us off the damn mountain with the way I felt. I needed Rosie to put me back together, but for all intents and purposes, she'd left me too.

"When you come to your senses and figure out you fucked up, you know where I'll be, Ash-hole," I called as I moved the broken front door away from the opening. "But don't expect me to drop everything when you come running back."

"W-what's going on?" Ben asked.

"I don't want to talk about it. Let's go. I need a drink."

We climbed into the truck, and I had to fist my hands on my thighs to stop them from trembling. I was so worked up that I couldn't tell if I wanted to cry or punch something. Maybe both.

I'd never had to deal with a breakup before. How the hell did people work through this? Ice cream and rom-coms didn't seem like they'd cut it. Maybe a gallon of rum and self-flagellation? That seemed most likely to send me into oblivion for a while. Or some of my good weed. Though my stupid shifter metabolism meant none of that would work for long.

Fuck.

I hadn't realized I'd said it out loud until my twin's eyes met mine after I punched the dashboard and dented it.

Nope. Didn't feel any better, and now I had to fix it. Perfect.

Thankfully Ben stayed quiet as he drove down the mountain, the truck bouncing with each pothole he couldn't avoid. Except, as I zeroed in on the terrain in front of us, I realized these weren't potholes at all.

"Are those birds?" I asked.

The sky was just dark enough as the sun set for everything to be a little hard to see.

Normally we had to deal with deer leaping in front of the truck at this time of day, not bird carcasses littering the road.

"Th-there's something w-wrong with this place."

"You think? What gave it away, Sherlock?"

Ben raised a brow, his silent warning for me to watch it before he was the one throwing punches. I knew it wasn't fair to take my temper out on him, but he was the only punching bag I had. And the only person I could count on to take my shit and not leave me.

"Sorry," I sighed, leaning my head back on the seat. "We need to get Rosie and get the fuck out of here. It might be time to find a new town. Close up the bar and leave all this behind."

The way my twin's jaw clenched told me I'd said exactly the wrong thing. "W-we're not t-taking her anyw-where."

Oh, goodie. This again.

"You're going to have to come to terms with her being a vampire sooner or later."

His grip on the steering wheel tightened, his knuckles white. "N-no, I d-don't."

"She's our mate, Ben."

"My m-mate is d-dead."

"No, she's fucking not. You saw it. She is alive and working through her transition. She's ours, Ben. You can't change that just by saying it."

"If y-you want her s-so bad, y-you keep her."

For the second time that day, it felt like something vital was being stolen from me.

"No. Fuck no, Bentley. You are not ruining this for me. I've already lost everything else. Don't make me lose her too."

"I'm n-not. I h-hate this. What s-she is. You m-make your choice. I'll m-make m-mine."

I couldn't breathe. "We do everything together. We always have. You can't leave her. It won't be right without you."

"You'll s-survive."

I raked my hands through my hair, gripping my skull and squeezing tight. "Is everyone taking crazy pills today? It's like I woke up in the goddamn Twilight Zone."

"I'm n-not the one w-wanting to be a v-v-vampire's blood bag. It's not m-me making bad d-decisions."

"Ben, it's Rosie. *Our* Rosie. Not some nameless, faceless monster.

She's still the same at the core, you'll see. You just need to give her a chance to adjust."

My twin was done speaking on the matter as he pulled up in front of the bar and cut the engine. "D-drop it. I j-just want to m-move on." He got out of the truck and stormed to the front door, his body vibrating with tension.

"I hate this," I muttered as I followed him, knowing that I'd be assaulted by the scent of her and memories of the life I'd almost had as soon as I walked inside the building.

I'd get her back somehow.

I had to.

CHAPTER

NINE

BEN

"Fuck," I muttered as the pint glass slipped from my fingers and shattered on the floor. "Get it together, Bentley."

"You okay, boss?" Darla asked, coming around the bar with a freshly washed rack of glasses, the steam billowing from them as she set them down on the counter.

"D-do I l-look okay?"

"Not really. I mean, don't get me wrong," she said, crossing her arms and settling in as she leaned against the counter. "You're always smoking hot, but you've taken broody to a whole new level. I half expect you to break one of those beer bottles and threaten a customer with it if they sneeze in your general direction."

I raised a brow. "Th-that bad, huh?"

"It's rough. But not the sexy kind." She looked around, her shrewd gaze picking up on exactly what was amiss. "Where's Nadia?"

Jesus, even her fake name sent a spike through my chest. "She l-left."

"What? Why?"

"Her h-husband took h-her b-back."

63

"Took her? Like against her will?"

"Th-that's the p-part you're hung u-up on? Not th-the husband?"

Darla shrugged. "I assumed she was running from something. Dickwad husband makes sense. But her leaving? She was so happy here with you and Remi. Finally coming into her own, you know? I can't imagine she'd just leave that all behind."

"Y-yeah, well . . ." I didn't know what to say. If she kept me talking, I'd probably do something mortifying, like break down crying. And not even a single man tear, but full-on sobs that end with me curled up in the fetal position.

Thank fuck the door opened, bringing us our first customer of the day. My relief was short-lived when Asher strode in, confident, cocky, and smiling like he had a secret. For someone who just crushed my brother, he seemed really damn happy. Then again, he was also the only one of us Rosie had mate-marked, so maybe he *was* happy. Just because I had a major issue with her turning didn't mean anyone else did.

No. I was the only one whose life had just ended as he knew it. I didn't understand how they could just so readily accept it. I'd watched the life leave her, watched her fall to the ground, avenged her, carried her lifeless body inside . . . lost her. The moment that spark inside her was snuffed out, so was mine. It didn't matter that she'd come back. It wasn't her. Vampires were tricky creatures. They could make you think they still held onto their humanity, but I knew better. I'd seen it firsthand, the carnage that followed in the wake of a blood-crazed monster with an angel's face.

Asher snagged a seat at the bar.

Even though I wanted to pour a pint in his lap, I couldn't afford to start shit with a customer. Business was still sluggish, and we could use all the paying patrons we could muster.

"D-Darla, your customer."

"Aw, c'mon, Bentley, I thought we were pals," Asher said, locking eyes with me. "I'm sure Darla has plenty to do."

I nodded at the woman in question before pulling Asher a pint without asking what he wanted. He'd take what I fucking gave him.

"You sure look cheery for a guy who was mooning around about puffins the last time I saw you," Darla said.

A vacantness filled his eyes for a moment before he huffed and shrugged. "Yeah, well. You can't save them all."

Darla and I exchanged a look. Asher really had done a one-eighty in the last few days.

"Did sh-she brainwash y-you when she g-gave you that bite?" I asked him, setting his glass down with more force than was strictly necessary.

"She gave me the goddamned world when she did that. You couldn't understand. And you won't, will you?"

My wolf growled low in my throat, a warning that Asher was about to find himself without a throat if he kept it up.

"Now, now, who's a good kitty?"

"Asher . . ."

He laughed. "So uptight. You should try laughing once in a while, Mercer. It would do you a world of good."

What's there to laugh about?

"She's g-gone. H-how can you l-laugh?"

"She's not gone. She'll be back, and I, for one, can't wait." He shuddered in pleasure. "Those teeth felt good."

"Teeth?" Darla asked, her face going pale.

I cut Asher a glare. We couldn't let anyone know she was a vampire. They'd kill her, and then us for hiding her. I told myself it was the second part of that sentence that bothered me. Even if my heart said otherwise. Love was a real pain in my ass.

The door opened again, breathing new life into the pool of grief and anger I was stuck in. Until I saw who it was. Sheriff Dallas Walker strode inside, thumbs hooked into his belt, head held high, chest puffed out.

"There's been another murder, y'all. Mayor's on her way to

Anchorage right now. There's going to be an official press release. Seems we've got a serial killer on our hands."

My first thought sent fear skittering across my skin. *Rosie.*

"Who was it?" Darla asked.

"Not one of ours, thank the Lord. A moose shifter passing through on his way to Canada. Man by the name of Michael Brady. Guess he went by 'Big Mike' according to his belongings. Near as we can tell, he was a loner, no herd or family to speak of. We found him face down in Devil's Lake. Throat torn out. Just like the rest."

"V-vampire?" I asked, proud as fuck I only stammered once.

"Possibly, but seems more like a shifter. Vampires are notoriously neat feeders, unless they're feral. Since we've ruled you out, I have no leads. You haven't seen any vamps in the area, have you?"

The way he stared at me made me uncomfortable. He was sizing me up, trying to see if I'd give him any information that would connect me in even the smallest way. My biggest fear was that this time, I really was part of this. What if Rosie had broken free and killed this guy?

"Unless, of course, that's just what the killer wants us to think . . ." Dallas was taunting me. Waiting for me to make a mistake and out myself.

Well, joke's on you, pal. It ain't me.

"Where's that pretty little mate of yours, Mercer? Already bare-foot and pregnant back at home? You work fast." The glint in his eyes told me he knew he was spouting bullshit.

"She l-left for a w-while."

"Back to her husband, then?"

My jaw clenched. "Something l-like th-that."

Dallas raised a brow. "Seems I recall telling her not to leave town. Mite suspicious we've got more bodies right around the time she conveniently takes off."

"Y-you'll have t-to take it u-up with h-her. I d-don't know w-where she is." I stood my ground, flicking my gaze to Asher, who just sat there smirking. "Is th-there anything else y-you need, Sheriff? I'm b-busy."

Dallas huffed out a laugh. "You look real busy to me. You just keep close to town. I'll need a word with you as the investigation continues."

I didn't say a word, just gave him a hard stare as he tipped his hat and sauntered back out the way he came.

Good fucking riddance.

Asher snickered as he brought the pint glass to his lips.

"W-what are y-you laughing at?"

"Cops. They never look in the right places."

I narrowed my eyes. "D-do you know w-where they should be looking?"

It wouldn't be unusual for the hacker to know something the rest of us didn't, but that seemed like a stretch, even for him. If he could stop a serial killer from running amok in our town, he would. Wouldn't he?

Instead of answering, all he did was shrug and take another long pull from his beer, which didn't remotely make me feel better.

What had gotten into him lately?

CHAPTER
TEN

PAN

There was just something . . . magical about people appreciating your work. The fear in that ridiculous sheriff's voice, the fear he tried to cover with bravado, was like food for my non-existent soul. Chicken Soup for the Demonic Soul? That had a nice ring to it. Perhaps it would be my great American novel once the Apocalypse was over.

I could see myself now, Rosie at my feet, me at a desk, a roaring fire as she sucked me off while I sat at my typewriter waxing poetic about things that did a demon's body good.

I did have a rather nice smoking jacket. Perhaps Mother would send it to me now that it seemed I'd be stuck topside for the foreseeable future. They'd never catch me, no matter how hard they tried. More fodder for my memoir. How I got away with murdering an entire town and they smiled while I did it.

I snickered and brought the pint glass to my lips.

"W-what are y-you laughing at?"

"Cops. They never look in the right places."

"D-do you know w-where they should be looking?"

Right bloody here, I wanted to say. The truth was, I needed the focus of this town to be on the murders, not the pestilence ravaging the animals. Humans and supernatural creatures were crafty, and they'd do something accidentally brilliant if I let them pay attention to the infection that was spreading. How do you think we got vaccines? Those damnable things had foiled many a global pandemic.

Ben stared at me as if waiting for me to solve a mystery. Oh, right, he asked me a question. I shrugged in response, then sucked back half of my pint. The quizzical expression on his face sent alarm through me, though. If I was going to pull off this broody hacker costume, I really needed to up my game.

The door opened, and three obnoxious gargoyles tumbled inside, loud and brash until their gazes found me. That was my cue to excuse myself. I didn't like the way they watched me.

Draining the rest of my beer, I slammed the glass on the bar and stood.

"I think I'll go for a walk. It's getting too busy in here for me."

"Off to visit . . . what was his name? Toderick?" Darla asked with just enough smugness I knew it was some sort of joke at my expense.

"So what if I am?"

Who the fuck was Toderick?

She shook her head and rolled her eyes. "You really need to get better hobbies."

"L-leave him alone. H-he's anti-s-social."

"Like you?"

"I'm quiet. Th-there's a d-difference."

Shrugging on my—*shudder*—hoodie, I zipped it up and covered my head with the aforementioned hood. Then I left them all to their own devices, wishing I had even an ounce of the power I needed to infect them all and get them out of my way.

I despised Aurora Springs. I despised the way everything smelled so crisp, the bright sunlight during the day, the blue—*gag*—sky, the babbling creeks. No sulfur anywhere. No hellfire. No brimstone. No hellions to order about. And worst of all, no Rosie to make things tolerable. If she were with me, I could withstand the . . . humanity of it all.

I walked without aim, not paying attention as the buildings grew few and far between. My handiwork really had spread beautifully. But then it always does. I am a master at my craft. As I am with most things.

What? It's not bragging when it's the truth.

Anyone who tells you to be humble is selling something. Or trying to dim your shine.

Looking at the town through Asher's eyes was different from those of my poor Scottish meat suit. It didn't take long for his vision to weaken as my essence ravaged his system. And I'd been rather focused on Rosie and my goal of separating her from her mates at the time. Things were different now. My perfect vessel might be missing a few key parts, but he'd been made to last.

I found myself stopped in front of a secluded cabin, not sure how and when I'd arrived. My thoughts had taken center stage, mainly thoughts of *her*. I hadn't seen her since the night she marked me, and blast it all, I think I *missed* her. Oh, bloody hell, was this nausea crawling up my throat? Was I going to be sick? Talk about irony.

"Look at you, you disaster of a demon. You can't even exist without her anymore. This is what you get for letting her mark you." I loathed the sound of the voice that came out of my mouth. Asher may be brilliant—for a human—but the American accent was just shameful. I never will understand why my mother preferred it. Must be her appreciation for rebellion or something. She thrived in chaos.

Curious what it was about this place that had snagged my subconscious's attention, I crept closer. Stealth probably wasn't necessary, there weren't exactly people milling about, but one never could be too careful.

A thrumming pulse in my ears had my breath catching until I

realized it was Asher's heart hammering. My stomach twisted as something drew me closer to the dwelling. Need coiled inside me, begging me to break down the door and get to whatever was in there.

If I wasn't trapped in this form, I'd be able to home in on what this pull was. I could do what I needed to and either dispatch the threat or take the prize hidden behind the walls. Instead, I stood there, useless and human. As I turned away, forcing myself to leave the property, a low growl hit my ears.

A thrill ran up my spine at the sound. *Ma petite monstre.* I'd found her.

I had already started to turn back around when I caught the *snick* of a door opening. I was slammed up against the side of a tree, the sweet, citrusy scent my only clue as to what happened.

"Rosie," I groaned as she ran her nose along my throat. The feel of her curves pressed up against me was a balm to my restless soul.

"Mate," she snarled, a second before her teeth found purchase.

"Roslyn, no!"

Blinding pleasure raced through me but was almost instantly replaced with agony as she was ripped away from my arms. Oh, I was going to have a field day when I got to stake that vampire duke. She was the reason I was here. I craved being inside her as much as she craved the taste of my blood.

"Fuck, man, what are you doing? We were fine."

He held a fighting Rosie back with a grimace on his haggard face. The vampire had certainly looked better. Here he was, keeping her all to himself, probably fucking himself to death. What a way to go.

"You were *not* fine. Who told you to come here? You've probably set us back days. Do you even have any idea what you've done?"

"I went for a walk. Chill."

I gave a little shudder at the colloquialism, but when in Rome, as they say.

"Let me have him," she wailed. "Gavin, please."

"See? She's lucid. She knows what she wants. Me." I puffed up at the statement. She was begging for me.

"She might want you, but you're human."

No, I'm bloody not. Seeing as how I couldn't very well deny it given my sausage casing, I just swallowed back a sigh as he continued.

"Even being her mate, she might drain you. I don't want to have to create a new vampire just to save her the guilt."

No, there would be none of that. This body was already full on occupancy. No additional monsters required.

"Please, my lord. I need him."

Gavin's eyes shuttered as he locked himself down. "I said *no*. Go inside, Roslyn. Right now, or I will chain you up again."

She looked at us in turn, her expression torn between hunger for me and the need to obey.

"I'll come back, Rosie. When you're ready." Why the devil did I sound so sweet? I was *not* sweet. "I promise." There I was, a simpering fool. Oh, hell.

"You won't return unless I summon you. Is that clear? We have work to do. At this rate, it could be months before she's trustworthy."

I stared at the erstwhile duke. "And here I thought you were good at taming wild things."

"I am. Unlike you. I know how it's done and that it requires time to do it correctly."

As far as insults went, it was hardly the worst, yet it crawled under my skin anyway. I resented any and all implications that I was *less than* any of these wankers. They had no idea. None.

"You know where to find me, Gavin. If she needs me—"

"She won't. I'm her husband. Her mate. You're an extra distraction she doesn't need." He snagged her by the wrist and stared deep into her eyes, putting my mate in a sort of trance. "Go inside, petal. I'll see to you. He won't be bothering you again."

Without even a passing glance my way, she walked into the cabin and Gavin followed, bolting the door behind him.

I watched as their shadows moved behind glowing windows. Watched. Waited. Planned.

He thought he could dismiss me like I was one of his submissives? Please. There were very few people I took orders from. One, in fact, and it sure as shit wasn't him.

Just try and keep me away, Your Grace. I'll be the one collecting your tears before long.

CHAPTER

ELEVEN

ROSIE

The urge to break through the door was so strong I had to clench my fists and dig my nails into my palms. The pain gave me something else to focus on. Something to stop me from shoving Gavin aside and chasing after my mate.

"I thought I was doing better," I mumbled, shame creeping up my neck.

"You are. I've told you, petal, this isn't going to happen overnight, but you're getting there."

"I want him."

"I know."

"Gavin, I don't like feeling this way. My skin is crawling, my gums ache, there's this emptiness in my belly, and I'm . . . on fire all at the same time."

"It's your mate bond fighting with your thirst. You won't kill him, but you could still hurt him so badly he'd never be the same."

"But you're my mate too. Why am I so much more in control of myself around you than the others?"

He took my hand, unclenching my fist and stroking his thumb along my skin. "Because we're the same. You can't kill me or hurt me

—not beyond what I can withstand, anyway—and I've already had the pleasure of marking you as mine."

"Wouldn't it be the same with Ben and Remi, then? They marked me too."

Gavin shrugged. "They're wolves. You and I are vampires. It stands to reason our bond would be strong from the start. It was made to withstand this very thing. In fact, now that we're the same, it's likely stronger than ever. We're natural mates, whereas you and they are not. The rules could very well be different."

"And Asher?"

"He's bonded to you just as you were to me when you were human. You'll crave him, and he will be drawn to you regardless of his own safety."

"Does that mean I'll always be a danger to him?"

"Only in the way I was once a danger to you." He stroked my cheek. "You will learn your limits. How much to take, how much he can withstand. You'll always need to be careful with him. He's breakable. But it will become instinct in time."

His warning rang in my head. He's breakable. Asher wouldn't like knowing I thought that about him, but it was the truth. I'd seen first-hand what vampire strength could do to someone. I'd never hurt him if I could help it.

"Can you sense him? Now?" Gavin backed away from me and busied himself by opening a bottle of red wine and filling a glass for each of us.

"Sense him?"

"Yes. Close your eyes. Think about Asher and what he is to you. You should be able to sense him."

I did as he told me, letting the picture of my black-hatted knight form in my mind. Just like Gavin suggested, I could feel him there, just out of reach. Like there was an invisible cord that stretched between us, and with every step he took away from me, it pulled tighter. A bit like a rubber band, though I knew our bond would never snap. It was more like living in a constant state of anticipation, of waiting for the moment he would come back.

Need crashed through me, but Gavin's lessons about control echoed through my mind, and with effort, I was able to push past it and focus on the man himself. His hair, tousled from running his fingers through it while working. Those bright blue eyes, filled with the usual mistrust and suspicion he reserved for everyone except me. A pang of deep longing stabbed my heart.

But then the scent of brimstone curled in my nostrils, and a low hum filtered through my thoughts. It was one I hadn't experienced in a long time.

"Pan?"

I didn't intend to send the thought; it was more a reaction than a choice, so I was surprised when his smoky croon filled my mind.

"Miss me, ma petite monstre?*"*

Unsure how to respond with Gavin so close, I simply attempted to block Pan out. He wasn't interested in leaving. His presence overwhelmed me.

"You can't hide from me, my filthy little slut. You're mine. No matter what you try to do to get rid of me. Even your death can't part us."

I swallowed, not remotely prepared for the bolt of lust his words sent straight to my core. I'd forgotten how potent he could be. Or was I simply more amped up because of my transition? No . . . I'd always had this reaction to Pan. Turning hadn't changed that.

"Are you wet for me? Tell me, since I can't make you show me."

"That's never stopped you before."

"You're the one who changed the terms of our little arrangement."

In the wake of everything that happened, I'd forgotten about that. And the part Lilith played in ending it. *"You shouldn't be able to be in my head like this. We don't have an arrangement anymore. "*

Something in him jolted, unease, perhaps? But he seemed to shake it off and steamroll right on through my statement.

"Oh, but we do. You gave me your soul. I won't give it back. Not even

the mother demon herself can make me. You are mine, Roslyn. My good little whore. Forever."

"I'm not yours."

"It's only a matter of time before you're begging me to claim you, mon ange."

I shoved him out of my mind, opening my eyes and finding Gavin staring at me curiously.

"I'll take that as a success?"

"Yes. I found him." *Among others.*

"So now you know what the bond feels like. You could try it with your shifters as well. That should answer your question about whether their links to you are intact."

Still a bit on edge from the unexpected run-in with Pan, I took a moment to shake out my limbs and clear my mind before creating my mental image of Ben. The second I did, the fresh scent of trees and outdoors washed over me, followed by a pulse of anguish right on its heels.

My eyes flew open, and my hands reached up to rest over my heart, as if that would somehow ease its ache. I'd found him, meaning our bond remained, but his pain was unlike anything I'd known. I couldn't walk through it without falling victim to the grief and hurt, all wrapped in a layer of hatred.

"He despises me," I whispered.

"Bentley?"

I nodded.

Gavin took my chin between his fingers and made me look at him. "Try the other one."

"What if he feels the same?"

"Then at least you'll know."

I couldn't imagine living out my days as an immortal, knowing I had a mate who turned their back on me. From a logical perspective, I understood it. After what he and Remi suffered, of course I did. My heart, on the other hand, would never get over his rejection. I didn't think I could take it if Remi felt the same.

"I don't want to. If Ben and I are still linked, so are Remi and I."

"I didn't take you for one who'd rather bury her head in the sand than face her problems head-on. What happened to the woman who faked her own death rather than accept the hand fate dealt her?"

"This is different. It's self-preservation. This way, I can hold on to hope. But if I know . . ."

I had to look away from his dark gaze. He was far too intuitive, and I wasn't ready to face the truth just yet. When in doubt, pivot. I knew one way to change this subject and get us something we both wanted. Something that would only hurt in the best kind of way.

"Gavin?"

"Yes, petal?" He toyed with the rim of his wineglass.

"If you've marked me, wouldn't it stand to reason I should mark you?"

His eyes flared with the banked heat I'd grown to know all too well. "That is the usual way of things, yes."

"Then why haven't you mentioned it?"

"You were hardly in a state to do anything about it."

"I seem to have claimed Asher just fine."

He quirked a brow, his lips curling up in that sensual smirk that melted my insides. "Is that how you remember it?"

"Well . . . he didn't die."

"Only because we were there to intervene."

Concern made my belly knot. "Is that why you haven't brought it up? You're worried there's no one here to intervene on your behalf?"

He snickered. "Not remotely. The day I need a wolf to save me is the day I'll gladly go meet the sun." Seeing that I didn't share his amusement, his expression sobered, and he set the wineglass down to take my face in both his hands. "I may be a dominant, but I also would never take advantage of you while you're not yourself. You should be fully cognizant of your choices regarding matters like these."

The thought of marking him made my fangs tingle with the urge to descend. It was a feeling I had grown accustomed to in a short time, one I welcomed now. I wanted to mark Gavin, feed from him, bond with him. Memories of our night in the church as he'd done the very same to me caused a flood of slick arousal to pool between my thighs. He inhaled sharply, eyes burning with a need that echoed mine.

"Let me mark you, mate. I've already felt the sting of rejection once tonight. Don't bring me that kind of pain again. Make me cry for other reasons. Please, my lord. You made me yours. Now let me make you mine."

TWELVE

GAVIN

Dear God in heaven. How could anyone resist her when she laid herself bare like that? No wonder she had four of us salivating on our knees. Metaphorical knees. I didn't kneel for anyone.

But she would.

"On. Your. Knees."

Her lust shot through our bond, amplifying my own. The way she responded to me without fail sent pride and pleasure coursing through me in equal measure. But here, it was watching her sink slowly to her aforementioned knees that nearly did me in. My cock was hard enough that I worried it would punch through my trousers.

"Like this, my lord?" she asked, all innocence and wide eyes, except for the hunger. That newfound unquenchable thirst she so recently tamed flared back to life, leaving her teetering at the edge of control.

I stroked her hair, taking the length in my fist and giving it a gentle—for me—yank.

She swallowed, her tongue darting out to wet her lips. "Do I need to start the scene?"

"No. Not for this."

"Really?"

Jerking her hair again, I made her stare at me. "What was that?"

"Nothing. Forgive me, my lord."

"You're forgiven. I would forgive you anything, petal."

Her brow furrowed, fingers twitching as she worked through something in her head.

"What is it? What do you want?"

"To touch you. To take you in my hand. My mouth. But you haven't given me permission."

I stroked her velvety cheek with my other hand. "You are such a good girl, duchess. You may touch me."

She didn't waste a second reaching up to undo my zipper and release my swollen length. My breath left me in a hiss of pleasure, and I didn't miss her eyes widening at the sight of what she brought out in me.

Those amber irises drifted away from the insistent erection in front of her and focused on my inner thigh, an altogether different sort of need evident in her expression almost instantly.

That wouldn't do. Not at all.

With a harsh tug of her hair still wrapped around my fist, I forced her attention to my eyes. "Did I say you could feed yet?"

She blinked a few times, fighting through her bloodlust. "N-no."

"Poor petal. You're so thirsty, aren't you?"

"Yes, my lord."

A wicked grin curled my lips. "If you want my blood, darling . . ."

Her breath hitched.

I bit into my wrist and allowed my blood to drip onto my erection, painting my shaft until it was coated in the red liquid. "You may suck it off my cock."

She swallowed audibly, her whole body tight. I could see her nipples pressing against the fabric of the shirt she wore. My shirt. It was her only covering. She was surrounded by me, my scent permeating the space. No one would question who her mate was. And after we finished what we started tonight, no one could challenge it.

My thighs trembled in anticipation of everything we had within reach for our future. She wasn't breakable any longer. I could be as rough as I liked, and my beautiful doll wouldn't shatter under my attentions. The best part? She would let me. *Beg* me.

Now *my* mouth was watering.

A drop of blood hung off the tip, threatening to spill onto the floor. "Go on, petal. Don't waste my gift. I don't want to be cross with you."

"Thank you, my lord." She leaned forward, greedily sucking me into her mouth.

The groan I let out as I hit the back of her throat was loud enough to startle the neighbors. It was a good job we didn't have any. My knees nearly buckled when she swallowed around my length.

"Fuck, petal. Where did you learn to do that?"

Did I really want to know?

"On second thought, just keep going."

She hummed around me as her tongue laved my cock, collecting the blood I gave her.

My grip tightened in her hair as she worked me, my orgasm cresting far sooner than I'd expected. "Are you ready for my cum, petal?"

She swallowed again, and I clutched her hair harder, bringing tears to her eyes.

"Take it. All of it."

A lone tear slipped down her cheek as she looked up at me, my blood staining her lips. That was it. My shredded control was burned to a cinder under her tongue. I came hard, my vision graying around the edges, and she reached up, grabbing my arse as she worked me over, sucking me down like I was her favorite treat.

"Fuuuuck, petal. You're going to be the death of me."

She leaned back, releasing me with a wet pop and then licking her lips like a cat who'd just gotten the cream. "At least we know you'd go out with a smile."

"Impertinent brat," I said, but there was no heat in it. I was still in the throes of my climax. "I should spank you for that."

"Yes, please."

"You'd like that, wouldn't you?"

"Can we play priest and penitent?"

I smirked. "Role-play? That's not something I ever envisioned for us. But I'm not opposed." I could see how much she enjoyed the idea, her lips curling up in a slight smile. "Focus. If you want someone to play priest with, I can arrange that, but right now, you and I have a mate bond to complete. I want you coming on my cock as you mark me."

Just like that, her attention was wholly on me once more. I reached down, grasping her beneath the shoulders and lifting her up as if she weighed no more than a sack of feathers. Her legs wrapped around my waist on instinct, allowing me to shift my grip so I was holding her by the arse.

With every step toward the bedroom, the heat of her sweet, slick cunt rubbed against my already hardening cock, as if I hadn't just come like a fucking fountain down her throat seconds prior. Thank fuck I hadn't insisted she wear more than my shirt. Sometimes I was quite brilliant.

"Gavin, I'm still thirsty. I need more."

"Of course you do, wife. And more you shall have. As soon as I'm ready to give it to you. Now ride my cock."

I sat back on the bed, and she sheathed me inside her in one smooth glide of slick warmth. I could go to my death with her wrapped around me and never know I was denied entry into heaven. She was everything I'd ever needed.

"I said ride me, petal."

She didn't say a word, simply rolled her hips and threw her head back. It didn't take long before I ripped the shirt from her, baring her beautiful curves to me and committing every moment to memory.

My palms skated over her ribs, cupped her breasts, rolled those nipples that taunted me like ripe berries ready for my teeth. I needed her pain just as much as her pleasure.

Wrapping my fingers around her throat as she chased her release, I watched her eyes for any sign this was too much as I tightened my grip. All I got in response was a flushing of her skin and straining of those buds at the tips of her breasts. She loved it. Just as much as I did.

Knowing I couldn't truly hurt her, I let the sadist free and choked her even harder until her eyes rolled back in her head and a wordless gasp left her. My balls drew up, a second orgasm hovering just out of reach. The flood of her arousal and the fluttering of her pussy told me she was close too.

I needed this, her, us. Pulling her close until we were pressed chest to chest, I held her tight to me. Her lips were nestled against the hollow of my throat as my hands, which had been constricting her perfect throat only moments ago, held her hips steady.

"Now, petal. Mark me. Make me yours."

She sank her fangs into my flesh, a ragged moan escaping her as she fed from me, pussy clenching, body shuddering. Her pleasure was beautiful, but her pain would be exquisite.

I bit down on her shoulder, doing nothing to protect her from the pain as I took the blood I knew I'd need to solidify our bond. My mark had given us the same link afforded vampires with their humans. But this? She was the same as me now. We could join on the deepest level possible for our kind by exchanging mating marks. We were destined.

My cock jerked as my orgasm barreled through me, and I filled her with my cum as the bond between us finally snapped fully into place. There was nothing quite like a fated mate connection between vampires. I could sense her every emotion, and she could sense mine. Her pain ramped up my pleasure, which in turn bolstered hers in one perfect cycle. We were linked so completely that it triggered another release for us both right on the heels of the last.

She pulled away from me, her breaths coming in sharp gasps as she stared down at me. Both of us bared to each other, our walls gone, our souls open and vulnerable.

"Gavin . . ." she whispered, the one word reverent.

I cupped her cheek, knowing she didn't need the words since she could feel the truth already, but wanting to give them to her—to anyone—for the first time. "I love you, petal."

A smirk twisted her lips. "I know."

I surged up, slapping her arse. "Brat."

She squealed, but the sound was filled with joy. Wrapping her arms around my neck, she held me close, whispering in my ear. "I love you too, my lord. Thank you for giving me what I need."

"Always."

"Careful, I'm a vampire now. Always is a long time."

"I said what I said."

"Yes, my lord."

"Good girl."

CHAPTER

THIRTEEN

PAN

"Who needs this many computers? Go out and touch some grass, you pasty git," I muttered as I stood in front of Asher's monstrosity of a desk. Six, count them, six screens were currently black, but this infernal beeping wouldn't cease. I'd tracked the sound over here but still couldn't locate the source.

I pushed one of the buttons on the board of keys, and all six screens flared to life. The glow from them had me shielding my eyes like a vampire who'd been assaulted by sunlight, but then I heard the moans.

"Hello, what's this?" I pulled my arm away from my face and snickered as I took a seat in the overstuffed chair that looked like it belonged on a spaceship rather than in a human home.

"Come to daddy." There was something equal parts exciting and hilarious about finding Asher's porn. Hilarious because he was such a twat. Exciting because . . . porn. Specifically, my little monster on her knees, crawling naked toward a St. Andrew's cross.

Before I could settle in and enjoy the show, the screens went black. I hit some buttons trying to get it back, but that beeping started again, this time combined with the subtle vibration of wood.

"Bloody hell, things were about to get interesting. Can't you leave me in peace? Captain Aubergine just reported for duty." Somehow, the joke didn't land. It lacked that certain *je ne sais quoi* only my natural sex-riddled voice could provide. Damn, I missed it. And my tail. And my horns. Fuck, I hated it here.

I tore open the desk's side drawer hard enough the face ripped off, but there it was. The fucking phone that never quit. Well, one of. It would seem I just discovered a damn cellular graveyard. I pulled one out that looked like it belonged back in the 1980s. "What could you possibly need this for?"

A slim device that was all screen and no buttons lit up as the chirp began again. Was that a puffin as his phone's wallpaper? Who did that?

Snatching it from the remnants of the drawer, I stared down at the screen and smirked when the security notification popped up asking for my fingerprint. "Don't mind if I do," I murmured, pressing my forefinger to the device and frowning as I was denied.

"Really, Asher? Can't you just use your index finger like a normal human?" I rolled my eyes and went for the least obvious option. Pinky. No one gave the little finger enough credit.

"Eureka!"

A flood of text notifications raced across the screen faster than my eyes could track. "Good fucking hell. Do these miscreants have nothing better to do?"

First there was a thread of texts from one contact labeled *Fuckboi*. I was positively giddy to know who that was.

FUCKBOI:

We need to talk.

FUCKBOI:

Asher. Answer me.

FUCKBOI:

It's important.

FUCKBOI:

Did I do something wrong? At least tell me
what so I can fix it.

Aʜ, Remi. I'd really done a number on him. My devilish little heart
swelled at the thought. I almost wrote back, 'No. Shan't.' But I
contained myself. Aren't you proud of me?

Since this was surprisingly good fun, I clicked on the next
unopened message.

MOIRA THE GOOD(ISH):

How are you doing? Any more episodes? I'm
looking for a more permanent spell to help
with you know what.

Wʜᴏ ᴡᴀs Mᴏɪʀᴀ? Some witch he was fucking? Intriguing. Dismissing
that, I moved on.

Yet another notification with thirteen missed texts loomed. It
was labeled *Sausage Party*. I smirked. He might be annoying, but
Asher was funny.

FUCKBOI:

We need to have a meeting.

THE COUNT:

I'm rather busy.

FUCKBOI:

Seriously? You've been radio silent. We need to talk about her.

LUMBERSNACK:

No.

FUCKBOI:

It's only a matter of time before fangface gets her under control. She's going to want to come back to work and be part of the real world. We need to get things in order before not one, but two vampires start walking around town and people get out the pitchforks.

THE COUNT:

Do. Not. Call. Me. That.

LUMBERSNACK:

She's not coming back.

FUCKBOI:

Stop being a dick. She belongs here. We need her, even if you don't like it.

LUMBERSNACK:

Rosie is dead.

LUMBERSNACK:

Leave me alone.

Lumbersnack *has left the group message*

Lumbersnack *was added to the group by* ***Fuckboi***

THE COUNT:

The way she just rode my dick says otherwise.

LUMBERSNACK:

Good for you.

FUCKBOI:

Ben, if you leave this chat again, I'm just going to add you. This is serious. We need a plan.

WELL, this was quite entertaining. I supposed I should respond. It wouldn't do to be discovered as an impostor yet. Not until my reveal would benefit me.

ME:

Fuckboi is right. We need to make sure they can stay in town.

FUCKBOI:

Excuse me? Fuckboi? Is that me?

ME:

Yes.

FUCKBOI:

Wow. Changing your name to Ash-hole in my contacts.

ME:

Whatever helps you sleep at night . . . fuckboi.

THE COUNT:

As entertaining as this is, I'm in the middle of something. Our mate is insatiable. Which reminds me, if anyone is feeling up to donating some blood, she could use it. I only have so much.

LUMBERSNACK:

Go to the mayor and plead her case, Remi.

LUMBERSNACK:

But leave me out of it.

FUCKBOI:

Maybe I will. Let's just hope that creepy ass cat of hers didn't survive the winter. Once fangface clears her to come back and Mayor Dubois gives her blessing, Rosie is coming home. She belongs with us.

LUMBERSNACK:

Debatable.

LUMBERSNACK:

She can come back to the bar.

LUMBERSNACK:

But if she attacks a customer, she's out on her ass.

LUMBERSNACK:

And she's not sleeping in our house.

THE COUNT:

Roslyn will be staying with me. Obviously.

LUMBERSNACK:

Also, don't schedule her to work when I'm there.

FUCKBOI:

You're always there, dumbass.

LUMBERSNACK:

Exactly.

Lumbersnack *has left the group message*

I LAUGHED and then instantly sobered. Fuck, I needed to get out more. If this pitiful mortal drama was enough to entertain me, I was sadly lacking in hobbies. Fucking Rosie had been my favorite pastime. Speaking of, my cock was hard as stone after that little home movie I'd stumbled upon. I wondered if I could get it to show up again.

The phone vibrated in my hand, making me groan. They never stopped. I shouldn't have acknowledged them. What was that human saying? Don't feed the trollops? Or was that troll?

This time the incoming message was on a private thread, just me and my best mate Fuckboi.

FUCKBOI:

Why are you being this way?

ME:

What way?

FUCKBOI:

Treating me like shit.

ME:

Isn't it obvious?

FUCKBOI:

What changed?

ME:

Desperation doesn't look good on you, Remi.

FUCKBOI:

Jesus, I forgot what an asshole you could be. I really thought we were past this hot and cold shit, Asher.

FUCKBOI:

Was it all just some kind of game? Did it really not mean anything to you?

ME:

Do yourself a favor. Lose my number.

Oh, my host didn't like that. He'd been dormant since I sent him away last, but now he hammered on the barrier keeping him locked up. He wanted out. He wanted Remi.

Closing my eyes, I tossed the phone on the desk and pulled together what minimal power I had, shoving him as far back into his memories as I could. Revisiting those dark times his mind had protected him from might be just the thing.

Asher needed a reminder of who was in charge here.

Me.

Asher

Fᴜᴄᴋ. I didn't want to be here. Not again. I'd sworn I'd never come back to this fucking place, but here I was, those cruel women in their black-and-white habits staring me down with fear in their eyes.

Nuns. I hated them. With their crucifixes and prayer beads and those stupid rulers. Oh God, and that acrid pine and bleach scent that permeated everything. *Gag.* And the vinegar and chalk. Jesus, I'd forgotten about that stench. To this day, I couldn't see a chalkboard, even on a TV show, without shuddering at the memory of the feel of sponges in my hands as I cleaned until my skin was raw.

Have I said that I hated nuns? Because I do. With a passion.

I'd spent a lot of time in this orphanage, on and off over the better part of a decade, actually. It was hard to know *when* I was. I didn't remember this moment. Clearly it was locked away, a repressed memory that fucking asshole who'd stolen my body was forcing me to see. When I got out of here, I was going to kill him.

Somehow.

"Hold him still, Sister Mary Elizabeth. He'll fight us."

A woman built like a linebacker came at me. I was pretty sure she had a mustache to go with those muscles too. In fact, pointing it out is probably what got me in trouble. Or maybe it was the mole on her cheek that seemed to move of its own free will.

"Are you certain the binding will work?"

"It has to. Father Tate assured me this was the only thing we had left that would save him."

"He's so young, though. How can you think he's evil?"

Sister Margaret trained her gaze on me, pinning me to the spot even if I hadn't been restrained.

So I must've been little. Maybe seven or eight? Old enough for them to fear me for some reason, but young enough they could stop me. Why couldn't I remember this?

"Evil can come in many forms, sisters," Father Tate said as he strode into the room.

Father Dreamy. I remembered him. All the girls were in love with him. He was nice. Always had hard candy for us kids. Butterscotch usually. Sometimes cinnamon. He was our confidant. The one who stayed on our side, the one we trusted. Not like those evil nuns who punished us for breathing the same air as them without being penitent.

"I'm not evil."

My voice was small. Afraid.

I had no clue what was happening, but I was terrified.

Father Tate crouched so he was face to face with me, one hand cupping my cheek as he stared into my eyes. "Oh, but you are, Asher. Now close your eyes. This will only hurt a little."

FOURTEEN

BEN

No matter how hard I tried to make things normal, the energy at The Tip just felt wrong. There was no way around it; without Rosie here, it would never be *right* again. She'd only been in town a few months, but she'd left her imprint on my bar just as deeply as she had on my soul. The place was fucking haunted. No matter where I looked, all I saw were the spots she was supposed to be. Behind the counter, pulling pints and serving the gargoyles. Sitting on a stool in the kitchen while I prepped in the morning, swinging her legs and teasing me. Leaning in the doorway of the office, keeping me company while I did paperwork.

Fuck, I'd bottled this all up inside, and it finally couldn't be contained any longer. It hurt. Worse than anything I'd experienced. Every memory stabbed through my sternum like a red-hot poker. She was missing from me because I couldn't come to terms with what she'd become. Aisling may have murdered her, but *I* killed us. That was the bitter truth.

As much as I told myself she was gone, that she wasn't my mate anymore because *my mate* died, it was a lie. One that didn't make things any better. How the fuck would I survive it if she came back to work like Remi insisted?

It had ruined me to see those fangs glistening in Rosie's perfect mouth. To watch her go after my brother as she tried to feed from him. Wild and uncontrollable, vicious. I'd never expected to see such bloodlust in her eyes. She was deadly and dangerous. Like a wild animal. They couldn't be trusted in your home because eventually they'd go for your throat.

"Those are some dark and stormy clouds over your head, boss." Darla's voice was gentler than I'd ever heard as she pulled me from my downward spiral.

I blinked, my head snapping up as I realized I'd gotten lost in my thoughts and completely overfilled the drink I'd been pouring for our lone customer seated in the back corner.

"Fuck."

"Wanna talk about it?"

"N-no."

"Might do you some good."

What the hell was I supposed to say? Vampires were outlawed in Aurora Springs. Darla had her own issues with the bloodsuckers; she wasn't exactly going to offer me a shoulder to cry on. She'd be more liable to snap a leg off a barstool and offer to stake her for me.

Christ, even the thought of that made my stomach churn. As hard as I tried to ignore them, the remnants of my bond with Rosie still sang in my soul.

"I l-lost her."

"Nadia?"

"Y-yes."

Darla grabbed a bottle of moonshine from under the bar and poured us each a shot. "I think you need this."

"I'm w-working."

"I won't tell the boss."

Sighing, I knocked it back and let the burn of the alcohol spread through me. "Sh-she's . . ."

How did I finish that sentence? Gone? Dead? Turned? All were technically true, but none of them would get me out of having to explain what really happened.

"Wh-what would y-you do if y-you found out y-your m-mate was . . ." God, my throat was tight, and my mind couldn't settle on what to ask her. "B-became something y-you hate?"

Darla's expression flickered, grief flaring in her eyes as she set her glass down and considered me. "Does it mean Jax could come back to life?"

Swallowing hard, I nodded.

"Well then, the answer's simple. I would learn not to hate it anymore."

A bitter taste filled my mouth. It wasn't so easy. Not when the actual prospect was presented to you. She didn't have to stare Jax in the face and know he could kill her at any moment.

I could feel her shrewd stare as she studied me. "I see those wheels in your head spinning, Mercer. You're thinking about all the reasons what I said can't possibly be true, but I am standing here telling you it is. When faced with the reality of what it means to spend forever without the other half of your soul, there is nothing, and I do mean nothing, that would keep me from having him back. So whatever hurdles I had to jump over to make that happen, I would get right with myself and do it. Nothing is more important to me than him. Especially not some stupid grudge."

I felt like such an asshole for being the reason she had that wobble in her voice. "E-even if h-he c-came b-back w-with f-f-fangs and on a l-liquid d-diet?"

"Even then. It's not like I don't have my own set of fangs. The monster isn't in control of us. I don't think it's in charge of them, either. Lots of vamps coexist peacefully in the world. Evil creatures are that way because of their hearts, not their species." She shrugged and snagged both shot glasses from in front of us. "So if Jax walked in that door today and wanted me to open up a vein for him, all you'd hear me say is, 'which one?'"

My brows pulled together as I let her words sink in. Was I holding on so tightly to my hatred of vampires that I was ruining my one chance at happiness? I didn't know how to reconcile myself with the conflicting emotions warring for dominance inside me. I had learned to tolerate being around Gavin for Rosie's sake, but we weren't exactly singing Kumbaya either.

But this was different. Wasn't it?

Or did it only seem different because Gavin had years of control under his belt and Rosie was just starting out?

I couldn't watch her kill my brother. That moment she'd lunged for him was already burned on my retinas. It would haunt me for the rest of my life, right along with the sight of Aisling taking out my parents.

What if by trusting her, I made us both vulnerable to the one thing I'd spent my entire life trying to protect us from? Opening my arms to her could lead us right down the path of our destruction. I couldn't just let Remi walk into something like that. I'd sworn to watch over him. What kind of Alpha would I be if I willingly let danger into our pack?

I couldn't do it.

I couldn't be that selfish. So no matter how much my heart begged me to let Rosie back in, I had to be strong enough for everyone and stay away. It was the only way to keep my twin safe. Remi would go to her like a moth drawn to a flame. He always let his heart lead him, ever since we were kids. It's how we got into our situation with Aisling. I cleaned up after. But if I gave in this time, it would be Remi's blood on my hands.

"Th-thanks, Darla. I'm g-going t-to the b-back. P-paperwork."

She offered me a sad smile, nodding as I made my way to the hall. Before I was more than five steps toward my office, the three gargoyles burst inside in a cacophony of shouts and grunts.

"Oi, get yer fat arse through the door so I can come in, Harry. We've got juicy news to share."

"Has there been another murder?" Darla asked.

"No, well, nae here," Tom said. "Quick, turn on the telly, lass. Channel four."

Exchanging confused glances with me, Darla snagged the remote off the wall and did as he said in time to catch the end of the newscaster's report.

"The body is the latest to be found in Whitechapel, hidden in plain sight, several organs extracted with surgical precision. This marks the fifth victim in as many weeks, causing British media to dub the killer Ripper due to his copycat style—" She brought her hand up to her ear, stopping mid-sentence as something prompted her to change her report. "I'm sorry for the interruption, but we have breaking news on a developing story outside of Boston, Massachusetts, where an outbreak of . . . what?" Her face paled. "A new super virulent strain of what experts have now confirmed to be the Black Plague has quarantined an entire town."

Dick groaned. "Bollocks, turn it off. I just wanted to hear about the new Ripper. Viruses are boring."

But my skin crawled at the fear in the newscaster's voice. Sure, we couldn't get sick—right now. I wasn't a stranger to biology. In fact, I enjoyed learning about the history of things like viruses and pandemics. It fascinated me. If a plague like that one could show up again centuries later and mutate, who's to say it couldn't evolve enough to come for us? We'd be arrogant as hell to think otherwise.

I should ask Asher about this. He was invested in that bird flu; he'd probably already looked into this one too. He'd know if we needed to worry. Wouldn't he?

FIFTEEN

REMI

Feathers, blood, and glass. Not the best sight to walk in and see, but I'd expected it. I hadn't been home since the birds went psycho on us, but now that things were on the skids with Asher, I needed to face the music. Without his house as an option, we needed a more permanent arrangement, which meant it was time to move back into the cabin.

I was tired of the couch, and Ben and I were all but on top of each other in the apartment above the bar. This was our home. We needed to be able to live here. Even if it smelled like Rosie and my chest hurt just looking at her bedroom door.

"Goddamn birds," I muttered as I swept up the broken shards of window pane and dumped them into the garbage. "Have to buy a new sofa. I loved that couch. I had it broken in perfectly."

The ruined piece of furniture was still out back, picked to bits by sharp beaks and claws.

"Hey, Siri, add a new couch to my shopping list."

"Okay, Sexy Beast. New porch added to your shopping list."

"No. Couch. COUCH, you freaking robot."

"Hmm . . . I'm sorry. I didn't quite catch that."

I swallowed back a scream of frustration, Asher's voice floating through my mind as it had nearly constantly since he ripped my heart out and threw it in my face.

"Don't go apeshit on the robot, man. There's going to be an uprising one day, and when there is, you want to be on the right side of it."

A hollow laugh escaped before grief rushed in to replace it. Stupid fucking hacker and his conspiracy theories. Like it or not, the asshole had gotten to me. I'd shown him my soft, vulnerable parts, and he eviscerated me. My traitorous lower lip trembled, but I willed it away. I wouldn't cry like a baby because of him. I had plenty of other reasons to be sad. Asher Henry couldn't be one of them. Not if I wanted to survive living in this town with him around.

"Fuck you, Asher. And fuck you too, Siri."

"I'm sorry, Sexy Beast, what was that?"

I flipped off my phone, about to chuck it across the room just for the satisfaction of breaking something, but stopped as the screen lit up with an incoming text.

"What now?"

I knew who it wouldn't be. It wouldn't be Asher. And it sure as shit wouldn't be Rosie, which meant the likelihood the text was something I would actually be interested in was slim to none.

Stop being a pouty bitch. It could be Gavin. Maybe he has good news.

With a sigh, I swiped my thumb over the screen and opened my messages. My stomach did a full-on backflip when the name popped up.

Two new messages from Baby Girl.

Fuck me. My stomach fluttered with butterflies. She was texting. That had to be good, right?

> BABY GIRL:
>
> I need your help.
>
> BABY GIRL:
>
> Please. Hurry.

Or not.

That definitely didn't sound good.

Instead of responding, I clicked the call button, turned around, and jogged to the truck.

She answered on the second ring, and my knees nearly gave out at the sound of her voice.

"Remi."

That was it, just my name, but I'd missed her so much it knocked the air out of my lungs for a second. It wasn't until that moment that I realized part of me had been afraid I'd never hear it again.

"What happened? What's wrong?" My voice came out gruffer than usual, emotion lending it a deeper edge. I was halfway to curling up in a ball and sobbing at the sound of my name on her lips, but she needed me, so the last thing I could do was fall apart.

"He said I couldn't kill him . . . but he's not waking up."

She was frantic, her words trembling.

"Who? Gavin? Where are you?"

"Yes, Gavin. He's been unconscious for twenty-four hours. I knew he was weak, he's been feeding me daily, but we haven't been able to hunt because the animals—"

"Are sick, right."

"He said he'd be fine, but . . . I don't know what to do. I can't leave. I'm so thirsty, Remi. I'm afraid I'll kill someone if I go out."

Running my fingers through my hair, I took a deep breath as I got into the truck and started the engine. "Tell me where you are."

"Didn't Asher tell you?"

His name sliced through me, but I pushed the pain aside. "What do you mean? He knows?"

"He came to me. To us. I'm not sure of the address. Gavin found this place, and I haven't exactly been . . . well."

Her admission sent another pang through me. I could vividly recall just how unwell she'd been. The last few days couldn't have been easy for her. This situation with Gavin had to be her worst nightmare.

"Is it safe for you to run outside and check? Or is there mail lying around? Magazines, maybe?"

"Um . . . wait. Yes. There's a copy of Reader's Digest here somewhere."

Reader's fucking Digest? What is this, 1982?

She rattled off the address, and it instantly registered. Secluded, private, snobby. Just like Gavin. Of course he'd taken the high-end cabin as his own.

"I'll be there as soon as I can."

My foot was lead, and I white-knuckled the steering wheel as I drove to the cabin with my heart racing. I was really going to do this. Let her feed from me. Fuck, Gavin would probably need my blood too. Could I do it? Give myself willingly to a vampire?

The answer came immediately. Yes. For her, I absolutely could.

A flicker of guilt flashed in my mind for Ben and everything he was struggling with. Maybe because I hadn't seen everything he did, it wasn't the same for me. I hated the monsters who killed our parents, but when I looked at her, I didn't see a monster. She was just Rosie. *My* Rosie.

Which meant I couldn't tell him about this. Not yet. But if I didn't, would he forgive me after? I didn't want him to think I was turning my back on him and everything he'd done for me.

I slammed my hand on the steering wheel. Fuck, why was everything so damn complicated all of a sudden? It's like every important relationship in my life imploded at the same time.

Shaking my head, I turned my focus back to the moment. I couldn't worry about Ben right now. This didn't affect him. This was about serving my mate. He may have tossed her aside like a piece of trash, but I hadn't. I wouldn't.

As soon as I parked in front of the house, I saw her in the window. She looked exactly as I remembered—big beautiful eyes, heart-shaped face, perfect lips I wanted to taste.

I was out of the truck and up the drive so fast I almost beat her to the door. There was a suspended second where we just stared at each other, and then she was in my arms. I breathed her in, stupidly thinking she smelled the same. That sugar-citrus scent that reminded me of freshly baked cookies. But then I caught a whiff of something new. The metallic tang that marked her as a full-blooded vampire.

My wolf let out a little warning rumble, reacting to the presence of its natural rival.

"Are you okay?" Rosie asked, pulling back slightly so she could meet my gaze, and it was like everything locked into place. All the confusion of the last few minutes faded away.

She wasn't my enemy. Or a threat. She was my mate.

Mine.

"I sure as hell am now, baby girl." In the space between my heartbeats, I took her lips in a bruising kiss. I couldn't help myself. Breaking the kiss, I dragged in a ragged lungful of air. "Fuck, I thought we lost you."

Her relief was palpable. "I was so worried you'd hate me . . . like Ben."

"He'll come around."

The look we shared told me we both weren't sure that was true.

She gave a little nod. "I hope so."

"You mentioned being thirsty."

Her gaze trailed away from my eyes and to my throat. Yep. That flare of her nostrils, the dilation of her pupils, the way she rolled her lower lip over her teeth. She was hungry.

"We have to see to Gavin first. He's not dead, but he needs to feed. We can't go on like this, being each other's only source of blood while I'm...adjusting."

That was a cute way of putting it. Made it seem like she was just recovering from an illness and less like she was learning how to wrangle her inner stone-cold killer. I could understand why she wanted to downplay it.

Unaware of my wandering thoughts, she continued with her halting explanation. "I require more than he can afford or I can replace. It's not sustainable."

My stomach rolled, but I nodded. I'd guessed as much. "What do you need me to do?"

"Well, I'll give Gavin my blood, so long as you're okay with me feeding from you after."

There was a hesitance to the question, like she wasn't sure it was a good idea. Something told me she couldn't afford to give away any blood.

"What if I feed you both? Is that safe? For me, I mean."

"I . . . uh . . . I don't know. This is all still so new to me."

"But haven't you seen this before? Your brothers turned, didn't they?"

"No, actually. I mean, yes, they turned, but I was kept away from all of it until the danger passed and they could be trusted. All I know about being a vampire is what I've learned from Gavin. And even that's a bit spotty because I've been mostly feral until a couple of days ago. We tried to go hunting, but . . ."

"It's okay. We'll figure it out together. All right?"

"You can chain me up if need be."

"Are you flirting with me right now, baby girl?" I was trying for a little levity, but honestly, the idea of restraints was hot.

Her nostrils flared, and that hazy look swept through her eyes again. Hunger, just of a different sort this time. "No?"

"Are you asking me?" I laughed, feeling like myself for the first time in days.

She licked her lips, shaking her head like trying to clear it. "If this part goes well, we can discuss the flirting later."

"We have to *discuss* flirting now? Since when?"

"Since I grew a pair of fangs and lost all semblance of control."

"Touché."

Her smile was exactly what I needed. "I just don't want to hurt you."

"I get it. I promise. Now, take me to your unconscious paramour. I have a donation to make."

SIXTEEN

ROSIE

Gavin's eyes were open by the time we entered the room. He was still on the bed where I'd dragged him after his collapse, but at least he was awake.

"I don't recall lifting the ban on visitors," he rasped, his eyes tracking our movements the same way a jungle cat tracks its next meal.

If there was ever any doubt Remi was walking headlong into danger, that predatory gleam just sent it up in smoke.

"You lost consciousness. I'd say that means you haven't been able to impose said ban. And if you're not even capable of standing, I doubt you can send me away. You need to eat. That's what Rosie says."

Gavin raised a brow, the only part of his body to move beside the shallow rise and fall of his chest. "Is that so? And that makes you what? Takeaway?"

"Just consider me Aurora Springs' only Uber Eats delivery wolf. Be sure to tip your driver."

"A bloodmobile, then?"

"Hey, look at you making jokes. It's almost like you've got a sense of humor tucked away beneath those stuffy shirts of yours after all."

"Piss off."

"And leave you two high and dry? No can do, amigo. I'm here to earn my Good Samaritan badge for helping out the world's douchiest duke."

"I'm fine." He tried to get up but failed and flopped back onto the pillow in a graceless heap.

"You're not fine, Gavin. You're whiter than your shirt."

"I would have said Casper's asshole, but yeah, our girl has a point."

"I can't keep feeding off you like this. I had to do something. We need him, Gavin."

I knew I'd won when he sighed as though incredibly put out by the whole thing. "Fine. I don't like shifter blood. It's too . . . gamey."

"Says the man who was planning to feed off actual game," Remi muttered.

"It's different. The beasts in the forest don't have magic in their blood. Though to be fair, any blood but Roslyn's will taste off to me."

"It will?" I asked, his assertion sounding vaguely familiar. My family rarely discussed the nuances of such things with me, seeing as how none of us believed they'd ever be relevant.

Gavin gave a weak nod. "Side effect of mating. Vampires prefer their mate's blood above all others. It's sort of like becoming accustomed to a rare vintage of wine and then being asked to drink toilet water. A bit disgusting, really. But I guess it can get the job done in a pinch."

Despite the insult Remi's brows rose, and he smirked. "Well, preferred vintage or not, this magic blood is about to save your ass, so scoot over so we can get this over with and then never talk about it again. I don't want to lose all my street cred."

"What street cred?"

"Ouch, baby girl. That smarts."

My belly gave a little flutter. I'd missed this. The easy back and forth we had. Remi made me feel normal. Safe. Better than I had since I woke up and found myself starring in this nightmare. He made me believe our happily ever after might not be quite so impossible after all. It just looked a little different now.

Remi climbed onto the mattress next to Gavin, looking for all the world like they were about to have a proper cuddle. I almost giggled, but the gnawing ache in my belly started up again, and my gums tingled as the fangs I'd been working so hard to keep hidden threatened to make an appearance. I was hungry. Famished, really. But Gavin came first.

"How do you want to do this? Me on top? You sucking my neck? My wrist? Are we going formal, shall I fetch you a chalice? What's your pleasure, your dukeness?"

Gavin frowned. "Your wrist will do."

"Afraid to get too close to me, huh? Never had a power bottom before?"

Heat swept through me at the image of those two tangled up in each other, but before the fantasy could really take hold, Gavin sent it packing with a snarled, "You wouldn't last two seconds with me."

As much as Gavin was posturing, I could see the fatigue taking charge. He wouldn't be conscious for very long if he didn't feed. "Oi, you two. Just get on with it. This isn't a pissing contest."

"I'm just making sure he's comfortable, baby girl. Letting him think he's in charge."

"I am always in charge."

"See?"

I rolled my eyes and got on the bed with them both, snatching Remi's arm and biting down on his wrist. Then, without further thought, I shoved the bleeding appendage at Gavin. "Drink."

They both stared at me, shocked.

"What?"

"You . . . shouldn't have been able to stop like that." Gavin's voice was soft and filled with awe.

I licked the blood from my lips, and the instant Remi's wild magic hit my tongue, I realized exactly what he meant. If I'd given myself enough time to taste him, I wouldn't have stopped. Oh, hell, I might not be able to keep my fangs off him now. The urge to swallow him down was burning through me. I needed it.

His pulse sounded like a drum in my ears.

Feed, a dark voice crooned in my mind. *Drain him dry.*

No. I blinked and tore my gaze away from the dripping wound at his wrist. I needed blood, but I needed Remi more.

With the last shred of my control, I blurred myself off the bed, holding on to the door frame with enough force that it groaned beneath my white-knuckled grip. "Don't just sit there staring at me, Remi. Feed him. Then it's my turn."

"Your mark is the only thing keeping her from killing you, Remington. Do as she says. She's hanging on by a thread, and she shouldn't even have that much control."

Gaze focused on the door, avoiding the blood and the men I wanted, I waited. Remi let out a soft gasp as Gavin must've bitten into the already torn flesh of his wrist. My tongue swiped over the tips of my fangs, the insistent throb impossible to ignore. It didn't help that my bond with Gavin had his pleasure crashing against me in waves. I could hear every suckle, every groan from my husband hitting me in the gut, but also sending lust straight between my thighs.

Now I had two very different needs spiraling through me, each one feeding the other. It was all I could do not to give in to the urge to slide my hand between my legs and take care of the growing ache.

I whimpered as I lost the battle to keep my gaze trained away from the men I wanted to feast on. In every sense of the word.

"Fuck, baby girl. I can smell how much you like this." Remi squirmed on the bed, his eyes locked on me.

Gavin released Remi's wrist, his lips stained crimson as his hooded gaze met mine. "She's ravenous."

"Come here and take what you need."

There was an edge of alpha command in his words. I couldn't have resisted them if I wanted to.

And I didn't.

I was on Remi almost before he finished telling me to come to him, pinning his shoulders to the bed and straddling his hips.

"Goddamn, you're hot when you're dominating me." Remi's hands found my waist, but I stopped him by bringing his still-bleeding wrist to my lips. "Yes, baby girl. Take it. It's yours. *I'm* yours."

Mine.

The word echoed through me, reinforcing the connection between us. Remi was mine. My mate.

Claim him.

Mark him.

I was lost to instinct now, unable to separate my baser urges from my conscious thoughts. All I knew was that I wanted him. Forever.

"She's going to mark you, Remington." Gavin's voice broke through the haze of need. "Don't worry, petal. I'll help you stop if you don't do it on your own."

"Do it," Remi gritted out as I rocked my hips, grinding against the steel-hard erection behind his fly.

He was as lost to the pleasure as I was. A moth to my flame. I pulled back from his wrist, licking my lips, not about to waste a drop. I reached for his jaw with one hand, turning his face so I could meet his gaze. There was very little *Rosie* left right now, but the part of me that was still *me* needed to know he truly wanted this.

"Are you sure?"

"Green," he groaned, reminding me of the night with Asher.

That reassurance was all I needed before I latched onto his throat, marking him as mine.

"Oh God, Rosie." His moan was low and guttural, a little desperate, as I fed from him. His hips bucked wildly beneath me, seeking out the friction our bodies craved.

I'd never done this with anyone but Gavin before, not while I was driven by more than instinct. It was a miracle I hadn't killed Asher.

"That's enough, petal. Give him your blood to seal your bond. Make him yours."

I shivered as Gavin's voice coated me like warm velvet. I wasn't sure I could stop. Remi tasted so good. He was fresh and pure, with a bite of moonlight and stars. I needed more. I needed it all.

A harsh tug on my hair had me torn from my mate, Gavin's lips at my ear, his strong chest pressed to my back. "I said, enough."

"I need him, my lord," I whined.

"Yeah, she needs me."

"What she needs is to give you her blood and complete the bond. We've both fed from him, petal. You take any more, you risk doing harm. Do you want to hurt your mate?"

"No." Even the idea of it sent a twist through my stomach.

Gavin's lips brushed against my neck, the gentle caress soothing and arousing at the same time.

"Then don't. Give him your blood." He lifted my hand, his lips ghosting down the sensitive skin of my inner arm before he bit down and opened my vein, stealing a taste for himself.

Remi watched with wide eyes. It wasn't in his nature to crave blood, but mating magic was at work here, and as soon as he caught my scent, the black of his pupils obliterated the blue of his irises. "Please, Rosie."

"We can't go back after this," I warned, proud of myself for having enough strength to warn him.

"I don't fucking want to. I dove off the cliff the moment I met you."

Then he grabbed my hand and latched onto my wrist. Pleasure exploded through me with the first lap of his tongue. It was similar to what I'd felt when he and Ben marked me, but more, so much more now that it was enhanced by my supernatural senses. Like this was the culmination of what began that night. A completion I never would have known was missing until I experienced it.

The bond snapped into place, syncing our pulses in beautiful symmetry.

Gavin's large palm wrapped around my nape, as though he was ready to pull me away from Remi again should the need arise. Or perhaps he just wanted to be part of this. But it wasn't necessary. I wasn't going to bite Remi again. I didn't need to. My unquenchable thirst was sated for the first time since I'd woken as a vampire. Because of him? Of them? Or was it simply due to the control I'd gained these last few days?

With a groan of pleasure, Remi kicked his hips up, grinding against my core. I felt his release wash over him through our bond, which triggered my own.

"Gavin, I need . . ."

I couldn't finish the request, but my duke knew exactly what I was asking for. He slid his palm off my neck and brought his lips to the side of my throat. "With pleasure," he whispered before his fangs pierced my flesh.

A sense of near completion caressed the innermost part of my awareness. That hidden, primal part I couldn't deny. The one that begged me to claim my mates so no one else could.

Gavin, Asher, Remi. I was only missing one piece. One vital part of my soul.

Ben.

SEVENTEEN

Remi trailed his fingers over the bare skin of my arm in slow, featherlight touches. It tickled and sent a wave of contentment through me I hadn't realized I'd been missing. No, that wasn't true. Remi had been missing from me until now. They all had. Save Gavin.

And a part of me had known it, even if I hadn't been fully . . . present.

Remi pressed his lips to my forehead. "What's up with the storm clouds, baby girl?"

"What storm clouds?"

"The ones in your eyes. You went from all smiley and dreamy to serious in a matter of seconds. You even have the cutest little furrow between your brows." He traced the tip of his finger along said furrow, smoothing it out.

"I've been . . . not myself these past few days, and it's just strange to be here like this with you now. Like everything's back to normal when I don't trust myself not to hurt you. Gavin's kept me restrained for the better part of three nights."

He waggled his brows. "Ooh, restraints. We haven't played with those yet."

I slapped his chest playfully, but he let out a little grunt of pain.

"Careful. I bruise easier than you do now."

"Oh, bugger. Do you see? I'm a menace. I don't know my own strength, and I'll never get out of this place."

He took my face between his large, warm palms and stared hard into my eyes. "You can come home with me tonight. Who cares what that puffed-up duke says."

From three rooms away, I could hear Gavin clear his throat, which reminded me that he might have left to give us the illusion of privacy, but he could still hear everything we were saying. Vampiric hearing really was amazing.

"I do?"

Gavin laughed, as did Remi. I could also feel the warmth of Remi's amusement and Gavin's approval flickering along our mate bonds. I was so deeply attuned to them now, in a way I couldn't have ever anticipated. I didn't think I'd ever get used to the feeling.

"Besides, I'm not ready yet. No matter how much I want to be."

"Because of the hunger?"

I nodded, already sensing the rise of my thirst. It had remained assuaged for far longer than before this time. That was progress.

Remi tugged at his shirt, ready to strip down and let me take from him again, but I rested my fingers on his sternum, silently asking him to stop.

"Do you think . . ." I bit my lower lip as I thought about what I was going to ask. "Could you call Asher? Bring him here? I'm going to need to feed again soon, and you've given me so much already. It would be best if I found another source before taking any more from you or Gavin. And it's safest for me to feed from those I'm bonded to since I'm less likely to hurt you because my instinct will always be to protect you." I knew I was rambling, embarrassed by this new need of mine, but it wasn't until Remi stilled and I was assaulted by a flood of his grief and anger that my words dried up.

The emotions weren't aimed at me, though. These were a result of my mention of our black-hatted knight.

"Remi, what happened with Asher?" I asked, sitting up so I could see his face.

"He . . . uh . . . decided he didn't want me anymore." The way his voice broke, mixed with my connection to him, had my gut clenching.

"Wait. What? That doesn't make any sense. He's head over heels in love with you."

Remi grimaced. "Not anymore."

I wrinkled my nose, trying to think about what could have possibly changed in a manner of days. There was only one answer. Me.

"You don't think my marking him had anything to do with it, do you?"

"What? No. Why would you think that?"

"Because we were so happy before. The things we did together, they were powerful." A lick of heat went through me, along with a shiver of arousal at the reminder of our night with Lilith's tonic. "There was nothing casual about that."

He scrubbed a hand through his hair, letting out a heavy sigh. "I wish I had answers for you. Trust me, I want them myself. But 'fuck off and die' is pretty hard to misinterpret."

"He said that to you?" I asked, infuriated on his behalf.

"Well, no. Not in so many words, but he may as well have."

"Give me your phone right now. I'll call him and get to the bottom of this."

Remi gave me a sad smile and shook his head. "No."

"No?"

"I appreciate you wanting to fight my battles for me, but this is between him and me. I don't want to come between you two."

He was aching. I could sense it the same as if Asher had broken my heart. How could this happen? As much as he'd told me this wasn't my fault, I couldn't wrap my brain around any other possibility. Asher loved Remi. Even when the two of them tried to deny it, they loved each other. I had to fix it.

"I can see you trying to figure out a way to put these pieces back together, baby girl. I'm telling you. Leave it. Asher Henry isn't a forever guy. At least not with me. I'll be okay. I still have you." He curled a hand around my cheek and pulled me down so he could feather a kiss over my lips. "And the way I see it, that makes me the luckiest guy in the world."

"Remi . . ."

Tears pricked my eyes at the devastation I could feel rolling off him. This thing with Asher was no regular breakup, no matter how much Remi tried to play it off as one. I knew without his having to say a word that Remington Mercer would never get over Asher. And the piece of his heart that belonged to our hacker would never sit quite right without him.

He kissed me softly, his lips trembling as he fought against the sorrow taking us both under.

With no solution in sight, at least for the moment, I decided to pull us from one tragedy and headlong into another.

"How's Ben?"

Remi winced. "You're not pulling any punches tonight, are you?"

"He's the metaphorical wolf in the room. You knew I had to ask."

"I did. But I hoped you might spare yourself anyway."

"Masochist, remember?"

"I have a feeling this isn't the kind of pain that gets you off."

"No, but I won't spare myself from it anyway. It's better to know how bad it is so I'm prepared to face it."

"That's my girl." He hugged me and cuddled me close. "Ben is . . . Ben. Grumpy. Stubborn. A massive pain in my ass. I'm not going to lie to you. This is a lot for him. The person he loved most turned into the thing he hated most. Worse, he watched his biggest fear come to life when he saw you go for me. His heart doesn't know what to do with that, and he's tearing himself in two trying to reconcile the parts of him that are desperate to be with you with the parts that tell him he has to run the other way.”

It hurt. I knew it would, but hearing the words from the person Ben trusted most in his life sliced at me as surely as a bite of a blade. I couldn't do anything to make this better for Ben. He'd be lost to me if he couldn't come to terms. What would that do to him? Wandering through life knowing his mate was out there but never being able to be with me because of my new nature? What would it do to me? Never being complete without that final piece of my soul?

A prickle of foreboding skittered down my spine.

Nothing good would come from our division.

I could feel it.

Fate brought us together for a reason. I had to find a way to mend this. As impossible as it was, I had to. Even the most broken pieces could be put back together. Made into something more beautiful than before when the right thing was used to bond them.

And what was stronger or more beautiful than love?

Gavin opened the door, a stormy expression on his face.

“We're a little busy in here, fangface,” Remi muttered, cupping the back of my neck as though he was going to kiss me.

“You have been with her long enough. I need you to make your phone cease its incessant pinging before I throw it in the fire.” Gavin chucked the aforementioned device at Remi, the shifter catching it easily. “Next time, tell your brother you're busy so he doesn't continue his barrage of messages, will you?”

Remi's eyes widened as he tapped the screen and began scrolling through an endless string of texts. “Oh, Jesus.”

“Is everything all right?”

He shot me a sheepish grin. “I probably should have updated him before I headed over here. He's threatening to go full Van Helsing on Gavin. Thinks you might have kidnapped me and Gavin is helping you hold me against my will.”

Gavin huffed and crossed his arms. “I think I've proven myself up to the task on more than one occasion. But please, by all means, invite him over and we can go a round or two."

"Nah. I'll give him a call in a minute. Proof of life and all that. First, I think our girl needs a snack. Isn't that right, baby?"

He wasn't wrong. My throat burned with hunger. "Just a little nibble. If you can spare it?"

"For you? I'd let you bleed me dry and die a happy man."

"Don't threaten her with a good time."

"Listen, you gave me my requisite cookie and OJ. I'm good to go. Suck away, baby girl. And then kiss it better when you're done."

Gavin rolled his eyes, but left us to our own devices.

I stared deep into Remi's blue irises, needing him to know he was more than a blood donor. Especially after everything he'd told me. "Remi, I—"

"I know, Rosie. I love you too."

Then he bared his throat and gave me what I needed.

ME:

Where are you?

ME:

Remi.

ME:

We're supposed to have a meeting.

ME:

Remington.

ME:

What the fuck? Answer your goddamn phone.

ME:

Seriously, Remi. Stop fucking around. Where are you?

ME:

It's been two hours.

ME:

Do I need to send out a search party?

ME:

Stop ignoring me.

ME:

Fuck, Remi. I'm getting worried.

ME:

Something's going on with you. I can feel it.

ME:

I know you're not with Asher. That asshole is parked at the bar.

ME:

Answer me.

ME:

Remi. Come on. It's not funny.

ME:

Where are you?

ME:

Where's my brother, Gavin?

ME:

What did you do to him?

ME:

I swear to fucking God, if you don't answer me, I'm going to the sheriff. You're lucky we haven't notified anyone of your presence here yet. But that can change, and then what good will you be to her?

ME:

Answer my goddamned calls.

ME:

Remi!

ME:

Gavin, goddamn it. Where is he?

ME:

Rosie . . . is he with you?

ME:

Please. Don't hurt him.

ME:

He's all I have.

CHAPTER

NINETEEN

REMI

"I should have brought a change of clothes," I murmured, a little uncomfortable after the effects of bonding with Rosie. Then again, no one warned me I'd come in my pants like a damn teenager, so how was I supposed to know?

Rosie let out a soft laugh from where I had her cradled in my arms. "You could always shower and change."

"What would I change into, baby girl?"

"I'm sure Gavin has something you could wear."

I smirked. "They wouldn't fit through the crotch. They'd be too tight."

"Maybe the original owners left something behind." She swung her legs over the side of the bed, and I immediately missed her warmth.

"Huh."

"What was that?" she called over her shoulder, already rummaging through the dresser.

"I just realized I always thought vampires would be cold. You know, walking corpses and all, but you feel the same."

"You're right. I think it has something to do with my heartbeat.

Gavin would know more. My family left me in the dark about a lot of this because they never thought I would turn."

"If not for your fangs and crazy eyes, I never would have realized something was different. Well, and the scent, I guess."

"What do you mean, crazy eyes?" she demanded, turning to face me fully, a pair of rolled-up sweats in her hand.

"Well," I slid off the bed and approached her, running my hand across her shoulder, then up to cup her nape. "You get this intense stare thing going when your hunger hits. And your irises . . . they kind of flare. They go molten, like warm honey. It's hot as fuck."

"But also crazy?"

"Also that."

A phone chirped from the desk at the other end of the room. Then again. And again. Rosie tensed.

"Is that yours?"

"Yes."

"Are you going to answer it?"

"I haven't decided." Her focus was locked on the phone across the room. Uncertainty shone in her eyes. She looked almost afraid.

Given the way my phone had been blowing up earlier, there was only one person it could be.

"Want me to check it for you? Act as a buffer?"

"I'm a grown woman, Remi. I can read a bloody text."

I held up my hands in assent. "Okay, okay. You just look pretty worried."

"He hates me."

"He's afraid of you."

"Exactly."

Taking the sweats out of her hand, I left a soft kiss on her forehead. "I'm right here if you need me."

Secretly, I was glad to know Ben was texting her. In fact, I should probably send the grumpy asshole a message and let him know I was alive. Reaching into my pocket, I pulled out the slim device, and my heart sank at the black screen. Dead. *Oh, shit.*

Her expression went from cautiously optimistic to heartbroken as she read the messages from my brother. Then she flicked her gaze to me briefly before returning to the cell.

"What did he say?" If he kept hurting her, she was eventually going to let him go. Maybe that was his plan.

She didn't answer, her fingers a blur as she typed.

"Rosie . . ."

She tossed her phone on the bed and shrugged. "If no one else was going to answer him, I had to."

"Fuck. You told him I'm here, didn't you?"

Rosie nodded.

As if summoned, his wolf called to mine, the pull between us, our twin connection twisting me up inside. He was desperate. Frantic. Terrified. And on his way here.

"He's coming."

"I figured."

"If you're hoping for some sort of joyful reunion, I should warn you that's not what this is going to be."

"Maybe if he sees me, sees how in control I am . . ."

"Maybe, if he was a rational dude, but he's not thinking straight. Fear has him all twisted up inside. Right now, baby girl, all you are is the enemy. You're a monster who took his mate from him."

It killed me to be so brutally honest, but I rather she be prepared than watch his indifference eviscerate her. Maybe that made me a bastard, but my connection to both of them meant I'd feel both sides of their torment, and I just didn't think I could handle it.

"I didn't choose to be this."

I wrapped her in my arms. "I know."

Releasing her, I stared into those eyes I dreamed about. "I'm gonna change clothes, then I'll deal with him. He'll handle this better if he sees me first. Safe. Whole."

She touched the bite marks on my throat, then my wrist. "Marked."

"He'll get over it."

"No," she said sadly. "He won't."

She was probably right, but admitting it wasn't going to help anybody. I kissed her forehead and shucked off my jeans before pulling on the gray sweats with the US Navy logo down the side. "Navy, huh? What do you think? Would I make a good sailor?"

"They certainly do a lot for your . . . package."

"Hot guy uniform, baby girl. Henleys and gray sweats. They're like an accent."

"Or a watch."

"Exactly. Put one on and you're instantly ten times sexier."

"Can confirm."

"Careful. You keep looking at me like that, and Ben's going to barge in here and find me balls deep. He might get the wrong idea."

"There's nothing wrong with it."

I winked. "Later."

Almost on cue, my wolf perked up.

"He's here," Rosie said, her head already turned toward the door. I still wasn't used to her enhanced senses. She could smell and hear just as well as I could now. Better, probably, when I wasn't in wolf form.

"Stay put, all right? This won't take long."

She gave a hollow nod as I jogged out of the room and down the stairs. Gavin was waiting on the landing, arms crossed. He didn't say a word but tossed me a warning look that spoke volumes. If things went sideways and Ben came for Rosie, Gavin would be right there to protect her.

I tossed him a little nod to tell him I got the message loud and clear before making my way to the door. With a little exhale, I shoved my apprehension away and pulled it open, all charm and patented Remington swagger.

"Hey, big brother, what took you so long?"

Ben stood at the edge of the walkway leading up to the house. His eyes still flashed the electric blue of his wolf as his breaths heaved and he clenched his fists. "A-are you f-fucking k-kidding?"

"It's a little cold out. You should have brought some pants. I'd offer you mine, but uh, they're a bit stained."

"Remington."

It was all growl and temper.

"Bentley," I mimicked. "Look at that, we know each other's names. Guess those Flintstone vitamins are working."

As always, my twin was not amused. "I th-thought you were d-dead."

I waved a hand, trotting down the steps and joining him on the driveway. "No, you didn't."

He reached out and grabbed me by the chin, turning my head this way and that as he inspected me. "Sh-she b-bit you."

"Multiple times. So did he. Once. All of which was consensual, I might add."

A low growl rumbled from deep in his chest. "Leeches."

"Dude. Don't knock it 'til you try it. Out of this world orgasms."

My twin visibly shuddered. "Never."

"You say that, but her lips on me . . ." I had a full-body reaction just thinking of it.

"Th-they could have k-killed y-you."

"And. They. Didn't." I spoke slowly just to get the words through his thick skull.

"B-but. They. C-could've."

"And I could also get hit by a car. Or fall off a cliff. Or be poisoned. Or hell, a piece of space trash could come crashing down from the sky and pulverize me. That's fucking life, man."

"Th-that's not the s-same, and y-you know it."

"Yes it is."

"No. Sh-she's an abomination."

"Oooh, breaking out the big words. Do you want a gold star, Bentley? You're a real dick when you're stubborn."

"How c-could you d-do it?" he whispered, his voice harsh and low.

"Because I fucking love her, butthead. You look at her and see the monster that killed our parents. I look at her and see my mate. That's the difference. You need to change the lens. Remind yourself she's the woman you love. Rosie is *not* Aisling. Stop blaming her for someone else's actions. Before you fucking lose her. And me."

Ben jerked as if I'd hit him.

"That's what I'm a-afraid of," he muttered softly. "I c-can't l-lose you, Remi."

"Then get your head out of your ass, because I made my choice. And I chose her."

I would never actually turn my back on Ben. I don't think I could if I tried, but maybe if I forced the issue, it would help him deal with things.

"Sh-she's n-not Rosie anymore. M-my mate is d-dead. I f-felt her d-die."

"So did I, you musty scrotum. Do you think I went through that all smiles? I felt everything you did. The broken bond between us, the moment her heart stopped, the agony of knowing we'd failed to protect her. You're not the only one who lost her, and it pisses me off that you seem to think you are. But what you're missing is the miracle we've been given. She. Came. Back. Stronger and more powerful, but still her. Can't you feel the mate bond? It's there. Weaker, but still intact."

Mine wasn't weak. Not anymore. It was alive and thriving inside me since she'd completed it with her bite. I hadn't even realized this level of connection was possible. This must be what it feels like for a mated shifter pair. Our two marks were like twin chains woven together. Unbreakable. Infinite. So much stronger than the single link my lone bite had been.

Which was saying a hell of a lot, considering how that had felt at the time.

But then how could you wrap your head around something this all-consuming until you experienced it firsthand? I never would have known anything was missing.

"Give her a chance, Ben. Let her prove she's not a monster."

My twin's eyes searched mine, and for a second, I could see the hope flickering in their depths. But then his gaze shifted behind me, and all hint of vulnerability vanished. I could feel it, though, the pain slicing through him. He was a man at war with himself, and it was slowly killing him.

"No," he said firmly, his throat bobbing as he swallowed and turned away from the house. "G-glad you're n-not dead. N-next time a-answer your fucking ph-phone."

Sighing, I ran a hand through my hair. "Well, that went over well."

I turned around and saw her standing in the window, like a beautiful ghost watching mournfully after her lost love.

We'd just have to keep trying.

Every word that came out of Ben's mouth hit me with the force of a sledgehammer. It wasn't just the words themselves, it was the weight of the emotion behind them. The anguish. The hatred. The finality.

My Ben, my protector, was broken. And it was my fault.

All I wanted to do was make it better. Go to him. Hold him in my arms. Tell him I love him. Complete our bond.

"He's a fool, petal. You deserve so much more." Gavin's lips were at my ear, whispering words I didn't want to believe. Ben wasn't a fool; he was hurt.

"Do I?"

Gavin's hand on my hip forced me to turn away from Ben's retreating back and face him. "Remington warned you, as did your connection to the wolf. You knew what to expect, and yet you insisted on eavesdropping anyway."

"I thought you'd be happy I was using my gifts. Isn't that what you've been harping about the last couple of days?"

Gavin wasn't impressed by my small display of sass. "I don't like to see you willfully hurt yourself."

"Really? Isn't that sort of your thing?"

"I love to watch your skin go red and bloom with bruises during our play. To collect your tears on my tongue and your cries in my mouth. But this, what you're doing to yourself now, is a different kind of pain. Your heart is my responsibility, mate. Mine to protect. That is the one thing I never want to see harmed, because that kind of damage doesn't heal the way your skin will." His lips twitched in the smallest hint of a smirk. Then he leaned forward, dipping his head until those same lips brushed my throat as he murmured, "Nor does it make you come. If anything, it gets in the way of your pleasure."

I swallowed, my body responding to the seductive promise in his voice, even though my heart was being pulled farther away from me by the invisible thread connecting it to Ben. I'd never been so sad and so aroused at the same time. It was hard to wrap my head around the conflicting needs of my body.

"Show me how to control my senses, then. I only wanted to see him, not listen in on the conversation. I couldn't help it. I could hear his pulse pounding from the bedroom. I had to . . ."

How could I finish that sentence? I had to do what? Torture myself? Make him aware of my presence? See me as a woman and not a monster? I'd achieved all but the last. That one ended in spectacular failure.

Gavin backed away and stared hard into my eyes, that furrow between his dark brows growing deeper. "I suppose it's not unlike the way you block out unwanted visitors to your thoughts."

"What do you mean?"

"Your mental shields. I know you've mastered those. I've come up against them."

I smiled, proud to know I'd successfully kept him out of my mind. *Thank you, Mum and Dad.* That little trick had come in handy against my brothers on more than one occasion. Humans usually couldn't defend themselves that way, but my witchy ancestry had come to my aid.

"All right, I'm following."

"You can do something similar with your enhanced hearing. Tune it out, so to speak. Put up a type of shield, or a veil. Something to dampen the noise. You've already started using it to ease your need for blood. Think of the moment I tore open Remington's wrist to feed. You didn't lose control because you blocked it out. It's the same for your hearing. Choose what you want to let in."

I closed my eyes and visualized a curtain dropping. The overwhelming noises muffled instantly. The rustling of leaves, the chitter of bugs crawling along the insides of the walls, the steady rush of Gavin's blood as it pumped through his veins. Even with my senses dampened, I could clearly make out the sound of Remi's footsteps as he came back into the house, the soft thud of the door as it closed behind him.

Gavin and I were still standing by the window when Remi joined us.

"So . . . that went well," he lied.

"Don't bother trying to sugarcoat it. I heard everything."

He winced. "You did?"

"Super hearing, remember?"

"So just for curiosity's sake. What's the range on that? You know, in case I want to make sure no one's listening to me rub one out."

I snickered despite myself. "Because that's what you'd want to keep secret?"

"Wank time is sacred time."

I knew for a fact that Remi loved to put on a show. He caught me watching him in the shower one morning, much to my chagrin. After he'd finished, he turned around and winked at me, asking if he'd drawn it out enough for me to fully enjoy the experience.

I had.

"I suppose it's just a good thing Ben didn't try to stake me tonight. We're lucky you were able to talk him down."

Remi cupped my face and pressed our foreheads together. "He'd never hurt you. No matter what. It goes against every instinct he has."

"I don't know what to do to fix this. He hates me."

"I think all you can do is give him time."

"And what am I supposed to do with all this *time*? I'm not technically allowed to be in this town anymore, and I will go mad if I'm locked away in this house much longer."

That trademark smirk of his twisted his lips. "Actually . . . I have a plan for that."

"Are you going to go to the mayor and plead our case on your knees?" Gavin asked drily.

Remi gave him a withering stare in response. "Way to steal my thunder, Lestat."

"I'll take that as a compliment. Lestat was a legend."

"You really plan to go to the mayor?" I asked, hope fluttering inside my chest as I let the emotion free. I'd never met the woman, but the gargoyles mentioned her and her pretentious feline every so often.

"Do you think she's ready?" The question wasn't aimed at me. Remi trained his attention on Gavin with a solemnity I rarely witnessed flickering in his eyes.

"You're still alive, so . . . I'd say yes. As ready as I can make her anyway. The real test will be seeing how she handles herself in a crowd. It's going to be an overwhelming experience for her the first several times. Especially if she's distracted."

"And by distracted, you aren't talking about mixing drinks, are you?"

"He means Ben," I said, easily following the thoughts Gavin didn't speak out loud. My heart gave a pathetic squeeze. Yes, being near Ben but not being allowed to touch him and coming face to face with his icy indifference would be agonizing. But if that was the only way for me to stay here and be with the rest of my mates, I would have to learn to live with it.

Somehow.

"So we get the mayor's permission to allow you both in town. Then ease you back into life with us. I'll make sure you're never alone with Ben. It'll be you and me all the damn time, baby girl. Nothing will happen if we're together. I can help you."

Gavin raised a brow, silently reminding Remi of his existence.

"Oh, well, I mean, you can take shifts too. If you want. Not sure The Tip is ready to have a resident corpse in the corner, but hey. You never know, right?"

"I'm not undead. I'm a born vampire. My heart never stopped—you know what? It's not worth it." Gavin dragged a hand through his hair, a telltale sign he was reaching the end of his rope.

"Am I undead? My heart technically stopped."

Gavin frowned. "I don't think so. You are the child of a vampire and his mate, which places you in the born category. Even if you didn't go about things in the traditional sense."

"It doesn't fucking matter if you're undead or not. You're alive now, and I can feel your heart beating through our bond," Remi said, his tone resolute. "Ben will figure his shit out. He just needs to look into your eyes and he'll let you in."

"I think you're very optimistic."

"I have to be. It's you and me, baby girl."

His voice was steady, but I felt the tremble along our connection. The reminder that it wasn't supposed to be just the two of us. That Asher was yet another missing link, at least in this equation. We couldn't be a triad without him. I was the center of all of us, but with Asher and Remi together, the three of us had something powerful.

"Well, I guess no matter what happens, the first step is this meeting, right? So what do I need to know?"

Remi shot both vampires in the room a teasing stare. "Rule one. No biting."

TWENTY-ONE

PAN

Oh, sweet mystery of life. I was me again. I reached down to cup my beautiful dick before I even opened my eyes. I knew it was fleeting. I wasn't going to be able to stay here. But perhaps I could get some alone time, just me and my aubergine.

"Get your hand out of your pants! Satan's ball sack, it's like you're a teenager again. I'll never forget the time I walked in on you looking at . . . angel porn." Mum shuddered. "I had to scrub my eyes out."

My cock wilted. So much for a happy reunion. "It's called experimentation, thankyouverymuch."

"It's called betrayal. Angels. Really?"

"You're one to kink shame. 1960s sitcoms, Mother? Do we need to talk about your obsession with Captain Tony Nelson?"

"You leave the captain out of this."

"I bet he could get you to call him master. You forget I found your Jeannie costume that one time. Your stained—"

"That's enough. I brought you here for a reason, not to suffer your nonsense."

"You started it," I muttered, feeling very much like the teenager she accused me of being rather than a several millennia old demon.

"Do you want me to send you back already? Because I can, you know."

"No, Mother."

"Good. Now, tell me what you've achieved thus far. Have you been able to get more of her blood?"

I rubbed at my neck, my body instantly reacting to the place Rosie had bitten me. "Not since the last time. Though not for lack of trying," I was quick to add. "The vampire has her locked away at the moment. Getting to her has been impossible, though I think we may be about to turn a corner there."

She arched a brow. "Really? Do tell."

"She's gaining control. There's talk of pleading her case with the mayor, trying to get permission to let her rejoin the town despite the vampire ban. If they can make that happen, she will be all mine."

I knew I'd piqued my mother's interest when her eyes took on that particular gleam. She was scheming. This didn't bode well, although it was too soon to say for who.

"Good boy, Pan. This is finally turning around. You might even say everything's coming up Rosie."

I rolled my eyes. "Not the wittiest you've ever come up with, Mum."

"Says the man whose working title for his opus was 'Wingspan.'"

"That was Sir Paul McCartney's greatest album."

"No. Just . . . no." She frowned. "We all know it was The White Album."

There was no use arguing with her; we'd never see eye to eye. On our porn selections or musical preferences. Lucifer trussed up and dressed as a bleeding angel? I mean . . . come on, who could look away?

"Go make sure all your loose ends are tied up, Pandemic. We must ensure your trail is hidden before she returns to town. I know what you've been up to. Making these deaths look like vampire attacks isn't serving you any longer. It might have been a smart tactic when you were trying to get rid of the duke and her shifters, but we need them to fear something worse than fangs."

"You say that as though you have something in mind."

"You know I do."

"Well then, don't keep me in suspense."

Her lips curled up in a smile so sinister it sent a shiver of apprehension down *my* spine.

"Me. My moment has come, Pan. Ready the stage. It's showtime."

WET, ragged breaths and the stench of rot hit my nose the instant I opened the door to the basement where I'd been storing Hamish. I couldn't believe he was still alive, honestly. Perhaps Mummy dearest had done that on purpose? I wouldn't put it past her.

"Honey, I'm home," I crooned, jogging down the steps.

My poor Scottish meat suit was slumped into a pathetic heap on the concrete. His skin was sallow, flesh sagging over his now skeletal frame, dark hair sweat matted and clinging to his face and neck. I almost felt bad for the tragic sod.

"Lovely."

"Who . . . the fuck . . . are you?" he rasped out between disgusting phlegmy coughs.

Whoopsie. I'd forgotten he hadn't had the pleasure of meeting me in my new form.

"Oh, don't you recognize me? It's your friendly neighborhood demon. I took on a new vessel since my most recent one was a weak sack of shit."

"Hope he"—a cough racked his emaciated frame—"asked for something good."

"Sadly for him, no."

"Poor bugger."

"I really can't believe you aren't a rotting corpse by now, Hamish." I sat on the step and stared at him.

"Me either. And"—another cough—"don't you think I at least" —a pitiful wheeze masquerading as a cough—"deserve my real name?"

I rolled my eyes. Wanker had a point. "Today's your lucky day, *James Marcus MacGregor.*"

"Jamie."

"Ugh, of fucking course. Jamie. Riding that Outlander train all the way to the station, I see."

"Just kill me and"—Lucifer save me, was he ever going to just stop with the incessant coughing?—"be done with it."

"Okay."

Jamie blinked at me. "O-okay?"

"Are you deaf now? Yes. *Oui. Da. Hai. Si. Ja.*" I smirked at him and wiggled my fingers, forcing my unfortunately weak power to the surface. It was enough to keep him standing. *Thanks for that parting gift, Mum.*

"Wh-what are you doing?" he spluttered.

"Taking you for your last drink, of course. You deserve one for the road. Can you think of a more proper send-off for a Scotsman?" I dealt with his chains and then helped him up, slinging my arm around his neck like we were the best of chums. "All right then, Jamie. Here's what you're going to do . . ."

I WAS POSITIVELY giddy as the patrons of The Tipsy Moose chattered happily, drinking their pints down as though it was a normal night in Aurora Springs. That surly, stuttering wolf was manning the bar tonight, his scowl permanently etched in place. The entire town had shown up this Friday evening.

Lion shifter, gargoyles, and bears, oh goodie.

"What can I get you?" the little biker babe waitress who wasn't my Rosie asked.

I had to fight a snarl. I didn't like it when she paid me attention. I wanted Rosie here. Not this poor substitute. But I did want a drink. Perhaps a scotch . . .

"Macallan."

"Sure thing." She smiled at me, and I forced a nod in her direction.

Frowning at the door, I glanced at the time and shook my head. Did he not know how to count? Oh, hell, had he died before coming inside? Was a Scottish corpse lying willy-nilly on the pavement somewhere in town? That would be bloody anticlimactic.

But then the door swung open, and in stumbled my masterpiece. For a second, no one said anything as he stood there, face downcast, body a stiff breeze away from collapse. One by one, faces turned his way as the patrons waited for him to either come inside or leave. As for me . . . I was just waiting for his big moment.

Finally, the not-Rosie sighed and called out, "Hey, my dude, close the door."

"Christ on a cracker, what's wrong with him?" Sheriff Walker shoved back his chair as he stood.

"Careful, Sheriff. He looks . . . sick." This was from his deputy. What was her name, Starla? Oh well, whatever.

"W-water," Tragic Jamie rasped, reaching out for the nearest of the three gargoyles before falling to the floor with a splat.

He began seizing a heartbeat later, his eyes rolling back in his head, pink foam escaping his lips, and blood leaking from all—and I do mean *all*—of his orifices. It was disgusting. And brilliant, if I do say so myself. Which I do. Bravo, Panny boy.

"Oh my God. Someone call an ambulance," not-Rosie squealed.

"It's too late for that," the Scottish gargoyle muttered. "Look at him. He's practically—"

"Melting," the scouser said, his upper lip curling in disgust as he used the tip of his boot to kick my masterpiece further away.

"D-don't t-touch him," Benny boy growled. "H-he m-might be c-contagious."

"We're not norms. We won't get sick." The sheriff, such an arrogant man, was all swagger as he strode up to the puddle that used to be Jamie. He stripped out of his uniform as he approached, with a sort of grace I'd have reserved for an exotic dancer if I was being honest. *My, my, Sheriff Walker, what kind of stories do you have to tell?*

He shifted into the form of a bloody great lion right there in the middle of the bar, his mane a luscious ring around his face. Simba had nothing on him. I tilted my head and got an eyeful of what he was packing beneath his tail. All that swagger made a lot more sense. *Welcome to Club Aubergine. With balls as big as those, you can be my sidekick. We'll call you . . . The Mighty Coconut. Coconuts? Melon Man. Eh, it's a work in progress. I'll keep workshopping it.*

He gave the body a sniff, and the fur along his back stood on end as he growled and backed away. Then he returned to his human form, and again, I realized exactly where the swagger came from. *Perhaps we call him Cucumber Man instead.*

"Ben's right. Don't touch him. We need a hazmat team in here. Bar's closed, everyone. Get out. Go home."

"Asher!" Ben called, and given the annoyance infusing his tone, it didn't sound like the first time.

I blinked, belatedly realizing that was me. "What?"

"W-why are you just s-sitting there sm-smiling?"

Busted.

"I've never seen a lion before. Up close, I mean. Illuminating."

"N-not the t-time. H-he's h-human."

"So?"

"So *you* c-could g-get sick." Ben scowled at me. "Go h-home."

"Right. Yeah. I'll . . . uh . . . see you around."

It took every ounce of self-control I had not to skip out of there like King George thinking he was on his way to a tea party in Boston. But while I did manage to contain my glee in that regard, nothing could keep me from whistling my favorite tune.

Ring around the Rosie . . .

In fact, perhaps I deserved a little celebratory rendezvous with my mate. I had some blood to collect, after all.

But first, I needed to find a new victim I could kill to take the heat off my lovely vampire. Perhaps a slashed throat? A broken neck? Something that left all their blood in their body but did the job just the same.

A lone fae woman sat on a bench as I walked past, her easy smile saying she already trusted my friendly face. Poor choice, love. Poor choice indeed.

TWENTY-TWO

ASHER

The wild swirl of color that overwhelmed my vision made my stomach twist and roll with nausea. This part of the ride sucked big fat monkey balls. Was I in hell? Probably, that witch (*I say it with a w, but I mean it with a b*) did say the curse would kill me. Now I'm damned to relive my horrible childhood, face the mistakes I made, suffer for my crimes.

Keep your arms and legs inside the ride at all times, kids. We wouldn't want you to fall out and die now. Not that it matters because you're already dead!

Weeeee.

Oh God, I was going to hurl. This had to be hell.

I finally came to a stop inside a graveyard I knew all too well. Not one of the nuns' more creative punishments, but forced solitude and manual labor was torture for a small boy who just wanted to make friends and play.

My hands were buried in the weeds surrounding one of the headstones, small, chubby hands belonging to a much younger version of me. I watched through my own eyes as I pulled weed after weed and discarded the plants in a bucket to my left. I'd hated this even more than the chalkboards or polishing the hardwood floors. Because I had to be alone when I was out here. My past and current selves bled together. Thoughts I'd been plagued with overturning in my mind as my six-year-old self took center stage.

The cemetery gives me the creeps. What if zombies claw their way out of the graves and eat my brains? What if they turn me into one of them? What if I eat all the nuns as revenge?

Okay, that part doesn't sound so bad.

"Oh, Mister Henry, I see you've found yourself on the tail end of Sister Margaret's favorite form of isolation. What happened this time?" Father Tate's warm, kind voice tore my gaze from the small scattering of graves I was supposed to tend.

"I don't know. She said I'm bad and can't be trusted."

"What were you doing before she said this?"

"Honest, Father Tate, I didn't do nuthin. I was just sitting there drawing my pictures, and she called me a demon and kicked me out of class." I smacked a rock to show how stupid I thought the whole thing was.

"Hmmm. Are these pictures, by any chance, the same ones you were told to stop drawing when you arrived?" He crouched down next to me and began helping me pull the weeds one at a time.

"Maybe."

"Don't you think that's a little inappropriate?"

"It's not like they're naked ladies or anything."

He chuckled. "No, definitely not. But you were asked to stop, and you chose not to. That's obstinance. Disobedience. And now you've earned yourself hellfire rained down by the scariest creature I've ever met."

My eyes were huge. "Who?"

He nudged me with his shoulder. "Sister Margaret."

I was laughing before I realized it and immediately stopped, slapping my dirty hands over my mouth.

"Asher, you must learn to school your expressions and your

power if you're going to survive in this world. That's what I'm here for. To guide you through and help you. Not all of us are bad guys."

"What power? I'm just a kid."

Father Tate raised a brow. "Everyone's got something special they can do. What's your superpower, huh?"

"People don't have powers. That's in movies."

"Are you sure?" He blinked, long and slow like a frog I'd seen once. When his eyes opened again, the brown irises were bright yellow.

"Cool!"

He grinned, and I would have sworn he had fangs like the Cheshire Cat, but I didn't get a good look before he said, "See? What about you? What can you do?"

I shrugged. "I don't know. One time I knocked a kid over with my hands."

"You shoved him?"

"No. I didn't touch him. I promise. It was light. Like Ironman, but without the suit." I jumped up and shoved my hand forward to show him what I meant. "Kaboom!"

But nothing happened. Just like every other time I'd tried to make the light shine out of my hand again.

"Oh, watch where you're aiming that thing," he said, jumping out of the way with a laugh.

"Sorry," I whispered, casting my gaze to the ground as I dragged the toe of my ratty Converse through the dirt. "Nobody believes me."

"I believe you. I've known since the day I met you that you were special. Just like me."

"You mean it?"

"Sure do, kid. I wouldn't lie about something that important. It's against the rules, you know."

"God's rules?" I asked, wrinkling my nose.

"The superhero guild's rules."

"There's a guild? Oh man, can I join?"

"Well, first we need to get a handle on your power. And you can't tell anyone you're a member. It'll be our little secret, all right?"

I nodded, because that made sense. Every superhero had a secret identity. I'd get some glasses, and then I could be just like Clark Kent!

"But how do I make it go when I want to? How do you do it?"

He smiled softly, then tapped his temple. "It's in my head. I think of it, and"—he snapped his fingers—"I do it."

"That didn't work when I tried it."

"When does your light work?"

I shrugged, because I'd never been able to make it happen on purpose.

"Okay, how about this. What happened right before your power showed up?"

"The last time?"

He nodded.

"I was being chased by that jerk Tommy."

"So you were scared? Trying to find a way to defend yourself, maybe?"

I shrugged again, because who wanted to admit they were a fraidy cat?

Without warning, Father Tate picked up a big rock and threw it at me—hard. I acted before I knew what I was doing, my hand lifting to protect my face. Purple light came out of my palm, and the rock flew back at him.

"Hells bells, I was right." He wasn't smiling. Father Tate's eyes were narrow and mean. He was staring at me the way Millie stared at ice cream sundaes. "Won't Minerva be happy to hear I found you? I might even get a promotion out of the deal."

"Priests get promotions? Or is that a superhero thing? Is Minerva your boss? Will she be mine too?"

"If you're lucky, but I'm sure she'll find some use for you either way." He winked at me. "Come on, kid. Time to get you back where you belong."

"I thought you said we were going to meet the mayor," Gavin said, his eyes raking over the three-story Victorian looming over us.

"We are."

"Then why did you bring us here?"

I gave him a slow once-over. "Because it's her house."

"Is it normal for your public officials to take meetings at their homes?"

It was official. The duke was dense AF. Handsome, yes. But there wasn't much going on upstairs. "Uh, yeah. Clandestine ones. I can't very well waltz into city hall with two vampires in tow, now can I?"

"What's to stop her from killing us all? There'll be no witnesses," Rosie asked, her gaze darting to mine.

"Me," I growled, my wolf reacting to the idea of anyone harming her.

"And me," Gavin agreed.

"All right, then. Looks like the testosterone we ordered has arrived."

"You weren't complaining about my testosterone this morning," I whispered, nipping her neck.

She shivered, her tongue darting out to wet her lips. "No . . . no, I was not."

I couldn't stop the smirk that twisted my mouth as I recalled bringing her out of her dreams with a screaming orgasm using nothing but my tongue. God, I missed her even though she was right here with me. That low hum of arousal buzzing through our bond couldn't be ignored. It wanted more.

After the storm cloud that was Ben shit all over our evening, we hadn't exactly been in the mood for sex last night. Understandably so. And with the way she and Gavin had been talking about her lack of control, I'm not sure she's ready for that yet. Even if she had been, there wasn't time for her and I to do more this morning because her duke had to feed and refresh his UV protection via our girl. But man, I was fucking desperate to be inside her again.

"Do you think she was trying to burn us to cinders before she even had to open the door?" Gavin asked, the sunshine filtering through the trees surrounding the property hitting his pale skin.

Not a sparkle in sight. I checked.

"One hundred percent. Too bad for her, our girl has magic sun blood. Yay, Blackthornes," I said, but the cheer was half-hearted at best.

I rang the bell and waited with the two of them at my side. Fuck, I was nervous. My wolf was on edge. What if I was taking all of us to our deaths?

Rosie's small hand linked with mine. "We're going to be fine. You said so, remember? No one gets to hurt me. And if they try to hurt either of you, they'll learn what happens when they come up against a Blackthorne vampire."

Something dark and dangerous laced the words, and fuck . . . I was hard.

Dangerous Rosie was an aphrodisiac.

Adjusting myself, I smirked. "Keep talking like that, and I'll come up against a Blackthorne vam—"

The front door opened, halting all conversation.

"Well, well. Remington Mercer. Right on time." Mayor Delta Dubois stood on the threshold, looking like a cross between a 1980s beauty queen and an extra from Dynasty with her power suit—with shoulder pads—and her hair a blond helmet teased to within an inch of its life. I could smell the Aquanet hairspray holding it in place. Jesus, I probably could have bounced quarters off it.

"Madam Mayor. Thank you for seeing us. You're looking more like Miss America every time I have the pleasure." Charming should be my middle name, really.

She beamed at me. "Well, the bigger the hair, the closer to God. Isn't that what they say?"

"Then you're damn near angelic." I winked.

My mate gave my hand a warning squeeze, not as appreciative of my flirting as the good mayor.

Before I could lean down and whisper for Rosie to go with it, the demon spawn Mayor Dubois called a cat wove its way through her owner's legs, then hissed at us.

"Now, now, Lady Godiva Sassafras, that's no way to treat our new guests." She scooped the feline into her arms and began slowly stroking her back. "She's just a little uppity about new people. I'm sure she'll warm to you. Sassy is an excellent judge of character."

Gavin's eyebrows were in his hairline, and Rosie looked like she was a second away from bursting into laughter. I guess that was better than the alternative, but it wasn't going to win us any points. Seriously, did no one understand the importance of greasing the wheel? You catch more flies with honey and all that.

Good thing I was here.

Remi Mercer to the rescue.

"That must be why she loves me so much. I promise, Lady Sassafras, we won't take any more of your mama's time than necessary." I reached out to pet her, but the little asshole swiped at me with her claws.

"Sassy doesn't like anyone to touch her but me, I'm afraid."

"Weird. I've yet to meet a pussy that didn't love me."

"Remi," Rosie hissed.

"Cat, baby girl. Pussy*cat*. Get your mind out of the gutter."

Although, between you and me, the statement was true both ways. Yeah, it was a flex. I know.

"Follow me," the mayor said, turning away but stopping with wide eyes. "Oh, do I need to officially invite you inside? Isn't that customary with you . . . vampires?"

"No." Gavin strode inside with his head held high. It didn't take much to imagine him in a crown and red velvet cape. If he was into role-play, he'd make an excellent king. He had the calves for stockings.

"It's a myth," Rosie offered, her sweetness hiding the killer under the surface.

Delta gave them both searching looks, wariness lurking in her blue-green eyes. I had to give the woman credit. Despite decades of hate and fear for their species, it was the first outward sign of apprehension she'd shown.

"You'll have to fill me in on what else is a myth."

"We're great lovers. That's not a myth," Gavin said from behind her. "Humans grow addicted to the pleasure. That's what makes us deadly. We'll love you to death."

Jesus, he was ridiculous. We were pleading our case here, not trying to steal her panties. I shuddered inwardly. Gavin just couldn't help himself. Everyone had to know he was a knicker destroyer.

"Pot meet kettle." Rosie's voice floated through my mind, reminding me of her new gift. Apparently telepathy ran in her bloodline as well, and hers kicked in along with her new taste for blood. Handy, but I'd have to be more careful about my wandering thoughts.

"Something tells me the mayor doesn't like sandwiches as much as you do."

Delta's brow furrowed. "What do you mean? I love a good Reuben."

Rosie snickered. *"Just think it next time."*

"Right. Still learning the new ins and outs."

"Shall we have this conversation in the parlor? I have a spread laid out for us. A bit of coffee and pastry. My chef is the best in three counties."

Didn't seem like a hard feat when the majority of the county was backwoods, but hey. Who was I to judge?

I smiled and offered her my arm. "Lead the way."

A few minutes later, we were all seated on ornate Victorian-style sofas. It looked like a fucking dollhouse. The carpets *literally* matched the drapes. Jesus.

"Do not say that out loud, Remington Mercer."

My lips twitched.

After pouring four cups of coffee, Delta paused. "I should have asked. Can your sort . . . ingest human food? Should I have prepared something more exotic? You'll have to forgive me. I'm not used to entertaining creatures of the night."

The flair she added to that last bit. You'd think the woman was auditioning for *Gone With the Wind*.

"We prefer blood, but can imbibe other liquids," Gavin said, taking the offered cup. "Many times we mix the blood with wine or other spirits. It gives the illusion of humanity."

She shuddered. "Oh, I see."

"Don't worry, Madam Mayor. I assure you, we are very conscious of only feeding from willing donors. And we are quite adept at blending in. After a while, you won't even remember our penchant for blood." Gavin flashed her a hint of fang that had her visibly paling.

Not if you keep reminding her, you asshat.

"Yes, well. That brings us to the reason you three requested this meeting, doesn't it? You want to petition for two vampires to be permitted to live and work in Aurora Springs, Remington. Explain, please, why in Hecate's name should I allow that?"

I cleared my throat and straightened, feeling like I was a kid back in the principal's office about to plead my case. That woman loved me. I got away with everything.

"Well, as you can see, Roslyn and Gavin aren't like your run-of-the-mill bloodsuckers."

Gavin let out an offended cough at my choice of words, but Delta nodded along.

"They can walk in the daylight, for one thing. But also, Rosie is my mate. Ben's too. Aurora Springs is our home, so if she can't stay here with us, we'd have to move, leaving a huge deficit in the community. I mean, The Tip is basically a staple of the town, wouldn't you agree?"

The mayor let out a noncommittal murmur. I could tell I had her on the fence. What politician could argue with the bottom line? But needing to really push her over, I blurted, "And they have impeccable control. They're basically vegetarians."

I could feel Rosie shoot me a look. *"Overselling it a bit, aren't you?"*

"How is that possible? The only vampires I've ever heard about are feral killers."

Gavin's stiff posture tensed even more. "That's because those were *made* vampires. Roslyn and I were *born* this way. We retain our humanity from the time we turn. Made vampires must cultivate their control and be nurtured before they can behave like civilized creatures. It's a shame, really, how persecuted we are because of them. You will never hear of a massacre led by born vampires, I assure you."

Lies. Rosie's grandfather was proof of the opposite, but I wasn't about to throw the duke under the bus.

"Still, you could turn on us at any moment." Mayor Dubois narrowed her gaze as she took a sip of her coffee.

"So could the bears, or the wolves, or anything with claws and fangs," I protested.

"True. However . . ." She stood and walked across the parlor to a large rolltop desk situated under a stained glass window. Opening the piece of enormous furniture, the woman puttered around before returning with a carved wooden box. Dread curled up like a stone in my belly as she sat. "While I do not doubt your word, I require more than that in a case like this. I'll need insurance if I'm going to risk the people of Aurora Springs for you."

The scent of herbs and incense hit my nose as she opened the lid. Delta Dubois was nowhere near as powerful as the Belladonna witch that saved Asher's ass, but she came from a long line of witches. Whatever price she requested would be binding, and it would pack a punch.

"What is this?" Rosie asked.

Mayor Dubois pulled out two clear crystal pendants and held them up to the light. "Magic, my dear. I'll need a drop of blood from each of you for this spell, but it will allow you to safely interact with our townsfolk. The only way you can feed is if the blood is offered freely, and you won't be able to kill."

"So you're essentially de-fanging us?" Gavin protested. "That's ludicrous. What if we need to protect ourselves?"

"Then I suggest you rely on your other assets. These are my terms. Take them or leave this town." Her tone brooked no argument.

"Indefinitely?" I asked, trying to find a way to compromise. "What if it's like a trial period? You know, sort of a ninety-day probation thing."

"Any monster can control their urges for ninety days. It will take more than that to convince the people of this town their enemy can be trusted. The amulets will make them feel safe. But I'm not unreasonable. After a time I deem appropriate, we can revisit whether they are still required."

It was something, I guess.

Before I could say anything else, Rosie held out her open palm. "Fine. If it will get me back to my life, I'll do it. I only want to feed from my mates anyway."

"I'm more than willing to help you with that, baby girl."

"As am I," Gavin agreed.

The mayor pricked each of their fingers, then smeared the crystals with a drop of blood before murmuring an incantation that turned the stones a pulsing crimson. Then as the spell was set, the crystals cleared. You wouldn't even know they were radiating magic.

"Good, that's settled. Speaking of probation, you'll need to return to me monthly to refresh your amulet. It takes a great deal of power to keep this spell controlled. We wouldn't want the magic to weaken and have you meet an untimely end by accident."

Rosie eyed the pendant that was now cradled in her palm like it was a snake.

"Are you sure this is safe?" I asked, my stomach suddenly uneasy. As if offended by my question, that fucking cat jumped up on the table, looked straight into my eyes, and swatted my cup right onto the floor. Then she went about bathing herself as if we weren't there.

Unbothered by the display, the mayor met my gaze. "Perfectly. So long as they don't set a"—she let the sentence hang, her lips curling up in a dark smile—"fang out of place. In that event, things will get a bit messy, but as you said, we have nothing to worry about on that front, right?"

"Right," Rosie said.

"Wonderful! Welcome to Aurora Springs. I'll have my eye on you."

TWENTY-FOUR

ROSIE

"Such a little thing, but I wonder if you might be the answer to my troubles with Ben."

I held the crystal pendant up until the firelight glimmered through the clear stone. The quartz sparkled innocently, but I knew better than most the dangers of accepting such items from a witch. Not that it mattered. As soon as she'd said the magic words 'you won't be able to kill,' I was sold. That was what my Alpha wolf was most afraid of, so if he saw that I was practically harmless, perhaps he'd be more willing to spend time around me. And then, hopefully, he'd see I wasn't the monster he feared.

I let the necklace fall back against my chest, a shiver running up my spine as my eyes drifted to the fireplace. I'd been holed up in the living room of our pilfered cabin, fire roaring, blankets draped across me, since we returned from our meeting with the mayor. I couldn't seem to stay warm without at least one of my mates nearby. That was why Remi was currently outside chopping wood.

I could have told him it wouldn't help, but he was determined to fix it, so I let him. My issue ran deeper than just heat, as if it wasn't my physical body but my soul that was cold. I'd yearned for them before, but since turning, my need for my mates had become a living thing. I was restless without them near. I should just tell Remi it wasn't the fire, but *his* warmth that would soothe me. Or ask Gavin to touch me and connect us in some small way, maybe he'd even let me borrow one of his shirts. Today was the first time I'd worn anything other than his white button-down, and I could feel the lack of his scent surrounding me like an actual ache.

It wasn't just the two of them I was missing either. It was Ben, for all the obvious reasons. But also Asher. I needed to hear his voice while he rambled about his puffins, run my fingers through his golden hair and watch for that mischievous gleam to fill his bright blue eyes.

And if I was being really honest . . . it was also Pan. I never thought I'd crave the scent of brimstone and degradation, but here I was. The echo of his sensual rasp as he called me his little monster ran through my mind, and my lips pulled down in a soft frown.

I stroked along the outline of Lilith's mark, the red kiss still there despite my transition. What would the mother of all demons say when she learned about the situation I'd gotten myself into? She'd probably rejoice. She'd have me forever now. But was that a bad thing?

Warmth bloomed across my shoulder as Remi ran a palm over my skin. "You're thinking awfully hard over here, baby girl. And by the feel in the air, not all of your thoughts are sexy fun things."

I shivered and leaned into him, searching for more. "I'm . . . a little adrift."

His exhale was heavy as he threw his legs over the couch and plopped down beside me. Without missing a beat, he hauled me up into his lap. "How can I help?"

Breathing in deep pulls of his scent, I sighed and snuggled closer, letting his heat radiate through me. "I never felt like this before . . . before I turned."

"Like what?"

There wasn't a word to describe how everything in me called out for them. But I tried my best. "Like without you all, I'm untethered. Each one of you is a piece of my soul, and when you aren't here, I can feel the missing pieces. You all exist independently of me, but I can't be whole without you. Especially now. I don't think I would've come back if it weren't for the marks you gave me before Aisling ruined us."

"Nonsense," Gavin said as he came down the stairs. "You were destined to turn. Because you're mine."

A soft growl left Remi as he protested the declaration.

Gavin rolled his eyes, but he didn't bother correcting himself. My stubborn duke never would. In his eyes, he didn't make mistakes, only choices.

Even as he glared at Remi, I ached to have him near. Reaching out with my mind, I asked in a soft, submissive way if he'd touch me.

One brow cocked and his lips twitched, but he stood behind the sofa and collared my nape with his large palm.

"Better, petal?"

"Yes, my lord."

"What's that? What's happening right now? Are you two doing some weird vampire stuff?"

Gavin smirked. "Yes."

"Rude. Don't make me the third wheel. We've shared blood. I think that earns me some privileges."

I reached out and squeezed Remi's knee in apology. "He was just checking on me."

My wolf hummed in his throat, seeming mollified. "It made my brain buzz. Like a conversation just out of range."

"It would seem our little mate is dealing with more than her change." Gavin's thumb traced the line of my neck. Up and down. Slow and sensual.

"What are you talking about? I'm fine."

Remi's body tensed. "Yeah. What else could be going on?"

Gavin's expression shifted, his gaze growing distant as he searched his mind for the answer. "That's what I was researching, actually. Some of her behaviors these last few days made me recall something I'd stumbled across in my studies of ancient vampiric lore."

"Nerd," Remi coughed under his breath.

I pinched him, secretly loving the idea of a rumpled and studious Gavin. "What are you talking about?"

Ignoring Remi's insult and massaging the tight muscles of my neck, my husband continued. "Wolves have Alphas, but vampires have Queens."

"Like bees?" Remi asked, his nose wrinkling.

"Not really, but for our purposes, sure."

"I'm a bee?"

He chuckled. "No, darling. You're a Queen."

I shook my head, no more familiar with the term now than the first time he'd said it. A Queen? Did I want to be one? Why did it make my skin all prickly and my palms sweat?

"Why have I never heard of that before?"

"Because it's rare. We're talking only two instances on record rare. I'll have to do more research and see what I can find, but I was able to locate some mention of what you're going through. There's not a word for it in the modern tongue, but I suppose the closest translation would be nesting."

"She's not pregnant. Why would she be nesting?" Remi asked. Then flicking his gaze to me, he ventured, "You're not, right? That's not possible."

"No, she's not pregnant," Gavin said with a world-weary sigh. "I don't mean nesting in the traditional sense. But like newly mated Queens—who also have more than one mate, by the way, although five is the traditional number—her instincts demand she surround herself with them. Not only does she need to feed from them regularly, but she also needs to touch them. Scent them. It's her way of ensuring they are safe. Without the mate bond secured, she won't be able to settle into her new role. Eventually the pain of denial will cause her to wither. We'll lose her."

Everything he said made sense, like little tick marks beside the list of things I'd been unconsciously feeling. If Queens were as rare as Gavin said, it begged the question: why now?

Or, more importantly: why me?

Remi's full lips pulled down. "So what you're really saying is my brother needs to get his head out of his ass."

"In a word, yes. We'll need to get Asher too."

My belly erupted in little flutters at the thought.

"Well, what are we sitting around here with our thumbs up our asses for? Come on, baby girl. Pack your shit. We're going home."

I was shocked Remi didn't even flinch at the mention of Asher, but it was a testament to how much our mating meant to him. He wouldn't risk me to save his own bruised heart. I loved him even more because of it.

"I can't come back to the house." Fear sent a shudder through me. "Ben won't like it."

"Ben can kick rocks. You're a fucking Queen."

"No, Remi. None of that. I won't make him uncomfortable in his own home. We can stay here."

"I'll get him on board," Gavin said, confidence pouring out of him.

"You really think you can do a better job than me?" Remi asked with a laugh. "Good luck, buddy. Can't wait to see this play out."

"Just wait and see."

"No using your fancy compulsion stuff, either. That's cheating."

I rolled my eyes, but pulled Remi's arm around me and cuddled into his side before asking the hard question. "So are you calling Asher, or am I?"

TWENTY-FIVE

GAVIN

The odors of beer, sweat, and shifters assaulted me as soon as I opened the door to The Tipsy Moose. I hadn't been here when it was filled with actual patrons. This was more than I'd been prepared for, and honestly, I'd expected the Mercers to be only marginally successful proprietors. Not this.

Bloody hell, were they actually good at their profession? It would seem so.

I did a quick scan of the room, knowing the precise second they became aware of me. The laughter died down, conversations halting midsentence as heads began turning my way. The jig, as they say, was up.

No matter. A gang of bears and a lone lion were no match for me. Nor were the shitfaced gargoyles or handful of fae tittering in the corner. My speed alone would protect me. And if that witch thought a measly amulet was enough to neuter me, she clearly didn't know what she was up against.

Darla's gaze shot to mine, all wide eyes and a little excitement. *No, little shifter, I'm not here for you. Unless I need you, that is.* She could be useful if the surly Mercer wouldn't see reason. Where was the stuttering lumberjack?

"What the hell are you doing here, fanger?" a burly bear snarled, two of his brothers right behind him.

I raised a brow. "The same as you, I imagine, but with a bit more panache."

"You're not welcome here, vampire. Hold him, Ivan. I'll pull out his fangs." Another bear put himself directly in front of me, staring me down with his eyes blazing as the one who'd spoken—Ivan, I presumed—shackled my biceps.

"You touch my fangs and you'll live to regret it. Now, unhand me." I didn't struggle. No point adding to the scene these bears had already dusted up.

"I think it'll be you regretting it. Yuri, get the pliers from my truck," Ivan said, his voice low.

"The mayor might have something to say about that, gentlemen. I'm sure you're already on her radar. Do you really want to test this?"

"She'd hand over the key to the city if I dropped a dead vampire on her doorstep. We could have a, what's the word? Cookout."

"Let him go, fellas. The vamp has the right of it."

Shocked gasps rang out as the lion pushed up from his seat in the corner to join us.

"What?" Ivan snarled, incredulous.

"Seems the mayor decided it was high time to explore reopening our borders. This here is our first guinea pig."

"Is that wise? I mean, we have a damn serial killer on our hands. Who's to say it isn't him?" Yuri asked, laser focus never leaving me.

"Well, for one thing—Gavin, was it?" he asked, addressing me directly for the first time. At my nod, he continued, "Gavin volunteered for some new protocol that would ensure our safety while everyone got used to the idea. He can't feed on anyone without consent, nor can he kill."

The bears grumbled, the fae tittered—again—and the gargoyles drained their glasses. This was going swimmingly.

"Wh-what's all th-this?" Bentley stuttered as he strode down the hall toward us.

"Ah, Mercer, would you please vouch for me here? I'm all for playing with restraints, but I'm not sure these gentlemen would enjoy my games. Especially since I'm always on top."

"Wh-why are y-you h-here? Remi?"

"Unharmed. Just as you left him."

"Is sh-she—"

"Right as rain. For now."

Bentley leveled a look at Ivan. "L-let him g-go. You h-heard the sh-sheriff."

The bears unhanded me with soft growls and a shove. Another time, another place, and I would make it a point to teach them a lesson, but I had more important matters to see to. Smoothing out the wrinkles they left in my suit jacket, I sauntered over to meet Bentley at the bar.

The wolf stared at me, blue eyes untrusting, tension knotting his muscles. When he didn't say anything, I sighed.

"Well, now that you ask, I'll have a dram of scotch. A Speyside or Highlands if you have it."

He reached beneath the bar, not even looking, and pulled out a bottle of some random amber liquid. My gaze drifted to the top shelf where anything even palatable would reside as Bentley poured my drink. As I suspected, a perfectly acceptable Macallan 18 year sat front and center.

Prick.

"This smells like motor oil."

"Y-you'll take wh-what I g-give you and b-be grateful." His scowl darkened as patrons began standing and leaving. "I'm l-losing m-money because of y-you."

I took out my billfold and dropped a thick stack of American notes on the counter. "That should more than cover it."

When he reached to scoop up the money, I used a small burst of my speed to catch hold of his wrist.

He growled and tried to pull away, but I sent my thoughts into his mind.

"We can do this here in front of everyone so they can all know our business, or I can talk to you in your head. Which is it, wolf?"

His lip curled, but his voice sounded back, strong and stutter-free. *"I don't love the idea of holding hands with you, vampire. Make it quick."*

"She needs us all. That means you."

"What the fuck are you talking about? Is she that much of a crazed monster that two of you aren't enough? Wait, three. Asher is part of this bloody gang bang of yours, isn't he?"

I tightened my hold on his wrist.

"Call our mate a monster one more time, shifter. I dare you."

Bentley couldn't know that it wasn't just his thoughts I could read this way. His emotions came through loud and clear too. Posture all he will, there was no hiding the desperation bubbling inside him. Or the pain. He was in agony without her, the same as she was with him. Denying their bond was doing neither of them any good. It would only see them both destroyed in the end.

"I can't, Gavin. I just . . . can't."

"You must. She'll only wither away if you don't. She's rare, Bentley. A Queen."

"I thought she was a duchess?"

I barely resisted the urge to roll my eyes. *"Not that kind of queen. A vampire Queen. Much like your wolves and their Alphas. She's precious. I've only just begun to research what this means for us, but the little I've found was unfailingly clear on one point. The kind of power she's capable of wielding requires a significant supply of blood. It's why she has so many mates. She needs each and every one of them. Trust me. Do you really think I'd be here right now, sitting on this sticky barstool and dirtying up my second favorite suit if I didn't have to? I'd be more than happy to be Roslyn's sole provider. But in this, even I must acknowledge my inadequacy. Remington and I cannot care for her on our own."*

I saw the flicker of indecision in his eyes. That anxious energy.

The buildup to some sort of solution. He was warring with himself. I knew that feeling well. I'd done the same the moment she threw herself at my feet.

"Do you two need a minute alone? We can leave," the gargoyle nearest me said, his cockney accent so thick I barely understood him.

Bentley snapped his attention from me and pulled away. "N-no. W-we're finished."

"You know where to find us when you change your mind, Mercer."

I knocked back the god-awful scotch and fought a shudder, then stood, ready to return to my wife. I would give the wolf a chance to come to it on his own, but if he forced my hand, I would come back here and use my compulsion to make him do what needed to be done. My mate would have everything she needed. I couldn't lose her, not again. Especially not when there was something I could do about it. She was already feeling the effects of her uncompleted mating bond. It wouldn't be long before she began to fade. I wouldn't allow that to happen.

As I reached for the door, it swung open, and a harried-looking fisherman tumbled inside, his expression grave. "She's dead. Oh God."

The sheriff stood, his chair scraping loudly on the wood floor. "Who? Where? I need more info from you, Whalen."

"Livvy Barrows. Poor girl. She's in the woods, Sheriff. She's been dead a while. I was on a hike, cleaning up some of the trails. You know how the kids like to venture out now that the weather is nice." He took a shuddering breath as Darla passed him a shot of whiskey.

"Did she have all her blood?" he asked, not bothering to disguise the mistrustful look he shot my way.

"I suppose? She had no marks that I could see. Granted, I didn't take much more than a glance once I realized she wasn't breathing. And her neck was turned wrong." He lifted the shot glass to his lips with a trembling hand, then swallowed it down in one gulp. Good man. Drink it fast so you don't have to taste the swill.

"First Ginny, now Livvy," the Scottish gargoyle said with a deep frown.

"Yet another fine set of mommy milkers lost to us," the scouser added, staring sadly into his pint glass.

Darla reached over and smacked him upside the back of his head. "Hey! The women of this town are more than just their tits. Show a little respect."

He scowled at her as he rubbed his head. "You mourn your way, and I'll mourn mine."

"Mourn all you want. At home. I'm shutting this down, y'all. We need to implement our curfew. There's a shark in our waters, and we need to find it."

"I'm not sure the mayor will agree with you, Sheriff. A lot of business is done after dark." Ivan crossed his arms over his chest.

"We'll see about that." The sheriff pushed past me and headed outside for his patrol car.

"This town, never a dull moment," I grumbled.

TWENTY-SIX

BEN

"She'll only wither away if you don't. She's rare, Bentley."

That fucking vampire wasn't even here, and I couldn't get his words out of my goddamned head.

I wasn't sure what pissed me off more—that Gavin had gotten to me, or that he was right.

He'd said almost all the same things Remi had, and maybe it was the fact that there was no love lost between us, but coming from Gavin, they hit a hell of a lot harder. I was hurting her. No matter how I felt about this awful situation, the truth was staring me in the face. Rosie would suffer without my blood.

But what the fuck was I going to do about it?

There was no way I could let her feed from me. My wolf wouldn't allow it. Even the thought had my fur ruffling the wrong way. But the idea of her suffering, when there was something I could do about it . . . that wasn't sitting right either.

It went against my fundamental need to take care of and protect her.

"Sh-she's not m-my mate," I growled, though the words lacked the certainty they once had.

If she wasn't my mate, if our bond was truly severed, I wouldn't feel this torn up about it.

I flipped open my ancient laptop and waited for the thing to boot up, hoping inventory would distract me. Remi used it as a coping mechanism every time Asher pissed him off. Maybe there was something to it. After what seemed like a thousand years, my screen finally displayed something other than a spinning wheel of death.

"You've got mail," the annoying man in my computer said. Dammit, I wished Remi was here to give me shit for still using AOL like he always did.

"F-fuck off. I d-don't w-want it."

Despite my words, I clicked on the mailbox icon to see that I had several unread messages. The most recent of which caught my eye with its subject line. I clicked the envelope icon, opening Mayor Dubois's email.

To: JustTheTip@aol.com
From: MayorDeeDee@aurorasprings.gov
Subject: ☠ URGENT UPDATE REGARDING FALSE SERIAL KILLER CLAIMS!!! ☠

My dearest and most valued members of the Aurora Springs Chamber of Commerce,

You may have been witness to our FORMER Sheriff Dallas Walker's wild ravings. It has come to my attention that he wrongfully imprisoned our esteemed barkeep Bentley Mercer in his mad quest to solve crimes that have not been classified as actual murders. In an attempt to control the narrative, FORMER Sheriff Walker has spread lies, unfairly imposed curfews, and pushed for the immediate shutdown of all businesses in the town.

Fear not! I, your beloved mayor (seven years running unopposed), have once again gone to bat for you. There is no threat. His claims cannot be verified. The vampires in our town have been collared by yours truly, and they are no danger to you or yours. These tragic deaths are not the work of a serial killer as the FORMER Sheriff would lead you to believe. Rather, it has been determined by experts that these deaths were unfortunate accidents. A rogue mountain lion has been caught and killed. I have his skin displayed on my office floor in celebration. If you would like to see it for yourself, please make an appointment with my secretary, Billy.

Please join me in congratulating our NEW Sheriff, Scarlett Bell. She has taken the mantle immediately and has committed to keeping our fair city safe.

In closing, business will proceed as usual. Tourist season seems to be starting early, and by the looks of it, we're in for a wild ride. Yeehaw!

Ever your faithful public servant,

Mayor Delta Dubois
(and her eternally devoted Lady Godiva Sassafras 🐱)

"Wʜ-ᴡʜᴀᴛ ᴛʜᴇ ꜰ-ꜰᴜᴄᴋ ᴡ-ᴡᴀꜱ ᴛʜᴀᴛ?" I frowned as I forced myself to read the ramblings again.

I should have been happy to see my name so publicly cleared and to find out that I wouldn't have to close down the bar, but something about the message rang a bit off. Delta had always been an odd duck, but this was a whole other level. I don't think she'd ever emailed me before, let alone sent a group message. Billy Hawkins, however, loved to call me up and bend my ear about all the reasons the mayor was a beautiful genius. I was 90 percent sure she had him under some kind of spell.

"Yo, bossman! The gargoyles are getting restless, and I really need that case of whiskey." Darla's strident call came through the open door, and I cursed under my breath. I was only supposed to be in here for a breather, but that email read like the Declaration of Independence, and I got distracted.

I slammed my laptop closed and stood, hefting the box of spirits as I headed out.

"S-sorry. Just g-got word from th-the mayor."

"Oh? What did the crazy bitch have to say?"

"No c-curfew. And D-Dallas has b-been sacked."

"Say whaaaat?" She grasped my bicep and stopped me from stalking past. "She really fired him?"

I nodded. "Yup."

"Oh shit. Prepare thyself for the mother of all benders. That man isn't gonna know what to do with himself." Then she grinned. "I know what to do with him, though."

"D-Darla . . . s-stop. P-please. No."

"When did you turn into a prude?"

"Wh-when you g-got h-horny eyes f-for D-Dallas."

"They're not horny. Just a little . . . thirsty. And it's not my eyes, it's my Justin Beaver. Have you seen what he's packing? Jesus. I wouldn't walk straight for a week." She winked at me. "Can you handle the three stooges? I have a pack of bears who ordered enough fries to kill a man, and Dante is out again."

My frown deepened. "Does h-he even w-work here anymore?"

Darla slapped me with her apron as she squeezed past. "You know his mate just had triplets. Give the guy a break!"

A pang went through me at the thought of a family. Rosie and I would never have that, not before she turned, and definitely not now. God, I had to get my head on straight and stop thinking of her. Unfortunately for me, that was impossible, and I knew it.

"Och, lad, get yer braw self over here and fill 'er up, will ye? We're in mourning, and Darla seems to have forgotten about the importance of the holiday pour." Tom scowled at me as I rounded the bar.

"What are y-you idiots m-mourning?"

"Nadia, obviously."

That stopped me dead. I dropped my box and slowly turned to look at them, my heart a cold pit. "Wh-why are you m-mourning her?"

"Cause she ain't here," Dick said, as if it was the most obvious thing in the world. "And no one treats us as good as your sweet gal."

Harry frowned at his glass. "Only one in this place that knows how to treat a man."

"Wh-what was that?" I growled on pure instinct.

All three gargoyles blinked at me.

"Nothin'," Harry said.

"But seriously, lads, those beautiful . . ." Dick started, his hands cupping imaginary tits, but at the storm clouds in my eyes, he nearly swallowed his tongue before redirecting his words. "Um . . . lips."

"Wh-why are you l-looking at her l-lips?"

"Nostrils?" he offered, doing nothing to soothe my angered wolf.

"How about y-you d-don't look at her a-at all."

"How are we supposed—" Tom was cut off by a well-timed elbow from Dick. "Nevermind," he croaked.

"F-finish your d-drinks. It's l-last c-call." Technically we still had half an hour before last call, but I didn't give a damn.

"What? Aw, mate, don't be that way," Dick whined.

"Shut yer piehole, Dickie. The wolf is on the edge, can't ye see that?" Tom knocked back his whiskey and dropped some bills on the bartop as his friends did the same. "I liked you better when you didnae talk."

"And I l-liked you b-better when you d-didn't sexualize m-my mate."

It took two full heartbeats for my words to register.

I scrubbed a hand over my face, sighing heavily. No matter how much I tried to deny it, Rosie was still mine. My wolf knew it, my heart knew it, and my dick sure as shit knew it. My brain was the only organ that couldn't seem to grasp it.

Which meant I couldn't leave her in need.

It might take time to come to terms with her transition, but there were more ways to feed a vampire than baring my throat. I could help her without letting her feed directly from my veins.

Snatching a mason jar from under the bar, I stormed into the back office. "D-Darla, close up for m-me. I've g-got something I n-need to do."

~

I LOOKED up at the house Gavin had commandeered, the weight of the cooler in my hand growing with every second. My arm throbbed from where I'd opened my vein for her and filled the mason jar with my blood. God, I couldn't believe I was doing this.

You already did the hard part, Bentley. Just leave it by the door and text Remi so it doesn't spoil.

It took everything in me to get my feet to move, but once again, it was the echo of Gavin's words that got me moving.

'She'll only wither away if you don't.'

"Fucking d-do it, asshole." Clenching my fist around the handle, I took the stairs one at a time until I stood on the porch with my heart in my throat. As soon as I leaned over to set it on the mat, I felt her.

She was standing on the other side of the door, holding her breath. I could picture her so easily. Her small palms pressed to the wood. Her amber eyes bright with hope while she bit down on her bottom lip. Jesus, how could I hate what she was but want her so badly? My cock was rock hard at the thought of that perfect mouth.

"D-don't, sugar. D-don't open th-th-the d-door."

There was a beat before she whispered, "I wasn't going to."

God, that voice. It nearly brought me to my knees. I hadn't heard her speak in so long. I fucking missed the melodic tone. I couldn't do this. I couldn't stand it.

"Why are you here, Ben?"

"Y-you n-need m-m-m—" My throat tightened, imprisoning my words.

"Your blood?"

"Yes."

She didn't pacify me with pointless apologies. "Thank you. I know this is hard for you."

"A-are you r-really s-s-still in th-there?" Remi said she was, but I had to ask. Something in me was desperate to know. Hell, I knew exactly what it was, my mate bond. My wolf. He needed her as much as I did.

"Yes. Underneath my new cravings, I'm still me."

I wanted to believe her so badly I had to fight back a sob. Realizing I was seconds away from a complete meltdown, I straightened and took a few steps away, shoving my hands in my pockets. "Th-the b-blood's on ice. I c-couldn't k-keep it warm."

"That's okay."

"I . . ."

"It's okay, Ben. That fact that you're trying is enough. You don't need to explain yourself."

I cleared my throat, on the verge of telling her I missed her. That I loved her. That I was going out of my fucking mind without her. But I didn't say any of those things. Instead I just nodded.

"R-right. Well . . . Remi w-wants you to come b-back to the bar, and I know about the mayor's protective m-measures, so if that's something you w-want, it's f-fine w-with me."

"Is it really?"

No.

"Yes."

"Thank you, Ben. I . . . I've missed—"

"This is all I c-can d-do. I c-can't b-be everyth-thing you n-need. But I'll b-be this."

"Okay."

The heartbreak in her voice nearly sent me to my knees.

I had to get the fuck out of here.

She sounded too much like the Rosie I wanted forever with. I wouldn't survive her if I let her in now. She'd show her fangs, and the truth would come out, and then where would I be? Dead? Alone? Sitting next to the graves of every single person I loved?

This would have to be enough. It was the only olive branch I had.

As I turned away and walked down the drive toward my waiting truck, I heard the door creak open. If I looked back, I'd see her. I'd be able to take in the perfect woman made for me and know she was whole and real and within reach.

That's exactly why I didn't.

TWENTY-SEVEN

I pounded on the door of Asher's hidden fortress, wishing he hadn't fixed the place up after the attack so I could shove my way inside. But the fucker had probably done that as soon as we all left. He probably changed the locks too. A quick glance showed that, yes, he had changed the locks, but it wasn't the high-tech automatic system he preferred. He probably had to special order that shit, which meant he was left with a good ol' deadbolt like the rest of us.

Sucker.

Either way, it was still a lock I didn't have a key for, but that was fine. I could wait. I'd stand out here yelling for him to answer until I lost my voice if I had to.

After a string of unanswered calls and texts, I'd had enough of his radio silence. He could hurt me all he wanted, but Rosie deserved better.

Before I resorted to shouting myself hoarse or throwing a rock through the new window, I spotted a new statue in the corner of his porch. "What the fuck is up with you and puffins?"

Asher wasn't exactly a guy who cared about curb appeal. Everything in his life was clean, bland, and utilitarian. He didn't like clutter or mess, nothing that made his world homey. I knew that was the side effect of needing to be ready to run at a moment's notice. It was easier to leave everything behind when you weren't all that attached to it.

Which made the little bird statue even more suspect. With as anal about security as he was, he didn't strike me as the leave-a-key sort, but . . . stranger things had happened. I snatched the ceramic figurine and flipped it over, hoping desperately I was wrong, but finding nothing.

"Goddammit, Asher. Couldn't you be lazy just this once? Answer your fucking door!" I threw the puffin as hard as I could onto the cement stoop, a sense of pure petty satisfaction washing over me as it broke.

But the tinkle of metal on stone drew my gaze. A fucking key. "I was right!"

I swooped down to pluck it up and moved back to the door without giving myself a chance to think through my plan. I was doing this for Rosie, not me, which meant I didn't give a single fuck if he wanted me in his house or not.

As soon as the door was open, the smell of old sweat, stale air, and alcohol hit my nose.

"Great," I muttered. "It's probably coming out of his pores."

Drunk Asher and I had a history. One I wasn't eager to revisit, but at least I knew what to expect. I moved through his house, turning on lights and wrinkling my nose at the destruction I found. Empty pizza boxes and take-out containers littered the kitchen, along with an open jar of peanut butter, gallon of milk, and some rotten bananas.

"He's really let himself go," I said, mostly as a way of dismissing the little flutter of concern the mess sent through me. *This* wasn't like Asher. Blackout drunk? Sure. But never a slob.

Maybe the breakup is hitting him harder than he wants to admit.

I only entertained the idea for a second before snorting to myself. *Yeah, right, it was his fucking idea. He threw you away like an old shoe.*

"Asher, I swear to God, if I find you dead in your bathroom, I'm going to buy a ticket to hell and bring you back just so I can kick your ass."

The anxiety clawing up my throat meant my threat lacked any heat.

Please don't be dead.

I'm not going to make it if you're dead.

I hated that I still cared about him after the way he treated me, that I still wanted him to be okay. But I couldn't help it. I wasn't the kind of guy who just stopped loving someone with the flip of a switch. Hell, until Rosie and Asher, I wasn't the guy who loved anyone—period.

Besides my twin, but that was different.

The faint glow of a screen as it flickered came from under a door down the hall. The computer lair. Of course. The creep was probably in there watching us all as he jerked off. I hope he strained his wrist. Or gave himself dick burn. No one liked a chapped joystick.

Through the crack of the partially open door, I could just make out the line of his long legs.

Hoping to scare him a fraction as much as he scared me, I slammed my palm against the wood and sent it crashing open. "Found you, you soggy ball sack."

Not even a flinch. Oh God, was he really dead?

"Asher?" I shook his shoulder and he groaned, lifting a heavy hand to bat me away. Thank fuck.

Just passed out then. Eyeing the bottles decorating his desk, it was easy enough to see why. *Moonshine.*

I grimaced, not quite in sympathy, but familiar enough with how he was going to feel when he woke up to know that anyone who willingly put themselves through that kind of hell was trying to escape something.

"You're lucky you haven't died of alcohol poisoning, human. You drank enough to kill a shifter. Come on, let's get you in bed. You won't be any use to her until you sober up."

I allowed myself a second to enjoy the thought of Rosie tipsy on blood and made a mental note to try it out with her one night soon.

His head lolled as I hoisted him out of the chair, and I had to fight the pang in my chest at his nearness. Even when he smelled like ass, something about him called to me.

He wasn't awake, not really, but he leaned against me and staggered along. I caught myself wanting to just stand there with him tucked into my side, and when he brushed his lips over my skin and hummed, my throat went tight.

"Remi," he mumbled, taking another deep inhale as he burrowed into my neck. "Missed this smell. You're not on my sheets anymore."

I stiffened, hardly daring to breathe as his drunk confession washed over me. "Whose fault is that?"

He didn't answer, proving that he wasn't fully coherent. This was a special brand of torture. I needed to get out of here before I did something stupid like let him fuck me or broke down crying in his arms. Maybe both.

I got him to his room and helped him onto the bed, thankful I didn't have to worry about taking off his shoes or anything that would make me have to touch him more than strictly necessary. When I pulled away and made to leave, his hand shot out, grasping my wrist. "Don't go. I don't want to be alone here." His words were slow, deliberate, serious.

"Asher . . ."

"Everything's a nightmare. I just . . ." He sighed heavily, sounding like he was already on the verge of falling back asleep. "I need you to be real."

"Fuck my life," I groaned, knowing there was no way I was going to be able to leave him now. "Scoot over."

He didn't budge, so I climbed over him and laid on my side, my gaze boring into the back of his neck, hands trembling with the need to touch him. Then, before I could protect my heart, he rolled over and stared into my eyes, vision clear and determined.

"Thank you for finding me," Asher said, a breath before he kissed me and sent my carefully constructed walls crashing down.

I didn't care that he was three sheets to the wind, that he probably wouldn't remember this come morning. I wanted to have this one thing for myself. A moment I could survive on for at least a little while. Cupping the side of his face, I returned his kiss, but his body went slack as he drifted back to his dreams.

"I always will," I murmured, pulling away and seeing that, yes, he was sound asleep again.

Heart heavy, head a mess, I rolled onto my back and stared up at the ceiling, knowing I was the world's biggest fool as I wished with every fiber of my being that he'd still want me when he sobered up.

I ROLLED OVER, distantly noting the sound of the shower cutting off as I buried my face into the pillow and inhaled Asher's scent. I'd known I missed him, but not this much. Being surrounded by him reminded me of every single moment we spent together. The bathroom door opened, and the man himself strode out, wrapped in nothing but a towel, water still glistening on his shoulders and dripping from his hair.

Hellooo, nurse.

I sat up, my body on instant alert. Maybe he'd let me lick the droplets off his pecs. Wait, where the fuck was his tattoo? No, not tattoo. His curse.

Asher's eyes found mine, his lips curling up in a cruel smile. "Oh good, you're awake. Now you can get the fuck out."

I blinked, my fantasy destroyed with one sentence. "What the fuck is wrong with you?"

"What do you mean? I'm fine."

"No. You're not. It's like you're possessed or something. Last night you were *you* again. Now you're back to being this raging cunt.

Whatever the reason, I'm really fucking tired of this Dr. Jekyll Mr. Hyde bullshit."

For a second something flickered in his gaze, but then he scoffed, speaking to me over his shoulder as he dropped the towel and opened a drawer, pulling out a pair of boxer briefs.

"You know what I think? I think you're so desperate for me to love you that you didn't ever take the time to learn who I really was."

"I'm the desperate one? You were the one who always came crawling back to me."

He shrugged. "I knew you wouldn't turn me down. You were nothing more than a means to an end. Seriously, you're a waste of space, Remi. No one really wants you. Not even Rosie. She's saddled with you because of your twin bond with Ben. Can't you see that? You should just let her go."

Ouch.

"Fuck you, Asher. I'm done trying to salvage anything between us. Don't expect me to help your drunk ass again. I did it for Rosie, who needs you, by the way. I wish like hell she didn't, but it's the truth. If you'd bothered to answer any of my texts or calls, you'd know that. Get your ass to the cabin and be the mate she needs."

He tugged on a t-shirt and raked his fingers through the damp strands of his hair. "My pleasure. Now get the fuck out."

"Gladly."

I stormed past him, my wolf barely contained. The last thing we needed was for me to rip his throat out.

"Don't let the door hit your ass on the way out!"

I gritted my teeth, forcing myself to keep walking away, because if I went back there, I was going to beat the shit out of him. I didn't recognize that person. And if that was the real Asher, my new mission was protecting Rosie from him in any way I could.

TWENTY-EIGHT

PAN

It was different returning to this place now that I knew what—or rather who—was contained within. And that I was actually welcome this time around.

Not that something as paltry as an invitation had ever stopped me before. But Gavin had no leg to stand on now. She *needed* me. My presence was *requested*. She'd likely die without me. Oh, that felt good.

Excitement bubbled up in my veins. Or maybe that was anticipation.

I'd missed my little monster.

The thought made my lip curl. I hated that mortal weakness, but it was true. Reminding myself that she was my mate made the emotion's presence within me tolerable. Mate bonds were magic; there was no getting around them, so these *feelings* weren't my fault.

They were hers.

I'd just have to accept it. Let them happen. Then perhaps I could use them to my advantage. Somehow.

Standing in front of the door, I raised my fist to knock and stopped myself, frustrated beyond belief I was being lowered to announcing my presence with something as pedestrian as knocking. I was a demon of the first order. I shouldn't have to . . . *knock.* I should be announced to great fanfare and trembling.

Thankfully, Roslyn took the choice out of my hands by throwing open the door and launching herself into my arms. For one blissful second, I drank in the feel of her pressed against me. Her delectable scent hit me as her hair tickled my nose.

And then she ruined it.

"Asher!"

The smile that had stretched across my face withered. She wasn't happy to see *me.* She thought I was *him.*

Of course she does, you bloody fool. You're playing a game, remember?

"Miss me, did you?" I ran my fingers through her hair and breathed her in, using her comfort with this man to my advantage.

"More than you know."

"Remi said you needed me."

She pulled back, a furrow between her brows. "What's going on with you two?"

I shrugged, not remotely interested in discussing the shifter. "Change of heart."

The furrow deepened. "Asher . . ."

"Hush, I'm here for you, not him."

I could tell her obstinate streak wasn't going to let it die, so I stopped her with a kiss. It wasn't my preferred method of shutting her up. That would require her choking on my cock or tail even, but beggars and all that. We were playing a part, after all, and I doubted a human would just whip his dick out on the front porch as a matter of course.

It took a moment for me to realize this was my first official kiss. I had no interest in that sort of thing usually. Why would I? Mouths were made for sucking. And the parts I was most interested in were below the waist, but this . . .

This was eye-opening. What was this feeling? Her lips on mine were soft and pillowy, and the way she sighed into me, bloody hell, I liked it. Why hadn't we done this before? It made my wicked heart flutter.

"Don't try to distract me, Asher Henry. I'm wise to your tricks," she murmured against my mouth.

"Seems like it worked pretty well."

"For now. We're going to talk about Remi. After we see to this situation."

By situation, I hoped she meant my raging erection and her already elongated fangs. "Hungry, love?"

"Love? Are you poking fun at my accent again?"

I froze for a millisecond, realizing my misstep. Fuck, she was making me careless. What was something the human would say?

"Would you rather I call you something generic, like baby?"

"I prefer when you call me princess."

Her smile was soft, and once again I was struck by the realization her adoration wasn't for me.

The world had officially gone tits up.

"To answer your question, yes, I'm so hungry I can barely see straight. I shouldn't be, though. I just fed from Remi not long ago, and Ben brought me his blood. Gavin says it has to do with the fact that I'm a Queen. That you're all stuck with me forever because of it."

Well . . . that's going to be a problem. But not one I'm in any state to deal with.

Nor did I much care, to be honest. I was more interested in sating her hunger. This mate bond was turning me into a sap, but I couldn't do a damn thing about it.

"That's not how I see it. Take me inside and let me give you what you need so I can show you just how fun being stuck can be."

She finally seemed to notice we were still tangled in the doorway. "Goodness, where are my manners? Come on in, Asher."

My lips twitched at the reappearance of her posh and proper ways. She was so much fun to break. Especially when I reduced her to little more than tears, pleas, and moans.

Lucifer, I missed my body.

"Where are we doing this?" I looked around and found Gavin seated in a leather club chair, a stern expression on his face, jaw clenched, eyes hard. He didn't like me. I didn't give a fuck.

"The bedroom? Or perhaps the shower? I'm not the neatest feeder yet. There's a bit of a learning curve."

"Why not both? We start in the bedroom and make our mess and then end with the shower so we can take care of the cleanup."

I hadn't taken her in the shower. That could be fun. All I cared about was being inside her again, honestly. She was addictive. I needed a fix.

Oh, and her blood.

One mustn't forget the blood.

I winked at the vampire in the corner. "We'll call you if we need you."

Not stopping to think about whether this was something the human would do, I grabbed Roslyn around the waist and then tossed her over my shoulder. "Which way's the bedroom?"

"Upstairs," she gasped, once she caught her breath. "Second door on the left."

She squealed when I slapped her round arse as I climbed the staircase. "Don't wait up, grandpa!" I called down to Gavin. I could feel the rage rolling off him. It was fantastic.

With a sharp kick to the already partially open door, I carried her inside the rustic bedroom and dropped her unceremoniously on the mattress. "Get naked, now."

"My, my, you're eager."

"It's been too long since I've had you. Show me that body I love to defile."

She raised a brow and giggled. "Asher, I've never seen you like this before."

I had to swallow back a groan. I would eat my own arm before I had to vanilla up my sex life. "You've never kept me away before."

"It was for your own good. You know that. I nearly killed you the first time."

"But you didn't. I love it when you lose control."

"Be careful what you wish for."

I knew my smile was all demon. "Do your worst, sweetheart. I can take it."

Her shudder of pleasure had me palming my already throbbing cock. I was going to destroy her pussy tonight. She'd have me dripping down her thighs all night, and any time she moved, her vampire would smell me on her.

Not you. The human.

A snarl slipped past my lips. I couldn't bear the thought of *him* getting all the credit when I was the one bringing her pleasure. Perhaps I could work this to my advantage. I could fuck her with this body, but ensure she was thinking of me—the real me—the whole damn time.

"Do you want to play a game, Roslyn?"

My unintentional use of her full name didn't register, praise Satan. She was too hung up on my offer to notice the slip.

Rising to her knees, she asked, "What kind of game?"

"How about a little role-play? You seem to think I'm such a good boy. Your knight in shining armor."

"Technological armor, actually."

I chuckled lazily as I tugged my shirt over my head.

"Asher! Your tattoo. It's gone. The curse? Does this mean it's . . ."

I followed her gaze to my bare arm, vaguely recalling the stars that had once decorated the back of my vessel's hand and arm. "Oh. Right. I guess you broke the curse when you mated me." She opened her mouth like she wanted to say something, but I was a demon on a mission. "Anyway, back to the fun stuff. I've heard you like a bad boy just as much as your heroes. Maybe even more."

"H-how bad?"

"Demon bad. You craved your demon, didn't you? What was his name again?"

Here it was. The moment we've all been waiting for. My grand return.

Ma petit monstre didn't disappoint. Her cheeks turned a fetching shade of crimson.

"Pan."

The breathless cadence of her voice had my eyes rolling back in my head. It was glorious. Nearly orgasmic. Oh yessss. This was just what the demon ordered.

"I'll be Pan, and you'll be my . . . what was it he called you?"

"Dirty little bitch."

Fuuuck. That wasn't what I was going for, but I'd take it.

My smile stretched. "And you'll be my dirty little bitch." I crawled up on the bed beside her. "Tell me what he did to you."

As much as I wanted her to mention my forked tongue and tail, I was also hoping she'd bring up the things I might actually be able to replicate. No amount of role-play could recreate that.

Fuck. Have I mentioned that I miss my body?

"He . . . degraded me. Marked me with his . . . spend."

I smirked. "Spend? Come on, Rosie. Say it. His cum."

She bit her plump bottom lip and batted her eyelashes at me. "He covered me in his cum, and I loved it."

Now we were talking. "What else?"

"He . . . he choked me. And was rough. Really rough. He used me." She squirmed, unconsciously rubbing her thighs together in search of friction.

What had started out as a way to ensure she was thinking of me had turned into something else entirely. I was so turned on I knew I'd be leaking like a damned faucet the second I pulled my cock out. I almost regretted taking her womb. I'd knock her up for sure if I hadn't.

"And you liked it? You wanted him to use you like a whore?" Was it just me, or did Asher's voice get sexier? Maybe I could get used to this accent.

"I wanted it. Every time. I still do."

Motherfucking hell yes.

"Call me by his name, Rosie. I'll give you what you're missing. I'll be him for you tonight."

"A-are you sure? I don't want you to be something you're not, Asher."

"But that's the whole point of the fantasy. I'll give you anything you want. Everything."

She nodded, eyes shining with her arousal. "Okay. Gavin and I usually start our scenes with a word so we both know it's begun. Is that something you want to do?"

I didn't give a single fuck, to be honest. This wasn't a game for me, but maybe it would help her. "Sure. Whatever you want, princess."

Gag.

"Brimstone. It's the scent that makes me think of him."

She thinks of me. Of course she fucking does. I'm her god.

"Brimstone it is. And if I take it too far?"

"Red. Let's keep it the same as always."

Oh, so perhaps the hacker wasn't as vanilla as I thought. Interesting. "I'm ready when you are."

She stared at me, her eyes bright and cheeks flushed, then with her breath hitching, she slowly unbuttoned the shirt that covered her and whispered, "Brimstone."

"Tell me, my dirty little slut, why do you like it when I'm mean?" The way she licked her lower lip and dropped the shirt from her shoulders made my mouth water.

"I don't know. But something about it makes me hot all over."

"Liar. You know why."

She started to shake her head in denial, and I caught her chin in my hand, gripping her tight enough that my fingers dug into her soft flesh. She whimpered, but not in pain.

"There's something freeing about being reduced to my basest state."

I could tell there was something she was holding back, so I pressed her. "And . . ."

"And when you do it, degradation feels a whole lot like adoration."

I almost sighed in pleasure at that. "Much better."

I didn't know why I enjoyed hearing the truth so much, in knowing that it was something she found specifically with me, but I did. Fuck, I did.

"And when you're with them, you miss me, isn't that right? They treat you like the beautiful precious thing you've always been told you are, when really the only way you feel whole is if I'm with you, reminding you how depraved you truly are."

"Yes," she hissed when I reached down and pinched her nipple. The nipple that was supposed to bear my ring. Where the bloody hell had it gone? When I found out who took it, there would be hell to pay.

"What's this scar from? Who hurt you without my permission?" I had to play this carefully, but I needed to know.

"It's from where you pierced me. G-Gavin didn't like it. He said you weren't mine and didn't deserve to mark me."

I supposed I'd be cooking vampire for supper. I never much liked the taste of ashes, but he deserved to end up as nothing more than a pile of shit.

I forced her head back, still brutally holding onto her face. "But we both know that's not true, don't we? I owned you first. My claim supersedes all of theirs." I was perilously close to blowing my cover. I'd already almost called her *ma petite monstre* once.

"They don't like to think about you. But I can't help it."

"Hmm, as it should be. If you're a good girl, perhaps I'll pierce your pretty little clit this time. Would you like that? Knowing that no matter who touched you, a part of me was always bringing you pleasure?"

Her breath hitched as she nodded. "Yes."

"You need to feed from me before I take what I'm owed."

"I-it's better when you're inside me," she whispered.

Who was I to argue that?

"Part your thighs like you were born to do, then. But I won't be done with you until you've come on my cock at least twice while my hand is around your throat and you've let me taste you."

"Taste me? You mean my . . . my . . ." Her blush deepened. "My pussy?"

"I was referring to your blood, but now that you mention it . . . why not both?" I asked, repeating my earlier question.

"You want my blood?"

"You taste fucking divine. If it's anything like last time, it will only heighten things for both of us."

"Fork me, why is this so hot?" she asked, falling out of the scene for a second.

"Because this is who you are and what you need."

I am what you need.

"Your cunt is glistening for me like the filthy slut you are. Let me have it."

She nodded and leaned back, spreading her legs wide and welcoming me. It seemed oddly . . . tender. I'd have to change that as soon as she fed. I'd pull her hair and slap her arse until it hurt to sit to make up for this romantic shit.

But for now, I joined her on the bed after shucking my jeans. My dick was straining toward her, a rigid, dripping length desperate to get inside her and make her moan.

"Please, Pan," she whispered.

I was gone at the wanton sound of my name on her lips.

I drove into her in one hard thrust, bottoming out and making us both scream.

"Yes, say it again."

"Pan, God, I need you."

My grip on her hips tightened. She'd be wearing my bruises if I wasn't careful. Which, come to think of it, I didn't need to be. My mate was a vampire now, and I a mere human. I could push her to the very brink and not worry about causing any permanent harm. Of course, she could break my pathetic human body with one too-strong clench of her thighs. But she wouldn't. I knew that deep in my bones.

The change in our dynamic was heady. I'd never been at anyone's mercy before. But the thought of being at hers . . . fuck, it stripped me of my control. I could see now why she craved my subjugation. Why pain brought her such pleasure. I wanted to experience that high for myself.

"Take what you want from me. Use me the same way I use you. Feed from me, Rosie."

The feral growl she let out had my dick swelling even larger inside her. Bloody humans. I wasn't ready, but Asher's body was raring to find its release already. What a two-pump chump.

She grabbed me by the neck and pulled down, my body flush against hers, the scent of sex heavy in the air. I needed her to come while we were still playing this game. If she cried out his name while I was inside her, I'd slip and tell her exactly who I was.

The roll of my hips became erratic the second she sank her fangs into me. It was no longer just Asher's body on the verge, but my entire being was lit up with the need to find release with my mate. To fall over the edge with her and float away on a sea of our pleasure-born oblivion. Apparently I wasn't the only one who thought so.

Deep in the back of my mind, I could feel Asher's consciousness stretch and wake.

I had a brief moment of panic at the thought of him fighting me, of the arse ruining my orgasm by running his mouth. What if she sensed him through the bond as well? We couldn't have that.

"Fuck, yes, Rosie," I groaned, threading my fingers in her hair and fisting the strands. "You're mine, aren't you? Drenched for me like the needy whore you are."

She couldn't answer beyond a hum of agreement as she took her fill, but I could feel her reaction to my words. The flood of arousal, the telltale flutter of her vaginal walls. She was close.

Thankfully, I knew exactly what she needed to push her over the edge. A rush of fear, its own kind of pain, to send her careening off the cliff. She broke the seal she had on my neck and stared up at me, lips stained with my blood, cheeks flushed. I in turn wrapped a firm hand around her throat and tightened my hold on her, feeling the wild flutter of her pulse under my thumb.

It was no tail, but the immediate dilation of her pupils told me she didn't mind the lack of my second favorite appendage. She detonated around me, her body milking me insistently until I was helpless to do anything but join her.

A sheen of sweat coated my skin as we both came down from the euphoric wave of our releases, my heart racing, her grin devilish.

"You're rather good at this game, Asher. Who knew you had it in you?"

"You don't know the half of it."

But I wasn't done with her. I had a job to do. A world to end. A soul to claim. Oh, it was fun to play the wolf in sheep's clothing. As long as she didn't figure me out. Eyes were the windows to the soul and all that. If she saw beyond me and into the prison I'd created for the other spirit that lived in this body, I was done for.

"Now, close your eyes and let me have the taste you promised."

In the back of my mind, Asher pushed for control. He didn't like that I was with her. But there wasn't anything the human could do. Rosie was all mine.

TWENTY-NINE

ASHER

My freefall stopped with an abrupt crash to the ground, my head cracking on a smooth, hard surface, breath knocked out of me, and a pained "oof," escaping my lips at the same time.

Shit. I was here again. In the place I'd first woken when the demon had taken me hostage. Not that I was really sure where *here* was. My mind, maybe? Or a blocked-off section of it, at the very least. There wasn't a whole lot to go by to clue me in.

Endless darkness stretched out in every direction. Inky and black. All-consuming. It had an almost glossy quality, as if it was liquid, or maybe a mirror. The only source of light came from me. Like maybe a spotlight was overhead, but when I looked up, there was nothing there.

"Hello, darkness, my old friend," I muttered, dread coiling in my stomach and apprehension slithering up the back of my neck.

Wherever I was, this wasn't a 'good' place. I wouldn't say it was evil exactly, but it was definitely wrong. I wasn't supposed to be here, trapped between reality and my memories.

This prison was the one thing I couldn't take. Sensory deprivation. I could be isolated, alone, quiet, but this was an oppressive and dead space. Nothing but me as a frame of reference and no stimuli to help me get my bearings. At least when he knocked me through my own memories, there was something for me to hold on to. A way to orient myself.

This was . . . hell.

"Of course the demon sent me to my version of hell." God, not even the sound of my voice was right. It came through dull and muted. Not bouncing off anything around me. The unease I was already experiencing only grew with every breath.

I hadn't had much time to get used to this place when he'd first put me here. The fucker threw me headlong into traumatic moment after traumatic moment from my past. I was stuck in them. My own special quicksand. Each one sucked me in and pulled me down until I drowned in it.

This was my first chance to come up for air in . . . fuck, who even knew what time was anymore. Had it been days? Hours? Months?

How long had he been wearing me like a costume? I was certain he'd been doing his best to ruin my life and make it into his. Fear skittered along my spine. What had he done to Rosie while smiling with my face? Or Remi?

I remembered the brief instances of anxiety that had shot through me, flickers of what was happening with my body. Something was very wrong in the real world, but I didn't know how to get back.

The last thing I remember was walking through the woods. Was I even in Alaska anymore? I was pretty sure I had to be, but my panic spiral was growing with every unanswered question.

And then, out of literally nowhere, I caught a hint of *her*. Rosie.

It was faint, little more than a phantom, but in this void, it was *everything*.

"Rosie?" I called, knowing it was pointless but unable to stop myself from hoping that maybe she'd hear me, or fuck, I don't know, feel me.

A twinge of longing started in my heart but grew to a painful tug, like something was wrapped around it and pulling. I pressed my palm over my chest and took a few deep breaths, attempting to curb the nervous energy from building into a storm I couldn't control. The last thing I needed right now was to lose hold of my senses. They were all I had.

But instead of losing them, I seemed to be gaining them. My neck tingled, like someone was rubbing a feather over my skin. I shivered, need and hunger unlike anything I'd ever known holding me fast.

The tug grew stronger, like it was pulling me up. A rope guiding me to safety.

I had nothing to compare this to, no explanation for what was happening, but I knew it was her. My light in the darkness.

And I wasn't just waxing poetic. Around the same time as that neck tingle, a light blossomed at the far end of this . . . prison.

I blinked. Or thought I blinked, but it was still there.

A literal light in the distance. One that definitely hadn't been there before.

That featherlight touch turned to deep pressure, and I brought my fingers to the spot where the sensation was strongest. The raised scar from her bite, the one I'd been vaguely aware of before the body snatcher sent me as far away as he could.

"I'm coming for you, Rosie. I swear." I ran, my legs pumping and pushing as far and fast as I could, but fuck if I wasn't going anywhere. The light was still impossibly far. It was like I was trapped in a damn hamster wheel. Or better yet, like Rosie was the carrot on a stick I could never reach.

Faint whispers filtered to my ears as I raced toward the only possible opening to get to her. A low rumble followed by the sweet melody of Rosie. He was fucking her; I knew it. Taking her and lying to her about who he was. When I got out of here, I was going to kill him. Send him back to hell where he belonged.

Wait, was I getting closer to my goal? The light was bigger, brighter. Fuck, I could see her. She was right there, staring up at me with love and sated lust shining in her topaz eyes. I wanted to scream for her to notice me, but she smiled and let out a soft giggle.

"You're rather good at this game, Asher. Who knew you had it in you?"

"You don't know the half of it."

That was my voice, but it wasn't me.

Something like electricity crawled along my senses, sending me on high alert.

No.

No. No. No.

Right on its heels came the softest croon in my ear. It swirled around me, so close it was practically a part of me. The voice was dark, carnal, filled with sinister promise. And definitely *not* mine.

It took a beat for me to place it as the inner thoughts of the monster who'd taken my body hostage.

I'm not done with her. I have a job to do. A world to end. A soul to claim. Oh, it is fun to play the wolf in sheep's clothing. As long as she doesn't figure me out. Eyes are the windows to the soul and all that. If she sees beyond me and into the prison I've created for the other spirit that lives in this body, I am done for.

This was him. Rosie's demon, Pan. Of course. How could I have been so stupid? This wasn't some random possession. He was after her.

"Now, close your eyes and let me have the taste you promised."

I screamed and pushed forward as the demon's thoughts infiltrated every cell, reaching the tear in reality, trying to come out on the other side, but something was keeping me back.

"Oh no, you don't, Asher."

I was so startled by him speaking to me directly I forgot what I was doing, and some of that light dimmed.

No. He couldn't have her. I pushed back, trying like hell to break through the film keeping me out of the place I wanted so badly to be.

"Fuck. You. Demon."

"Oh, ouch. I'm hurt. Your words are so cruel and painful. However shall I go on?"

I could still see her through the gap in the darkness, baring her throat, waiting for him. She didn't know that what she was doing was going to help a demon end the world, but I heard him. I felt his intention. I had to save her.

Somehow.

Without a body, all I had was my mind. *My* intention. Maybe even my voice.

"Stop!" I roared, infusing my shout with every ounce of my fear and fury.

I wasn't sure what I was expecting, but I'd clearly caught Pan off guard.

He faltered, and my girl opened her eyes. I willed her to see me, to recognize that something wasn't right.

"Asher? Are you all right?"

Before I could try anything, the light was all but gone. Nothing more than a glowing crack in a black wall.

"Now you've done it. This just won't do. I'd say enjoy the ride, but I'm going to make sure you don't." Pan's snarl was laced with vitriol, and my stomach churned as reality once again turned to a swirl of nothingness I recognized all too well.

Fuck, I didn't want to keep bouncing around in my memories. I needed to get back to the surface, back to Rosie. I had to warn her. She had no idea how much danger she was in.

But of course, Pan didn't give a flying fig what I wanted. So here we were again, strolling along memory lane. I was maybe five this time, based on the size of my chubby fist wrapped around that crayon. Which would mean I was with the Rochesters. The first of my many foster families.

"Thank you for agreeing to see him, Father Tate. We just don't know what to do." My foster mom's voice wobbled as she spoke in hushed whispers. I could still hear, though. They didn't realize just how much listening a little kid could do.

"Of course, my child. Don't worry."

"We're just quite gobsmacked by this whole thing. First it was the animals, then the attack, and now these . . . drawings." Ah, yes, Martin Rochester III. The man who should have entered the priesthood himself rather than become a lawyer like his father, and his father's father. He did love a sermon. Or just to hear himself talk. I spent most of my waking hours wishing he would shut up.

"Where is he?" The priest's voice was calm and soothing. A sharp contrast to my high-strung foster parents. If ever there was a couple who could benefit from a joint or seven, it was these bible thumpers.

"In there. Do we . . . have to go in with you?"

"No, Dee Dee. Father Tate will sort it out."

The doorknob turned, and I dropped my purple crayon as my gaze lifted to meet his.

"Hello, Asher. What are you drawing there?"

What the fuck does it look like, padre? A cucumber? It's a giant purple demon.

Of course that's not what I said. I didn't speak a lot in those days, but as soon as little Asher opened his mouth I felt our consciousnesses merge, just like they had the last time.

"A superhero."

"Oh, wow. Does he have a cape?" he asked, coming to crouch beside me.

I shook my head. "Just a tail and some horns."

He raised a brow. "Horns? That doesn't seem like something a superhero would have. A monster, maybe."

"Pan's not a monster! He's my friend! Don't be mean to him."

"Okay, I'm sorry. I understand that now. Is that why you draw him all the time?" The priest placed a hand over mine. "May I see one of those pictures?"

I narrowed my eyes. "Why? You gonna copy it?"

"I just want to see if I know this friend of yours. I know a lot of superheroes."

"Not this one. He lives in my dreams." My shoulders drooped. "He's not real."

"Be that as it may, let me have a look."

I shoved over the stack of drawings I'd been working on. My comic book, as I called it. I wasn't very good yet, but if I kept practicing, maybe I'd get as good as Stan Lee.

"These are very detailed, Asher. So cool. Can I keep this one?"

"What?" I didn't want to give him that. I worked hard on it.

"Yes. I want to show my friends."

I bit my lower lip. "Fine."

"I know you love to draw, but if you don't want to be sent away, you have to stop drawing Pan. The Rochesters won't understand. They think he's bad."

Crossing my fingers behind my back, I nodded. "Okay. I won't draw him anymore."

The priest stood and rumpled my hair. "That's a good boy. I'll see you soon, okay?"

"Okay! Hope your friends like my picture!"

He winked before tucking it in his jacket. "Oh, I'm sure they will."

THIRTY

ROSIE

Being back at The Tip was harder than I'd anticipated, and believe me, I'd expected it would be akin to being starved and then sat in front of a buffet without permission to eat. It didn't help matters that my 'easy' shift had turned out to be absolutely bananas. Wednesdays were notoriously slow nights, which is why Remi suggested it for my first night back, but this was unheard of. Regulars and visitors alike had flocked to our little bar like booze-happy moths to a whiskey-fueled flame.

Thus why I was currently hiding out in the back alley. Even with all of my mates present—though Ben was also in hiding—I just needed to put a little space between me and all those thrumming pulses. With each new arrival, I'd felt myself get more on edge.

I wasn't hungry, per se. But I was definitely uneasy. I think Moira referred to this feeling as stabby.

Remi had finally sent me off on break. He'd offered to come with me, but there was no way in Hades I'd let Darla handle the crowd alone. Ben wasn't any use, holed up in the office, Gavin was too busy glowering at anyone who looked his way, and Asher . . . he was . . . off. The hermit had become Aurora Springs' new welcome wagon. He was chit-chatting like he was being paid by the word, and the newcomers loved him. Gone were the prosthetics and fake tattoos. Now he was dressed like a GQ model with his hair slicked back and white teeth flashing with every smile.

Had Scarlett drugged him?

What the devil was going on with that man? He'd been acting strange for a couple weeks now, and I'd definitely caught a hint of it myself the other night. For a second there—

The chirp of my phone interrupted my musings, and I glanced down as I pulled it out of my pocket. Seeing it was a photo from my brother, I clicked it open, giggling instantly at the sight of my niece dressed up in a Halloween costume. She made an adorable wolf pup.

I responded immediately.

ME:

You do know it's not even summer yet, right?

NOAH:

Try telling Kingston that. He's insisted she needs to learn about her roots from an early age.

ME:

LOL

I SMILED AT THE PICTURE, her chubby cheeks and red-faced scowl telling me all I needed to know about how much she liked wearing that.

ME:

Speaking of learning about roots. Do you think you could help me with something? Gavin's so protective he filters what he says, but I need advice.

INSTEAD OF RESPONDING, my phone rang with an incoming video call. I answered with a raised brow. "Video? What a bold choice. I could have been in the loo. Or naked."

"I would hope if you were naked, there'd be no chance of you answering." Noah looked relaxed and happy with a sleeping Eden on his chest.

"Fair. But with all these mates of mine, you never know when you might get an eyeful of something you would rather not see."

He laughed. "Don't I know it. How's it going? They handling your transition well?"

"Mostly?" The one-word answer sounded more like a question, and he sat up straighter, the laughter leaving his eyes.

Before Noah could respond, Kingston popped into the frame, a wide grin on his handsome face. "Hey, baby sis!"

I wrinkled my nose, charmed by him as always. "Two brothers is enough for me, thank you very much."

"Oh, shots fired. You only say that because you're stuck with this guy. I'm the best big brother. Ask T."

"Do you mind?" Noah asked, annoyance in his voice, but a sort of resignation too.

"Nope. Scoot over. I want to be part of the Nosie reunion." Kingston shoved in next to my brother and scooped Eden out of his arms.

"Nosie?" I asked, feeling like I was either being insulted or missing a joke.

"You know, your celebrity name. Noah . . . Rosie . . . *Nosie*. I mean,

I guess we could go with Roah, but it doesn't roll off the tongue the same way."

"Don't." Noah groaned as Kingston smirked.

"Oh, c'mon. Just because your stupid name doesn't go with anything isn't a reason for you to be pissy about it."

I let out a giggle. "Oh, please, tell me more."

Kingston preened. The man lived to be the center of attention. "Well, you see—"

"I said don't. My sister was in the middle of asking me something important, and like always, you're butting in where you don't belong."

Kingston raised his brows, wholly unfazed. "Agree to disagree, my man. My ass is right where it belongs."

"And where exactly is that? Because if Caleb catches you with your arse on his countertops, you know he's going to Irish you about how they aren't for sitting."

"Of course not. Everyone knows the kitchen counter is made for . . ." He waggled his brows instead of finishing the sentence.

"I hate you."

"Sure. Keep telling yourself that." A huge hulking Norse god walked by in the background, protein shake in one hand and a whole turkey leg in the other. "Tell her, Alek! Noah loves me."

Alek chuckled and shook his head, not saying a word as he continued down the hall.

"Okay, but celebrity names. Please, I need to know." I wanted more of this distraction, more proof it could all turn out happily.

"Rosie, trust me—"

"Just because Sunston and Kingsday are way cooler than Noday doesn't mean you can s-h-i-t all over our fun."

"Hey, look at that. You can spell now. Good job, Kingston. Try this one. P-i-s-s o-f-f."

Kingston shook his head. "Too many letters. I got bored just listening."

"I should win a medal for not smothering you in your sleep."

"Sunday would never forgive you. She loves my face. Speaking of places to sit . . ."

"Kingston, fuck off and let me chat with my sister."

The wolf placed a large palm over his daughter's ears, face twisted in mock outrage. "How dare you use foul language in front of my perfect little sunbeam. What are you going to do when that's her first word? I'm telling Sunday what you said. Just wait. You're going to get all the spankings."

"Oh, go tune your banjo or something, will you? I'm busy."

Kingston tossed me a cheerful wink, seeming far too pleased with himself and his work here. "Good seeing you, Nosie. Maybe someday soon you can come snuggle your niece, huh?"

I smiled. "I'd love nothing more."

Then the man swaggered away, baby in tow, and I understood exactly why Sunday kept him around.

"So what kind of advice do you need, Winnie?"

My heart flipped over as a wave of nostalgia blasted through me. Noah hadn't called me that in years. Not since we were small. I couldn't remember where the nickname had come from, only that he'd had trouble with his Rs and Ls, and that's what he'd settled on. It made no sense, but children's nicknames rarely did.

"When you transitioned, how did you manage being around creatures without being so edgy all the time?"

His dark brows drew together over eyes so like my own. "What do you mean? Thirsty?"

"Nooo," I said, drawing the word out as I struggled to explain what I was feeling. "It's more like a general sense that something is about to happen. Like something is wrong or, I don't know, off."

"I'm going to need a little more to go on than that. What's happening right before you feel that way?"

I shrugged. "I dunno. New people. Unfamiliar faces. Strange scents and a barrage of thoughts I can't home in on. Everything is a mashed-up jumble of words, and I can't get a strong read on anyone. Especially when they put themselves in the proximity of my mates."

His expression cleared, and he gave me a smile filled with understanding. "That doesn't sound like a vampire thing. That sounds like a mate bond thing."

"Really?" I rubbed at my chest, at the ache that had settled there the second I'd left my men in the bar.

"Your instinct is to protect them from any and every threat. With so many new people and scents around, you don't know who is trustworthy or not, so the bond has you on alert, ready to defend at a moment's notice. I'm a nervous wreck any time Sunday and I are out in public. Constantly on edge, waiting for someone to threaten our bond."

As he explained it, it made so much sense. I'd just assumed it was part of my transition, but since that happened at nearly the same time I'd acquired my first full mate bond, I suppose I didn't really know how to separate the two in my mind yet.

"What do I do?"

He sighed. "The same thing I do. Be with them. Wrap up in their scents and assuage that need in you to be around them. You can use your connection to them as well. You should be able to get a read on what they're feeling. Are you able to talk in their minds?"

"I . . . think so. I've done it before."

"Okay, so reach out. Assure yourself they are safe. Talk to them and just check in. It will help."

I nodded. "Right. Check in. Don't murder anyone."

"Definitely don't do that. Stay fed and connected to them. Keep them close."

Easier said than done with some of them. Well, one broody wolf in particular.

"You make it sound so easy."

"Easy?" Noah laughed. "No. Nothing about being a mate is easy, except loving them. That's the easiest thing in the world."

"Thank you. I love you, Noah."

"Love you, Winnie. You can do this. I know you can. You're a Blackthorne."

"Technically I'm a Donoghue now."

He scowled at me. "You're a Blackthorne. Always."

I blew him a kiss. "Chat soon. Kiss your baby girl for me."

The moment I hung up, that curl began to build strength in my belly again. The one that made me uneasy. I took a deep breath and reminded myself I was a forking Blackthorne vampire and Noah was right. I could do this.

I hoped.

~

I COULDN'T DO THIS.

The bar had only grown more crowded since my break. I could just barely make out my broody husband perched at his table in the corner. Asher was speaking to what appeared to be a group of musicians. And Remi was hurriedly slinging drinks, but with enough grace it looked like a choreographed ballet. Ben was still hiding in the flat upstairs.

Each one of them made my heart flutter in a different way. Gavin with anticipation of time with him. Remi with pure affection. Ben with longing. And Asher, well, that was more complicated. A cocktail of feelings rather than just one. Love, of course. But also a bit of concern and mild apprehension. He just wasn't acting like himself. First with Remi, and now here with all these people he was playing cruise director for, then there was the other night when I'd thought . . . Had my mate bond changed him that drastically?

Stop it, Rosie. You're borrowing trouble, and you already have more than enough to go around. Focus on getting through the night unscathed, then you can worry about Asher.

"Come on, baby girl. Break's over. We've got a line nearly out the door, and I could use your help," Remi called, breaking me out of my self-imposed worry dungeon.

"On it!" I called back, squeezing through a couple of nereids, more commonly but less accurately known as sea nymphs. "Oof, sorry," I apologized distractedly when I accidentally caught my fingers in the long strands of one woman's waist-length hair.

Was it naturally seafoam green? Moira would be jealous.

"What on earth is going on?" I asked as soon as I joined Remi behind the bar.

He shook his head. "I have no idea. It's never been like this before. We aren't exactly a hot spot for tourists, but it looks like a whole caravan arrived in town this week."

"No kidding. Where do you want me to start?"

Using his chin, he gestured at a rowdy group of sailors. "See those guys over there? I need you to make them seven duck farts."

I blinked at him, certain I'd heard him incorrectly. "I'm sorry, what?"

He grinned. "Duck farts. They're an Alaskan tradition."

"You're having me on."

"I'm not. They're shooters. Layer Kahlua, Baileys, then Crown. Equal parts."

Eyeing him dubiously, I said, "And you want *me* to make these? I'm barely able to make a cocktail without poisoning people. Do you remember my egg fiasco? Asher still can't look at one without turning green."

"This one's hard to fuck up. And by nature, they're not pretty. So it's basically made for you."

I pinched his arse.

"You keep flirting with me like that, I'm gonna have to take us both on a break and leave Dante in charge."

"Dante's here?" I looked around, trying to spot our elusive chef. He was absent as often as not, and I wasn't sure how the man still had a job. Unless he was secretly the invisible man or something.

He chuckled. "No. So I guess it'd be the gargoyles. We'd be out of whiskey by the time I let you come back to work, bow-legged but smiling."

"Ha! That's optimistic. You'd be out of whiskey by the time you got my knickers off."

His answering smirk was pure sex. "Happy to test the theory. I'm on inventory this week, so it would only help me out."

"Until Ben did the accounts."

My stupid heart squeezed at my mention of Ben. Remi gave me a tender smile, then handed me the Kahlua. "Get to work, baby girl. We can play later."

I moved down the bar, setting the bottle down and pulling out the shot glasses. Then with a dubious look, I began pouring the layers. It looked bloody awful. A mix of brown and white snot. I shuddered. You couldn't pay me to try one, even if the ingredients were delightful on their own.

"All right, lads! Order's up."

The man sat in the middle of the group turned and faced me, his gaze promising wicked things if I only came to talk to him. His dark blond hair was somehow both slicked back but tousled, like not even his curls wanted to behave. The scruff lining his chiseled jaw was a shade or two darker, only enhancing his dark and sexy vibe.

"On second thought, maybe I'll handle that table." Remi came up next to me, one hand possessively on the small of my back.

"I've got it, boss."

But before either of us made a move, the man was stalking toward the bar, his smirk rivaling that of even Remington Mercer. Oh, bloody hell, he had a dimple. And swagger. So much swagger. He could have easily been a model working the runway in his skintight black leather pants and white button-down open to nearly his waist. His rolled-up sleeves showcased a myriad of tattoos. He was a bit too far to make out the details, but one appeared to be the coils of a snake.

"Allow me, love. This lot is too crude for the likes of you. You're much too pretty to spend time in their company. Believe me, I know. I have to do it at all hours of the bloody day."

His voice rolled over me, drawing me in as surely as a wave to the shore. It was a velvety rasp. As seductive as any of my men, and a whole lot more dangerous.

I placed each shot on a round tray as he leaned close and said, "Perhaps tonight I might find myself some other accommodations? Care to pass the witching hour in bed with a pirate?"

My cheeks burned as he reached out and brushed his fingers over mine. Large rings adorned two of them, one a skull and the other a deep red ruby as large as his knuckle.

"She's busy, and her bed is full up, man. Take your drinks and stop harassing my mate." Remi's growl was so ice cold goosebumps erupted on my skin.

The pirate winked at me and took the tray. "The name's Caspian, love. In case you need anyone to fantasize about tonight after this one falls asleep." His eyes flicked over Remi, the curl of his lip growing. "Or you're welcome to join us."

Remi and I both stood transfixed as the man sauntered away, neither of us immune to the drive-by sex bomb that was Caspian the Pirate.

"Who the blazes was that?" I breathed.

"Hook," Scarlett muttered, our new sheriff staring after him with a hard look in her eyes. "That was Hook."

"As in . . . Captain?" Remi asked, his voice holding no small amount of awe.

"Yes. The very one. Or this generation's iteration of him, anyway."

"What do you mean?" I poured her a second glass of ice wine—the pixie liked her drinks sugar-sweet—and waited for her to elaborate.

"The curse is passed down."

"Curse?"

"Oh yes, the one thing the mortals always get wrong is that there are no true heroes or villains. Only curses. Someone must always bear the mantle." Scarlett began listing names on her fingers. "Maleficent's line continues to this day. Same with Peter Pan, Captain Hook, the Sea Witch, that poor headless horseman, and even The Beast. All of them live on, no matter how many times we try to break the cycle. Sadly, it's usually those that slay them who take on the curse. Tricky business, faerie magic. But then, they need someone to keep the tales alive, don't they? Belief feeds the fae realms."

"So you're saying he's Captain Hook, but not the original?" Remi asked.

"Yes. By the looks of him, he was once called Peter."

"*Peter* Pan?" I asked, my eyes going wide, remembering teasing *my* Pan about this very name.

Scarlett nodded. "Exactly so. Like I said, it's usually the ones who slay them that take on their curse. He'll have no memory of his past. He's simply Caspian now, and there's another lost boy out there going by Peter in his stead."

"Wow, Peter Pan really had a glow up." Remi's voice was low in my ear, and I couldn't help but nod as I stared at the handsome pirate. "What is he doing here? Doesn't he belong in Neverland?"

"Actually, the island is called Ravenndel. Barrie changed some things to protect us."

"Wait, wait, just one second. If he's here and there are a bunch of pirates in my bar, does that mean there's a real live pirate ship out at the harbor?" The excitement in Remi's question had me on the verge of giggling.

Scarlett sighed, far less excited by the prospect. "Yes. And a gossip of mermaids, several selkies, a few naga, and I'm 90 percent sure that tentacle I saw belonged to a kraken. So . . . cheers, the world is ending." She lifted her glass and nearly drained it.

I swallowed back the lump of dread in my throat. Was she just having a laugh, or was the pixie onto something?

"Is it really so bad?" I asked. "Business is booming."

"I wish Dallas wasn't fired. With the influx of tourists, the inns are all full, traffic is already out of control, and the way things are going in this bar, I'm going to be so busy I won't have time to wipe my own ass."

"You know there are people you can pay for services like that," the pirate crooned, causing a blush to steal over Scarlett's neck as he snuck up on us. We'd gotten so distracted by our conversation that none of us realized he'd come back. "Oh, hello, you look quite familiar. Have we set my ship a'rocking?"

"No, but your ancestor killed mine." Her gaze was icy, even if her cheeks were still pink.

"Ah, a Bell. Now all we're missing is one of the Darling bloodline, and the gang would all be here."

"Don't forget the crocodile."

He laughed. "You've got me all wrong, pixie. We don't have to be enemies. We can write our own history." He leaned even closer and put his lips at her ear. "And, for the record Miss Bell, I do believe in faeries."

"If you're Hook, where's your . . . you know, hook?" Remi asked, a clear attempt to distract Caspian.

It worked, but the sexy scoundrel turned his attention on us. "Wouldn't you like to know?"

I glanced at my blushing mate, then back to the rake before us. I was wrong. *That's* a sex pirate.

"Are you . . . did you just say that in front of me?" Remi asked, affronted.

"What? No. Oh, bloody hell. Excuse me. I need a breather."

"But you just had a break," Remi protested.

"I'll join you," Caspian offered.

Before I had a chance to respond, Gavin appeared behind him, one hand fisted in the back of his shirt. "That won't be necessary, *Captain*. I'll accompany her."

Caspian grinned. "How many mates have you got, love?"

"Enough," Gavin answered.

"Is there really such a thing?"

Gavin's voice dropped even lower, a growl weaving through it. "Her dance card is full."

"Pity."

"I'm sure you'll find somewhere to dip your wick. From my experience, pirates aren't picky."

"Are you offering?"

Gavin's jaw ticked as he rolled his eyes. "You couldn't handle me." Then he looked at the rest of us. "Can someone kill him? I'm not allowed."

"No death or dismemberment in front of me, please. No matter how frustrating he is." Scarlett took a long glug of her wine. "I'm off duty and really rather not have to arrest anyone tonight. We only have the one cell."

"She pretends to hate me, but she wants me." Caspian shrugged out of Gavin's hold. "Though his hot and cold act of yours begs the question. If you didn't want me here, why did you summon us?"

"I didn't summon anyone."

"Someone did."

"Some*thing*, not someone." Asher's voice broke through the din of the crowd. "It took me a few minutes of hackery, but I figured out what's drawing everyone here. Aurora Springs is a hellmouth, and . . ." His dramatic pause had us all ready to punch him. " . . . it has been opened."

Well, that was just bloody brilliant.

Noah got an Apocalypse when he mated. I got a hellmouth.

Asher and the fae might not be the only ones with curses. The Blackthorne children weren't faring much better.

THIRTY-ONE

PAN

I waited as my words settled over the crowd. Instead of the shocked gasps I'd expected, I got a few shrugs before most people returned to their drinks. I suppose it wasn't exactly news to the newcomers, since that was the reason they were here. But my Rosie and her menagerie of buffoons didn't react either.

"Helloooo, did you hear me? I just said the hellmouth is open. You know, as in the mouth of hell." As they should have in the first place, everyone in the bar trained their attention on me.

Darla scoffed. "Okay, Joss Whedon. Hellmouths aren't real. They only exist in fiction. We've all watched Buffy. Talk about a sexual awakening. I'd forgive Spike anything, even being a vampire." She gave Rosie a lascivious wink. "Am I right? All that show was missing was a hot priest."

"What kind of stupid stick did you get hit with as a child? All of you are technically fiction, and you're going to stand there and tell me the literal mouth of hell doesn't exist?" I was far more livid than I should have been, but this was my big moment. My grand reveal. The pièce de résistance, if you will. They'd taken the wind straight out of my sails and then shat all over said sails before lighting them on fire.

Miserable bastards.

If I'd been in my true form, my tail would have literally drooped. *Sigh*. I missed my tail.

"That's uncalled for, lad. She cannae help how she was born." Tom the gargoyle took a swallow of his pint and smiled at Darla, who simply growled in response.

Remi stared hard at me before flicking his gaze to Darla. "It's a legend. Remember, Darla? That's why we were all taught to stay away from Devil's Lake. They said it was a portal straight to hell."

I cocked a brow. Interesting. A whole portal? That could be worth investigating.

"It's not a legend. Trust me. I know these things."

I wasn't sure if that was strictly true, but the hacker did have a reputation for ferreting out information the others couldn't, so it was plausible at the very least. I, the demon, however, absolutely did know about these things. Not only that, my mother had told me she'd done as much.

Remi's lips twitched, but my sweet Rosie at least seemed inclined to give me the opportunity to explain myself.

So I did.

In rather glorious fashion, if I do say so myself.

"I find it quite ridiculous that the legend of Devil's Lake was all you lot were taught."

Remi and Rosie locked eyes, and he mouthed, "You lot?" to her before she shrugged.

Well, bugger. I'd forgotten myself. But how could I be a proper showman without all of my assets? I refused to reduce myself to my vessel's subpar level. This was a tale that deserved my very best.

"You could have spent your summers in that lake and not had any problems. Not until now. All it was doing was acting like a low-frequency beacon. A signal. But now . . . well, it's open and calling every supernatural creature across the globe, even other worlds. Hell, its reach is infinite. And they don't even know what's happening. Like moths to the fucking flame."

"Like Zuul," Rosie whispered.

"What?" I asked, frowning. "I don't know anyone by that name." Zuul? Was she fucking another demon I didn't know? Oh, I'd have his horns for earrings if I found him.

"Dude. Ghostbusters. You know the scene with the light blasting out of the skyscraper and the chick in the catsuit?"

I had no fucking clue what Remi was going on about. "Oh, right. Ghostbusters . . ."

Rosie gave him a secret smile. "Who ya gonna call?"

The three gargoyles held up their pint glasses and shouted in unison, "Ghostbusters!"

Remi feathered a kiss over her lips. "And here I was thinking you slept through the whole thing."

Lucifer save me from the people in this town.

"Right, moving on from your pop culture derailment. We should be prepared for even more creatures to come to town. Even ones from the bowels of hell itself. They're probably already here."

"You mean demons?" Rosie asked, her voice breathless.

Oh, ma petite monstre, *I can see the way your eyes spark with excitement even though you're trying to hide it.*

I couldn't help the smug curl of my lip. "Yes. Demons."

Color burned in her cheeks, and there was no missing the flare of arousal that sent through her. She was remembering our little game the other night. And if the sudden interest in Remi and Gavin's eyes were any indication, they'd caught on to it as well.

"What am I missing?" Gavin asked, the vampire grasping her nape and tilting her face to his.

"N-nothing," she stuttered.

Oh, a secret. Are you ashamed of your depravity, mon coeur?

"I'll get it out of you later." He grazed his thumb along the vein in her neck like no one was watching.

"Get a room, you wanker!" Harry shouted, tossing a balled-up napkin at Remi.

"What are we meant to do about this? Is it a problem we should be wary of?" Dick asked, his voice just a touch worried.

"This can't be a good thing, what with the murders and all. Now there are just more victims at risk of getting themselves killed." Every head turned toward the president of the North Star MC, surprised Ivan was the voice of reason.

"Didnchu see the mayor's email? S'not a bunch of murders. S'a bunch of unforschunate accidents." Former sheriff Dallas Walker sat in the back corner, his face covered in an unkempt, scraggly beard. The man was well in his cups, as liable to topple out of his chair as he was to pass out. Oh, how the mighty have fallen.

Sorry old chap, that was my fault, but I couldn't allow you to keep interfering with my plans.

"Cut him off, ladies. He's had enough," Remi muttered.

"We haven't served him in an hour. I think he's got his own supply." Darla filled a pint glass with water as Rosie was pouring piping hot coffee into a mug. "We'll do what we can."

"If we don't shtop them, they'll drag us all to hell. Mark my wordsss. Hell!"

You say that like it's a bad thing.

But he wasn't wrong. Once the Apocalypse started, they'd wish they were in hell before it was over. And when they finally arrived, oh, what fun we would have.

"We should hold a town meeting. Dallas is right. With demons and vampires running amok in the streets, it won't be long before there's a full panic. I'll reach out to Mayor Dubois, and we'll set something up."

"Thank you for taking this on, Asher. We're so lucky to have someone like you in this town." A flirty, busty redhead called from the group I'd been entertaining earlier.

"*Asher?*" Remi mumbled, incredulous. "Since when do you go around handing out your name like it's candy for trick-or-treaters?"

"Just doing my duty to keep this place safe," I said, addressing them both.

Dallas huffed, clearly put out by their worship of me. It was deserved, though. I was their hero. Their savior. The only one they could count on.

The way Rosie was eyeing me had my hackles up. Perhaps I'd laid it on a little too thick. If the human had given me access to his blasted memories, I wouldn't be flying blind. But Asher was mine now, and I'd mold him into someone I could stand to be.

"Don't worry, everyone. We'll come up with a solution. Just . . . watch your backs for now. Lock your doors. And whatever you do"—I flicked a glance at Rosie—"don't summon anything."

She bit her bottom lip as I winked at her. When I got her under me later, I was going to ruin her. But first, I had some demonic feathers to ruffle. I just had to find them.

THIRTY-TWO

ROSIE

My nose crinkled as I gathered up the last of the black rubbish bags. "One of the few times enhanced smell really works against you," I muttered, even as a voice in the back of my mind added, *but the super strength is always great.*

A task that used to take me several trips now only required one. So . . . I guess it wasn't all bad. I might be able to smell every awful thing, but at least it was over quickly.

I pushed through the door, using my backside to knock it open. Helpful when my hands were full, but not so much when I should be paying attention to my surroundings. That was my only excuse for not immediately noticing the man standing at the other end of the alley.

By the time I'd tossed the bags, he'd crept close enough that I caught the low thrum of his pulse. The unexpected sound startled me, my heart beating overtime at the flood of resulting adrenaline.

"Uh, we're closed," I called, not sure why my senses went on high alert. As far as I could sense, there was no immediate threat.

No reason for me to be afraid.

And yet when I finally spun to face him, my hands were balled into fists, my muscles tense.

"Are you? What if I told you I wasn't here in search of a drink?" His voice was pure sex, smooth and lilting with an Irish brogue I rarely encountered. He was too beautiful to be real, with an intense stare that caught and held my gaze, chiseled features reserved for models and fictional heroes.

"Then you've come to the wrong place. This is a bar. Not a brothel."

A low, sensual laugh filled the air as he closed the distance between us, and God help me, I leaned in to let the sound wash over me, right along with his scent. It was a welcome distraction from the rubbish bin nearby. A mixture of all my favorite things: cedar and woodsmoke, leather and vanilla, clean water and petrichor, along with . . . a trace of brimstone.

"That's right, lass. It's not a brothel. I'm not in the habit of paying my bed partners for their attentions either. It'll be you who pays me in return for the pleasure I'll bring you."

With every word out of his mouth, it was as if my annoyance and fear washed away, nothing more than dissolving bits of candy floss in water. I blinked, my eyelids suddenly heavy. I felt . . . drunk. No, not quite drunk. Languid. Or perhaps even sluggish. As if I was wading through molasses. I couldn't remember what I was supposed to be doing, how I'd gotten out here. The only thing my mind wanted to focus on was the beautiful male specimen before me.

He inhaled long and deep as he stepped closer, and I instinctively backed away until I hit the rough wood wall behind me.

"Mmm, you smell delicious. So many complicated emotions rolling off you."

He caged me with his body, his heat settling over me and making me swoon.

"My kind loves to feed on pleasure, but I prefer your pain."

My voice was softly slurred as I parroted him. "Mmm. I do love pleasure and pain."

Pleasure . . . and pain.

Gavin.

The thought of my mate sent a bolt of clarity through my mind, cutting through the lusty prison this creature had woven around me. I clung to the image of my husband, using it to bolster me as I reinforced my mental barriers.

The incubus had caught me off guard, but I wouldn't allow him to do so again.

"You have so much delicious torment in here for me. I can feast for days," he murmured, his lips closing in on me.

I reached up with both hands, gripping his exposed forearms and calling on my strength to push him off me. But he didn't budge, and the connection between us was amplified as soon as my flesh brushed his. Arousal punched through barriers I'd just put up, and I realized I'd just walked right into his trap.

A tendril of fear awoke inside me. *So much for that super strength.*

Think, Rosie. You cannot let him overpower you. You're not a helpless human. He'll suck out your life force and leave you an empty shell for eternity because you can't bloody die. You ran away to save yourself from becoming prey. Don't let it all be for nothing. Fight!

I channeled my fear into anger, raking my nails across whatever I could reach, squirming in his hold, intending to bite down and use my greatest weapon the second I got in contact with skin.

The incubus smiled. "Keep going. It's so good." He rocked into me, the ridge of his erection pressing against my lower belly and making me ill. "That's it. Look into my eyes, little vampire. Let me take it all away. All your pain, all your suffering. Every last drop can be replaced with pleasure."

BEN

THE TIP WAS FINALLY quiet after a long night of patron after patron stumbling in. They might not think I had any clue what was happening, but I knew how to use a fucking computer. I was watching it all from the camera feed. Asher had given us access to his creepy stalker video stuff after all our issues with the bears. Now I couldn't deny how helpful it was as I sat here with my eyes glued to the screen for hours.

No, I was lying to myself. I wasn't watching all of it. I was watching *her*.

Rosie flirting with that damned pirate.

Rosie smiling up at Remi.

Rosie.

She was all I saw.

"Fuck!" I shouted at the empty room.

Remi would be up here soon. He'd taken the cash bag to lock it away in the safe, which meant Rosie and he were pretty much done closing up. She was probably taking out the garbage before locking the back door for the evening.

My traitorous eyes turned back toward the computer screen. I told myself it was to verify my assumption, but I knew it was just more lies. I was hungry for more of her. I might not be able to touch her. Kiss her. But fuck, I could look. Drink in every microexpression, pretend those smiles were for me, dream her fingers brushed mine instead of Remi's.

She should have come back inside by now. Even if she stopped for a minute to stargaze or something, Rosie had been gone long enough to toss the trash into the dumpster. What if she was hurt?

You idiot. She's the monster now. She's the one they need to fear. Not the other way around.

I closed my eyes and took a deep breath, trying to calm the racing of my pulse. But with every inhalation, my unease only grew. Something niggled at me. A tickle in my mind told me there was danger. I could feel her. It was Rosie, her consciousness plucking at the cord still tethering us even after I lost her.

I stood, hands balled into fists. My mate wasn't safe. She was scared.

On instinct, I tore open the window and jumped out, not giving a shit that it was two stories up and the pavement below was unforgiving. I was an Alpha wolf. I'd be fine. I landed in a crouch, the vibration of the impact radiating through my bones. Then I followed the pull of our bond, hoping I was simply overreacting, until I found her pressed up against the wall, a hulking male caging her in. To her credit, she was fighting him, her fingers digging into the flesh of his forearms, blood dripping down his skin. The fucker was strong.

"That's it. Look into my eyes, little vampire. Let me take it all away. All your pain, all your suffering. Every last drop can be replaced with pleasure." He leaned close and inhaled, and I swear I saw some kind of glowing mist leave her and enter him.

An incubus. He had to be.

"L-let her g-go, asshole." My wolf was close to the surface, but I was still the one in control right now.

As much as I hated what she'd become, I hated this prick more.

Rosie opened her eyes, and her attention flicked to me, fear evident in those copper irises.

The demon slowly turned his head, and a punch of unwanted arousal pulsed through me.

"Don't fucking try it," I growled, my wolf fully in control of my voice. I welcomed him, handing over the reins gladly.

"Oh, this is the one who caused your agony, vampire girl?" He sucked in a slow breath, and his eyelids fluttered. "He's wallowing in heartbreak."

I hated that he was right on all counts. "Step away."

"No, I don't think I will. I haven't had a feast like this in decades. And lookie here, two for the price of one. My favorite."

"Ben, don't touch him. His influence is stronger with a physical connection."

Don't touch him? Then how am I supposed to—

The answer came by way of the crates and empty kegs lined up alongside the wall. Thank fuck Remi hadn't scheduled the pickup of those when I asked him to.

My gaze flicked to Rosie, a silent plea for her to understand what I was going to do as my hand flexed and the itch to get him away from her grew nearly unbearable.

"Aw, don't be like that. Touch me, Ben. Let me show you how life can feel when you're numb to all the terrible things you've experienced. I can take it from you."

Oh, this guy. Smooth-talking fucker thought he could seduce me into an anguish-free life? Was I burdened with trauma and years of anger and guilt? Yeah, sure. But the hard shit was what made the good so damn good. Without it, there was nothing to appreciate.

With every breath, I let the transformation build. It wasn't a full shift, not yet. But as I stalked closer to my target, my body swelled with my wolf's strength.

He grinned at me, a laugh building but dying as soon as I grabbed the keg nearest me and chucked it straight at his face. He spun to knock the metal barrel away, forcing him to release Rosie and allowing her to duck.

That's my good girl. Now stay down. I pleaded in my head.

"You really think that's going to stop me?"

"No. But this is." There was no mistaking the amusement or the threat laced through the words, my wolf as on board with the plan as I was, his tone still coloring my voice and keeping me blissfully stutter-free.

Still in this in between wolf and man state, I was the best of both of us. I had my wolf's size and strength, but my body. Twisting, I grasped the dumpster and hurled it straight at him. The only sound was the crash of metal as it connected with a car at the end of the alley.

"No one touches what's mine without her consent," I growled.

The incubus didn't make any noise, didn't reappear from where he'd been crushed. I hoped he was dead. Back in hell where he belonged.

Breathing heavily, I turned to face my mate, every protective instinct screaming at me to make sure she wasn't hurt.

She blinked up at me as she stood from where she'd been crouched. "What's yours, huh?"

"Yes."

Her pupils flared with interest, but she held back. I could understand her wariness. I hadn't exactly been accepting of her or her transformation.

"Oookay . . . and after the way you treated me, I'm supposed to what? Just roll over and let you have me?"

My wolf swelled, shredding the last vestiges of my restraint. He wanted his mate. And nothing, not even me, was going to stop him from reclaiming her. He was through letting me call the shots, fed up with my bullshit. Frankly, so was I.

But first, we'd play his favorite game: Chase.

"No. Not roll over. I want you to run." Excitement built inside me. "Now."

"Run?" she asked, hesitance lacing the one word.

A low growl hummed from deep in my chest before I could stop it.

"Run."

THIRTY-THREE

BEN

I had to hold myself back as she took off into the woods. If I went after her too soon, the chase would be over, I'd be balls deep inside her, and I wouldn't get what I really wanted. From the very first, part of me had craved this with her.

The hunt.

Stalking her through the woods I called home. Running her down. Making her mine in the most primitive, primal way for my kind. Getting her on her back under me as my teeth sank into that place I'd marked her and I gave her my knot.

I was humming with anticipation to follow her trail. Just a few more minutes. She was fast, but so was I. Especially in my wolf form.

Find her. Take her. Hold her down and breed her until cum is dripping from her and they all know what she let us do.

For the first time in a long time, it felt like my wolf and I were on the same page. As I prowled slowly behind her, still unerringly following her trail, I began to strip out of my clothes, leaving them on the ground, knowing I would come back and recover them later. Or not.

Fuck, I was already hard and straining, the cold night air doing nothing to lessen my need for her. I needed my mate in the worst way, and seeing her in danger, defending her, saving her from that incubus, had only added to the agonizing desire to have her.

It had been too long. I'd been denying both of us what we needed. Made us suffer because of what had happened in my past. All of this was my fault, and now I'd make it up to her.

"Daddy's coming, sugar."

Though the words were mine, my voice was still all wolf.

With that promise, I handed over control, welcoming the transition from man to beast. It's not like they make it out to be in the movies. All screams and agonizing pain. Sure, the first couple of times, it was a bit uncomfortable, but now it was as easy as breathing. It felt more like that first big stretch in the morning than anything. Muscles and senses coming alive that had previously been dormant. The wolf slid into place like a key into a lock, opening the door to this animalistic side of me.

When I was little, the wolf would take full control, sort of like a mentor showing me the ropes. Now we shared my headspace, equal partners in all things. And right now, our goal was singular. Rosie.

I caught her scent on the breeze, the citrus stronger now, with an undercurrent of copper and the promise of death only a vampire could cause. A shiver ran up my spine, ruffling my fur and causing already tense muscles to tighten even further.

She's our mate.

A low growl accompanied the thought, filling my chest and spilling out of me to join the melody of the night.

I padded forward, steps slow to begin with as I pressed my snout to the ground. Then I felt it, the tug of her heart on mine. I couldn't hold back any longer. My wolf wouldn't let me even if I wanted to.

Your Alpha is going to find you, sugar.

You can run all you want, but I'll catch you.

I'll make you feel so good, you'll have to forgive me.

Launching myself forward, I let my senses take over and gave in to the chase.

It felt better than I'd imagined as I all but flew across the forest, the scent of my mate leading me straight to her. She wasn't even trying.

I slowed back to a prowl as I approached her, leaning against a tree with her palms braced on the bark.

It's like you want me to catch you.

Is that what you want, baby? Do you want Daddy to find you?

As if she heard my thoughts, her lip curled up in blatant challenge. "Just didn't want you to get lost."

I noticed the subtle shift of her muscles, the coiling of tension, right as she said, "Catch me if you can, Alpha." She took off with a burst of vampiric speed, leaves and dirt flying into the air as she raced away.

Fuck me.

A rumble built in my throat as I dug my paws into the damp earth and went after her. The bell-like tinkle of her laugh mixed with her perfect aroma had my senses on overdrive. She was so fast, I worried for one brief moment that she'd be able to escape me, until I saw her, standing in the moonlight, a smile on her lips as she pulled her shirt over her head and dropped it to the forest floor.

"Catch me," she whispered.

I was on her before the last syllable fell from her lips, my body still in the middle of transitioning from wolf to man.

"Mine," I growled, claws shifting into human hands as I took her down to the ground.

Make her submit.

The thought flickered in my mind for just a moment, but I wasn't going to have to make her do anything. As soon as I pinned her, she turned her head away from me, baring her throat in submission. The spot where I'd placed my mark called to me as I stared down at my mate. My wolf drove me forward, had me rutting against her clothed pussy as I dipped my head and dragged my teeth across the rapidly fluttering pulse in her neck.

"Want to mark you all over again. Rub my cum into your skin. Scent you. Fuck you." My voice was all wolf, no stutter.

"Then do it. You caught me. I'm yours."

I reached down and tore her denim as easily as shredding cotton.

She released a breathless laugh. "Liked that, did you?"

I let out a rumbling growl in answer, then took her hand and placed it over my straining erection. "What do you think, mate?"

Her response was a long slow stroke of my cock, one that had my hips canting forward in search of more.

"Need to be inside you."

"No one's stopping you."

"Open for me."

"Yes, Alpha."

The way my wolf swelled with pride and primal lust had me nearly shifting back into his form. I wouldn't take her that way. I couldn't. Even if she wasn't nearly indestructible, I'd be afraid of losing control and hurting her. Vampires and shifters were enemies for a reason. We could kill them if we wanted to. Aisling was proof of that.

Even though she'd started to obey me, it felt like she moved in slow motion. I couldn't stand the thought of wasting another second without burying myself inside her. I grabbed her thighs and pushed them wide so I could lean down and sample her, needing her taste on my tongue as much as I was checking to make sure she was ready for me. She was. She so fucking was.

Rosie moaned as my tongue slid over her clit, whimpering in protest when I pulled away. Without giving her a chance to say anything, I flipped her over onto her hands and knees and drove into her in a single, powerful thrust. The cry that came out of her was ragged and desperate. My mate needed me to fuck her raw, and I'd be damned if we ended this night without me doing exactly that.

I fisted the hair at the base of her skull until she gasped and arched her back.

"More, Alpha. Please."

"Take it. Take every fucking inch I give you," I rasped out through clenched teeth as I hammered home over and over, the sound of my hips slapping her ass echoing around us. The woods were filled with my heavy breaths and her wanton moans. It was my favorite song.

Our song.

Wild.

Primal.

Fucking perfect.

Being inside my mate again felt like coming home. I'd missed this. Needed it. Denied us both for far too long. Never again.

The promise was accompanied by another brutal thrust that had me seeing stars.

Knot her.

Fill her until she drips with your spend.

Fuck, I was close. I didn't want this to be over, but I could feel the swell of my knot building. I shoved her down until her face was pressed into the grass and her ass was high in the air so I could go deeper. It felt so fucking good, but I didn't want to finish without looking at her. I needed her eyes on mine as we both came, because I was going to make sure she fell off that cliff right along with me.

Pulling out roughly, I yanked her up and turned her to face me before taking us both to the ground. She spread her legs as wide as possible, welcoming me even as I lined myself up with her soaked entrance and shoved inside.

"Touch yourself while I fuck you. Come around my cock. Milk me for everything I have."

She reached down between our bodies, the tips of her fingers brushing against me as she gathered some of her wetness to obey my command. That barely there touch ghosted along my skin, making me shiver and driving me even closer to the edge.

"Come for me. Now." My Alpha's growl was heavy in my voice, my body shaking with the need to knot my mate. But I wouldn't let myself come, not until she did.

Her head thrashed against the ground, tiny bits of leaves and twigs tangling in the purple and chocolate strands. "I . . . I'm so close."

Pain. She needs pain.

Bite her.

Leaning close, I bit down on the cord of muscle connecting her neck and shoulder. Her strangled moan of my name told me she was there. Her eyes fluttered, back arching, pussy clenching around me as she came, and I followed, my knot swelling as I pumped my seed inside my mate. Where it belonged.

We fell still, our breaths and heartbeats frantic as we came down from our joint high. I pulled back just enough to look at her face. The face of the woman I'd love for the rest of my life. Reaching up to skate my knuckles down her cheek, I finally let every piece of the protective wall around my heart fall away.

God, I've been such a fool. I'm sorry. I'm sorry. Fuck, I'm so sorry. I can't believe I doubted this for even a second. I can't believe I hurt you. I'll spend my life making it up to you. Please, baby. Please forgive me. I missed you so much.

Something flashed in her topaz irises, and she threaded her fingers through my hair, and I wondered for an instant if she heard my thoughts. I shuddered as the sensation of her touching me so tenderly sent a tidal wave of longing crashing into me. There would never come a day I didn't need her. I'd tried to live without her, but it wasn't even half a life. I'd died along with her, and it wasn't until right now, this precise moment when I'd given in, that I finally came back to life.

"I missed you, Ben." Her voice was so soft I'd have missed it if I wasn't intently focused on her. On us. On this.

I swallowed, my throat tight with emotion as I gave her what I could of the apology running rampant in my mind. "I kn-know. I'm s-sorry. F-forgive me?"

Part of me mourned the loss of my wolf, of the surety of his speech. But the return of my stutter was a signal to her that this was all me. That the apology was as real as the man in her arms.

"There's nothing to forgive. I know what my kind did to your family. I won't lie, it hurt, but I could never hold your trauma against you."

"Y-you sh-should. I l-left you."

Her lips were so close, and I hadn't even kissed her yet. I'd been so caught up in claiming her again that I'd done everything but the most intimate thing we could share. I cupped her jaw and brought our foreheads together, running my nose along the side of hers as I soaked up our moment.

"It'll n-never happen a-again, sugar. I s-swear to you."

"I know."

My thumb ran along her lower lip, a precursor to the kiss I wanted to give her. But there was more I needed to say first. I knew what needed to be done. She might think she believed me, but there was one surefire way to prove myself to her. To make her see I was all in. "I w-want you to m-mark me. L-like you d-did them."

She blinked up at me, and I didn't need our connection to sense that I'd shocked her. "Ben, we don't have to rush."

"I n-need it. I n-need to be yours."

"I'll have to bite you. Take your blood. And . . ."

"I h-have to take y-yours. I understand."

"Are you sure . . ."

There was so much unsaid in her lingering question, but regardless of the ending, my answer was the same.

"Yes."

She's my destiny. My gift from fate. I had let all my prejudices get in the way and almost rob me of this gift. But never again. She was mine. The other half of me. The fear I'd felt at almost losing her again, even when I was still trying to lie to myself, proved it. No matter what form she was in, I would love her until the day I died. I didn't want anything to come between us ever again.

But our bond couldn't be whole until this was done.

"D-do it. Mark me."

I was still knotted deep inside her, and I felt the answering flutter of her walls around me as the excitement of what we were about to do ran through her. Closing my eyes, I bared my throat to my mate and waited for the pain I was sure would come.

"I love you, Alpha," she whispered, her lips soft as butterfly wings across my skin.

Then her teeth sank into my flesh, and I groaned in pure pleasure. Surprisingly, there was no pain. I'd braced myself for it, but there'd been no need. Without conscious thought, I started rocking into her. My knot prevented any sort of true thrust, but I was more than able to apply the friction she craved where she needed it most.

I couldn't speak from the sensations flooding me, but my mind was one singular thought.

I love you. I love you. Fuck, I love you.

Then her voice echoed in my head, shocking me and sending satisfaction straight to my heart.

"I know you do, Benny boo."

Her hold on my throat loosened before she grabbed my hair hard and tugged. I wasn't sure what she needed or why she would want to move me, but when her fangs left my vein, she moaned and ground her hips against me.

"Your turn, mate. Bite me."

Still holding my hair, she pressed me down past her throat until my mouth rested just above her heart. Instinctively I feathered a kiss over it before turning my face to the side, calling on my wolf just enough to borrow his fangs so I could bite down into the soft mound of her breast.

"Yes, Ben. God."

It didn't take long. I felt the mate bond between us as it wrapped around the threads of our original connection, the one I tried to destroy. Now we were unbreakable. United.

Forever.

THIRTY-FOUR

ROSIE

I reread the recipe for the third time, taking notes in my book and underlining the part about the special herbed butter mixture several times. I bit down on my lip, making a mental note to take a trip to the *Kitchen Witch* to find myself some 'special herbs.'

A soft tug on my ponytail had me glancing over at Remi, who was seated beside me on the sofa, his phone cradled in his other hand.

"You're looking studious over there. I'm really digging the ponytail and knee socks thing. It's helping me live my dirty library fantasies."

I smiled up at him. "Oh, really? Do you have a dusty book kink? I didn't know that was a thing."

"Really. In fact, maybe we should head over to the stacks and make out. Do you have any panties on under that skirt?"

"Why don't you come over here and find out?"

He leaned forward, eager to do just that. "You know, there are other kinds of role-play scenes we could reenact while we're at it. Sexy library. Sexy bookshelf. Sexy desk. Sexy bear skin rug."

"Sexy ghostbusters?"

He arched one brow and chuckled. "Is *that* a thing?"

"Oh, yes." I trailed one finger up his torso before adopting a breathless tone and batting my eyelashes. "Are you the keymaster?"

"Oh, fuck. I sure as hell hope so."

His hand was on my thigh, phone forgotten on his lap as he leaned in to kiss me when it started going off with a series of notifications.

"Goddammit, Ben, you better be on fucking fire." Remi pulled away with a groan, picking up his phone and swiping the screen to pull up a slew of text messages from his twin. From my vantage over his shoulder, I could easily make out each one, my smile stretching as I read.

POOR MAN'S REMI:

Remi.

POOR MAN'S REMI:

I need you.

POOR MAN'S REMI:

Come to the bar.

POOR MAN'S REMI:

Now.

POOR MAN'S REMI:

Oh, tell Rosie I'll be late.

POOR MAN'S REMI:

We're swamped.

POOR MAN'S REMI:

Tell her I'm sorry too.

POOR MAN'S REMI:

And that I'll make it up to her.

POOR MAN'S REMI:

You know what?

POOR MAN'S REMI:

Nevermind.

POOR MAN'S REMI:

I'll text her.

POOR MAN'S REMI:

But I still need you to come.

"That's what I was trying to do, you fucking cockblock."

My own cell chimed from the side table where I'd laid it as soon as I found the cookbook.

"Your turn. Good luck, baby girl."

"Don't worry. I can handle him."

Remi nuzzled my neck before biting down lightly over his mark. "I wanted you to handle *me*." He sighed heavily. "Alas, duty calls. Are you going to be okay with Ben being late for . . . you know, his *appointment*?"

I rolled my lips together and nodded, belatedly realizing I'd forgotten to tell Remi Asher was on his way over. It wasn't like I was intentionally *Parent Trap*-ing them, though I was sort of hoping if they were in the same room with me as a mediator, maybe I could help them get through this rough spot of theirs. Honest. I just hadn't gotten around to telling Asher that Ben had volunteered to take his spot tonight. With everything that had happened yesterday, how was I to know Ben and I would make amends and he'd offer to join in my daily feeding rotation?

That sounded awful, a *feeding rotation,* but sadly it was necessary. Newly turned vampires required a lot of blood, and my mates taking turns was the safest way for all of us.

"I'll be fine. Actually, erm . . . Asher should be here any minute."

Remi sat ramrod straight. "What? He's not on the calendar."

"You made a calendar?"

"How else were we going to keep track of the shifts? I'm nothing if not organized."

"Remington Mercer, you are not."

"Hey, you're looking at The Tip's bookkeeper and shift manager. I am very fucking organized. Look." Holding up his phone with a smug smirk, he said, "Siri, open up my calendar."

"Okay, Sexy Beast. Would you like me to read your daily appointments?"

"No."

"Okay, reading your appointments—"

"I said no, you fucking—"

"9: 15 a.m., smirk practice. 9:45 a.m., manscape. 11:00 a.m., meet Ivan for vodka shipment. Noon, meditate (or take a nap). 1:00 p.m., call Rosie. 1:03 p.m., jerk off. 1:10 p.m., lunch. 2:15 p.m., blood donation."

"Okay, that's enough." Remi started frantically smacking his screen.

"Oh no, I'm quite interested in how the rest of your day plays out."

"It was supposed to play out with you riding me, but my brother shot that to hell."

"So . . . did you get your wank session in?"

He pouted. "No."

"Well, perhaps we can at least do something about that before you go. It would be a shame for me to not get to inspect your freshly manscaped form."

A slow grin lifted his lips as he sat back to give me access. "I mean . . . I did do it all for you."

I reached for his belt, happy to send him to work smiling, but the front door slammed, and Asher's voice rang through the house, stopping me in my tracks.

"Hello? Is anyone here? Bloody hell, she calls me and then expects me to wait for her. I don't wait for anyone. I make them wait for me."

Remi's eager smile vanished. "See? He's like a different person. Fucking dick. I know he's your mate and all, and I never thought I'd say this about him, but I can't stand to be around the guy."

"I don't understand what's going on with him. Maybe I did something, bonding with him the way I did."

Remi took my chin between his fingers and stared hard into my eyes. "Don't. You didn't do anything wrong. He's making a choice. Or maybe he finally decided to drop the act and take the mask all the way off. Either way, I'll get over it."

"It wasn't an act, Remi. It couldn't be. I was there, remember? I could see the way you two looked at each other. There's no faking that kind of emotion."

Asher strolled into the room, his expression bored as it raked over Remi and immediately brightening when it landed on me.

"You sure about that? Looks like it to me," Remi muttered bitterly.

"Are you hoping for both of us today, then? I wasn't told we'd be sharing." Asher's entire attitude was wrong. Even the way he walked, like he had something to prove, felt off.

What was going on? He'd been different since I turned, but every time I saw him, he was less of the man I loved and more of this cocksure person before me. Perhaps the curse being broken really had changed him. But with the way he'd been behaving, I didn't think it was for good.

"Do you need me? I'll happily make other plans if you're otherwise engaged."

"She called you, didn't she?" Remi's dry tone telegraphed his irritation with Asher clearly. No questions about it.

"And she looks busy. I'm not here to be sloppy seconds, Remington."

Remi scowled, standing up and shrugging on his leather jacket. "I'll see you tomorrow, baby girl. Unless you want me to swing back by and take the trash out. Oh, sorry, I meant unless you want company tonight." He winked, but there was none of his usual confidence and swagger behind it.

"Oh, ouch. I'm hurt. Perhaps it's me who'll take you and toss you in the rubbish bin."

"You already did that."

Oh, my heart. I hated the tension between them. I wanted so badly to fix it, but right now, there was nothing for it. Remi was right; Asher had switched into someone else as quickly as if he'd put on a costume.

Remi pressed a distracted kiss to my cheek, murmuring, "Love you." Before taking off. I frowned after him, not remotely immune to the heartbreak I could sense through our bond.

Asher had done a number on him, and I wasn't sure I'd ever be able to fully mend the broken pieces.

My hacker stalked over to me, taking my face between his hands and stealing a kiss. "Now that I've got you to myself, *ma petit monstre—*"

I snapped out of his hold. "What did you just call me?"

Asher blinked, looking absolutely flummoxed. "I've been, uh . . . practicing my French. You never know when we'll have to run. A new country, a new life. I might even purchase us a little château. Wouldn't that be nice?"

Dread sat heavy between my shoulder blades.

It was exactly the sort of thing Asher would do, but that phrase . . . that particular phrase, I'd only ever heard it used by one person in my life. Had I unknowingly sent it to Asher through our bond? I didn't think I had, but how else would he have stumbled across it?

Perhaps it was simply me being oversensitive, but after our little role-play session the other night, Pan refused to stay in the box where I'd shoved him in the back of my mind. I'd been thinking of him almost constantly, and in the throes of passion, who knew what errant thoughts I might have had. Still . . . it was troubling in a way I couldn't easily dismiss.

"I suppose it might."

"You and me, French wine, the sunset in a place no one knows us. I think it sounds perfect."

Something wasn't sitting right, so like the idiot I was, I poked the bear. "What other phrases do you know?"

"I've learned a lot, *ma belle*. But I don't want to talk to you. I want to fuck you."

"You're here to feed me, aren't you?"

"That's what I said."

"No, you said fork me. Feeding and forking aren't the same thing." Even if they did tend to go hand in hand.

"Can't we do both?"

Lips feathering over my neck, he pulled me into him, but I wriggled out of his hold. "Asher. I need to talk to you about Remi."

"No, you don't."

"Yes, I do. You two were in love, then suddenly you weren't."

He shrugged. "Things change. People change. He's not what I want. I want you."

Enough was enough. I'd done this. His statement made that clear to me. The bond was forking with his feelings for Remi. He wasn't allowed to love anyone but me because of some kind of vampiric ridiculousness.

I couldn't stand the idea that I'd broken his and Remi's heart in the process.

Perhaps you can fix it.

I knew vampiric compulsion wasn't strong enough to force someone to love someone else, nor would I ever dare. Love should always be a choice. But in this instance, since I was the one who'd ruined things, maybe I could undo the damage I'd inadvertently caused. Perhaps I could jumpstart things, or remove the blockage via a bit of mental surgery, if you will.

Kissing him deeply, I threaded my fingers in his hair and gave myself over to the pleasure of his mouth on mine. Then I trailed my lips down to his throat, sinking my fangs into the vein and feeding. His hands tightened on my hips, and he moaned in response. This was my moment. My chance to get in his head and see if there was anything I could do.

Eyes closed, I sent my power into his mind, hoping I'd find exactly what was keeping his feelings for Remi locked away. Instead, I came up against a blank wall of . . . nothing. Where Asher's consciousness should be was a vast empty cavern. Not even an echo of him existed in there.

Something was very wrong with my hacker.

I pulled away, staring at him in a combination of horror and panic, only to be met by a sleepy, contented smile. I had no reason for the suspicion taking root in my mind. None. Unless you counted the lingering taste of brimstone on my tongue, Asher's new interest in demon role-play, and his casual use of Britishisms and a pet name he had no business knowing. Oh, right, and the terrifying void in his mind.

"You okay, princess?" he asked as he sat woozily on the sofa.

"Right as rain. I just need to pop to the loo and freshen up. Why don't you have a lie-down, and we can pick up where we left off when I get back, yeah?" I needed to think, and I was terrible at hiding my emotions.

He grinned. "Don't be long."

"I won't."

Too afraid to voice my fear, I focused instead on the one person who could unequivocally confirm my new theory.

Lilith.

I needed to call Lilith.

THIRTY-FIVE

LILITH

I trailed my fingers across the smooth texture of one of the wallpaper samples I was considering for my office remodel. I was so bloody tired of red. Ever since War had tried to end the world, something about the color just turned me off. And we couldn't have that now, could we? I picked up a swatch of velvet in a shade of plum and then another in a damask pattern with tones of violet and lilac. Honestly, either would do, but perhaps I'd simply do black leather and call it a day. Easy to clean up any . . . messes made. And I could hang soundproof panels in each of these fabrics as accents about the room.

Look at me, so domestic. I was a regular Martha Stewart these days. And that, as dear old Martha says, is a good thing.

An irritated huff from the other end of the room had me smirking. Ah, my pet was cross with me. He didn't like being ignored or made to feel unimportant. Good. After what he'd pulled last night, he deserved every moment of silence. Honestly, I liked a bit of primal play, but not when I was the one being hunted. If he thought he could switch on me without so much as a discussion, he had another think coming. One would expect, after what he'd been through before coming to me, that he'd be averse to that sort of game. Although . . . perhaps this was something he needed? Was my fae prince asking me for this in his own special, spoilt brat way?

Something to consider.

Once I was through punishing him, of course. My Drystan needed to remember why he called me Mistress, and that my dominion over him extended far beyond the bedroom. What started off as a mutually beneficial deal between the two of us had shifted these last months into something new. Something neither of us expected. But I must admit, I quite liked it.

Well, that was interesting.

Surprising me was nearly impossible.

"What do you think? Blink once for velvet, twice for damask." I held up the samples and waited, knowing full well he could choose to break my order and speak if he wanted. But that meant I'd be able to punish him for it. A tingle of anticipation ran through me at the thought.

His eyes sparkled with challenge as he lay across my chaise, his long, lean body draped like a cat who was sunning himself. Why did the bastard have to look so good in black?

Because he was born to rule the night.

I'd had kings before. Emperors too. As well as artists, bakers, singers, politicians. You name it, I've had it. But this creature . . . he was special. As ruined as I was, and stronger for it. I might be the sole, well . . . soul, in existence capable of recognizing his pain and giving him the things he needed to conquer it.

Holding his gaze, I strutted across my office and dropped into the wingback chair across from him. Picking up my tablet from the side table and tapping away on the screen, I began intensely staring at him, then glancing back down, returning my gaze to him every so often.

Three.

Two.

One.

"What are you doing?" he blurted.

I win.

"What do you mean?" My lips quirked into a smile.

He waved a hand in my general direction. "With the stare and the concentration. What are you doing, Lilypad?"

I tugged on the magical chain linking us, reminding him who held the power. I'd given him far too much slack of late, even going so far as to extend the chain's length enough that the man could be in a separate room if he wanted. Not that he ever wanted that.

"Why, Drystan, darling, I'm drawing you like one of my French girls. Can't you tell?"

"What? You don't have French girls." He frowned and glanced around. "Do you?"

"Non." He could hear the laughter in my voice, and his frown deepened. He did so hate being the butt of the joke. Taking pity on him, I rolled my eyes. "It's from a movie."

He sneered, opening his mouth about to launch into what I was sure would be a scathing tirade about the film industry, when a soft *pop* had my head snapping to the corner of the room.

Saved by the . . . harp? Halo? Toga?

"Lilith, we need to talk." Gabriel walked over to my desk and settled himself in my office chair, kicking his motorcycle booted feet up and resting them on the shiny glass top.

"Please, do come in, Gabriel. I wasn't in the middle of anything."

I shot Crombie a look that said, *don't think for one second you're getting away with disobeying me.* He returned it with a smoldering silver glare of his own that I had no trouble interpreting as a haughty *don't be so sure about that.* Somehow, our bargain had become far more complicated than I'd anticipated.

"Oh, good. Because we have a problem."

Crombie opened his mouth as though he had something to add, but Gabriel shot him a look and said, "Quiet," and my fae prince's voice simply vanished.

I sighed and rolled my eyes. "Back to this problem. When do we not have one?"

Gabriel waved a hand, as if I'd entirely missed the point. Apparently it was my fate to be surrounded by males with no semblance of a sense of humor.

"Lilith." The angel stared hard at me, gravitas in the utterance of my name.

"Gabriel." I met his attitude with my own.

"The Apocalypse is nigh."

"That was last month's headline, darling. I do believe you're slipping."

"I'm not, and you know it. You've seen the signs. Pestilence is slithering into every living creature, and before long, she will win."

"So, what can we do about it?"

"That is the question, isn't it?"

"You're the one always saying we can't interfere. I don't see how you think the two of us can stop her."

"You know it's not about us. It's *them*."

"Yes, *them*," I teased. "The dreaded them."

Poor leather feathers had such a stick up his arse, and it wasn't even a fun kind. "Demon," he huffed. "Pestilence has opened the hellmouth. We can do something about that."

I sighed, already bored by this impromptu meeting. "You know the rules, Gabriel. We cannot take sides. The humans must sort this out on their own. Isn't that what you're always going on about?"

"Do not play the saint with me, succubus. I know exactly how much you meddled in the last round. Just as I know you're already dabbling in this one. And, the balance is uneven now that the demons can walk freely on the mortal realm."

"Oh, Gabriel. You're so uptight. Let me help you out with that."

I released my power, allowing it to creep toward the archangel like a dozen invisible tendrils. Well, invisible to him. To me, they looked like a soft pink mist. Absolutely harmless and nonthreatening in appearance, but undeniably potent. The moment the first wound itself around him, he stiffened and jumped out of his chair.

"Stop it this instant!"

"What?" I asked innocently. "You're in my realm, in my chair. It's only natural my gift would want to check your intentions, your desires."

"I don't have desires."

"Ruby red lies. I've tasted them."

The color drained from his face, his body drawn tight as a bowstring at the mention of his lost mate. But can one really be lost if one knows exactly where they are? Sacrificed might be the right word. Or perhaps, abandoned.

Collecting himself, Gabriel reclaimed his seat at my desk, his eyes shifting to my cell phone, its screen currently illuminated.

"Roslyn Blackthorne?" He cocked a brow. "Lilith . . ." He drew my name out like a priest's sermon.

"Yes? We've established you know my name, angel."

"Why is Roslyn Blackthorne calling you?"

I shrugged. I had no earthly idea.

Then he narrowed his gaze. "You knew."

"*You* knew."

"Of course *I* knew. I'm the Messenger of the Lord. How did *you* find out?"

"I sort of stumbled onto that little nugget."

I couldn't tell him I'd given her my mark as a way to get her out of Pan's clutches. That went far beyond the dabbling he'd accused me of and treaded dangerously in the outright interference category.

"Well, don't be shy. Answer your phone. Put it on speaker."

I stood with a put-upon sigh, taking a moment to smooth down my leather skirt and adjust the silk of my mostly unbuttoned blouse before claiming the little device.

"Roslyn, darling, what a lovely surprise. Calling to book your performance already?"

"Erm, no. Not quite. I have a . . . that is, I think . . . blast it all."

I raised a brow. "Well, don't be shy, dearest. Spit it out."

"What can you tell me about demon possession?"

My brows shot to my hairline, and Gabriel stiffened.

"That's quite the loaded question. Why are you asking?"

"I think . . . someone I know might be possessed."

Oh, Pan. What did you do now?

Clearly, he was the only demon in her life who would even dare to do such a thing. Possession wasn't easy on the demon or the vessel, and it rarely ended well for either party. There was a reason few priests could perform exorcisms. It took power to imprison a soul while it was still earthbound. Power only the strongest of us had.

"Well then, it sounds like you're calling the wrong person. You need a priest, not a succubus."

"Oh. Well, I thought you'd want to know, considering you're my—"

Gabriel's eyes shone with interest, and I knew I had to cut her off before she gave up all my secrets.

"That's enough, poppet. If you truly think this creature is possessed, an exorcism is the only way to flush out a demon who's unwilling to leave. Tell me why you believe your . . . friend is possessed."

She gave me her list of suspicions, and the more I heard, the more I wanted to grab my nephew by the tail and string him up for his idiocy. *Oh, Pan. This is going to hurt you so much more than it will me.*

"And just to clarify, this began *after* you marked your mate's body?"

"Yes. Not long after that."

I rolled my lips, pressing them together as I shot an amused look at Gabriel. *Which one of us is going to tell her that when she claimed the man, she also claimed the demon soul inside him? Not it!* The thought was pure reflex. That sort of mess wasn't my bag. I had no interest in getting in the middle of it. The mates, unwilling or not, could sort it out for themselves.

"It will be difficult to send him back."

"I don't know the first thing about exorcisms. Where do I even start?"

Gabriel's glare was all fire and warning, but a demon had to do what a demon had to do. I would not let Pestilence win this easily. I couldn't. I liked it here too much. If she wanted to end the world, she'd have to work for it.

And this could hardly constitute interfering. The girl called me with a question, and I was simply providing the answer. It's not like she told me who the demon was. How was I to know it was Pestilence's son up to no good? I couldn't possibly know a thing like that. And I'd swear to it in a celestial court of law. I'm a demon; deception is basically our first commandment.

Gabriel shook his head, but I simply smiled and said, "I happen to know a priest."

THIRTY-SIX

REMI

"This is fucking ridiculous. I've been working double shifts for the last four days while he's off chasing our mate through the woods and rolling around balls deep inside her. I'm in here cutting fucking lemons like a . . ."

"W-what was that? I d-don't think the b-bears heard y-you. W-want to s-say it louder?"

"Motherfucker," I hissed as the paring knife I was using sliced through the flesh of my finger as my brother spoke behind me. "Don't you know better than to sneak up on a guy while he's slicing his fruit?"

"D-don't you kn-know better than t-to air our d-dirty laundry at the bar?"

"It's my night with her. Excuse me if I'm a little pent up. At this rate, I'm never getting out of here." I gestured to the space, filled to capacity with creatures of all kinds. "I need to leave soon. It's the *literal* law. I am required to leave this place for my safety. I'm gonna report you to the better business bureau or something for unfair work conditions. Do we have a bartender's union?"

Ben rolled his eyes and then smacked me upside my head. "Fuck off."

"I'm trying to, asshole. You won't let me leave."

My twin looked pointedly at the crowd pouring through the door to escape the torrential downpour outside. "Y-you own h-half of th-this place. What d-do you w-want from me?"

"Call Darla. Where the fuck is Dante? Hire someone else. I don't know. But I can't keep working sixteen-hour shifts. My dick is going to shrivel up and die at this point. And what good will I be to her when my humper's broken?"

A flash of yellow was my only warning before a whole-ass lemon collided with my ear.

"Holy shit, it was a drive-by fruiting!" I hollered, holding a hand up to my ringing ear as I spun around to look for my assailant. My outrage was more from the shock of the attack than from any actual offense. Anytime I could quote a Robin Williams movie was a good day in my book. God rest his soul.

"Oi!" Harry shouted. "If you two don't mind, I'd love to get my hands on the pint I ordered twenty bleeding minutes ago."

"That doesn't give you the right to fondle my lemons. Hands off, Harry. I'm a mated man. I know they're big and juicy, but my citrus is off the market."

"You're lucky I didn't just come around the bar and serve meself, lad. I'm a fine barkeep. Better than the both of you."

I raised a skeptical brow. "If I could trust you to serve someone other than yourself, you'd be in a job, my man. Since I can't, maybe you sit your ass down and wait your turn."

"Is that any way to speak to your best customer?" Dick intervened on his behalf.

"I dunno. Is pissing off the man with the booze the best way to get your drink faster?"

"Best shut yer trap," Tom whispered loudly. "Them blue bollocks of his are getting the best of 'im."

"Cut him some slack, Benny boy. Poor sod has a mate, and his prick's as dry as Margaret Thatcher's cunny." Dick shuddered.

Ben and I exchanged a look before he smirked. "H-how do y-you know it's d-dry?"

"Trust me." The solemn look on the gargoyle's face had me near laughter.

"N-no."

Dick turned pleading eyes on me.

"Not if you were my long-lost uncle, buddy."

"Right tossers, you are," he muttered, snagging the last of Tom's pint and necking it.

"I beg your pardon?" Tom grumbled.

"What was that pretty boy going on about? It's a crisis," Dick said, snapping his fingers as though the word had just come back to him.

The Scottish gargoyle gave him a look shot through with confusion. "There are nae birds here."

"Who said anything about bloody birds? The crisis is me parched throat."

"No, it's my dwindling patience." I heaved a long-suffering sigh as the door opened and another flood of patrons filed in. I was about five minutes away from shifting into my wolf and eating them all just so I could call it a night. "Ben, seriously, call Darla. Pay her double. Give her all my tips. I need to get out of here or our mate is going to suffer because of it. Do you want that?"

I'd pulled out the big guns, and we both knew it. Since getting back in Rosie's good graces, the last thing Ben wanted to do was risk his place in the pecking order. He'd done everything but a fucking backflip trying to please her and make up for his behavior over the last couple of weeks.

"F-fine."

He stormed off to the back, leaving me to handle the crowd, but I knew it was a means to an end. I was getting my freedom. My time with Rosie. Fuck, my fingers itched to feel her skin under them already.

"Ah, speaking of the pretty boy! How are the puffins?" Tom crowed.

My gut clenched as my gaze found Asher at the tail end of the group of customers who'd filtered in. "Shit," I muttered.

The last thing I wanted right now was a confrontation with him. In the state I was in, I was liable to rip his cock off and shove it up his own ass. Or smack him in the face with it. Honestly, any sort of cock-related violence seemed imminent. And since that would be a travesty of the highest order—the man really was blessed below the belt—I decided to make a hasty retreat instead. That was until he opened his mouth and I stopped dead, slowly turning back around to face him.

"Why the fuck would I care about puffins?" Asher sneered.

"Aren't they sort of your cause? You were ranting like a madman not long ago." Harry asked, lifting his hat to scratch at his head.

"Beer," Asher grunted as he came up to the bar. "Now."

Who the hell is this asshole? Asher had always been a bit prickly, but it was like he'd had a lobotomy. Maybe he'd been body snatched. Eager to test the theory, I leaned forward and poked him in the cheek just to see if he had any weird sort of alien residue seeping out of him. I frowned when all I was met with was warm skin.

He jerked back. "What the fuck are you doing?"

"I thought you might be an alien."

"I don't know what she sees in you. Clearly, it's not your wits." When all I could manage was a slow blink, he drawled, "I'll take that beer any time."

If he wasn't a secret alien, he was just a regular old asshole, and I was done being his punching bag. "Sorry, we're fresh out."

Petulant? Yes.

Did I care? Not one single bit.

Asher raised his brows and offered me a sly smile I would have been aching for once upon a time. "Doesn't look that way to me."

"Maybe you need to have your eyes checked. I hear weakling humans do that yearly."

"Buckle up, lads. Shots fired." Harry's amusement only irritated me further.

I was peopled the fuck out. I needed to get out of this bar and under my girl. Stat.

Ben came out of the back with a permafrown still painted across his face. It got worse when he saw Asher.

"Sh-she'll be h-here in h-half an hour." He turned his attention to Asher. "W-why don't y-you g-go s-s-si—"

"Ye gods, spit it out, man! Did no one ever teach you how to hold a conversation?" Asher shouted.

Ben flinched. It was slight, but I noticed. Fucking Asher was really riding the asshole express straight to Dickville. I bet he'd be president. Also, *ye gods*? Who talked like that? My money was back on aliens.

But that wasn't what I cared about at the moment. I was too focused on the fact that Asher, of all people, thought he could treat Ben like that. No one talked shit about my twin. I hadn't let that crap slide since we were kids, and I sure as fuck wasn't about to let it happen now.

"I n-need y-you t-to go s-s-sit—" Ben started, but Asher laughed.

"W-w-where d-d-do y-y-you—" It happened in an instant. One second I was listening to the man I thought I loved make fun of my brother in the cruelest way possible. The next, my fist connected Asher's face with the force of an angel smiting the devil.

The look of utter shock on his face was a thing of beauty. Though there wasn't much time to appreciate it as Asher staggered back, losing his fight with gravity and landing on his ass. He almost took a couple of bears with him, but Ivan had a surprising amount of dexterity for his kind and pulled them out of the way, clearing the floor so everyone could bear witness to Asher's humiliation.

Before I could leap over the bar and finish what I had started, my brother wrapped an arm over my chest and pulled me back. But his words, when he spoke, weren't aimed at me.

"Get out," he snarled, his wolf heavy in his voice. "Now."

Asher let out a breathy chuckle as he wiped the back of his hand over his bleeding lip. "If you liked it rough, why didn't you say so?"

The taunt might have worked on me once, but all it did now was enrage me further. This anger was different, though. It didn't burn hot, but ice cold. This was it, I realized, the end of the road for us. I'd been holding on to hope that the man I thought I'd fallen for would come back to me, but there was no way I could forgive him for mocking my twin.

"I might have to deal with you outside of work, but I don't want to see you in here again, Asher. Don't come back. And if you try, you're gonna end up on your ass outside. Consider yourself permanently banned."

I wanted it to feel good, giving him what he deserved. Instead, it only deepened the cracks in our already weak foundation. Every interaction was slowly chipping away at the fragile bond we'd built. Asher Henry was tearing it all down, and this was proof of it. I'd endure him for Rosie, but he'd never find me vulnerable to him again.

With one poorly crafted joke, he'd just ensured it.

I didn't care what he—or anyone, for that matter—said to me, but no one, and I mean fucking no one, came after my brother.

CHAPTER

THIRTY-SEVEN

PAN

Who the bloody hell did he think he was, booting me from his grimy little pathetic excuse for a pub? The wolf was lucky I didn't send him off with a festering case of boils. Ha! He wouldn't feel nearly so cocksure if the appendage fell off, would he?

With every step, my ire grew until steam all but flowed from my ears. How could I get him alone so killing him would be an option? It would've been easier before I broke his tragic little heart. But if I ended him, as he rightfully deserved for publicly shaming me, I would destroy my mate in the process.

Gah, what a fucking disaster. Murder and mayhem were my bread and butter. How ever was a demon supposed to exist without them? Then again, perhaps a better question was how was a demon supposed to deal with a mate? It was all but unheard of for our kind. We were selfish, narcissistic assholes by nature. Putting someone else's well-being above our own was about as foreign as a damn halo. I was sure somewhere in the archives there were references to such a relationship occurring before. But with a vampire Queen? Surely I was the first.

Oooh, I liked the sound of that. Pandemic, a god among demons. Fitting, really. All I needed was my crown and scepter. Easily remedied, unlike my current situation. Not that knowing what my Roslyn truly was would have stopped me from accepting her mark.

Satan's virile bollocks, I'd bitten off more than I could chew. I was trapped in a cage of my own making. Oh, hell. I was her captive.

Somehow I was no longer her king, able to demand she kneel at my feet and impose my will upon her. Rosie had become my queen (no pun intended). How had this happened?

Rage boiled in my blood as I stalked down the quiet street, the townspeople and tourists all seeking shelter from the storm. I covered my head with my hood. I didn't particularly care if I got wet, but I sure as hell didn't want to be recognized and have to stop for a chat. However, if lightning struck me and sent me back to hell, perhaps it would free me of this mortal coil, and I could get my beautiful tail back.

Hmm. But the risk of becoming nothing more than an earthbound phantom, cursed to roam unseen for eternity, was too great. Mum had said if Asher died I would as well. I liked being the center of attention far too much to put myself in danger of death.

Mortality really was a finicky little bitch, wasn't it?

Alas, what a conundrum. I couldn't kill Remi. I couldn't rid myself of Asher. I couldn't do anything I bloody wanted. Not even properly fuck my mate.

"Fuck you, Remi!" I shouted, kicking over a rubbish bin and grinning as a pair of rats ran out from behind it. Lucifer's greatest minion after the raven. Bless them. Best little plague-bringers this side of the—

"God, rein it in. I'm walking here." Darla frowned at me from under her sparkly umbrella.

I turned to face her, my smile growing as my eyes landed on the woman. Speaking of plague-bringers. Maybe I *could* cause a little bit of mayhem after all.

And just like that, my night was suddenly looking up.

"Well, hello there," I whispered, low enough she couldn't hear me. I turned the smolder up to eleven and waited for her to flutter her lashes at me in desire. She just needed to be close enough for me to touch her.

"D-do I know you?" she stuttered, squinting through the rain to try and make out my face beneath my hood.

I grinned, knowing the most she could see were my lips, though my words were far too soft for her to hear over the storm. "That's right, sweetheart. Step right up. I've got just what you need."

ASHER

OH, no. Not again.

This time I fell right into the scene, landing in five-year-old Asher's body as he stared up at a face my adult brain recognized as a ghost. Young me didn't know it yet. To him, it was just his friend Friedrich, with his silly hat and tattered suit.

"How did you find me?" I asked him, my childish heart happy to see my one and only friend and not caring one bit that he shouldn't be here.

"I kept an eye out. No one likes to be alone, Asher. I couldn't leave you to fend for yourself." He smiled gently, his gloved hand holding tight to the top of his walking stick.

"I'm always alone. No one likes to play with me."

"One day, it won't matter. They'll see you for who you truly are and kick themselves for doubting your greatness."

I wiped a dirty hand beneath my nose, my stomach feeling all twisted up with how badly I wanted to believe him. "Wanna play hide and seek?" I asked.

"Sure. I'll hide, and you—" He stopped mid-sentence and glanced at the crest of the hill beyond us. "He's coming. Run."

"Huh? Who?"

"The one who watches you. Run, my boy."

My terrified gaze swept over the horizon, and I saw him, my foster parents' son Nathaniel. I bolted. Wind whipped my face as I ran. My heart hammered, and I shouted into the sky as he chased me with the stick in his hand.

"Get back here, Asher! You freak. Always talking to yourself. Doing weird things."

"Shut up, Nate. Go away!" I cried as I ran.

"I'm gonna tell my dad what you did! He's going to send you back to that orphanage. No one wants you here!"

"Ignore him, Asher. Keep running. You're almost there." Friedrich's voice seemed far away and in my ear all at the same time. But he kept me going.

I saw the trees up ahead. If I could make it to the woods, I could climb one and be safe. But Nate was fast. I was small. I couldn't get away. I didn't want to go back. The nuns were mean, and they smelled funny.

"No!" I shouted as I tripped over my own feet and fell.

The pounding of his footsteps made tears blur my eyes as he got closer. I rolled onto my bottom and stared at him, my lower lip wobbling. Friedrich was nowhere to be found. He'd abandoned me too.

"I've got you now, you turd. Aw, look at the baby. He's gonna cry."

Nate raised the stick he'd been chasing me with and swung it down at my face.

I curled up into a ball, my hands lifting protectively to cover my head. My eyes were squeezed shut so I didn't see what happened, but I heard it. Nate screamed, and when I looked up to see what would make the meanest kid I'd ever known make that sound, my eyes went wide.

Nate flew backward into a tree. His head hit the trunk with a smack that made my belly clench. Oh, no.

I stood, but my knees were so shaky I almost fell down again. "N-Nate?"

He didn't say anything. His eyes were closed like he was sleeping.

"Nathaniel?" I tried again, my whole body shaking as I reached out to touch his shoulder.

Bright red blood leaked out of his ear, and I whimpered just as Mrs. Rochester's scream filled the air.

THIRTY-EIGHT

ROSIE

"Petal, if you're going to continue to give all your attention to that infernal device, would you at least do it without your clothes on so I can enjoy the view?"

I looked up from my phone with a slight frown. "Sorry. Remi was just supposed to be here a couple hours ago. I've been getting twinges of stress from him all night. Just wanted to make sure everything was okay."

Gavin stood with a sigh, walking over to me with all the controlled grace of a jungle cat. My eyes lingered on his bare feet, finding his casual state of undress far more intimate than he probably intended. For a second I tried to picture him wearing one of Ben's Henleys or Remi's gray sweatpants, but my giggle was smothered the second his warm palm curled around the back of my neck.

"Something amusing you?"

"No."

"Little liar."

My phone chimed, making me jump as anticipation zinged through me.

THE KEYMASTER:

Sorry, baby girl, I'm stuck at The Tip. Darla's on her way though, so hopefully I'll be there soon.

ME:

Keymaster? Remi, did you change your name in my phone?

THE KEYMASTER:

. . .

THE KEYMASTER:

Everyone else got a cool handle. It's only right your favorite had one too.

ME:

So you're my favorite now? Do I need to widen the doorways so your overly large head will fit through them?

THE KEYMASTER:

No need. I walk dick first, and you know that's the largest head around.

ME:

Remi . . .

THE KEYMASTER:

Gatekeeper . . . I need a place to put my key. I'll be there as soon as I can. Make sure your lock is well-oiled.

ME:

Well, Gavin is here, so I'm sure I'll be nice and lubricated for you. I just can't help myself when he's around. So much animal magnetism and masculine energy.

THE KEYMASTER:

He wrote that, didn't he? Gavin, fuck off. You already get her in person. You don't need to bogart my sext time too.

ME:

THE KEYMASTER:

Cold-blooded, baby girl. The duke doesn't
do emojis. Stop playing with my heart. It's
been days since I've been inside you. I
need you.

ME:

Hurry up then.

THE KEYMASTER:

Trust me. The second I see Darla, I'll be off
faster than a prom dress.

I LAUGHED as I set my phone down.

"How did he know that was me?" Gavin asked, a sweet little wrinkle between his brows.

"Because I don't speak like that."

"But you covered for me."

I lifted a shoulder in a shrug. "Of course I did."

"Why?"

"It's more fun that way."

He leaned close and took a long inhalation, his lips at the hollow of my throat, palm now trailing down between my breasts. "And by the scent of you, it's the truth as well. I do make you wet."

"That's hardly a surprise."

"No, not a surprise. But I can't leave my wife in need."

"Gavin," I whimpered as he trailed little bites along my neck. "You can't give me any more tonight. Not without hurting yourself."

"While that may be true, don't think I won't be making up for it on my next turn with you. It's been a while since we've played, petal."

I shivered. It had been too long. Now that I had my bloodlust mostly in hand, I was more than ready.

"Yes, my lord. I want to play."

"Good. I've ordered us something special. It should arrive soon, and then you're all mine."

He grabbed a fistful of my hair and tugged my head back so his lips could crash down on mine. Upside-down kisses weren't the easiest to manage, but the way he took complete and utter control of me made them some of my favorites. I loved when my only purpose was to exist for his pleasure. I didn't have to think. I didn't have to worry. I just had to live in the moment and *feel*.

When Gavin pulled away, both of us were breathing heavily, fangs extended, hunger making his eyes nearly black.

"Don't stop," I pleaded.

"I have to."

I whined and reached for him, but he tsked, his lip curling up in a mocking smile. "You don't make the rules, petal."

"If you're going to get me all worked up, I will have to take matters into my own hands."

He took my wrist in an iron hold, preventing me from sliding my hand down my leggings. "You will not. Your mate asked for you to be wet and ready for him when he arrived. You will do as he says. In my absence tonight, you will obey his rules, petal. And don't think I won't know if you disobey me."

"I thought you didn't like others having sway over my body."

"They don't. I'm the one who has sway since I'm the one calling the shots, even from afar."

Oh, my. The things that did to me. There was no way I wouldn't be thinking of Gavin tonight, even if it was Remi driving inside me. From the look in his heated gaze, he knew it too. My dark duke was very, very good at keeping me in his metaphorical chokehold. He may not take care of me in the way Ben did, but he saw to my needs in his own special way. A way I needed and craved every bit as much as I did the tender care of my Daddy.

"In fact . . ." He tugged me up until I was standing. "Perhaps you should go to him now. Meet him at the bar so neither of you has to wait very long. Consider it a gift."

I wouldn't tell him no. Even if I didn't want to leave the house, I'd have gone.

"Yes, my lord. But how will you know if I do what you tell me?"

"I'll feel it through our bond. If you keep yourself open."

My aching breasts and hard nipples betrayed exactly how much I liked the feel of his thoughts brushing my mind. Gavin wasn't one for sharing, not in the way Asher and Remi or even Remi and Ben were. But this would be the next best thing. My duke crooning in my ear all manner of delicious filth while Remi used my body.

I practically skipped to the door, suddenly more than eager to get on with the night's festivities.

"Oh, and petal?"

I stopped and peered over my shoulder. "Yes, my lord?"

"He won't like it if you call out my name." Then he grinned, and the heat of it nearly incinerated my knickers. "But I will."

WATER DRIPPED into my eyes as I blurred as fast as my vampiric speed allowed. I really should learn to drive. Perhaps Asher would teach me? I was nearly to The Tip, the pull of my mates stronger with every passing moment. Three of them. Close enough that they had to be together.

Something about that sent a flicker of hope through me and brought me to a halt about a block away from the bar. Had Remi and Asher reconciled?

Before I could entertain the thought beyond the fleeting hope, the sounds of a scuffle had me turning more fully toward a darkened alley. Two shadow figures were on the far end. Obscured as they were by the rain and darkness, I couldn't see much of their features, but I assumed one to be a man based on his larger size and broad shoulders.

"Hello?" I called.

The man froze, turned his head my way, and then took off

running. The woman immediately slumped to the ground, and I realized with dawning horror that this wasn't some lover's tryst. I'd just interrupted an attack.

She let out a weak moan of pain, which died to a whimper as she rolled onto her side and curled into a ball.

"Help me," she croaked, her voice raspy but recognizable. While the heavy rain washed away the distinct scent I knew to be Darla, the voice revealed her identity instantly.

I bolted for her, crossing the street and dropping to my knees at her side. "Darla, what happened?"

Her answer came in the form of a chest-rattling cough, bloody spittle escaping her lips. The blood filled the air, but it was tainted and stronger than it should have been for the small amount staining her mouth. Darla's head lolled to the side, and I got my explanation for the brimstone-scented copper. That wasn't a man I'd seen with her at all. It'd been a demon.

"Oh my God, Darla!"

A large gash tore through the skin of her neck. She was bleeding out. Out of sheer reflex, my hands shot out, my first instinct to stem the blood flow.

Hunger wasn't even a thought in my mind as her blood stained my fingers. I was only concerned with how to save her. The color drained from her face as I sat there applying pressure to a wound I couldn't close.

"Don't die. This is too much blood. You can't lose this much. Not even if you're a shifter." I spoke into the silence, needing something to ground me as panic threatened to claim my rational mind. "Help! Help us! We need an ambulance!"

Oh my God, you absolute numpty. You're a forking vampire.

In the seconds immediately following my discovery, I'd responded as a human would. As I'd been trained to do my entire life. But I wasn't human any longer. I was a vampire. My blood could heal her far better than any other mortal methods.

Lifting my wrist to my lips, I bit down hard, grimacing at the taste of her blood on my skin. It was wrong. Sick. Tainted.

I spat out what I could before pressing my bleeding wound to her mouth and willing her to drink. Praying I would be able to heal her.

"You can't die. You're my only female friend here. I can't live surrounded by a bunch of males. Who will I get to joke about Mercer sandwiches with?" A tremulous laugh escaped, more a hysterical giggle than anything. I was terrified. Unsure of what I was doing. All I could do was keep my wrist pressed to her lips and pray this would be enough. That I hadn't wasted precious seconds and now it was too late.

It didn't take long before Darla was drinking from me of her own volition. Her cheeks went pink, the pained crease in between her brows vanishing.

My own heart, once a slow, steady thrum beneath my ribs, began racing as I broke out in a cold sweat. My head swam, my stomach churned, and I had to brace a hand against the brick wall of the building beside me to keep myself upright.

"Oh, sugar . . ."

Were my words slurred?

Something was wrong. Gifting my blood shouldn't leave me feeling like this. As if I was six years old again, stuck in bed with the flu.

As spots danced in my gaze and my eyelids began to close, a distant part of my brain recognized the danger I was in. That little taste of her blood was toxic, even for a born vampire. We were supposed to be impervious to all ailments, but this was different. More potent somehow. I couldn't be certain what sort of demon I'd scared off, but I'd bet my life it had been one of Pestilence's line. It was the only explanation that made sense.

I let out a small, hysterical giggle. I didn't need to bet my life. I'd just given it up to save Darla.

My vision blurred as I slowly turned my head toward the

panicked cries that came from the mouth of the alley. Ben and Remi stood there, eyes wide, expressions stricken.

I didn't want them to find me like this. To have to watch me die all over again. But, as I pitched toward the cool pavement, the chill a comfort on my fevered skin, I thought to myself, what a gift it was to see them one last time.

The darkness threatened to claim me as they approached, and fear for their safety kept me grounded long enough for me to warn them. "Bad . . . blood. Don't . . . touch it."

CHAPTER

THIRTY-NINE

GAVIN

The strains of the mournful violin filled the library as I attempted, in vain, to distract myself from Roslyn's absence. Wagner was a broody bastard, but I found the prelude to Tristan und Isolde calming, a way to center myself, and somewhere along the way it became my go-to. The scent of leather and oil permeated the air as I prepped the whip I'd commissioned specifically for my petal. I couldn't wait to introduce her to its lash.

My thumb traced the outline of a rose I'd requested along the handle, and I closed my eyes as the music swelled. A vision of Roslyn washed over me—her head thrown back in pained pleasure as I marked her skin. I needed her to come home to me, but I'd sent her off to be with her other mates. I'd been the good husband and given her what she needed. God, I was turning soft. She'd turned me soft.

For now.

I would fix that sooner rather than later.

A subtle tug beneath my ribs interrupted my reverie, and I scowled. With each passing heartbeat, it grew more insistent, and I was on my feet facing the door before I fully realized what was happening. It wasn't until the scent of her blood—her *tainted* blood —hit my nostrils that I understood.

"Roslyn," I growled, tearing through the house and throwing open the door.

What had those fools allowed to happen to my mate? I'd have their guts for garters if she'd been harmed.

As I blurred in the direction of the pull in my chest, rage and panic warred for control. But I stopped short when I caught sight of Remington struggling to get a bundled-up Roslyn out of their truck while Bentley took someone else from the other side.

As soon as my gaze fell on Roslyn's unconscious form, I bolted toward them, snarling all the way. "What did you do?"

I snatched her from his arms, the wolf growling in response, a warning flaring to life in his eyes, turning them a neon blue.

"Unhand her, wolf. You've done enough."

"I brought her to you, didn't I?"

That might be the only thing saving him.

"What happened?" I bit out.

"Sh-she was a-attacked."

"Yes, Bentley. I've gathered that."

"We need to get her inside. She's been unconscious since we found her." Remington watched her like a hawk as I cradled her close. "I don't know what happened."

"Put me down, you caveman!" Darla whined, wriggling in Bentley's hold. He had her wrapped in his shirt as though it were a straitjacket.

"N-no. Y-you h-have b-blood everywhere. Sh-she s-s-said—"

Remington interrupted his brother in a rare show of impatience with his stammer. "Rosie said the blood was bad."

"Who the fuck is Rosie?" Darla asked.

I tensed, ready to compel her into forgetting she'd ever heard my wife's true name. I'd already ensured she couldn't react to me through the thrall I had on her. It would be easy enough, but there was no need for me to do anything because

Remington shot back, "It's a long fucking story. Just go with it."

That would work.

Frowning, I replayed his earlier words in my mind. The blood was bad? Bad was an understatement. It was the same contamination I'd discovered amongst the wildlife weeks ago. But how had it come into contact with Roslyn?

"You," I snapped, my attention zeroing in on Darla's dark head. "She attempted to rescue you, didn't she?"

Darla nodded. "When I came to, she had her wrist pressed to my lips."

So Darla had been the source of the corruption. Roslyn must have come into contact with it when she'd happened upon her. And too focused on saving the woman, hadn't stopped to consider the potential risk to herself. The last few generations of Blackthornes were a far cry from their steel and shadow ancestors. They were bleeding hearts. Heroes. And once upon a time, I'd thought them weak.

"How were you infected?" I asked, but then thought better of it. "Come inside and get cleaned up while I tend to Roslyn. We will discuss this once she's safe and you're no longer contaminated."

Roslyn's blood would have cured whatever infection lingered in Darla's veins, but the remnants of taint lingered in the dried patches coating her skin and clothing.

"Can you save her?" Remington demanded.

I spared him a single glance over my shoulder. "Obviously."

"Th-then fucking d-do it."

If I didn't have my precious mate in my arms, I'd have thrown the shifter across the garden.

Her skin was clammy and cold as ice, lips blue, pulse barely a thread. She was ill. Vampires didn't get ill. Kicking the door all the way open, I strode to the fireplace, thankful I loved ambiance enough to keep the flames fed. I carefully deposited her on the plush rug in front of the hearth and brushed a lock of hair away from her beloved face. Beloved? Bloody hell, I was a sap when it came to her.

"Come now, darling. I need you to open for me."

"This is hardly the time for a seduction, Heathrow." Remington dragged a hand through his hair and paced like a caged animal as he watched us.

"That's an airport, you insufferable donut. You meant Heathcliff. Do me a favor and at least insult me properly in the future."

"I'm stressed out, man. Give me a break."

I rolled my eyes but could see that plainly enough. He was a coil of nervous energy. Both shifters were. Seeing Roslyn like this, so soon after we'd watched the life drain from her before, was playing havoc with us all. "This will go faster without your commentary. Now kindly shut up or fuck off. I don't care which."

Tearing open the flesh of my wrist, I pressed my skin to her mouth and willed my blood to heal her. She was my mate. My fated destiny. I wouldn't allow some supernatural pestilence to take her from me.

"Pestilence," I murmured as she began suckling my wrist.

"What?"

"It was a pestilence demon."

"Let me guess, the hellmouth unleashed them?"

I nodded.

"H-how can y-you tell?" Bentley asked as he joined us.

"Only possible way she could have taken ill. If Darla was infected by one and her blood got into Roslyn's wound, she'd suffer the effects."

"I thought vampires were immune to shit like that."

"We are, usually. But pestilence demons are rare breeds. It must be a very old or powerful one. Which tracks given the hellmouth situation. Their kind rarely make it to the mortal plane."

"I would hope not. Jesus. We're doomed if they're able to just start infecting us all over the damn place." Remington continued his pacing, muttering to himself as Roslyn fed. "First the birds, then the land, the hellmouth, now this . . . holy shit, Asher was right. It is a crisis. But not just for the puffins." He stopped and stared at us, whispering in a tremulous voice, "'Behold, a pale horse.'"

"W-wrong horseman," Bentley said, though he'd grown pale at his twin's intonation.

"But *Pestilence* is a horseman." He dramatically threw out a hand. "What if he got out? What if he's the one who got to Darla? You said he had to be old, right? And powerful? Well, who's more powerful than that guy? Don't you think that tracks? What about all that other end of the world shit going on a few months back? The boiling sea or whatever the fuck that was?"

"The l-lake turned to b-blood. Th-that f-freak storm in Ireland."

"You two need to settle down. Are you saying there's an Apocalypse?" I rolled my eyes at their dramatics.

"Maybe. Fucking demons are running amok in the town. Supernaturals are getting sick. That guy just fucking keeled over in the bar."

"He was a human."

"Don't care. No one gets that sick and turns to fucking goo like that."

Dread coiled in my gut, a snake about to strike.

"It was Asher," Darla said as she came into the room, hair damp, wearing one of my shirts. Oh, petal wasn't going to like that when she woke. We needed to get the shifter out of here before that happened. But then she kept talking, and I realized we had a far bigger problem than her attire. "The guy who attacked me. It was Asher."

The three of us exchanged an uneasy look.

"I'm sorry, what?" Remington asked, his eyes wide. "*My* Asher?"

She nodded. "I recognized his voice. I'm sure it was him. He slashed my throat, and then I got sick. Really sick."

Roslyn's grip tightened on my arm, but not to hold me closer, to pull me away. I shifted to support her weight as she sat up, her eyes fever bright as she looked at each of us in turn. "It's Pan."

"Who?" Darla asked as Remington said, "What?"

"My demon."

Darla frowned. "You named him?"

We all ignored her, my gaze intent on my mate. "What do you mean, it's Pan?"

"I think Asher's possessed by him."

Remington let out a soft, pained noise before his knees buckled and he crumpled to a seated position on the floor, a shell-shocked expression on his face. Then his gaze raked across us all before he whispered, "Holy shit."

"Uh, guys. I hate to interrupt what is so clearly a crisis, but I'm not sure you hear yourself right now. Possession?" Darla let out a hollow laugh and stepped further into the room. "That's a bit of a stretch, isn't it?"

"B-but a d-demon attack isn't?" Bentley shot back with an unamused lift of his brow.

She scoffed and waved a hand. "I can hardly dispute the existence of demons, but when have you ever heard of an honest to God possession?"

As she paced even closer, she found herself right beside Roslyn, completely oblivious to the danger she'd just put herself in. Idiot.

Sure enough, Roslyn tensed, her nostrils flaring and pupils overtaking the brilliant topaz of her irises as thoughts raced through her mind, unchecked, unguarded. I heard each of them loud and clear.

She smells like them.

Cedar and leather.

The sexy dungeon.

Mine. My mates. Not hers.

Why did they touch her?

A deadly growl built in her chest as she clenched her hands into fists. Roslyn was fast, but not so quick as to escape me as I wrapped my arms around her waist, stopping her midlunge. I flicked my gaze to Darla while Roslyn thrashed in my hold, her control obliterated in the face of this perceived threat.

She was a wild, feral thing, each progressive thought becoming more devolved and primal.

"Jesus, what's gotten into her?" Darla squeaked, backing away.

"Mine," Roslyn growled, this time aloud.

"She smells us on you. You're a threat to her mate bonds. It's triggered her bloodlust."

"Fuck," Bentley whispered. "W-what do w-we do?"

His willingness to help instead of run was such a one-eighty from his reaction the last time he'd seen her in a similar state. I was almost impressed by the shift, but then Roslyn squirmed in my hold, and my attention returned to the matter at hand.

"We need to get Darla out of here."

"W-what do you s-suggest? We c-can't exactly l-let her walk out w-without protection. Sh-she was attacked not even an h-hour ago."

"She'll be fine. I doubt that demon will be making the rounds any time soon. Not after Roslyn stopped him."

The woman in question wriggled in my arms and tried to break free. Her thoughts were a mess of angry and possessive threats aimed at Darla.

"Remington," I ground out, fighting with Roslyn to keep control. The man didn't respond. He simply sat there in a daze. Stunned. Processing. Heartbroken, perhaps. Unfortunately for him, there was no time for us to wait around for him to get himself sorted.

He'd have to deal with his feelings the same way as the rest of us. By ignoring them completely.

"Oi, Remington! Get your fucking shit together."

My enraged bellow caught his attention, and his head snapped up with a distracted, "What?"

"I need you to handle this situation. Take Roslyn out of this room. Distract her. Help her regain her resolve and focus unless you want to start interviewing new barmaids tomorrow."

Remington hesitated for the briefest second before his twin stepped closer. "I'll d-do it."

I shook my head. "No, you can't. Darla smells like the both of us.

If Remington touches Darla and adds his scent to the mix, hell, if he even gets a hint of his scent tangled with hers, Roslyn will overpower me and take out our little friend without batting an eye. Her mate bond is threatened already. Don't add fuel to the fire."

"I thought that's what the necklace was for," Remington said, but it was more idle curiosity than accusation as he pushed to his feet.

"Do you really want to test it?"

His blue gaze moved to Roslyn and widened when they took in her fangs and wild eyes. "Shit, okay. Come on, baby girl. Let's go play naughty nurse in the bedroom. This time, you can be the patient." She snarled, and he held up both his hands. "Okay, okay, fine. I'll be the patient. Same as always."

"Remi," Roslyn whispered as he put himself directly in front of her.

"Touch her, wolf. Remind her of the truth. Make sure she knows the bond is stable."

He reached out and trailed his fingers along the place he'd marked her. "See, baby? No one wears my mark but you. No one ever will."

She softened, that feral energy ebbing ever so slightly as her eyes focused on him. It was enough.

"Now," I urged.

"Let's go. I need my mate." Remington threaded their fingers and tugged her against his chest as I released her.

The two of them left, Darla standing stock still as they passed by. The oppressive heaviness in the air dissipated as soon as the bedroom door clicked shut, and Ben turned his attention to me.

"W-well? N-now what do w-we do?"

My eyes were already locked on Darla's, the compulsion to forget everything that happened tonight already forming on my tongue.

"Now we take care of this problem and then see to our mate."

"S-see to her? But, I th-thought Remi . . ."

I stared at him as though he were dense. What part of this didn't he understand? "She'll be in need after such an ordeal, Mercer. It's going to take all of us."

"Uh, guys? Can I go now? I'm really not here for an orgy."

My gaze swept back across the room, returning to the shifter woman. "You weren't invited."

FORTY

REMI

Thank God for Rosie. If not for her, I'd still be in the fucking fetal position trying to wrap my head around what the hell was going on with Asher. I was drowning in the cascade of emotions her revelation had unleashed until she gave me a lifeline, a purpose. Take care of my mate. Give her what she needed. Be the man she loved.

I could do that for her.

I may not be able to save Asher, but this . . . this I could definitely do.

We walked up the stairs hand in hand, neither of us speaking but both breathing hard. I knew she was hanging by a thread. My wolf could feel the tempest of her need through our bond, and he was more than ready to weather it with her.

"Remi," she whispered, her grip on my hand tight enough it almost hurt. "I need you."

"I'm always here for you, baby girl. I swear it. Nothing will take me from you."

Her eyes were fever bright when they lifted to mine. "I don't think I can be gentle right now."

My cock jerked to attention. "Who the fuck asked you to be?"

As if my words were the permission she'd been waiting for, she launched herself into my arms, lips crashing to mine in a kiss so hard and frantic I was pretty sure she drew blood. Her shuddered moan told me I'd been right even before the taste of copper filled my mouth.

Christ, it only made me harder. Especially when she licked at my lip and let out a ragged groan. I gripped her ass in both hands as she wrapped her legs around my waist and clung to me.

"Yes, fuck, I've missed you."

Her fangs dragged along my neck, making me shiver in anticipation of the sweet bite of pain that would precede the pleasure of letting her feed.

If I wasn't dressed, I'd already be balls deep inside her. But dammit, I had to be wearing pants because apparently it was frowned upon to walk around naked. Fucking puritanical society. Thankfully, pants didn't prevent my girl from grinding her hot little pussy on me. I could feel the heat of it even through the tented denim covering me.

Time to get to the bed and get a lot more naked. Tightening my hold on her ass, I walked us into the nearest bedroom and kicked the door closed behind us. Would it keep her other mates out? Doubtful, but it punctuated the frenetic desperation in both of us.

The slight graze of her fangs along my neck turned more insistent, and I felt a slight burn as she cut through my skin.

"Take it all, Rosie. I'll give you every drop. You can have it all if you want. Drain me fucking dry."

Something shifted in the air between us, a thick layer of apprehension coloring her scent and making her heart race. I pulled back enough that I could look her in the eye. She was gone before I could ask what was wrong, her tiny form now crouched in the corner, shaking.

"Rosie, what's the matter?"

Her lips were still smeared with my blood as she stared at me with wide eyes. "I shouldn't do this. I . . . I can't do this. I can't trust myself right now."

"You're stronger than anyone I know, baby girl. I trust you with everything I am."

"You only say that because you don't know what I'm thinking right now."

"Ooo, kinky. Why don't you tell me about it?"

"I'm serious, Remi." She held her hand out so I could see how badly she was trembling. "I feel like I'm going to die if I don't feed from you."

"I'm not seeing a problem here. You want to feed, I want you to feed . . . two plus two, baby girl."

"I'm afraid I won't be able to stop. I . . . I can't lose you too."

"You're not going to lose me. You're not going to lose any of us."

"Haven't we already lost Asher?"

I flinched but shoved away the pain, focusing on her and what she needed. "We'll get him back."

Rosie shook her head and stared down at the floor. "It's my fault. And all I want to do is sink my fangs into your throat so I can sate my monster's bloodlust. I practically invited the demon into Asher's body, and now I can't see beyond the thrumming pulse in your veins. If you don't walk away, I'll hurt you, Remi."

"You won't. You can't," I insisted, speaking over her next bout of protests. "Mates cannot hurt each other. It goes against our DNA. I don't doubt that you feel out of control, but I promise you, you won't do a single thing I don't want you to."

"You're not listening to me!" she shouted, picking up the nearest object—a fucking wingback chair, in case you were wondering—and chucking it straight at me. I dodged, staring at the splintered piece of furniture in surprise.

"I don't think that was supposed to be so fucking hot. But it really was." I started pulling my shirt off as I stalked toward her, not remotely fazed by her little display of temper. The show of strength was nothing but a turn-on for my wolf. Our mate was fierce and strong. If she needed a new post to sharpen those claws of hers, we volunteered as tribute. Especially when the strong pulse of her arousal resonated in our bond. She was questioning herself, but if she gave me a chance, I'd prove to her that she had no reason to be scared.

"What are you doing? I just threw a great bloody chair at your head."

"You missed."

The bedroom door burst open as I approached, Ben and Gavin both standing there, my brother's chest heaving, Gavin doing what he did best—brooding.

"Wh-what's happening in h-here?" Ben growled, taking in Rosie's crouched form and rounding on me.

"We're fine. Just some growing pains. She's—"

"Terrified. But why?" Gavin asked, bypassing me and walking to the corner where Rosie was still crouched. "Petal, look at me."

He took her chin between his thumb and forefinger, tilting her head back and forcing the issue when she didn't immediately obey.

"You need to feed."

"I don't want to hurt anyone."

"I've already tried to tell her—"

Gavin shot me a glare so heated, the rest of what I was about to say turned to ash in my mouth. "I'm not talking to you. Take off your clothes and take a seat. We'll be with you shortly."

I raised a brow, not sure about this 'we' he spoke of. Was it a royal we, or was he planning on taking a more hands-on approach? I wasn't sure I was here for that. I also wasn't sure I wasn't. How many wasn'ts was too many wasn'ts before it got ridiculous? Fuck, I was all turned around. It had been a confusing day.

"I'm sorry. Are you talking to me now?" I drawled, mostly because I couldn't resist.

"Sit," he growled. "Strip. And shut the fuck up."

"Ooookay. I'll take that as a yes."

I started unfastening my belt buckle as I made my way to the one remaining chair, not giving in to my instinct to be a smart ass and tell him I couldn't sit and then strip. I mean, I guess I could. But it made more sense to do it my way. Unbuttoning my fly, I caught my brother's gaze and rolled my eyes, silently asking, *'Can you believe this guy?'*

Ben wasn't as amused by the new turn of events as I was, but I caught a flicker of his interest. He might not be as kinky as me, but he wasn't a priest . . . although I'd heard things about priests, so maybe that wasn't much of a comparison.

While I shucked off my pants, Gavin returned his attention to Rosie. Her attention was locked on him, her eyes still holding that feral edge they'd had since she caught her other mates' scent on Darla, but she was no longer shaking. His firm touch and low, dominant voice seemed to ground her.

"You have two choices, petal. Start the scene, or safe word."

"What the fuck are you doing?" I asked, protective instinct rearing its head. This really didn't seem like the right time to bust out the chains and handcuffs.

"Let me handle this, wolf. I know what I'm doing."

"Do you?"

But even as I uttered the words, Rosie made her choice, her husky voice laced with desire. "Moonlight."

I looked at Ben, mouthing, "Do you know which one that was?"

He slowly shook his head, as absorbed by the situation unfolding in front of us as I was.

"Stand, petal." Gavin's words were cool and controlled.

I expected her to stay huddled as she was, but Rosie stood, her shoulders relaxed, eyes downcast, but attentive all at the same time. Gavin grabbed her hair and wrapped it around his fist, tugging hard. Then he leaned in until his lips were at her ear before whispering, "You're supposed to be naked and in position when we start a scene, duchess. I'll let it go this time, but if it happens again . . ."

"It won't, my lord."

He yanked on her hair. "Did I tell you that you could speak?"

Ben's wolf made his presence known in the form of a low snarl, and mine wasn't far behind, except, fuck . . . I could smell how turned on she was. Why was this so hot?

Gavin's gaze shot to me, and I swear I tried not to flinch. I failed.

"I thought I told you to sit," he sneered.

I obeyed without conscious thought, muttering, "Sorry, Daddy G."

Gavin shook his head. "Never call me that again."

"What should I call you then?" I asked, more out of curiosity than anything. I didn't really know if I was a prop or participant in this little show of his, but either way, if there were codenames, I should probably know them.

"When I'm in a scene, you may refer to me as . . . Gavin."

I really expected something, I don't know, more exciting than that. She's over there my lording him left and right, and I'm left with boring old G man. There was no hiding my disappointment. "Wow . . . real original. Here I was thinking I was going to get to call you 'your royal dukeness' or 'king of the duke-swingers.' But nope. Just Gavin." I rolled my eyes. "Cool."

He began to turn back toward her, but I shot my hand in the air like a fucking schoolboy. "Mr. Gavin, sir? What's my name?"

"What the fuck do you mean, what's your name?"

"Well, she's petal or duchess, and you're my lord, well, her lord, my Gavin." I waved a hand. "You can understand my confusion."

"No," he said with a slow shake of his head. "I can't."

"Remi," Ben hissed. "Shut the f-fuck up."

"What? It's a very confusing dance, and I'm just trying to learn the steps."

Rosie's lips twitched, amusement twinkling in her eyes as she fought the urge to laugh. Good. I'd happily take his disdainful glares if it made her smile.

"Don't you dare fucking laugh, petal. Not if you want to be able to sit down again any time soon," Gavin warned.

"No, my lord."

"Now, take off your clothes. When you finish, get on your hands and knees and crawl to him."

Oh, now we were fucking talking. This I was definitely on board with.

"Spread your thighs, Remington. Show her what she's got to look forward to."

When I again obeyed without question, a little tingle of surprise shot through me.

Do I like this? Him bossing me around and taking control of the situation? If he tells me to fuck, will I ask, 'how hard?' Does that make me a submissive? Can Alphas be submissives? Christ, I'm so confused and so goddamn hard all at the same time. Is this what they refer to as a sexual awakening?

But then Rosie did as she was told and began crawling to me, and I forgot about all my tumultuous thoughts. The look in her topaz irises said it all. I was making her happy by playing this game. I didn't care one bit if Gavin was here or not. All I wanted was for her to get what she needed.

And right now, what she needed was me.

And *Gavin* too, I guess, although I was totally coming up with a better codename for him next time.

"Stop, petal," he ordered, halting her progress just when she reached me. Dammit. I just wanted her touching me, but this bossy britches wasn't going to let me have any fun.

"Go, petal," I murmured.

Gavin growled. "She won't listen to you. Not until I tell her to."

"I thought that was her go word? Fuck, can I get a cheat sheet? Why are there so many rules?"

Gavin stalked over and gripped my face. "You have three rules. Sit. Strip. Shut up."

"About that, your order of operations—"

"Remington Mercer, you are one second away from learning the true definition of the word dickless."

My gaze trailed to Ben, who was simply leaning against the wall, smirking like an asshole. *We'll see how you feel about this when you're in the hot seat, Benny boy.*

"Touch him, petal. Slide your lips across his thigh until you find his pulse."

Oh, yeah, now we were talking. I spread my legs a little wider, reaching down to stroke my dick before she touched me. The resulting flickers of arousal that sent through her echoed in me. I loved this mate bond.

Rosie was slow and careful as she leaned in, almost hesitant, really. I didn't want her to ever hesitate with me.

"Go on, baby girl. I want it so bad." I threaded my fingers through her hair, encouraging her to come closer.

That seemed to do the trick. It wasn't as aggressive as the way Gavin held and guided her, but then that was their thing, not ours.

Her mouth feathered over my thigh, trailing higher and higher until she was right at the juncture of my thigh. I was trembling in anticipation. Ready to beg, borrow, steal, sell my soul—okay, maybe not that last one—in order to get her to just bite down.

I went with begging. "Please, baby girl."

FORTY-ONE

ROSIE

As he'd proven since he came in and took control of the situation, Gavin knew exactly what I needed. How to help me find control when it had felt like I was spiraling.

"She needs you to tell her what you want."

Remi gave my hair a soft tug. "Is that what you need, baby girl?"

I nodded, rolling my eyes up to look into his blues. He reached down and dragged his thumb across my lower lip, swiping away the blood I'd accidentally let trickle over my chin. Then he stuck his thumb in my mouth.

"Suck me."

I cleaned his thumb, releasing it with a pop, and sat back on my heels.

"Yes, Alpha."

A bolt of lust slammed through the bond, Remi's eyes flashing neon as his wolf growled in approval. That wasn't the only growl in the room, though Ben's was less approving and more grumbled protest.

I shifted my attention, finding his hooded gaze across the room. "You don't like it when I call him Alpha?"

"No. But it's f-fine. I'm your Daddy, isn't th-that right, sugar?"

A thrill ran through me, collecting between my thighs. "Yes, Daddy."

"Good girl. Now d-do as he says."

"Take him, petal. Unless you want a spanking?"

Forking hell. Three doms in one room. I was a puddle. It was a literal dream come true. It was hard to know which of them I was obeying at the moment, Gavin certainly orchestrated things, but every single one of them was dominant. Remi was just the most willing to go with the flow. As for me, I wanted to please them all.

Thankfully, their desires were aligned, so I didn't have to worry about going against any of them.

I raised up on my knees so I had better access as I took Remi's leaking tip in my mouth. The groan he released had tingles sparking through every nerve ending I had. His distinct flavor burst across my tongue, satisfying an ache I didn't even notice until it was sated.

"You can do better than that, petal. Give him your tears. Remington, don't hold back. Fuck her face."

"My pleasure, Daddy G."

Gavin snarled, and I had a feeling if Remi had been anyone else, he would have already felt the punishing bite of Gavin's whip. But Remi didn't belong to Gavin; he belonged to me. I could sense Remi's need to continue poking at him, so I used the best weapon I had. My mouth. I took him all the way to the back of my throat in a move fast enough to catch him off guard. His second retort melted into an incoherent groan.

"So that's how you shut him up," Gavin muttered darkly. I could just make out Ben's snicker over Remi's whispered, "Again."

More than willing to obey, I drew back, allowing my teeth to drag gently along his length.

"Fuck, Rosie. More."

I repeated the move, taking him deep and then raking my fangs over his sensitive flesh. Remi's thighs shook with barely contained pleasure. He wanted nothing more than to spill down my throat, but he was going to fight to make it last as long as possible.

"Look at her. She has such a needy cunt, don't you agree, Bentley?"

Ben was less willing to cede control to Gavin; I could see it in the tense lines of his shoulders, but he eventually agreed. "Yes."

"You want it. You want to taste it. Fuck it. Fill it. Don't you?"

This time his reply came faster and was all wolf. "Yes."

"Then take it."

I stopped what I was doing only long enough to train my focus on Ben. His muscles trembled from the effort to hold back, just like his twin. But he could have me. I'd always let him have me.

"Please, Daddy. I need it."

The second my voice filled his mind, his resolve crumbled. He didn't bother stripping. He just unzipped his jeans and stalked over to me.

"C-careful with those t-teeth, sugar. I'm n-not gonna be g-gentle."

Remi let out a pained laugh. "Funny, that's what she said."

Ben dropped to his knees behind me, his warm palms cupping my arse and spreading me open for his inspection.

"She is d-dripping."

"Of course she is. Our girl's a giver. Speaking of, can you keep on with the giving, baby? I'm dying."

As distracted as I was by the feel of Ben behind me, my need to please Remi pushed me to do just that. Ben must have been paying attention, because he timed his move with my own. As I slid Remi's swollen tip past my lips, Ben slid into me. I let out a garbled moan around the thick shaft in my mouth, and his fingers tightened in my hair.

"God, it's good," he said on a happy sigh.

"F-fucking heaven," Ben agreed.

"Don't forget, boys, she likes it more when it hurts."

A full shiver raced down my spine at Gavin's words. Knowing he was here, watching me being taken by my wolves, satisfied a heretofore unexplored kink. I'd had all of them alone, even a couple together, but this was the first time I'd had almost all my mates at the same time. It was wanton. Everything I didn't know I needed.

"Is that what you want, sugar? For it to hurt?"

"Yes, Daddy."

The burst of pain that accompanied the crack of Ben's large hand connecting with my arse had a muffled cry escaping me, which in turn sent Remi surging deeper into my throat.

"Fuck her, Ben. I can't last much longer."

I loved the way he pleaded. Increasing my efforts, I pulled back enough that I could roll my tongue along his head, drawing ragged breaths from him in response.

"Jesus, fuck. You deserve a gold medal," he panted, rocking into me while Ben set a relentless pace behind me. Everything was building. I'd been reduced to a toy made for their pleasure.

"I'm gonna come," Remi warned. "Make our girl sing for us."

Ben grunted and reached around me until his fingers played over my aching clit. My mate would never deny me my orgasm. That wasn't how Ben and I played.

"Gonna knot you," he growled. "Breed you." His wolf was in charge now, the deep bite of his voice only making what he was saying that much hotter.

I didn't care that he couldn't actually breed me. I only cared that he wanted to.

"Fill her up," Remi gritted out.

"You too, brother."

The second I detonated, they followed me. Remi spilled down my throat while Ben spurted inside me. Ben was still twitching inside me when Gavin's voice broke through our daze.

"Be a good girl, petal. Swallow every last drop. And then I want you to crawl over to me. It's my turn."

FORTY-TWO

BEN

Fuck, that was hot. I've never wanted another man to tell me what to do in the bedroom, but the way Rosie responded to Gavin was undeniably potent. The surge of arousal that dripped out of her every time a new command came from him was the only proof I needed that this was exactly what she wanted. My mate practically glowed with pleasure, obeying his orders and giving all of us her body.

"I said come to me, petal. Don't make me repeat myself. I don't like to waste my breath on sweet little sluts who don't listen."

Remi and I both bristled, but the flush that stole up Rosie's skin spoke only of desire.

I didn't understand how she could like this, but she clearly did.

Who was I to judge?

"G-go, sugar. Sh-show us wh-what he does t-to you."

Remi laughed. "Way to go, Benny boy. Getting kinkier in your advanced years."

I shook my head and ignored him, my focus wholly on Rosie and the way my cum leaked out of her as she crawled across the carpet to where Gavin perched on the bed.

The way her heart-shaped ass swayed had my spent cock thickening. But it was the red handprint that had me nearly ready to go again. I liked the sight of my palm marking her. Especially knowing she'd been desperate for it.

When she reached him, he leaned down and took her by the face, his fingers digging into her cheeks with far more force than I'd ever dare use. Rosie whimpered, but it was all pleasure, no pain.

"Are you ready to be properly fucked, petal?"

"Yes, my lord."

I'd already fucked her hard enough she'd feel me for days, but in this scene, the knowledge he was going to try and one-up me didn't bother me at all. She needed us all.

"Stand and face your wolves."

She did as she was told, her legs trembling.

Gavin brought his mouth to her ear. "I want you to look at them while I fuck you. I want them to see who owns this pussy. Who gives you what you need. Don't you dare close your eyes."

The fucker was going to put on a fucking show.

"God*damn*, dukie-pie, I thought you were all talk." Remi adjusted himself in his seat and smirked. "Guess I was wrong."

"Do shut up."

"No promises. I'm loud. Just ask Rosie. I don't suffer or fuck in silence."

"You d-don't do anything i-in silence."

"Pity we don't have that ball gag yet," Gavin grumbled.

Rosie listened to all of this with a soft smile. Like our casual commentary while she stood naked in the middle of us was the greatest gift we could ever give her.

Gavin pressed his lips to her shoulder before sliding his hands around her waist. "Watch them and let them see every single thing you feel, petal."

He ran his fingertips along her ribs and up until he reached her hard nipples, the flare of desire in her eyes and flood of arousal scenting the room, making it hard to breathe. He took one of the furled buds between his fingers and twisted—hard. I'd be shocked if he didn't leave a mark. My wolf bristled, but Rosie's moan was pure sex. I let out a confused whimper instead.

"She's okay, Ben. She's practically indestructible." Remi's voice was breathy, and when I risked a glance his way, I saw his arm rhythmically moving as he stroked himself. Of course he wasted no time. Remi did what he wanted. I was the patient one.

Gavin continued his exploration of her body, alternating gentle caresses with much more punishing grips. What he couldn't pinch, he bit and then would kiss and lick better. Rosie was a squirming mess in under a minute.

"Please, my lord. I need you inside me."

The sharp slap that rang out had my teeth on edge, but once again, being able to feel just how much she enjoyed his rough treatment kept my feet rooted to the spot.

"Would you like another spanking, petal? Or are you going to remember your place?"

"Yes, my lord."

I widened my stance to allow for more room between my legs. Fuck, I was so hard. I shouldn't be this hard watching my mate be treated like this.

"Which one?"

"Whichever one pleases you, my lord."

Gavin's eyes flicked to mine. "Bentley, come here."

Just like the first time, I stiffened in shock, but it was easier to give into his direction this time. I padded over to them, not sure what part I was about to play, but more eager than I'd have expected to join in.

"Stand in front of our little slut and let her brace herself on you. She'll need to hold on to something."

"Hey, what about me?" Remi asked.

"Your hands are already busy." The dry tone of Gavin's voice didn't betray any excitement about this, but there was no way he wasn't turned on just like the rest of us. He placed his lips at Rosie's ear and whispered, "Hold tight, don't close your eyes, and remember your safe word."

When those lust-drunk eyes found mine, I felt it straight in my cock. She looked on the verge of coming any second, and he'd barely even started with her. Fuck, she really did need this.

Her palms rested on my shoulders, but Gavin stopped us.

"On your knees for her, Bentley."

I sank to the floor immediately, and she bent at the waist, holding herself up using me for support but giving me a full view of Gavin as he opened his pants and pulled out his dick. I could understand now why he'd chosen me for the job instead of Remi. No way would my twin see what the duke was packing and resist making some sort of comment.

"English sausage is bigger than I thought."

Yep. I knew him so well.

"I'm getting you a muzzle," Gavin grumbled. "Don't let her fall, Bentley. She's yours to take care of."

Fuck yeah, she was.

She may have more than one Dom, but we played very different roles. Gavin gave her his pain, and I would take it all away.

"I've g-got you, baby," I whispered, staring into her eyes.

I saw it the second he pushed into her, that flicker of surprise and relief. She loved all of us, loved feeling us inside her, and we wanted to give it to her.

"Are her eyes open?" Gavin asked.

"Yes."

"Brilliant."

Then he unleashed on her, slamming into her with bruising force. Had she been human, her hips would have shattered; I was sure of it. Her expression was pained euphoria, her breaths coming in harsh little pants as she fought to keep her eyes open.

The closer she got to her orgasm, the darker the amber turned, until they were almost obsidian. Gavin must have been able to sense she was close, likely feeling those telltale flutters of her inner walls trying to milk his cock just like I had only minutes prior.

He reached around, his hand encircling her throat and clamping down. She gasped as he tightened his grip, and I nearly came unglued at the sight of her struggling to breathe until she fell over the cliff. Her cry was unintelligible, but I felt her through the mate bond. Fuck, my balls tightened, and another release barreled down my spine as she stared into my fucking soul and came, forcing me to join her.

Her lips crashed over mine. I had a feeling if he hadn't been in the middle of his own release, Gavin would have something to say about that, but fuck if I cared. I took her face between my hands and kissed her back, pouring every ounce of my love and devotion into it.

"Very good, Bentley. You're better in a scene than I expected." Gavin pulled out of her and tucked himself away as he stared us down. "Go on, take care of her. Clean yourselves up and give her the tender lover she's earned."

"At the risk of repeating myself, what about me?" Remi asked from behind us.

Gavin barely spared him a glance. "See to yourself, Remington."

"Uh, definitely already did. Twice."

"Then I don't see what you're complaining about."

"Remi, join us in the shower?" Rosie offered.

I shot him a glare, and he chuckled, shaking his head. "Ben's got you. I'll meet you two in the bed after. Your Daddy wants to take care of you, and I'm not gonna get in the way of that."

Thank fuck he knew how to voice what I wanted better than I did.

"Gavin and I can spend some quality time together," he teased.

"Never going to happen." Gavin was at the door before Remi called as he chased after the vampire, "Aw, c'mon, I bet you'd make a great little spoon!"

Rosie giggled when I scooped her into the cradle of my arms and strode toward the bathroom. "He's going to get himself whipped."

"He'd p-probably l-like it."

Her answering laugh was filled with mischief. "Not as much as I would."

"I s-saw."

"Are you horrified?" she braved while I checked the temperature of the water.

Jesus, no. It was the most erotic moment of my life, next to getting to chase her in the woods. "N-no. It w-was fucking hot."

"I liked it too," she whispered, allowing me to tug her into the shower stall with me.

"You m-more than l-liked it."

She bit her lip and nodded. "I did."

"Me t-too."

"Does that mean we can do it again?"

I used the showerhead to wet her hair, then began washing the thick strands slowly, taking extra time to massage her scalp where I knew it would be tender after our rough treatment of her. "Anytime y-you want," I promised, "so l-long as I always g-get to do this p-part after."

"Yes, please."

I brought her knuckles to my lips and kissed them softly, gaze zeroing in on the purple bruises blossoming on her pale skin. I kissed my way up her arm, paying special attention to the collar of markings around her throat. She was so precious to me. My mate.

"I love y-you, Rosie."

"I love you too, Ben. Thank you for giving me this."

I cupped her cheek, running my nose along hers. "You never n-need to th-thank me. I was b-born to take c-care of you."

"Hey, guys. Not to ruin this tender moment or anything, but we've got a problem," Remi called as he burst into the bathroom.

I stiffened. "What?"

"Asher's here."

FORTY-THREE

PAN

"Ring around the Rosie . . ."

That's right. It was my bloody turn with her, and I was ready to make her forget the rest of those blithering idiots. Tail or no tail.

I didn't bother knocking as I pranced up the steps and made my way inside.

"Honey, I'm home!"

But it wasn't my favorite monster who greeted me. It was the other one. That milksop wolf.

I couldn't resist taunting him. "Back for another round? I think you should swap places with Rosie. You might be more of a masochist than she is."

"Fuck off, Asher. We've got it handled." He crossed his arms over his broad chest and stared me down. From the rumpled state of his clothes and the pallor of his skin, I'd wager he'd been servicing our little mate.

"No. Shan't."

He dragged a hand through his hair and sighed. "Look, if we're going to exist in this dynamic with Rosie, you and I need to figure out a few things."

"What's there to figure out? I fuck her. She fucks you. We leave the rest in the past where it belongs."

"God, you're frustrating," he groaned. "Come have a drink so we can talk like grown-ups."

Suspicion took root. "Why are you keeping me from her?"

"Because Ben's not done yet."

"Well, the only drink I'm interested in is her cum, so thanks, but no thanks."

"Once upon a time, you would have lapped it off my dick."

"Once upon a time only works in faerie tales."

"Don't remind me." His gaze darted to the second-floor balcony, where I assumed my Rosie was currently being enjoyed by that wolf. "They should be done soon."

"Fine, I'll take two fingers of scotch. Neat."

Remi snorted. "Coming right up."

"Thanks, pal. It's a good thing you're a solid bartender. Serving me is the only thing you excel at."

This time his smirk held a distinct edge of violence. Oh-ho-ho, the pup was worked up. He wouldn't last a day in the demon realm. He was far too soft-skinned. But it made him oh-so-fun to play with.

"Far from the only thing. You thought I was pretty great at taking your dick too. And Rosie definitely has a list of my many talents." He opened the study door, and the two of us entered the cozy room. In a few short moments, I had a drink in my hand, and Remi gestured for me to sit on the leather club chair nestled in front of yet another fireplace. How many did one house need?

"Cheers," I said, knowing my friendly demeanor would set him on edge.

"Tell me, Asher. How's Toderick?" Remi asked, pouring himself a drink.

"Toderick? You mean that bloody penguin?"

Remi turned to look at me over his shoulder. "I think you mean puffin."

"What is it with you and your hard-on for waterfowl?"

"Uh, pretty sure that was you, buddy."

Right. Fucking Asher.

"It was a phase. I'm onto . . . moose now." Then thinking better of it, I snickered. "And beavers."

"So no more wolves, huh? I seem to remember the nights when you'd come looking for me, desperate for my mouth, for something to make you feel again." Remi's voice went from laced with derision to seductive with the flip of a switch. "You might not want more with me, but we could go back to what we had before. Hate fucking is always fun."

"Aren't you happy with Rosie?" I asked, hating that I could feel Asher's consciousness responding.

"I'd be happier if you were part of that equation again."

He was behind me now, the hurt in his voice betraying him. Maybe I'd string him along a bit. Torture them both. I did love a two-for-one deal. And was there really anything better than a plague of the heart? It was practically my wheelhouse.

When Remi spoke next, his lips were at my ear, his hand moving firm and sure down my pec. "So would she. You know how she loves it when we take her at the same time. Or when she watches you take me. You want her to be happy, don't you?"

I mean . . . I wouldn't be opposed to—the hand which had been on my chest only a moment ago was now across my body, gripping my other shoulder. I didn't have time to do more than suck in an enraged breath before Remi flexed his arm and his bicep cut off my airflow. Bloody fucking human strength. This body was no match for Remi's shifter constitution. He could crush my windpipe if he wanted. I clawed at him, but couldn't make purchase with his skin through the long-sleeved shirt he wore.

This time when his voice sounded in my ear, there was none of his flirty playfulness. "Fuck you, Pan," he hissed. "Give Asher back to us."

As my stupid, weak brain stopped functioning due to lack of oxygen, I had one last thought before going unconscious.

Lovely.

~

ASHER

"Come here, Cupid! Why are you running away, silly kitty? I just want to pet you!"

The orange tabby meowed, but it didn't sound scary like when he hissed at Nate, just sad. Like me.

"Cupid! Come here, boy. I brought you treats." I held out the can of tuna and gave it a shake. Milk might have been better, but it was harder to run with milk.

The cat tried to run but tripped. That made me laugh. He was clumsy. Like me.

I dropped to my knees and snagged him. "Gotcha!"

As soon as I touched him, my tummy felt weird. Sick. Twisty. Wrong.

I almost dropped Cupid, but the cat snuggled into me like he hadn't just made me chase him for three blocks.

The longer I held him, the less my tummy hurt and the happier Cupid got.

That's when I knew what I was feeling was him. His sickness. I was making him feel better. I was helping him.

His purr motor started going, tickling my arm as his eyes seemed to get brighter. He wasn't sad anymore.

"Asher! Put down that filthy stray cat!" Mrs. Rochester called, scaring me.

I dropped Cupid and ran away. I always ran when people yelled at me.

I dove into the bushes at the end of the block, making myself as small as possible so she couldn't see me. I didn't want to go back home yet. It wasn't my home. I didn't have a home. Just like Cupid.

It was no wonder he and I were best friends. We were just the same.

I could see her get closer, crouching down to pick up the can of tuna I'd dropped. "Stealing from us, Asher? After we put a roof over your head! Mr. Rochester is going to be so disappointed when he hears how you've been abusing our—what's wrong with you?" She reached out to poke at Cupid, who was still curled up on the sidewalk. Not moving.

"Come on, kitty," I urged. "Run away! Don't let her get you."

But he didn't move. Not even when she touched him.

The last thing I heard as I was ripped out of the memory was the sound of her screams.

FORTY-FOUR

ASHER

"He's not going anywhere any time soon. I'm going to nail this shitstain to the wall before I'm through with him for what he did to Asher."

Remi? What's Remi doing in my worst memories?

I blinked, my fuzzy vision clearing and bringing my surroundings into focus. This wasn't familiar. I'd never been here before, but I sure as hell was chained to an entire bed. Shit, was I free? Sort of?

"Uh, a little help here?" I called.

Remi spun to face me, a sneer curling his lip. "Not fucking likely. You're right where I want you."

I gave the chains binding my wrists a tug. "Kinky."

Hurt flashed in Remi's burning gaze. "Don't you dare. You don't get to pretend with me. Not now that I know what you really are."

Was he serious right now? I'm the one who'd been body snatched, and he's playing the victim card? "If anyone's supposed to be pissed here, I think it's me. Some boyfriend you are. You didn't even know I wasn't me."

"I still don't."

Goddamn demon. Pan had really done a number on Remi while he had me locked away. What else had he done?

"Where's Rosie?" I asked, knowing that if I could get in the same room as my mate—Christ, I had a *mate* now—she'd take one look at me and see the truth for herself.

"Not setting foot in this room. That's for fucking sure."

I rolled my eyes. "In case you forgot, I'm a human. It's not like I can do anything to her like this."

"How do I know you don't have demon voodoo?"

"Demons don't practice voodoo," I grumbled.

"Something a demon would say."

"Remi, come on. I'm really me. How can I prove it to you?"

"You can't. There's not a single word that can come out of your mouth that will convince me you aren't a manipulative hellspawn."

The hatred in his voice cut me to pieces. The sting of tears pricked at my eyes, and my throat was so damn tight I had to swallow past the lump that had settled there.

"After everything? I . . . Jesus, Remi, I love you. You're breaking my heart."

There was a spark of something in the shifter's eyes, but it sure as shit wasn't tenderness. "Fuck you. You don't get to say that to me. Not after everything. You're just throwing my own words back at me, you dick. You don't remember anything about my time with Asher."

Wow. The first time I tell the guy I love him and he rejects me. That feels awesome. Not.

"What's the point of keeping me alive, then? If you don't think I'm able to be saved, then why not just kill me and be done with it?"

"I didn't say Asher couldn't be saved. I don't give a fuck what happens to you."

"I *am* Asher." Frustration had my words bursting from me before what he said actually penetrated. "Wait. How are you going to get rid of him?"

"Wouldn't you like to know?"

"Uh, yeah. That's why I asked."

"That's for me to know and you to find out."

"Jesus, you can be such a fucking child. What if whatever you're going to do has side effects? Like what if you get rid of him, but then I'm in a coma for the rest of my life? I'd really rather not be a vegetable if it's all the same to you."

He snorted. "And you can be a fucking tool. Don't make me gag you."

Gags could be fun. We hadn't tried that before.

Wait. That's it. Pan might have been able to throw me around in my head, imprison me in my memories, but he didn't have access to any of my lived experiences. Maybe I could use that to my advantage. I racked my brain, frantically trying to think of something I could say to show him I really was myself again. At least for the moment. There was no knowing how long I'd have before he took the reins again, and I knew it was a matter of *when,* not *if.* I could still feel the fucker slithering around in my head.

"That's one we haven't tried before. Usually I'm the one shoving my fingers in your mouth and shutting you up."

There was that flicker in his eyes again, so I kept going.

"But if you want to gag me while Rosie uses that strap-on again and maybe even the glitter lube, I'd consider it."

His eyes narrowed. "Ha! You almost had me, but you didn't want the Uni-porn."

"Right, because I didn't want to shit glitter for the rest of my life. But you only live once, right? I want to live with you two. And if I have to do it with a sparkling butthole to prove that to you, I will."

Remi's throat bobbed. "Asher?" he asked, a wobble in my name.

"It's me, Remi. I don't know what happened or why, but I'm in control right now."

His expression crumpled, all traces of anger and suspicion replaced with raw vulnerability. He crossed the room in three strides, took my face in his warm hands, and kissed me like it might be the last time.

Because, let's face it, it very well could be.

I couldn't really touch him because of the chains, but the niggling sense of Pan's presence was still there in my head. They'd been right to lock me up. I was a wild card right now, and as far as we knew, I might always be.

Remi reached for the closest chain. "Fuck, Asher, I—"

"No, don't," I said, interrupting him before he could release me. "I don't know when he'll come back. You were right. This is safer for all of us. We can't let this guy anywhere near Rosie. He's bad news. He's doing something with her blood."

"How do you know that?" he asked, pulling back and studying me intently.

How could I explain this to him without sounding nuts? "Sometimes I break free of the memories and can hear him. I think his hold on me gets weaker when he's tired or something. Then there's the pull I feel to Rosie. And you. You two seem to be the key that helps set me free. My tethers to the real world."

Remi sat facing me on the side of the bed, his tense sigh adding to my own stress. "So she's really his target? Not just a soul he's trying to steal?"

"I don't know what his plan is, but I think he's had his sights set on her for a while. It's not a coincidence they're connected. Not with the way he was talking."

"Fuck."

I nodded, sharing his sentiment.

His eyes refocused on my face. "Do you know how he got ahold of you?"

"No idea."

"What's the last thing you remember?"

"I was taking a walk, giving Gavin and Rosie some space, and thinking about visiting the puffins. Toderick has been a little blue lately—"

"Jesus, it really is you," he said with a huff of laughter.

"You kissed me like that, thinking I might not be me?"

He looked a little bashful for a moment. "I've been wrong before."

When? I remembered every single one of his kisses. Just like I remembered Rosie's. But then it hit me. "Oooh, that night at my house."

"Wait. Was that you? I thought so, but when I woke in the morning . . ."

"He was back," I finished for him. "Like I said, I think his hold weakens when he sleeps."

"Or when he's drunk off his ass."

"That too. Pretty much anytime he's not mentally strong or focused enough to contain me."

"That makes sense. I knocked him unconscious tonight, which must have weakened him enough for you. Shit, Asher, I'm sorry I didn't realize something wasn't right with you. I was just so fucking hurt. The things you said . . . they fucking gutted me."

"*I* didn't say anything. It was all him."

"I see that now."

Taking a deep breath, I steeled myself in case I was about to make an absolute ass out of myself by trying to be honest like this a second time. But, if this was my only chance to make sure he knew what he meant to me, I had to take it.

"I love you, Remi. More than I thought I was capable of. More than I deserve. And there's nothing I wouldn't do to prove it to you and Rosie both. I'm so sorry this asshole made you doubt me. That he's wearing my face and using my voice to hurt you. I . . . fuck . . . I can't lose you." The way my voice broke would have been embarrassing if I'd been a weaker man. Instead, I just let all the emotions pour from me because this was Remi. He was mine, and I needed him to believe in me like I did him. "Are you . . . shit . . ." I had to stop because my throat was too tight.

Remi wiped a tear off my cheek with the pad of his thumb but didn't say anything as I worked up the strength to ask the question.

He'd had enough practice with Ben's stutter. He knew not to rush me.

I cleared my throat, trying a second time to get the question out, but there was no hiding what this was doing to me. I was basically an open wound, my heart bloody and raw, and all but right there in the fucking palm of his hand. Fear of what he might say in response to my question had me in a chokehold, but I'd never been one to hide from the truth. Whatever his answer, I needed to hear it.

"Is it too late? Did he . . . did he ruin us?" It was a chore not to break down again, but I made it through.

"No," Remi said with an emphatic shake of his head. Then he said it again, softer, his lips ghosting over mine. "No. He didn't ruin us, Asher. Even when I hated you, I couldn't find a way to stop loving you. I'm not sure there is a way, to be honest. I don't know how to quit you. I never did."

"Thank fuck for that," I whispered.

His lips twitched, but he wasn't done baring his soul to me just yet. "There's not a me without you. At least, not one I can stand to be around. I need you to stay. I don't think I'd survive losing you again. I love you too, Asher Henry."

Relief tore through me, sending a full-body shudder down my spine. I had to close my eyes as I sucked in my first full breath since asking my question.

"How long do we have before he wakes up?" Remi asked, his palm skating up my chest.

"No clue. I can't feel more than a flicker of his presence right now. Whatever you did to him, it did a number on him."

Remi smirked, looking pleased with himself. "Just a little light choking. Got the idea from Gavin."

"Explains why my throat's so sore."

"Shit, sorry!"

"Kiss it and make it better, Remington."

"With my dick?"

I laughed. The first laugh I'd let out in God knew how long. "That could be arranged. You'll have to straddle my face, though."

Remi was already up, pulling his shirt up and over his head, when a terrifying thought took root. "Wait."

He stopped, peeking over at me, still half inside the shirt. "What's wrong?"

"What if he comes back while your dick's in my mouth?"

Remi shuddered. "Maybe we table that for now."

"Agreed."

"But . . . we could keep doing the kissing. I really love the kissing."

I smirked. "And some touching?"

"Yeah. I've got you chained up and at my mercy. There's definitely going to be touching."

A bolt of lust hit me right in the groin. I didn't want to think about how Pan had most likely been using my dick. Right now, I was ready for some attention from the man who held half of my heart. If Rosie wasn't at the center of Pan's diabolical plot, I might have asked him again to see her, but I wouldn't risk her safety because of my selfish need to have them both.

Besides, Remi needed me more than she did right now. And truth be told, I needed the reassurance too. Pan had tried to destroy us. We needed to reconnect and prove to each other he hadn't succeeded. That all was truly forgiven.

"Then crawl up here and come kiss me, Mercer."

My cock was a length of steel at the look in his eyes as he laid on top of me, bracing his hands on either side of my face and lowering himself slowly until we were pressed against each other fully. His lips were so close I could feel the heat of his breath.

"I said kiss me, not tease me."

"God, I love it when you take control."

It was my turn to smirk. "I know."

"Even chained up, you fucking own me."

"Yeah, I do. Now shut up and kiss me. And while you're at it, grind that cock of yours against mine until we both come."

His eyes fluttered closed, and I could practically see the shiver racing through him. "Fuuuck, you could teach the duke a thing or two."

"I'll let him know you said so next time I see him."

He rolled his hips into mine, and I groaned at the friction before his mouth finally claimed my lips. I could float away on the sensation of Remington Mercer kissing the life out of me. Rosie's kisses were candy sweet. Tender. Sensual. Remi's were a goddamn siege. He wanted to take everything he could get and then come back for more.

But he didn't need to take anything. It was already his.

I was his.

His thrusts went from rhythmic and slow to more frantic as he moaned into my mouth.

"God, Asher," he whispered, desperation heavy in his tone.

"I want your cum, Remi. I may not be able to fuck you properly like this, but your orgasm is still mine. Give it to me. Get yourself off on me."

He growled, and before I knew it, his teeth were scraping my throat, and one hand was opening my fly, reaching down my pants, and fisting my cock.

"Wanna make you feel good too, Asher."

"Yeah, you do. You make me feel so good."

My body was on fire with need, but little pricks of ice crept down the back of my neck. Something was wrong. My brain buzzed, the sound in my ears growing to a nearly deafening roar.

No. God, please. Not yet. Not now.

I was determined not to let Pan steal this from me too. Not when he'd already taken everything else.

"Look at me, Remi."

His blazing blue eyes found mine, pupils blown wide with his desire.

"I love you. No matter what."

He swallowed thickly. "Love you too."

"Remember that."

He nodded.

"Good. Now, I need you to come for me, Remi. Right fucking now."

His eyes rolled back in his head as he followed my order, jaw clenching, that vein in his neck throbbing with his pulse. The last thing I saw before I was lost to my own release was the man I loved in the throes of pleasure he found with me.

Pan could steal my body, but he couldn't take *this*.

He'd never take Remi from me.

FORTY-FIVE

"Good. Now, I need you to come for me, Remi. Right fucking now."

As soon as the command left Asher's lips, my orgasm tore through me, lighting me up from the inside out. Fuck, I loved him. I had him back in my arms, and I wasn't going to let go of this man. I'd bring him home to Rosie. I'd deliver him to her, and the three of us could be a triad again. We could be exactly what we were supposed to be. To-fucking-gether.

Completion I hadn't felt since our night playing with Lilith's present settled in my limbs, sating a need I hadn't even fully recognized. I'd missed this, missed *him*, more than I could have ever known. I released a satisfied breath as I fell against him and just took in the beating of his heart and the scent of his sweat, the scent of . . . Asher. It comforted me more than I'd expected, but that was only because I'd never been loved by anyone aside from my Rosie.

Asher's breaths were still uneven beneath my ear, and the fact that he was as affected by our reunion as I was only made this moment sweeter.

"Think we'll have time for a second round?"

He stiffened . . . and *not* in a sexy way.

Then a sinister chuckle filled the room, and my world came crashing back down.

"Well . . . there are worse ways to wake up."

Pan.

That fucker.

I bolted. Panic thrumming in my veins, I stood at the foot of the bed and stared down at the man who looked like Asher but felt like a stranger.

"What? No kiss hello? I'd say I was disappointed, but"—he looked me up and down—"you're not really my type." When his gaze landed on my crotch, he smirked. "Oops. Guess I'm not yours either."

"Give him back."

"No. Shan't."

"Stop saying that."

"Why would I do that when it bothers you so much? I mean, the jig is up. No point in pretending to give one single fuck about what anyone other than my dirty little slut wants."

"Don't call her that."

His lips turned up in a wicked smile. "Clearly you're not fucking her right if you don't. She loves it. Fucking *gushes*."

My jaw ached from how hard I was clenching my teeth. I could feel my fucking molars cracking. "She's too busy crying out my name to complain. But I guess you wouldn't know what that's like since you stole Asher's body. How's it feel to know she doesn't even think of you, demon? Even when you're pretending to be him, she's forgotten you."

Anger flashed in his eyes, but his smile didn't budge. "I know for a fact that isn't true. I was her first. Did you know that? No one else will ever get that from her. No one else can possibly hope to replace me."

I raised a brow. "Pretty sure the four of us will do just fine spending the rest of our lives giving her everything you never could. I mean, you had to steal a human's body just to try and win back a piece of her attention. So trust me when I say I'm not that worried about you."

"You should be. Let me free, and I'll show you just how quickly I can turn her into a begging little bitch. She'll ask for me by name before you can blink."

"No. *Shan't.*"

His lips twitched with suppressed laughter, and he gave me an appraising once-over. This one filled with curiosity rather than derision. "Well played, wolf. Now, if you let me free, I'll give you Asher. I'll let him take you just like you're desperate for. We can come to some sort of arrangement. I get Rosie, you get your hacker."

I wish I could say the offer wasn't tempting. That I was strong enough to see straight through his bullshit, but there was a suspended second between heartbeats where I considered it.

"No. I won't settle for fucking weekend visitation. Asher belongs to me, and I'm going to get him back. For good."

"Is that so? What exactly do you propose to do with me?"

It was my turn to smirk. "The same thing people have done since the beginning of time."

Confusion flickered across his face, but when it was replaced with fury, I knew he realized what was in store for him.

"That's right, you fucker. Time to exorcise some demons. Namely . . . you."

Pan jerked in his chains, all traces of haughtiness vanishing. "You sure you want to do that, Remington?"

"Yup. Pretty sure it's going to rank among the best days of my life."

He bared his teeth in a snarl. "News flash, wolfboy. If I die, *he* dies."

I had to fight not to show how that statement affected me. I couldn't lose Asher. I wouldn't.

"I guess we'll just have to rip you out of his body and store you in an oil lamp or some shit. Maybe a litter box would be more appropriate. Maybe a lucky rabbit's foot?"

"You have no idea what you're getting into. There is no separating us. We are soul bound. Your hacker was made for me. A gift from my mother. His only purpose on this earth is to house my soul. There's no going back. Not now."

"He's a whole fucking person, not your toy. And your mom sounds like a real bitch."

"Oh, she is. The bitchiest. Perhaps you've heard of her. Pestilence? You know . . . *the* Pestilence."

"I fucking KNEW IT!" One brief moment of celebration for being the smartest wolf in the room before I realized exactly what that meant. "Wait, your *mother* is Pestilence, the horseman?"

"Horsewoman, if you want to split hairs."

"So the Bible is wrong?"

Pan exhaled heavily. "That and so many other things. I mean, technically, there are horsemen as well, but they're more figureheads than anything. Useless."

"Huh. Go figure."

"Are you remotely surprised?"

"No, just . . . paradigm shift." I shook my head and blinked. "All right, all caught up. So why did she name you after a runaway faerie?"

His lip curled. "She didn't. It's Pan, for *Pandemic*."

"Lame." I snorted.

"Okay . . . *Remi*."

"Remington, if you're feeling nasty."

"I always feel nasty. It's in my DNA."

I snickered, knowing he missed the joke, but amused despite myself. I was not flirting with this stupid demon. But he looked like Asher, and my smart mouth did whatever it wanted. It was as likely I'd pass up the opportunity to land a perfectly delivered zinger as it was you'd find a celibate unicorn. They were horny motherfuckers. Seriously, it was called Uni-porn for a reason . . . Glitter lube had to come from somewhere.

"Don't get too attached, demon. We're going to be sending you back to hell where you belong."

"So melodramatic. I think I see why Rosie likes you."

"She likes me for a lot more than my sense of humor—which is epic, for the record."

"That's a reference to your dick, isn't it? Because I assure you, she likes mine best. It vibrates."

Well . . . fuck.

He winked at me. "I can see you trying to imagine what it would be like. Trust me. It's as good as it sounds."

It took more effort than I cared to admit to shake off the mental image, mostly because it was Asher I was picturing, and I was interested in all things relating to *his* dick.

"So, are you going to release me or not, dog?"

"Not."

I had to get out of here. This demon was charming as fuck. I could see why Rosie liked him, how he'd manipulated her into accepting his deal. And to be honest, while he was wearing Asher like a goddamned costume, I barely had any defenses against him. I was trash for my broody puffin-obsessed hacker. Especially when I wasn't even twenty minutes post afterglow. I still had his cum on me, for fuck's sake.

"All right, well, that was a fun round of two truths and a lie. I'm gonna go be anywhere but here and leave you alone to do whatever the fuck it is you do."

"Currently, that's nothing since you have me chained up like chattel."

"Perfect. Good to see our Airbnb is living up to expectations. Just scream if you need anything. We won't answer, but I'll enjoy listening to you."

"You fucking bellend."

"Oooh, watch out there, Pan. Your British is showing."

"Do you have an accent kink?"

Yes, actually.

"Don't get your hopes up."

"You wish."

I turned away, not giving him the attention he so clearly wanted, and locked the door behind me. I fucking hoped Rosie had a plan, because the help she said Lilith had called for sure as shit hadn't shown up.

FORTY-SIX

BEN

Remi shot through the door, slamming it closed behind him before leaning back and closing his eyes with a heavy exhale. I took in his shirtless state and the large damp patch on his jeans and could piece together what he'd been up to.

"S-seriously, Remi?"

His eyes snapped open, and I could tell he'd been so distracted he hadn't even noticed me standing across from him. "He was back. It was Asher. He's still in there."

"R-right now?"

"Yes. Well, no. I mean, inside his body. The demon took control again, but the real Asher is in there too."

"H-how do you kn-know?"

Remi gave me a look that said I was being an idiot. "Do you think I would have gotten anywhere near him if I wasn't sure?"

Considering the shit I'd seen him get up to, I was pretty sure he didn't want my honest answer to that question.

We were attuned enough to each other's thoughts; he could read them on my face without me having to say a word. He rolled his eyes.

"Okay . . . fair. But it *was* him. I wouldn't have . . . you know . . . otherwise."

My twin blushed. He actually fucking blushed. The guy who used to take great joy in sharing every dirty detail about his conquests was suddenly shy about sharing anything about his time with Asher. That's how I knew. This was more than fucking. He was in love with the guy.

A pang of sadness swept over me for everything my brother must be going through. First with Rosie, now with Asher. I was glad he had two people to love him the way he deserved. Life hadn't exactly dealt us the kindest hand. I hated that he was still suffering now, when everything he'd ever wanted had been right there within his reach.

"W-we'll fix him. I p-promise."

Remi took a shuddering breath, which caught in his chest. I was all too familiar with that hitch. It was the one right before you either broke down or pulled your shit together. I was betting on the first option this time. He'd been strong for too long. So I did the only thing I could to help. I pulled him into my arms and held him together as he fell apart.

The Mercer twins weren't big criers as a rule. We tended to deal with our problems using our fists or our heads. Emotions were useless. Crying didn't solve anything. It sure as shit hadn't brought our parents back. But sometimes there was no other way to purge the overwhelming emotions gathering within. And if my brother needed a shoulder to cry on, you damn well knew I would be the first in line to offer one.

Remi broke away and sniffled a few times, wiping at his eyes as he came back to himself. "Thanks, Ben. I . . . it's just a lot. Seeing him like that, knowing for sure he's trapped and has been trying to break free, and that I had so little faith in us. It's so easy to believe the worst. I've come to expect it, you know? Everyone always leaves us. But it's Asher. I should have known better."

"Y-you're expecting t-too much of yourself."

"You would have known. If it was Rosie."

I gave him a look. "W-when Rosie turned, y-you were the one who s-saw the truth. That she w-was still her. *I* was c-convinced she w-was a m-monster. Seems t-to me, I'm n-no better than you. Stop holding y-yourself to impossible s-standards. You w-were trying to p-protect your heart. D-don't beat y-yourself up for that."

"I was pretty awesome."

The slight laugh that escaped me was a mixture of relief and annoyance. No matter the situation, Remi could be counted on to be the same loveable asshole he always was. Even so, I couldn't think of anyone I'd want by my side more when shit hit the fan. "Love you."

"You too, big bro."

I clapped a hand over his shoulder, about to suggest we head down to the living room, when a snarl and the rattling of chains came from behind the door. It didn't sound human, and for the first time, I thought of Asher as a demon rather than the man I'd known.

"Are y-you sure h-he's s-secured?"

"As sure as I can be. Don't exactly have demon tamer on my resume, you know? But so far he seems to be limited by Asher's humanity. No super strength or anything."

"F-for n-now. Who knows h-how long it'll b-be before s-something changes. Demons are p-powerful, and don't they g-gather strength over time?"

Remi frowned. "Maybe we need to watch *The Exorcist.* Oh! Or that Heath Ledger movie. You know, the one where he played a hot priest? He had an accent too. Irish maybe? No . . . that doesn't sound right."

"I w-wouldn't know."

"Listen, just because you're straight as an arrow doesn't mean you can't appreciate Heath Ledger in a priest costume."

"I th-think it does."

"You're missing out, man. Pretty sure there was a whole sex club cult too. Sort of an *Eyes Wide Shut* meets Catholicism thing. Honestly, it all felt kind of like a fever dream."

"Wh-what kind of m-movies are you watching?"

"Awesome ones. C'mon. Let's get the others and do some research."

It didn't seem like the right time to mention that, while based on true events, Hollywood movies didn't constitute actual research.

"Come on. L-let's go have a d-drink and s-see what our m-mate is up to. Y-you're going to h-have to t-tell her about Asher."

He sighed. "I hate making her sad."

"Pan already d-did that."

"The fucker."

"No argument h-here."

He gestured down his body with a smirk. "Why don't you go ahead? I need to get changed."

With a curt nod, I turned away and headed downstairs in search of Rosie. I'd fill her in as much as I could to avoid making Remi rehash the painful details. It was the least I could do for him.

Rosie and Gavin were cuddling on the couch when I joined them in the living room. Well, Gavin wasn't so much cuddling as he was playing with Rosie's hair while she tucked up against his side.

"Everything okay?" Rosie asked.

"D-depends on your definition of okay."

She stiffened and sat up, her focus intent on me. "Ben. What's wrong? Is Remi hurt?"

"N-no. Well, n-not physically."

"Oh, for pity's sake, spit it out, Mercer. We don't have all night." Gavin's words were laced with frustration.

I growled, far less interested in being bossed around by the vampire when it didn't revolve around taking care of our mate. "You g-got somewhere to be, duke?"

"Stop it, you two. Tell me what's going on, Ben."

Taking a seat on the coffee table directly in front of her, I gripped her hands and locked eyes with the woman I loved before I destroyed her. Then I gave her every piece of information I had without stopping because I knew if I took a moment to think, I'd try to spare her the pain of knowing what Asher was going through.

Rosie lurched to her feet, fury turning her eyes a blinding gold. Gavin hooked an arm around her waist and tugged her back down to the sofa.

"No, petal. You heard what he said. The demon is after you. You can't go near him."

"I'll do what I bloody well like, Gavin. He's gone too far. He deserves a piece of my mind."

"Stop," I ordered, my wolf at the forefront of the command.

She did, turning pleading eyes on me. "Ben . . . I can't leave him like this. Pan will listen to me better than any of you. I can give him—"

"You've already given him everything," Gavin growled. "He doesn't get more of you."

"He's r-right. It's your b-blood he wants. You can't g-give him anything else. Who knows wh-what he's using it f-for."

"Uh, isn't it obvious? The guy is trying to start the Apocalypse," Remi said, making his way down the stairs.

Rosie gasped, her fair skin leaching of all color. But there wasn't time to comfort her because thunder boomed loud enough to make the windows rattle, and lightning forked across the night sky as if it had been fucking choreographed.

Letting out a shaky laugh, she said, "Well, that was terrifying." She wasn't laughing anymore when the doorbell rang. "Were we expecting company?" she asked at the same time Remi growled, "Who the fuck is that?"

"Why don't you answer it and find out? Jesus Christ." Gavin didn't try to disguise his annoyance.

"Oh, you think? Fuck you, Nandor." Remi spat, heading for the front door.

Gavin frowned, the obscure vampire reference going straight over his head.

Remi opened the door, and another flash of lightning illuminated the sky as our guest stepped over the threshold. The man in the doorway shook some of the water from his dark curls as he removed his scarf, revealing a pristine white collar. "I hear you're in need of a priest."

"What in the Heath Ledger magic is this?" Remi breathed. "Fuck, I should have wished for a pony."

Rosie stood, her eyes locked on the man who was too good-looking to be a priest. "Father Gallagher?"

I didn't miss the way Gavin snatched her by the wrist and held on tight. He might not be vocal about it, but he was on guard. He didn't like this stranger coming into our space any more than I did. The only thing keeping us leashed was the fact that Rosie seemed to know him.

The priest nodded, his dark blue eyes landing on her as he offered her a gentle smile. "It's good to see you again, Roslyn. Your brother sends his love."

Remi grinned. "He even came with an Irish accent. Can we keep him?"

"No." The priest's eyes flicked over to my twin. "You must be Remington. Noah warned me about you."

Remi puffed up like a peacock. "Good to know my reputation precedes me."

"In a manner of speaking."

"Caleb, what are you doing here? You're not a priest anymore." Rosie stepped away from me and toward the man. I didn't want her near him, especially if he wasn't still a priest.

"He's a vampire," Gavin said under his breath, instantly setting me on edge.

"Uh, yeah," Rosie said. "That's part of his appeal."

"Appeal?" I asked before I could stop myself.

Rosie blushed and shrugged. "Remi's not the only one who fancies a hot priest."

Oh, she and I were going to have words about this. Eventually.

But Caleb took off his long black coat and set his leather satchel by the door, distracting me from my jealousy.

"As my wife likes to remind me, once a priest, always a priest."

"Lilith called you?" Rosie asked.

"Aye, that she did."

"So you're here to . . ." Remi gestured upstairs.

"Yes, Remington. I'm here to perform an exorcism."

FORTY-SEVEN

GAVIN

I'd never liked Caleb Gallagher, the pretentious, pious arsehole. In my years at Ravenscroft University, I'd never once managed to avoid his blistering stare. The Priest, as we'd called him, had been rigid, unmoving, and eternally judgmental of us all. Oh, how things have changed.

"Why do I feel like we're missing something?" Remington asked as Caleb waltzed into the kitchen and began opening cabinets.

"Oh, no, do please make yourself at home," I said, sarcasm dripping from every word.

He didn't spare me a glance. "I'm well aware this isn't your home, Mr. Donoghue. Don't you get uppity with me, lad."

"I'm not a child."

The priest turned his gaze on me then. "Aren't ye?"

Remington laughed. "Ooh, shots fired."

"Piss off," I bit out.

"No. Shan't."

Roslyn's brows rose. "Since when do you say *shan't*?"

He shrugged and offered her a wink. "It's just something I picked up. I think it's catchy."

Would I never be free from insufferable gobshites?

"Not likely," Roslyn murmured.

Had I been telegraphing my thoughts so clearly? It was like my days at uni all over again. My former professor had me spiraling back to those years, and I didn't like it one bit. It would seem he walked through the door and brought with him too many of the memories I'd hoped had been buried.

"What's going on? Do you have problems with Caleb?" My petal's voice was a gentle caress in my mind.

"Nothing beyond the fact that he's an absolute arse."

Her lips twitched knowingly. *"He gave you low marks, didn't he?"*

"No." Even in my head, the answer was pouty. *"Him being here dredges up things I don't want to recall."*

She squeezed my hand, offering silent comfort while Caleb continued rummaging.

"Is there something we can help you find?" she asked.

"I'd kill for a cuppa tea."

"Is he allowed to say that?" Remington stage whispered to his brother.

"I th-think so. He s-said he was m-married, right? Is h-he a real p-priest?"

"I was. Many years ago. But I haven't been able to perform a mass since I was turned." Caleb put the kettle on after plucking a mug from one of the cupboards.

"So you can just wear that getup whenever you want?" Remington stepped a little closer, something like hero worship in his eyes.

"Well . . . my wife quite enjoys it, so I usually reserve it for her. But for a situation like this one, I thought it was appropriate to bring it out of retirement."

"Does it still have, you know, God power?"

Caleb raised one dark brow. "Pardon?"

"You know, the big man's blessing. Or is it more of a supersuit situation?"

"Christ on the cross, you might be worse than Kingston."

"You know him? That guy's pretty fucking awesome."

Remington leaned against the kitchen island as though he and Caleb were now fast friends. Little did he know, the priest had once been a fearsome being no one wanted to piss off.

"Aye, I do. He's married to my wife."

"But you're married to her. So how's that work?"

Caleb raised both brows, letting out a long-suffering sigh, and he pointedly looked at each of us in turn. "Do you not realize what situation you're in here, Remington?" He flicked his gaze to me. "Has no one explained it to him?"

"Ooooh, she's your mate. Why didn't you say so? That's a horse of a different color."

"I'd appreciate it if you'd not refer to my wife as a horse."

"Sorry."

Roslyn moved to Remington's side and brushed a kiss over his cheek. "Caleb is married to Sunday. Who is also married to my brother, your best mate Kingston, and Alek."

"Have we met that one?"

She shook her head. "Trust me, you'd remember the Viking."

"He's rather hard to miss," Caleb muttered. "No matter how hard you try."

"Thor in the streets, Loki in the sheets," Roslyn said, seeming not to realize she'd said it aloud.

Bentley growled. "How w-would you know?"

Her cheeks went adorably pink. "Just something Sunday told me."

Once the priest's *cuppa* was made, he took a seat at the table and propped one ankle on his knee, professor expression on his face. All he was missing was a pair of black-rimmed spectacles.

Training his stare on Roslyn, he took a deep breath and said, "All right, Miss Blackthorne—"

"Donoghue. Mrs. Donoghue," I corrected.

His stern gaze snapped to me. "Noted. Roslyn, tell me everything."

"Shouldn't it be Mercer?" Remington asked. "I mean, there are two of us, so it's a majority rules thing."

"Yes, but she's only married to me."

"Easily r-remedied."

Caleb smiled softly into his cup as he took a sip. "I remember these conversations."

"He's a priest. He can go ahead and take care of that for us, right?" Remington pressed a kiss to Roslyn's temple. "What do you say, baby girl? Wanna change your name . . . again?"

I would have been jealous of the flood of lust that punched through our bond, but as she'd so recently proven, I couldn't deny her anything. That said, she'd only ever be Mrs. Donoghue to me.

A loud howl of rage filtered in from above our heads, thumps and crashes echoing on its heels. Bloody hell, had he escaped?

"What was that?" Caleb asked.

"The demon." I rolled my gaze upward and watched the flicker of the lights and the puff of plaster as it floated to the ground below.

"He's chained up," Remington offered. "He's not going anywhere."

"No, but he'll kill the poor bastard he's possessing if he can, simply to get free."

"How many exorcisms have you done, Father?" Roslyn asked carefully.

A muscle twitched in Caleb's jaw. "Enough."

"Were they successful?" I asked, seeing through his carefully crafted facade.

"Not all of them."

The mood in the room dipped when another bellow came from upstairs.

"How long has he been like this?"

"Do you mean possessed or . . ." Roslyn ventured.

Caleb pointed toward the rocking chandelier. "No. I mean specifically like this."

"Just an hour or so. He knows that we're onto him, and he's done playing nice," Remington supplied.

"That's good, at least. Things begin to go downhill fast once they realize they're in danger. We'll have to move quickly." His thought dipped inward for a moment before he refocused on Roslyn and asked, "Did he give you his name, lamb?"

I bristled at the endearment, as did Bentley.

"Mmm, lamb. I like that one," Remington said, trailing one finger over Roslyn's shoulder where he'd marked her. "I'll have to save that for our priest-y role-play. Speaking of, can I borrow that costume of yours, or . . ."

"N-not the t-time, Remi."

Thankfully, the wolf shut his gob so Roslyn could answer Caleb. "Yes. It's Pan."

"Pandemic, actually," Remington offered. "He made a point of correcting me earlier."

Caleb shook his head. "That won't be it. Not his true name, anyway."

She bit down on her plump lower lip, and my fangs tingled. It might not be the time, as Bentley pointed out, but I would never be immune to my petal's charms. "I can still recall his sigil, if that helps?"

"Aye, it might. Can you show me?"

Bentley was there with a pen and paper, but she shook her head. "I don't need that. But thank you."

Then my beauty shut her eyes, and a small furrow built between her brows as she concentrated.

The only clue she'd been successful was Caleb's sharp intake of breath. His expression darkened. "The White Rider."

"I FUCKING KNEW IT!" Remington pumped his fist into the air, crowing in victory. "Did I not fucking call that?"

He held one hand aloft, waiting for a high five from anyone, but

Bentley simply took his wrist and pulled his hand down. "No. L-leave it."

"How did you know?" the priest asked, suspicion in his question.

"Everything's dying. Supernaturals are getting sick. Shit's falling apart. The hellmouth is open. Oh, and he said his mom is Pestilence. I thought that was a big one."

Caleb pinched the bridge of his nose. "Christ on a bike, Mary on the handlebars, and feckin' Moses in the basket."

"Gesundheit," Remington said without missing a beat.

"It's started again," Caleb said, expression grim despite the shifter's antics.

"What has?" I asked.

I couldn't contain the fear skittering down my spine as he intoned, "The Apocalypse."

FORTY-EIGHT

ROSIE

We crowded outside the door to Pan's room. I couldn't think of him as Asher right now. It might be Asher's body, but there was no doubt the demon was in the driver's seat. Every cruelty, every slip, they all made so much sense now. But with clarity came guilt.

This was all my fault. I'd brought Pan into his life. If not for me and my deal, Asher would have never even been on his radar. I'd let him inside me, thinking he was Asher whilst pretending he was Pan. Oh my God. That sneaky, conniving snake. He'd known exactly what he was doing.

I was going to forking kill him.

His eyes found mine from across the room, a devious smile spreading his lips. "Couldn't stay away, could you?"

He rattled his chains, the cuffs biting into his flesh and sending a small trickle of blood down his right arm. He looked bloody awful. Feverish, perhaps. His blue eyes, usually the color of tropical waters, were bloodshot and underscored with dark circles. His blond hair was dark and matted with sweat, the strands plastered to his forehead.

"Don't speak to him, Roslyn. That's what he wants. The demon will try and manipulate you every moment he can." Caleb put himself in front of me, breaking the spell between Pan and me.

I licked my lips and gave him a shaky nod, upset with myself for being drawn in even when I knew better. That had always been the problem with Pan. He was intimately familiar with the darkest parts of me, and instead of running, he'd only wanted me more. It was an addictive feeling to be seen so thoroughly and not found wanting. Perhaps that was the true allure of demonkind.

"He's here because of me."

"Aye, and were you not the second most stubborn woman I've ever met, I would've sent you off somewhere else so he couldn't get to you now."

"Who's the first?" Remi asked, threading our fingers as he came up next to me.

"Sunday," I murmured. "My sister-in-law."

Ben gave him a curious look. "H-how'd you d-deal with her?"

Caleb smirked. "I don't think I know you well enough to give you the answer to that question, wolf." He pulled a rosary from his pocket and wrapped it around his fist. "Now, stay back. No matter what, do not interfere with the rite."

"Doesn't that hurt you?" I asked, knowing made vampires struggled to withstand holy objects while those who were born this way didn't.

"Aye, but it's a pain I can tolerate. Don't worry about me, Miss Blackthorne."

"Donoghue," Gavin corrected.

"Soon to be Mercer," Remi said.

Ben sighed and looked at me. "There'll b-be no l-living with him n-now."

The small moment of levity was almost enough to make me forget what we were doing. At least, it had been until Pan caught sight of Caleb.

A dark chuckle filled the room. "Oh, it's the poor sad priest of

Ravenscroft, come to send me away. Did you bring your cat-o'-nine-tails for a little penance, Caleb?"

Caleb ignored him as he set his satchel down on the dresser and began pulling out items and placing them neatly in a row.

"So that's how it's going to be? No matter. I'm more than capable of holding up a conversation on my own." There was a flicker behind those blue eyes I loved so much, and for a second I would have sworn they flashed purple. "I can smell them on you, you know. The family you lost to my mother's plague."

Caleb stiffened, but didn't falter as he smoothed out the length of cloth and set it next to his bottle of holy water.

"What was your youngest sister's name? Maisie? She was my favorite."

Bless the man; he didn't give Pan what he wanted. Instead, he murmured a prayer over his stole and made the sign of the cross before kissing the silk and draping it around the back of his neck.

As he did, he closed his eyes and prayed in Latin.

"*Deus meus, ex toto corde poenitet me omnium meorum peccatorum, eaque detestor, quia peccando, non solum poenas a Te iuste statutas promeritus sum, sed praesertim quia offendi Te, summum bonum, ac dignum qui super omnia diligaris. Ideo firmiter propono, adiuvante gratia Tua, de cetero me non peccaturum peccandique occasiones proximas fugiturum. Amen.*"

Pan sneered. "Your God can't forgive you, Caleb. You don't have a soul."

Caleb slowly lifted his head and turned. "Actually, I do."

For the first time, Pan seemed truly afraid of him. When he'd thought him nothing more than a vampire, he didn't believe himself in any danger. But now he knew better.

"*Good, Pan. You should be frightened. We won't let you get away with the things you've done.*"

"*Ah,* ma petite monstre, *you don't want me to go. Don't try to fool yourself with this charlatan. He's nothing.*"

Pan's smooth British accent flooded my mind and sent a wash of conflicting emotions through me.

"Roslyn, whatever you're doing, stop it." Caleb's words were tense and chastising. "So help me, I will send you out of this room."

I gulped and lowered my eyes. "Forgive me, Father Gallagher."

"Peace, my child. You must resist the pull to him. I know it's strong, but he will continue to use you to his advantage. Don't give in."

"But it's so much more fun to be bad, Rosie. Come play with me like you did the other day." This came from Asher's mouth, but even sounding like him, the attitude was all Pan.

How had I not seen it?

Because you're a bloody fool, Roslyn.

Remi's hand flexed on mine. I hadn't realized I'd projected the words to him until I caught his response. *"I missed it too. He's a crafty bastard."*

Caleb stood at the foot of the bed, staring down at the chained demon as Pan breathed heavily and snarled. Then the priest began.

"In the name of the Father, the Son, and the Holy Spirit, I command you to free this soul from your evil grasp."

Pan hissed, then laughed. "That's not how it goes, Caleb."

Father Gallagher ignored him and continued. "I adjure you, ancient serpent, by the judge of the living and the dead, by your Creator, by the Creator of the whole universe, by Him who has the power to consign you to hell, to depart forthwith in fear, along with your savage minions, from this servant of God, Asher, who seeks refuge in the fold of the Church. I adjure you again"—he pressed the rosary to Asher's forehead, and the demon thrashed in response— "not by my weakness but by the might of the Holy Spirit, to depart from this servant of God, Asher, whom almighty God has made in His image."

Pan laughed, his voice ringing out loud and clear. "God's not the one who made him."

Remi sucked in a shocked breath, his hand gripping mine so tightly. Were I human, my fingers would have broken.

Though his voice was strong, Caleb's brow was dotted with sweat and his shoulders were tense as he continued. "Yield, therefore, yield not to my own person but to the minister of Christ. For it is the power of Christ that compels you, who brought you low by His cross. Tremble before that mighty arm that broke asunder the dark prison walls and led souls forth to light. God the Father commands you"—he made the sign of the cross, and Pan growled, spitting in Caleb's face—"God the Son commands you; God the Holy Spirit commands you."

He continued, the whole time alternating between pressing the rosary into Asher's skin and making the sign of the cross over him. Pan didn't like it, but he seemed to be firmly rooted inside his host.

Caleb's words grew more insistent, but I could hear the strain in them as he opened his container of holy water and began dousing Pan with it. "Depart, then, transgressor. Depart, seducer, full of lies and cunning, foe of virtue, persecutor of the innocent. Give place, abominable creature; give way, you monster. For He has already stripped you of your powers and laid waste your kingdom, bound you prisoner and plundered your weapons. He has cast you forth into the outer darkness, where everlasting ruin awaits you and your abettors. You are guilty before the whole human race, to whom you proferred by your enticements the poisoned cup of death."

Throughout this, Pan was screaming as he thrashed and fought the hold of the chains. As I watched on in horror, his skin began turning purple, hair a deep aubergine, and all I could think was that if he got free, he'd kill us all.

"The longer you delay, the heavier your punishment shall be; for it is not men you are condemning, but rather Him who rules the living and the dead, who is coming to judge both the living and the dead and the world by fire."

His back bowed as he raged, but when Caleb's last words rang out, Pan collapsed and went silent. His features shifted again, returning to Asher's beloved form as he lay unconscious on the bed.

Caleb sagged, breathing heavily, skin paler than normal, and the dark strands of his hair were now streaked with white at the temples.

"I . . . is it done?" I asked, moving forward.

"Stop, petal. Don't move," Gavin commanded, reminding me he was here. We'd all been so focused on what was going on once Caleb started, I don't even think one of us blinked.

Remi was tense beside me, his body trembling with the restrained need to go to Asher.

"That g-goes for you t-too," Ben said, likely feeling the same coiled urge I was through their twin bond.

Caleb's breaths were still labored when his eyes found mine. "Aye, it's over. For now. I can't do anything while he's unconscious."

"So what do we do? Stand around and wait. Say a couple more Hail Marys and hope for the best?" Remi asked. His words sounded sarcastic, but I knew it was his fear speaking.

"No. That won't be necessary. Why don't you lot go downstairs and take a break. Maybe get something to eat or rest a bit. This could go on all night. Perhaps longer. We're all going to need our strength."

The thought of walking away now and leaving Asher alone terrified me, but none of us could argue against the logic of his words.

"Come on, petal. Your wolves need to eat, but they won't go without you."

It was quite possibly the only thing he could have said to convince me.

I nodded woodenly, feeling like I'd just run a marathon when all I'd done was stand near the door clinging to Remi's hand for the last hour or so. I squeezed it and tugged. "You heard them, Remi."

"I don't want to leave him."

"Me either, but we won't be any good to him if we're dead on our feet."

"Fine," he sighed, raking a hand through his hair and releasing me as he turned toward the door. Gavin and Ben had already made their way into the hall when it happened.

A cracking sound, so loud my ears hurt, echoed throughout the space. Faster than any of us could process, Asher was on me, shoving me against the wall with one hand clutching my throat as he pressed into me.

He ran his nose along my neck until his lips reached my ear, and in Pan's voice, he said, "I'll kill them all and take you as my prize, *ma petite monstre*. You'll never be rid of me. You couldn't leave me if you tried. Not now that you've marked me as your mate."

CHAPTER

FORTY-NINE

ASHER

"Uh . . . God? Is this thing on? It's me, Asher. You know, the one you sort of left up shit creek without a paddle since the day I was born? Anyway, I was just wondering, is my soul supposed to hurt? Asking for a friend. Okay, fine, it's me. I'm the friend, and I'm pretty sure I'm dying."

"God's not here right now, Asher."

"Excuse me, lady. I wasn't talking to you. Are you his assistant or something? 'Cause I totally understand the need for gatekeeping, but this is like an emergency situation . . ."

"No, you silly boy. God can't help you with this. No one can. No one but me."

"What makes you so special? Are you an angel or something? One of Gabriel's lackeys or something?"

"Pfft, that winged biker wannabe couldn't hold a candle to me."

"So you're not God. You're not an angel . . . I can't see you, but you sound familiar. Have we met before?"

"I've known you since the day you were born, Asher Henry."

"Lady, this is the weirdest game of twenty questions I've ever played. Who the fuck are you?"

389

"I'm the beginning of the end. Not to put too fine a point on it."

"Still weird, and now I'm pretty sure you're plagiarizing. Or dangerously close to it."

"Who amongst us hasn't misquoted the Bible a time or two?"

"Um . . . me?"

"Such a good boy. So sweet and stupid. That priest really robbed you of your glow up, didn't he?"

"What? Lady, I'm about to go apeshit on you in a minute."

"With what body? In case you haven't noticed, you're decidedly non-corporeal."

"Fuck, so I am dying, aren't I? I knew it. Just my luck, I get the girl *and* the boy, and then it's lights out for me. Fucking figures."

"Not yet. But you will. If they don't stop this pesky little exorcism, you'll follow Pan to hell, and there won't be any more ring around the Rosie for you."

"Wait. What?"

"Which part are you having trouble following?"

"Try all of it."

"You're the same as him, dear Asher. As much a member of the demonic legion as he is. And now you're bound to one another. So if he goes, you go with him. Straight to hell. And not just you, I'm afraid. But every other soul on the mortal realm. It will be game over. And I shall be the lone victor."

"Jesus, fuck, lady, WHO ARE YOU?"

"Why Asher, I know it's been a while, but don't you recognize your own mother?"

" . . ."

"I see you're speechless. Allow me to elaborate. Twenty-five years ago, my sisters and I made a wager. The first one to the Apocalypse wins. Of course, none of us could do it directly. We had to move our pieces around on the board. You and your brother are my pieces. I already had Pan in place well before, but he needed a vessel for my grand plan to work. Along came your stupid father, and then, bam!

You were born. Such a pathetic little human child, but perfect for my plot."

"H-how is any of this possible?"

"Well, it's really quite simple. A little absinthe, a Russian accent, and a black wig. It wasn't exactly hard. Well, I mean *he* was hard—"

"Gross."

"I left you to the nuns and simply waited for the right time. Unfortunately for you, there was a bit of an issue with your power."

"My power?"

"Yes, darling. Your power. Although let me tell you, when I found out you could *heal* things, I was quite disappointed. Whoever heard of a *healer* in our line? Talk about the black sheep of the Pestilence family. But I'm getting ahead of myself. That priest friend of yours, Father Tate, you know the nice demon-possessed man who used to visit you at the orphanage? He recognized what you were and walled away your gift as well as your memories of its existence. The wall has been crumbling for years, especially once you met your mate and she set everything into motion. Tonight, finally, that buffoon Caleb demolished what was left of it. So here we are. Reunited at last. Though you should know, if he doesn't stop soon, he's going to send you straight to me via a one-way ticket. Can't use you if you're dead, and then what was this all for?"

"I . . . don't understand."

"Of course you don't. But you can still serve your purpose. And, when we succeed, you'll sit at my side with your mate at your feet. All powerful. No one will ever abandon you again."

"I . . . that's not what I want."

"Are you sure? Sounds to me like *exactly* what you want. A mother knows these things, dearest."

"Get rid of him."

"Whom?"

"Pan."

"But he's your brother. Every fledgling demon needs a big brother to show him the way. You've always wanted a family, Asher.

Now you have one, and a mate to boot. Truly, I've made all your dreams come true. You should be delighted."

"Sure, but I want my body back."

"Of course. No problem. As soon as you help me with my Apocalypse, we'll take care of your little dual citizenship issue."

"You make it seem like a foregone conclusion. Won't the other horsewomen try to stop you so they can win instead?"

"You'd be surprised to learn that we are actually sticklers for the rules. They've been here this whole time, watching things unfold, but they know better than to interfere. Besides, War already lost her round. It's my turn, and I have no intention of following in her footsteps. The game is nearly won already, and you're going to help me ensure it. All you have to do is say yes, Asher. And you can have everything you want."

"Put me back."

"That isn't the magic word. You must agree to our deal first. Like I said, we're sticklers for the rules."

"Fine. I'll do it. Now get me back in my body."

"Good boy. I always liked you best."

FIFTY

ROSIE

'*You couldn't leave me if you tried. Not now that you've marked me as your mate.*'

Pan's words ricocheted in my mind as I sat at the kitchen table, head in my hands, fear and guilt swamping me. He hadn't been free for long; Gavin and the twins saw to that, but he'd caused absolute havoc in a matter of seconds. Especially when it was no longer Asher standing before us but Pan in all his purple demon glory.

They'd torn him off me, but it had taken all three of them to restrain him until Caleb brought the chains. And me? I'd stood there like a bloody great fool, watching on, fighting the truth and my unchecked desire for the arsehole demon who'd ruined my life under the guise of giving me a new one.

I shouldn't feel anything for him but hate. He'd lied to me. Manipulated me at nearly every turn. But it wasn't that simple.

Mate.

Pan was my mate. Every bit as much as Asher.

I felt the truth of it, that mystical bond tethering us to one another. With his soul residing alongside Asher's, I'd marked them both at the same time. And now there was no escaping him. Even if I wanted to, I couldn't hurt him.

Not without hurting Asher or myself.

Forking hell . . . no, I silently corrected. *Fucking* hell. If ever there was a situation that called for the full monty, this was it.

"Fuck!" I shouted, making all three of my mates jump at my outburst.

"S-sugar? Y-you okay?" Ben was right there, large palm on my cheek, blue irises searching mine.

"No. No, I'm not okay. I'm a disaster. It's all my fault."

"You d-didn't do anything w-wrong," he soothed.

"How can you say that?" I swept my arm out, dramatically gesturing to the stairs. "You heard him, Ben. I mated a bloody demon, for crying out loud. A demon who is trying to end the literal world. I'm the forking horse he rode in on."

Remi snickered. "So we're back to forking now?"

"Yes. I'll speak how I like, Remi," I snapped, instantly feeling guilty. He was a wreck, and I wasn't helping by being cross with him. Standing, I walked over to where he was leaning against the counter and wrapped my arms around him. "I'm sorry. I . . ."

Remi pulled me into him, resting his cheek on my forehead. "You're freaking the fuck out, baby girl. So am I. Where even is Asher right now? Why does he look like the purple people eater?"

"I don't know. But he's not dead. I can still sense him. I'd know if my mate died, wouldn't I? You said you can feel it."

Ben grumbled and nodded. "Y-you'd definitely f-feel it. Your heart w-would stop the m-moment he l-left his body. And if y-you were l-lucky you'd go w-with him."

Caleb joined us then, looking far more worn than he had when he'd arrived a few hours earlier. I knew he didn't have good news when I saw he was holding his kit and was bundled in his coat and scarf.

"You can't leave. The demon is still inside him," I protested, jerking out of Remi's embrace.

The priest shot me an accusing look. "You didn't tell me you mated the bastard, Miss Blackthorne. I won't kill you to attempt to cast him out. Noah would never forgive me. Besides, your Asher is not possessed. He's soulbound to the white rider. He's not who he said he was. He's not even human."

"W-what?" I asked, terror turning my blood to ice.

"The exorcism should have sent the demon back to hell, but your Asher is part demon too. So instead, the rite tried to send *him*. It's not going to work. There's nothing for it. At least nothing I can do. You don't need a priest. You need a miracle."

My eyes filled with tears, but it was Remi who spoke. "How long is he going to be stuck like this? Trapped inside our very own demonic Barney?"

"Barney?" I asked.

"You know, the big purple dinosaur from the kids' show?" Remi mimed T-Rex arms.

"No."

"Ugh, never mind. It's not relevant, anyway. The point is, he's not dead. You said the only way to save him is a miracle, so we need to find a fucking miracle." He dragged a hand through his hair and stood straighter. "I'm not giving up on Asher."

"He might never come back, Remington," Gavin offered, gentler than I have ever heard him speak to my wolf.

Remi cut a desperate glance at Caleb, his voice cracking as he said, "Is he right? Are we just stuck with Pan? Asher is condemned to being his hostage forever?"

Caleb's expression was a mixture of remorse and pity. "I cannot give you the answer you seek, Remington. I've never encountered anything like this before. All I can say for sure is there are two demonic souls in one mortal vessel that are somehow tied to each other. And right now, the one called Pan is stronger. So strong he was able to manifest his true form."

"So basically you were useless and sent the good guy away so the villain could rise up. Awesome. Great fucking job. I gotta get out of here," Remi spat, angrier than I'd ever seen him. Usually it was Ben who ran away when things got too intense for him to process, but this time it was Remi struggling under the weight of his emotions.

I reached for him, but he shrugged away, and Ben grabbed my wrist. "L-let him w-work this out, sugar. He n-needs to run."

Selfishly I wanted him to stay. I wanted everyone to be together. Not just to ensure that we were safe, but because I couldn't silence the little voice in the back of my mind telling me that Remi blamed me for all of this. I was the reason he'd lost Asher. I was the reason he may never see him again. How could he stand to be around me?

He couldn't, obviously.

Remi walked out the door without a second glance, but I had to trust that Ben was right. Remi needed time to process all of this, and just like his twin, he had to be alone to do it.

"How do we find a miracle?" I asked Caleb.

"Pray."

"That hasn't w-worked out v-very well in the past," Ben offered, and I knew he was thinking of his family and the events that took place that fateful Christmas Eve. "I p-prayed in an actual church as every p-person I loved was m-murdered and G-god didn't answer m-me."

Caleb stiffened, remorse flickering in his eyes before his expression went blank. "God works in mysterious ways, Bentley."

"B-bullshit."

"You can't understand it now, but I've seen it firsthand. I may not be able to give you answers, but I can assure you that He is watching over us all. The path before you is not set in stone. Your choices will be what determines the outcome. You've been chosen, all of you, because of the part you'll play in this game."

"So we're basically a bunch of pawns?" I asked.

Caleb's brow rose. "When is a Queen ever a pawn?"

"Um . . . try almost always. You're a professor. Surely you know your history."

"You were chosen for a reason, Miss Blackthorne. Gifted with a power not seen by our kind since the last plague. That's not a coincidence."

"W-what do you m-mean?" Ben asked, coming closer.

Caleb released a heavy, exhausted sigh, but set his satchel down and began. "Once upon a time, vampires roamed the earth without guidance or leadership. Until the great flood that restarted the world."

"I hardly think this is the time for one of your sermons," Gavin sneered.

Without blinking, Caleb continued, "Everything was wiped out save those chosen by God. We're told about Noah and his ark in the Bible, but you rarely see mention of what happened to the supernatural creatures. If not for the rise of a vampire Queen who was granted her power by the Fallen, the vampires would have been wiped off the face of the earth. She ensured their survival. It was her sole duty. Her strength was unmatched, and she was revered until she was betrayed."

"Someone killed her?" I asked.

"Aye. And her court. But what the Fallen put into motion never stopped. The bloodline has continued for millennia, and a Queen only rises during a time of great peril. You are the harbinger of our doom, but also our only hope."

"So . . . no pressure then," I muttered woodenly as I sat down heavily in my chair.

"You were born for this, and you are stronger than you know. Do not doubt yourself, Roslyn. We're counting on you."

"Lovely."

Ben took my hand, infusing me with his strength as he asked, "H-how do you kn-know all this?"

"I've been a professor for a long time, Mr. Mercer. And a priest longer still. You learn a thing or two."

"You can't tell anyone she's a Queen, Caleb. The Council will be afraid of her. You know what they do to things they fear. They rid themselves of the threat." Gavin's words cut through me because, for the first time, his voice held true unease.

"Aye, that they do. But who better to keep your secrets than your confessor?" He checked the clock on the wall and let out a heavy sigh. "I need to get back. There's nothing more I can do here anyway." Caleb came and pressed a kiss to my forehead. "That's from Noah. Take care of yourself. I'll be praying for you."

After he left us, the room still smelled of him, and the atmosphere was weighed down by everything he'd told us. I glanced at my two mates, desperate for reassurance.

"What do we do now?" I asked.

Ben squeezed my hand. "F-find a miracle."

"And stop the Apocalypse," Gavin added.

"Brilliant. And you always say Tuesdays are slow."

"N-not anymore."

FIFTY-ONE

PESTILENCE

Everything was coming up Pesty as I strolled down the main drag of Aurora Springs. The sun was shining. The world was dying. I was winning, as if there was ever any doubt.

Better still, no one had sniffed out my secret identity.

"Good girl, Lady Godiva Sassafras. You're such a pretty little minion. Cat scratch fever is one of my favorite maladies."

The Persian meowed and continued to lick her paw in her custom hot pink Louis Vuitton cat carrier.

"I know darlin', you didn't like me climbing that ladder, but it had to be done. How else were we supposed to reach the supply?" I pulled out the empty vial and grinned wickedly as I relived the euphoria of leaving my gift in the water supply.

It was only a matter of time now. One by one, they'd fall ill. And I'd revel in it. I did love a slow burn. Some went with the wham, bam, thank you, ma'am approach. Me? I preferred the silent spread before, voilà! Pandemic.

Well, perhaps there were a few I'd like to get rid of more expediently. I'd take care of them personally. Nothing wrong with a little southern hospitality. It would still be miserable, but I'd see to their deaths myself.

A little bit of having my cake and eating it too.

"Morning, Madam Mayor!"

I preened, waving at the passerby and his family like the dutiful civil servant I was. "Mornin' y'all. Beautiful day, isn't it?"

Hitching Lady Godiva's carrier a little higher on my arm, I pushed open the door to my next destination. Three sets of eyes found mine as soon as I walked inside.

"Good to see you three are already at your posts," I muttered.

Fucking vultures.

"We wouldn't miss this," Dick said.

"Not for the world," Tom agreed.

"More like the end of it." Harry laughed with a wink as he raised his pint glass for a cheers with the other two just as Remi walked in from the back.

"Celebrating already? What's the occasion?" he asked.

"Family reunion," I said, smiling.

Remi cast his gaze out behind me. "Oh? Where is everybody?"

"Closer than you might think."

His brow furrowed, but he shook it off. "Can I get you something, Madam Mayor?"

I reached out and trailed my hand over his cheek in a genteel gesture of affection. The southern bitch *would* be a terrible flirt. "Always such a gentleman, Remington. But I have to pass. I was simply stopping by to ensure all was well. I must take care of my constituents, after all. How else can I live up to my reputation?"

Remi nodded and started to turn away. As he did, he let out a dry cough.

I bit back a smile as I stood. "Oh no, Remi. You sound unwell. Perhaps you should go home and get some rest."

I winked at the gargoyles and sashayed my way back out into the Alaskan sunshine.

Oh yes, a glorious day indeed.

THE MATE GAMES PESTILENCE CONCLUDES WITH LOST TO THE MOON. KEEP READING FOR A SNEAK PEEK!

SNEAK PEEK: LOST TO THE MOON

REMI

I did up the buttons on my black shirt, staring at myself in the mirror and smirking. I couldn't wait for Rosie to get here for her confession. I was like a kid in a candy store. This was going to be the best anniversary, hands down.

Taking off my wedding band, I carefully placed it on the dresser before I adjusted the white collar at my throat, winking at myself in the mirror as I did. "Just call me, Father Ledger."

Hmm, maybe I should use an Irish accent too? Rosie had definitely enjoyed Caleb's. Fuck, so had I.

"Come here to me and unburden yourself, my child," I said to the empty room, an Irish lilt coloring my words.

It sounded good, but I wasn't sure I could keep it up once we really got going. That took a lot of brain power and I was pretty sure once the blood started rushing south, I'd be struggling to string together a coherent sentence in my normal accent.

A soft knock on my door had me giddy with anticipation.

"Remi? Are you in there?" Rosie's sweet voice was temptation itself. How fitting.

"Come in, Mrs. Mercer," I said.

She opened the door, laughing as she said, "Mrs. Mercer. So formal this morning, Re–oh, my—I mean, Father..."

My lips twitched. "Ledger."

"Of course. My apologies, Father Ledger. I wasn't expecting to see you."

"Neither was I. We don't have an appointment, my child."

"I wasn't aware I needed one. You've always accommodated me before." I could see the twinkle of laughter in her eyes at our game, but she was an expert at staying in scene these days. Gavin had seen to that.

"You simply assume I'm at your beck and call? How presumptuous of you. I'm a very busy man. Confessions to take, absolution to give, rites to perform."

"Punishments to dole out?"

My grin was sin itself. "Oh yes." My cock twitched before I let my next words free. "Do you need to be punished, lamb?"

She bit her lower lip and heat flooded her cheeks in the form of a blush. "Yes."

"How does your husband feel about what we do in my office?"

"Which one?"

"Such a sinner."

"I just can't seem to help myself."

"Perhaps you should get on your knees for me then." Fuck now I understood what hot under the collar meant. I was sweating. Kind of uncomfortably, if I was being honest.

She sank to her knees, raised her face to look into my eyes, and moaned.

"Are you feeling all right, Remington? You look a little flushed." Rosie's mouth was moving but the voice that came from her was all wrong as the dream faded into darkness. "My, my, I fear you may have taken a turn for the worst."

THIS IS ONE FINALE YOU DON'T WANT TO MISS.
PRE-ORDER YOUR COPY NOW!

The Mate Games Universe

by K. Loraine & Meg Anne

War

Obsession

Rejection

Possession

Temptation

Pestilence

Promised to the Night (Prequel Novella)

Deal with the Demon

Claimed by the Shifters

Captive of the Night

Lost to the Moon

ALSO BY MEG ANNE

BROTHERHOOD OF THE GUARDIANS/NOVASGARD VIKINGS

UNDERCOVER MAGIC *(NORD & LINA)*
A SEXY & SUSPENSEFUL FATED MATES PNR

HINT OF DANGER

FACE OF DANGER

WORLD OF DANGER

PROMISE OF DANGER

CALL OF DANGER

BOUND BY DANGER (QUINN & FINLEY)

THE CHOSEN UNIVERSE

THE CHOSEN
A FATED MATES HIGH FANTASY ROMANCE

MOTHER OF SHADOWS

REIGN OF ASH

CROWN OF EMBERS

QUEEN OF LIGHT

THE CHOSEN BOXSET #1

THE CHOSEN BOXSET #2

THE KEEPERS
A GUARDIAN/WARD HIGH FANTASY ROMANCE

The Dreamer (A Keeper's Prequel)

The Keepers Legacy

The Keepers Retribution

The Keepers Vow

The Keepers Boxset

The Forsaken

A Rejected Mates/Enemies-To-Lovers Romantasy

Prisoner of Steel & Shadow

Queen of Whispers & Mist

Court of Death & Dreams

Prince of Sea & Stars

A Standalone MMF Romantasy Adventure

Gypsy's Curse

A Psychic/Detective Star-Crossed Lovers UF Romance

Visions Of Death

Visions Of Vengeance

Visions Of Triumph

The Gypsy's Curse: The Complete Collection

ALSO BY K. LORAINE

~

STANDALONES

CURSED (MFM SLEEPING BEAUTY RETELLING)

~

REVERSE HAREM STANDALONES

THEIR VAMPIRE PRINCESS (A REVERSE HAREM ROMANCE)

ALL THE QUEEN'S MEN (A FAE REVERSE HAREM ROMANCE)

About Meg Anne

USA Today and international bestselling paranormal and fantasy romance author Meg Anne has always had stories running on a loop in her head. They started off as daydreams about how the evil queen (aka Mom) had her slaving away doing chores, and more recently shifted into creating backgrounds about the people stuck beside her during rush hour. The stories have always been there; they were just waiting for her to tell them.

Like any true SoCal native, Meg enjoys staying inside curled up with a good book and her fur babies . . . or maybe that's just her. You can convince Meg to buy just about anything if it's covered in glitter or rhinestones, or make her laugh by sharing your favorite bad joke. She also accepts bribes in the form of baked goods and Mexican food.

Meg is best known for her leading men #MenbyMeg, her inevitable cliffhangers, and making her readers laugh out loud, all of which started with the bestselling Chosen series.

ABOUT K. LORAINE

USA Today Bestselling author Kim Loraine writes steamy contemporary and sexy paranormal romance. **You'll find her paranormal romances written under the name K. Loraine and her contemporaries as Kim Loraine.** Don't worry, you'll get the same level of swoon-worthy heroes, sassy heroines, and an eventual HEA.

When not writing, she's busy herding cats (raising kids), trying to keep her house sort of clean, and dreaming up ways for fictional couples to meet.